IVORY TOWER

IVORY TOWER

Grant Matthew Jenkins

atmosphere press

to the countless victims of sexual assault
who did not have a voice or a champion

Part 1: A Convocation

I.

The thing about Margolis Santos—a sign she is slightly *off*—is that she sees ghosts. Real ghosts and not-real ghosts.

Start with the real ghosts. Well, one ghost in particular, her dead father Cicero.

He didn't want her to go to graduate school or become a film professor—no money in it—he didn't want her to marry Frank Sinoro—too much of a dumb jock—and Cicero certainly didn't want her to go against her university's president in her first year on the job as an Assistant Professor—no tenure to protect her.

But she did it all anyway, perhaps to spite him, though she didn't think so at the time. She thought she was just following her dreams, as they say in the chick-lit novels on her night stand. But the constant negativity would creep into every decision she'd made, to the point where it seemed like it didn't matter if any choice was good or bad, so she might as well choose bad.

Like this morning. A not-real ghost. She thinks back on it as she drives to campus.

Why did she let Frank come over before their 17-year-old daughter, Brie, woke up, just so he could pretend everything was alright, to keep up appearances? Why didn't she just tell him to fuck off and tell Brie the truth? She's 17.

Margolis reassures herself: she wasn't the one who had messed around with a graduate assistant when she thought her spouse was away at a conference. That was Frank. Sure, she had wanted to seduce students too—it was kinda easy and not that sexy for all that—but she had a rule, despite another not-real ghost—having a thing for younger lovers. That rule was: no students. At least while they were in her classes and hadn't yet graduated.

"Thanks, Glee." Frank reaches for an orange and tosses it into the air. As it lands suavely in his hand, he leans over and smooches her on the cheek. "I'll see you at school."

Margolis reaches up and rubs the wet left by his lips.

"Bye, Bee." At the breakfast table, he kisses Brie on the head as he walks by. She doesn't even stop munching her Cheerios.

"Mbye," she mumbles sleepily.

The morning ritual having been accomplished, Frank grabs his keys off the kitchen counter—*nice touch of verisimilitude,* Margolis thinks—and he glances back at her.

For a moment, she wants to wish him a 'kick-ass day,' like she used to. She catches herself, swallows the reflex, but that look in his eyes—she almost wishes this ritual was real, that he were here, had been here, in her bed. She can almost feel his fingertips on her skin, like it used to be. It felt so real. But it wasn't.

Real or not-real, nothing can keep her demons away—not graduate school smarts, not middle-age maturity, not a hearty Midwestern Catholic upbringing, not even her cynically wry sarcasm. The visitations are starting again, now that it's fall. She looks over her shoulder half-expecting Cicero to be in the back seat. She swallows the feeling as she parks the car and heads for class.

So, fade in on 'The U,' short for Athens University where Margolis teaches television and film. The august, southern university, vivacious and verdant, spreads across rolling, urban hills. Imposing buildings lord benevolently over ancient stone pathways and ivy-covered walls. A parents' wetdream of future prosperity and security for their precious spawn.

Through this sylvan scene, Margolis leisurely makes her way dressed in a flowing floral toga. She's tall, like Jennifer Beals from *The L Word*, and just settling into her early 40s. Her face is angular and a tad severe, but the dark brown eyes and high cheekbones give her a grace that defies age.

Margolis's overconfidence flows from the belief that hers is an enviable life—nobly pursuing knowledge, furthering the progress of humanity, shaping the young minds of tomorrow's leaders—all of that happens here, she thinks, inside the hallowed walls of the Ivory Tower. Margolis knows there's a reason why people rank being a college professor as the most respected profession behind Supreme Court Justice—because it's ideal, in a word, *cushy*. Summers off, flexible hours, getting paid just to think. Hundreds of young nubile bodies prancing around half-naked. A veritable paradise before the Fall.

Margolis stops in front of her lecture hall. Hesitates.

That's when it happens. Another visitation.

Margolis is transported to the middle of a desolate field landscape in middle America, the overcast grey sky and leafless trees give a sense of endless winter cold. In the distance the skyline of some nondescript city rises dark and foreboding. Maybe it's Omaha. Or maybe St. Louis. Maybe Minneapolis. It doesn't matter.

Margolis grew up in this lifeless exurb with Cicero, whose voice she hears, almost as if in a memory or a dream. Flashes of the dead Cicero stand in her mind's field like a warning. He's tall, dark-haired, with sallow cheeks, a ghostly pseudo of Edwards James Olmos. But it seems so real, his voice, as it spews from his mouth.

"The world is full of predators, Margolis. You eat or get eaten. Weakness—for money, for blood, for lust—gives the beast a place to sink his fangs."

A phone buzzes. His twisted face disappears. And Margolis suddenly finds herself back on campus at the front of a large auditorium classroom.

Usually when she teaches, Margolis doesn't just stand, she *presides* over her class. But she's rattled after seeing Cicero. She takes a deep breath and rallies at the thought of finishing up a series of lectures on the rise of the sexual thriller in film history. For the students.

The lights go down, and a projector lights up. Glenn Close from *Fatal Attraction* in all her frizzy 80s glory rolls on the screen above the chalkboard. In this scene, Michael Douglas follows her into her apartment after she's invited him in. He's here to end their torrid and adulterous love affair, but she drops the bomb on him that she's pregnant. Feeling that he's being manipulated, Douglas tells her that this affair is over. That rejection sets Glenn Close off, and she demands to be part of his life, exclaiming the famous line, "I'm not going to be *ignored*, Dan."

The clip stops with Glenn in mid rant and menacing glare.

Margolis flicks on her laser pointer and makes circles with the red dot around Close's face.

"You see her, Glenn Close? The classic femme fatale, threatening this normal American man's perfect, happy life."

Margolis turns on the lights and resumes her lecture—it's like nothing else has happened today. She's on.

"But Glenn Close takes it to a new level. She's authorized by history, in a way that no femme fatale before her really ever had been. In the wake of the Supreme Court's 1972 *Roe v. Wade* decision legalizing abortion, Douglas's condescending line, 'That's your choice, honey,' takes on a much weightier and sinister meaning." Margolis looks at the clock and sees it's time to go. "But we'll have to stop at that cliffhanger."

Margolis raises her arm for attention as the students start to pack up their things.

"OK," Margolis increases her volume over student rummaging, "we'll finish the discussion of *Fatal Attraction* next time. Be sure to read the chapter in the textbook on Film Noir, or you'll learn from me the true meaning of femme fatale!"

With the screen behind her, Margolis rewinds the clip. She puts her laser pointer's red dot right on the nose of Glenn Close and mouths along: "I mean, I'm not going to be ignored, *Dan!*"

The class laughs collectively and shuffles out.

Margolis puts her own things into a tattered leather valise and hauls the strap over her wiry shoulder. At the front of the stage she stops for a moment and takes in a long, satisfied breath. *God, I love this gig*, she thinks to herself. What would she do without it? With one more look around, she strides, satisfied, out of the room, down a hall, and through the front door to the quad.

In the humid air, Margolis walks down the tree-lined walk. The sun is lower in the sky. Warm orange light glints off buildings and glows in trees. It's what filmmakers call the 'golden hour.'

Frank Sinoro jogs up behind her.

"Margolis."

She doesn't answer. She keeps walking.

"Margolis, wait." He reaches for her arm and pulls her gently to a stop. "Glee, hi. I'm glad I caught you."

Margolis turns, nonplussed. She feigns indifference to seeing her husband.

"Frank, I'm late." At six feet plus heels, Margolis towers over pee-wee Frank.

"Please? Just for a minute?"

She folds her arms and waits for him to speak.

"I need to ask you something. A favor."

"A favor? Really?"

"It's not a big deal, but I need you to go with me to the athletics banquet this weekend."

"A banquet." She chuckles. "Honestly, how can you expect—"

"I know I should have asked you this morning, but with all that's been going on—"

She folds her arms and looks around, impatiently now. "It slipped your mind."

"Yeah."

"It's a lot to ask, Frank. I'm done with that kind of—"

"Come on, Glee, you owe me this. At least this."

"Owe you? I owe *you*?"

"OK, OK. Listen. I'm asking you. Nicely. As a favor. Would you please go with me? It's a crucial time, and I need supporters to think that—"

"Everything is golden in Coach Sinoro's landscape, like that charade you pulled this morning for Brie?"

"Yeah," Frank wilts slightly. "Yeah, exactly. At least for now."

Margolis stands silently for a moment, considering the trees and looking like she wants a smoke. She turns her head down the quad as anger swells inside of her.

"I know it's been tough. But please, this one last time. Will you go?"

Margolis thinks back to last year's banquet. It was a blast, maybe the last time they were happy. Before he fucked it up. *Why can't we go back there?* she wonders.

Gradually Margolis softens and gives a nod of assent. *There is no sense in saying no.* Anyway, the pretense that they are still a couple will give her a little more time to maybe figure out a way to fix things, maybe to reconcile. At the very least it will give her time to break the news to Brie. She doesn't know that three months ago, her father secretly moved out, waiting until she goes to bed to head to his small apartment closer to campus and then coming back early in the morning before she gets up.

"Great, I've got a meeting with Lane, but I'll be by to pick you up in a few hours—"

Margolis doesn't wait for him to finish but simply turns and walks. Frank watches her go, shading his eyes against the late-afternoon sun.

*   *   *   *

Angle on a classic southern mid-century motel. Vintage neon sign, a pool shimmering in the later sun. Cars whiz by.

Track in through a part in the sun-gauzy wool curtains and over the cliché of shag carpet. Margolis lies leisurely in bed with a sheet barely covering her naked body. She takes a drag from a cigarette.

Next to her is Ford Reinhart, 19, maybe 20 at the most. On

the outside, he looks just like another douchebag: toned physique, his hair crew-cut blonde. His accent, southern. His face, a blueberry pie.

Ford flops out of bed, scantily clad in underwear only, looking for his jeans. Can't find them.

That's because Margolis has them. She takes a pack of smokes from the back pocket, pulls one out, and lights it.

"God, that tastes good." Exhales, "I haven't smoked a cigarette in years." A beat. "How come so many of you kids smoke these days?"

She takes another drag, watches him. He's clearly sober and a bit nervous. He stops.

"Kids?"

"You know what I mean."

She offers him a cigarette, and he takes one. Lights it.

"Margolis, can't you—" Ford starts but she interrupts.

"It's pronounced Margo-*lee*. Rhymes with *glee*."

"Margolis, can't you..." He pauses a beat. To Margolis's expectant eyebrows: "Can't you, like, get in trouble for this?"

She laughs. "For what, smoking?"

"No, for this." Standing in his underwear, he gestures back and forth between himself and her.

"Oh," as if considering it for the first time. "Oh, no. No. What do you mean?"

"I don't know. I've never done this before, like, been with a professor."

"Shut up! You're not even my student."

"I know. I just thought maybe there were, like, rules and stuff. You know, ethics."

"Ethics?" Margolis stares at him. Incredulous, then annoyed. "Look, I have a rule: No students."

Ford shrugs, "OK."

This talk has clearly taken the savor out of the moment for her. She wants to get it back, so she watches Ford pick up a shirt and put it on over wash-board abs.

"Look, we met on Farrah's set. *She's* your film professor, not me. She's my friend. I was only there as a consultant, not a teacher."

It's like she's rehearsing a poorly prepared script. He doesn't know it consciously, but he hears that in her voice. You can tell from his reply.

"You're also an investor, right? A producer from the U?"

Suddenly worried, "Yeah, well, that's true. But that doesn't mean anything. It can't."

"Couldn't you, like," Ford presses, "get fired?"

Margolis confidently, "No, not fired. I'm tenured. You have to basically break the law to get fired as a professor."

Ford continues putting on his clothes. She watches his legs, his bulge. He speaks as he slips on his Calvins. "I mean, I like you and all, but I don't think we can keep doing this."

Margolis smirks. "Come on, haven't you ever done anything that was a little, um, frowned-upon?"

"Yeah!"

"Like what?" Margolis teases in a dubious tone.

"I picked a lock on my uncle's liquor closet so I could get some of his booze."

"What? Really? You can pick locks?"

"Yeah, and it's something he taught me, just to give me a real skill. 'In case the social order breaks down,' he used to joke."

"Ah come on, we're not breaking the social order, Ford."

Ford doesn't respond but keeps dressing. Margolis exhales, relaxes.

"Hey, stop. Come here." She pats the bed and gives him a come-hither smile. He pauses, then relents, diving on the bed next to her.

She folds him in: "Don't worry, OK? It's all going to be golden, Pony Boy."

Then she kisses him, long and firm, on the mouth.

In the gap, Ford: "*The Outsiders*. Nice."

She kisses him on the neck and reaches under the sheets between his legs. She moans seductively. He reluctantly is getting aroused.

"You know, your parents, salt of the earth that they are, will eventually find out about us. You ready for that?"

Ford, suddenly with a start, "Oh, shit. What time is it?" He jumps out of bed and looks furiously around for his phone. "I haven't talked to my parents since Tuesday before the shoot. Fuck! Where's my phone?"

"Well, of course you haven't talked to them," she jokes. "You've been too busy diving for pearls with your tongue."

He finds the phone, unlocks it. "Shit, shit, shit. There's 30 messages, like 14 from them."

Margolis takes another drag.

Ford reads through texts, eyes darting back and forth. He thumbs out a reply quickly.

"Ah hell." Margolis watches disappointedly. "Smart phones—world's greatest buzz-kill device."

"Great. Everyone on Facebook is wondering where I am. They think I'm missing."

"What? It hasn't even been a day since you talked to your folks."

"Two days."

"Two days?! Whatever." Margolis dismisses.

"Since I live at home, Professor Santos, they're always up in my business."

"If my parents had ever overreacted like that, I would have told them to go fuck themselves. But they weren't like that at all—I would have been shocked if they cared where I was at all." Beat. "And call me Margolis, please. Jesus."

"I told them I was staying at a friend's house."

"You lied?"

Ford isn't listening, he's reading text messages. The phone suddenly dings, vibrates. "I gotta get out of here. They are pissed. Even called the cops!" He grabs his stuff and runs out the door without waving goodbye.

Dissatisfied, Margolis lies still for a minute, the only motion the smoke rising and fluttering from her fingers.

Suddenly, a sick feeling comes over her. Was she really living out this cliché, the student-teacher affair? Jesus, she thought she was above that.

Guess not.

She'd rationalized it by constantly reminding herself he's not her student. But, fuck, what does that matter? She may have just gotten the poor kid in big trouble. Why did she have to be so self-indulgent?

She doesn't have an answer. She just mushes her cigarette out in an ashtray on the bedstand, pulls back the covers, and reaches for her bra.

II.

Track through Athens University President Art Lane's oaken office. In the reception area, the school's storied athletic trophies stand, sadly proud. Colorful memorabilia covers the walls. A black, grey and pink Athens University pennant. A signed jersey. All the typical rah-rah *Scheisse*: It's like Knute Rockne got tanked on official sponsor beer and spewed team spirit all over the place. The "Raven" they're called. Singular, as in Poe's "quoth the raven."

Of course, there's a TV here, like a sports bar, and it plays a recent interview with the University's president defending the football team's performance. The coach's photo appears as an inset over the President's shoulder.

President Lane (on the TV, to reporters): "Now, boys, whatever I say you're going to speculate that it means the opposite, so I'll be clear: Frank Sinoro's job is 100% safe. One 4-7 season tells us, tells us nothing about what he can do. His potential. He hasn't even had a full recruiting class..."

But we can't listen to all that propaganda. We've got to see what's happening in the inner sanctum, so we move in through the heavy oak doors.

Predictably, President Lane leans forward emphatically over his blotter and pen set, a signed football sitting proudly on his desk. Lane gestures at someone with his finger on the table. He's playing the good cop.

The presidential finger points to Frank Sinoro, the midlife crisis of early 40s eeking out of his pores. He sits meekly across from the president in a chair that seems too small. Frank is dressed in his team warm-up, as if he just came off the football field, and he tellingly wrings his baseball cap in his hands. His gorgeous hair sitting smack on top of his skull, Frank listens to Lane intently.

"It's just that I've got these gall-darned boosters breathing down my neck to fire your ass before your contract is up."

"I understand, sir."

"I'm not sure that you do, Frank. During the search when we hired you, they wanted a local boy, a southerner, for this job. Someone who understands the hard-nosed style of football we play down here." A beat for emphasis. "But I liked you. And I was willing to take a chance on you."

"And I appreciate this opportunity, I really do."

"The game is changing, Frank, and I'm gambling that you know which way the wind is blowin. But I have got to see results." Lane straightens the football in line with the desk edge. "Another losing season is just not gonna cut it. Hell, a mediocre 8 and 5 Holiday Bowl season won't be enough. We need championships. Without one soon, I won't be able to keep the heat off you."

Frank shifts uneasily. "Exactly what are these 'boosters' saying?"

"Well, they're not happy." Lane sounds like a kid with hurt feelings.

"Is it play-calling?" A gesture of exasperation, "Every armchair quarterback wants to second-guess—"

"No, no, that ain't it, exactly. It's not really what you're doing on the field they find problematic."

Lane catches Frank's eye for more than a moment.

"In a way. It's more what you're *not* doing."

"Not doing, sir?" Frank twists the cap in his hands a little tighter.

"They don't think you are doing enough off the field to win." Just a slight pause for emphasis. "They think you could be more creative. Out of the camera eye. But I told them—"

"Jesus, Art, what the hell does that mean, 'out of the camera eye'? I pride myself on running a clean—"

"Now, listen, Frank. I'm not—" A breath. "Don't get all riled up over what these guys say. What the hell do they know about running a football program?"

Frank, feeling exonerated, understood: "Damn right."

"I aim to make sure that you have every resource at your disposal to make the most out of our program." The president picks up the football, leans back in his chair. "All I need to know is that you are committed to doing what it takes to win."

"Sir, you know that I am." Frank leans slightly forward.

"Then I'm sure you will find all the necessary ways—maybe ways you haven't considered yet—to do just that." The president stands and extends his hand. "That's all for now—I'll see you at the team banquet with that lovely wife of yours." A smile.

Uncertain at first, Frank stands and nods in acquiescence as he shakes the president's hand. "Oh, Dr. Santos. Margolis. We're not—" He pauses.

"Not what?" Still grasping Frank's hand.

"Noth—nothing. It's just she feels awful for what happened last year, during the vote of no confidence. Now that she knows you better, she fully supports you. She says she's sorry and hopes that—"

Lane raises a hand to cut him off. "Water under the proverbial bridge, Frank. Anyway, she's married to my superstar head football coach, right? As long as you two are happy, I don't care about the past."

"Well, okay then. She'll be there with bells on." Frank flashes a stiff smile.

"Good, good to hear that. I look forward to seeing her in all her finery."

Heading toward the door, Frank puts his baseball cap back on.

The president sits down. "Oh, and Frank."

Frank stops at the door and turns back.

"I was able to keep the boosters at bay last year, but now they want to get to know you better. So, I've set up a meeting for you with Chet Orchard tomorrow at practice."

"Chet Orchard. Who's that?"

"A concerned citizen. Just stop by Susie's desk on the way

out. She'll give you the details." The president turns away from Frank and picks up the phone, summarily dismissing him.

*   *   *   *

Emma Barnes, 21, sits alone at an island in the middle of the large, commercial kitchen of the Delta Delta Theta sorority house. She nibbles at a piece of chocolate cake. The recessed lighting shines down on her like a spot. Her walnut-brown hair glosses with the flood of light. Her olive face, soft and delicate, is bowed in the shadows.

She holds a bill from the university: TOTAL DUE FOR FALL SEMESTER: $25,459.00.

She sighs and looks into the distance for a moment then back down. She shuffles to another paper.

It's membership dues from Delta Delta Theta. Under the chapter logo, it reads DUES TOTAL: $3,600.00. ROOM AND BOARD: $4,500.

Emma frowns and slams the papers down on the counter.

Enter the sorority housemom, Lucille Bontemps, a white, Cajun spinster pushing 60, who putters around wiping counters and putting away dishes. She notices Emma and stops for a second. Lucille's hand reaches instinctively for the fridge and pulls it open. Without taking her eyes off the girl, Lucille pulls out a gallon jug of milk and walks over to the island. She fills Emma's cup.

"You've been down in the mouth all evening, child. Didn't touch your dinner, and now... You're eating chocolate."

Emma picks at the cake with her fork; it's true, she hasn't eaten very much. She doesn't look up from her plate.

"It's nothing, really. It's just..."

"Come on now, Emma. It's Lucille you're talking to! You can't hide a sniffle what I don't suss it out."

Emma doesn't look at her, as she decides what to reveal. "I know." A beat. "I failed my first Brit Lit quiz of the semester."

"It's not like you to get riled by a little ol' quiz." Lucille notices the papers scattered under Emma's plate. "Those don't look like schoolwork."

"No, they're bills. Tuition and stuff. Due soon."

"Ah, I see. So that's what's gotten you so upset. Money."

Emma looks back sadly. "My folks are going to flip."

"You haven't told them you lost your scholarship, have you?"

Tears welling up, Emma looks at Lucille. Answer, no.

Lucille grabs her by the shoulders and squeezes her gently but emphatically.

"Now you buck up, li'l' Theta. I know your folks are going through hard times—so many are these days. You just hit those books, study hard, and things'll all work out just fine. You'll see."

Emma lowers her head, not totally convinced.

Lucille insists, "You hear me?"

Emma nods and smiles weakly. Lucille takes her to her voluminous bosom, but the smile disappears from Emma's face. Somehow the hug seems disappointing.

Looking over Emma's head on her breast, Lucille sees Brooke Golindy, 22, college senior and sorority president, standing behind them in the doorway. Brooke gestures roughly to Lucille, who releases Emma and walks over. Brooke pulls Lucille into the adjoining hall.

Lucille whispers, admitting guilt for something. "What?"

As Brooke talks her perfectly straight, blonde hair shakes. "Has she paid her dues yet?"

"No, not yet."

"They were due at the beginning of the semester. It's your job to make sure she does it."

"I know. I'm working on it. Right now, she's going through some—"

Brooke points at Lucille. "I don't give a flip. We've all got to pull our weight." And with that, she turns on her heel and emphatically exits.

Lucille looks sadly through the doorframe and sees Emma, slouched at the counter, take a big bite of chocolate cake.

*   *   *   *

Home from her encounter with Ford, Margolis slumps into her William Sonoma kitchen and unburdens herself from keys, purse, bookbag.

The family's Golden Retriever, Benny, wags his way up to her. She crouches down and pets the dog, rubbing her face into his with kissing sounds. She pulls back and looks him in the eye, searching for a friend. She's a bit miffed with herself having given in to Frank by agreeing to go to the stupid football banquet.

Margolis stands up and looks around, a bit dazed for a moment, and then remembers what she wants. There's a habitual rhythm to her motions. She moves to the wine rack, grabs a bottle, and opens it. She takes a deep drink, puts down the glass, and sighs.

Of course, in that moment of solitude is when Brie slouches into the kitchen and plops herself down at the table without saying a word. Brie is a senior at Athens Westside High. She's tall, a little curvy, and a lot dramatic.

"Hey, Brie." Margolis looks expectantly at her over her wine glass and waits for her filial greeting. It doesn't come. " 'Hello, mother, it's nice to have you home,'" Margolis puppets in a high voice. No response.

Brie looks silently down at her phone, which she swipes thoughtlessly.

"Hey." Margolis puts her hand under her child's chin and gently pulls it up. She suddenly looks terribly young. The sad eyes that meet hers are almost heartbreaking. They're blue, like Frank's, and sit deeply in her round face. "What's wrong?"

Brie realizes her mother isn't going to give up. "I found a

key on the counter this morning. When I asked Dad what it was, he told me it was to a new apartment."

Margolis is stunned but tries to hide it. "I see," Margolis sighs and leans back in her chair. "I didn't want you to find out this way. Not yet."

Margolis waits for a long moment, and then Brie finally says, "I just feel so out of it. Lied to. You two have just been pretending this whole time. For my sake."

"Not this whole time, only a few months."

"A few months?" Some anger now. Benny's golden head turns at the raised voice. "You've known for months that you're getting a divorce and you didn't bother to tell me?"

"Not divorced, not yet. Just separated. I had hoped...we just needed some time apart."

"Separated. Like that's better?"

A few blinks. "You're right. We should have told you earlier. I just thought, during that time, that maybe..."

"Maybe what? That I'd never find out?"

"No. That your father and I might..." A long beat. "Look, the important thing for you to know is that I love you. We both do."

"But you don't love each other."

Margolis looks down at her hands. With the right, she rubs a small brown spot on the back of her left. She doesn't know how to answer, so she just starts: "Of course we do, baby. I'll always love your father. It's just that—"

"You two are always working. You never take any time for each other."

"No. I mean..." Margolis stops, looks up. "Is that how you see it?"

"You're always working. And you don't even have to. Dad makes enough money."

"But money is not the only point, Brie-Brie. I work to be fulfilled as a person, to be a role model for you as a strong woman who—"

Brie suddenly scrapes her chair back with a thrust. Benny

jumps to his feet.

"What a role model." She stands staring at Margolis a moment and then turns away.

Margolis, paralyzed with guilt, can only watch her walk out. Benny comes up to her and wags his tail reassuringly. She doesn't reach down but stays still, thinking that she owes Brie this emphatic moment.

*   *   *   *

Her eyes red from tears, Brie climbs some metal fire-escape stairs, stands at a back door of the Theta house, and knocks. Emma opens it and melts in sympathy when she sees Brie. Emma looks around to see if anyone sees, then smiles slightly as she takes Brie by the hand. Emma gently pulls her inside.

Through the door, Coltrane's "Naima" plays on Emma's stereo.

Emma hugs Brie and just holds her for several bars of the song. She knows the story of why Brie is here—there's trouble at home.

Emma releases and looks Brie deeply in the eyes. She embraces her again, this time harder and longer. More than friends.

She releases Brie and takes her face in her hands. She kisses Brie softly on the mouth. Brie opens her eyes and looks searchingly into Emma's.

Brie grabs Emma and kisses her back, hard.

III.

On the practice field, Frank stands, arms folded, with a whistle in his mouth and a clipboard in one hand. All around him in a green dust of dirt and mulch swirls a madness of machismo as thin cover for pubescent youth in tight pants. In the middle of hundreds of armored boys, looking way older than they actually are, Frank anchors the still point.

Frank blows his whistle and, suddenly animated, yells at the players doing blocking drills: "No, Wakowski! No! You gotta get your hands under there, like this."

Frank squats down and fires off against the sled, pushing it with all his built-up stress and anger.

"Now do it again. All of you." He spits. "Right this time."

That's when Chet Orchard, mid-50s, white fishy-out-of-water in his jet-black Zegnas and Hickey-Freeman suit, strides through the choreography of human beef. Next to him saunters Mickey Andouille, early 40s, former athlete, no taller than Chet but clearly still in shape with muscles taut under his pink golf shirt with the Raven logo. Branded with Greek letters from his black fraternity house, his biceps display intricate tattoos of African design that spiral out of his sleeves and down his thick arms.

"Tough to get a box of rocks to jump up and do pirouettes, ain't it?" Chet grins at Frank, his crooked old-man teeth showing over his bottom lip. "Almost takes a magic wand." He reaches his hand out. "Frank Sinoro, I'm Chet Orchard. This here is Mickey Andouille."

"Mickey Andouille?" Frank reaches back to Chet, shakes his hand, and then offers it to Mickey.

"Just like the sausage." Mickey smiles. "You may not remember, but we played against each other in the Cotton Bowl, 1989."

Suddenly, the stress drains from Frank's face: "Oh yeah, yeah. I know who you are. Defensive back. I took you deep in the third quarter on a second-and-ten. You stepped inside, and Freddy Jackson stepped outside and went 89 yards for the TD."

"That's right. And on the next series, I stepped in front of Jackson, picked off your badly underthrown ball, and took it to the house!"

"Yes, you did!"

With both men laughing full-belly, Chet watches them in delight, sensing that the chemistry is working, but he wants to move things on past memory lane. "I believe Lightning told you we were dropping by."

"Lightning?"

"President Lane. We called him 'Lightning' back in the day. Played tailback right here at the U. Ladies' man. Could hit any hole like lightning. And he was a damn fine running back too!"

Chet laughs heartily and habitually slaps Mickey's shoulder.

Mickey ignores the sexual innuendo: "Those were some good teams at the U, weren't they, Frank?"

"Damn straight. Better than what we have now." Frank turns to watch his players for a moment. Chet stares, smiling at him the whole time. Frank then blows his whistle loudly. "That's a wrap! Hit the showers!"

Exhausted players jog by with helmets in their hand. Frank and Chet follow them slowly, Mickey lagging behind.

"What can I do for you, Mr. Orchard?"

"Chet, please."

They take one step in dry grass. Two. Their strides don't match.

"OK, Chet."

"Well, Frank. Mickey and I are here to talk to you about making the most of your opportunities."

"Opportunities, sir?"

Chet likes the deference and formality of "sir." It's southern. It shows respect. He smiles. "Frank, I don't need to tell you that we play in the most competitive conference in college football."

"No, sir."

"Then I don't need to tell you that the difference between winning and losing is sometimes a razor's edge."

"Nope, Chet. You do not."

Mickey is watching carefully now.

Chet continues: "But what I do need to tell you is that there's those who think you're leaving too much on the table. Too many missed opportunities. To get that edge."

Frank, hastily with hands up: "Look, Mr. Orchard." A skip. "Chet. I appreciate your coming, but I don't need you or anyone else to tell me—"

Sensing Frank's defensiveness, Mickey steps between them, all three now even. "Of course, you don't, Frank. You're the expert on the field. It's almost like you were born to coach. That's why you were hired."

The flattery simmers Frank down. His shoulders relax. "And I appreciate that, Mickey. Honestly, I do." Now grudgingly, "So what do you have in mind?"

Chet looks around and moves close to Frank, then lower.

"These five-star recruits visiting this weekend?"

"Yeah, what about them?"

"They ain't going to be impressed with a 5 win and 6 loss team, no bowl game even. No pomp and pageantry."

Frank shifts restlessly under Chet's gaze, so Chet takes advantage: "We need to find another way to dazzle 'em. Make unforgettable memories of the U."

"And exactly how am I supposed to do that? Our million-dollar facilities and the excitement of this college town obviously aren't enough."

Mickey fields this question: "No, unfortunately, they're not. It's just the world we live in, Frank. With all their gadgets and gizmos, today's youngsters are hard to impress. You know this. And we're not talking about paying players either. Buying them fancy cars? No. We're way past that."

"Hell," Chet stops and the other two gather round him. "All of 'em already have cars they got from playing high school ball, so that old trick pony won't ride no more."

Mickey: "They're looking for something exciting. Something they don't get anywhere else but here at the U."

Frank's interest piqued: "How are they going to do that?"

Mickey steps back to let the boss answer.

Chet puts hands on hips and leans forward. "Let's just put it this way. There's a certain institution on campus that's having some major financial difficulties."

Chet looks over at the Delta Delta Theta sorority house and pauses for impact. "I'm sure they'd be grateful if my organization, The Raven Foundation, mostly boosters for football, would step in and sponsor some of their activities. To help alleviate their troubles, you see."

"What activities would those be?"

Mickey: "Activities that could reciprocally help the football program, of course."

Frank looks blankly at Mickey and then Chet, who continues: "Now everyone knows that a night on the town is more fun with some company, especially the company of lovely young ladies."

It suddenly dawns on Frank what they are talking about. "It's the 21st century, gentlemen. Do we really want to do this, ask young girls to make themselves available to athletes?"

"Hell no!" grimaces Mickey, shaking his head a definitive one time.

"We didn't say anything about asking anyone to do anything," Chet adds with a serious, sideways look.

"We're only talking about some social events, a match-up between football and Delta Delta Theta."

"Think of it as USO for those boys serving on teams out there in the hinterlands thither an' yon." Chet swings his arms wide, off toward the horizon.

"Just giving them a little taste of what's to come," Mickey

shrugs innocently, "when they commit to the U."

Frank, relieved, ever so slightly: "Well, clearly then I need counsel from someone who obviously knows these opportunities so well. It's just that I've never done anything along, uh, such grey lines."

Chet cuts in. "Opportunities, Frank. Nothing grey about opportunities. They're golden!"

"If you want me to stay clean, then why are you telling me all of this?"

Chet removes his hand and steps back. His face now is very bright, so bright it's almost menacing. "So you'll stay out of the way."

*   *   *   *

During her film genre class, Margolis stands at the podium at the front of a dark, windowless auditorium. Spots shine down on her as if she herself is in a movie. The rest of the room dims in relative shadow. As she speaks, her gestures get larger and more emphatic.

"Film Noir was not supposed to be art. It was often made in Hollywood on low budgets with unknown actors and shot on cheaper black-and-white film. Scripts were taken from the pulp fiction of hard-boiled detective writers like Dashiell Hammett."

She pauses and then clicks a remote. The iconic final image from *The Big Combo* flashes up on the screen. It shows Cornel Wilde and Jean Wallace walking out into the fog.

"Film Noir equates dark cinematography, the high contrast of black and white, with the dark side of American civilization. A civilization that is ultimately corrupt. The institutions we depend on to protect us and nurture us—the criminal justice system, the federal government, universities, families even— are really out to destroy us."

She again pauses to let her words sink in. She scans the

room with her eyes for emphasis and walks out from behind the podium to be the center of the students' attention.

"But noir doesn't deal just with society; it deals with the human condition. This is what makes it art. It shows us the dark side of the human soul and its futile aspirations for light. In film noir, we see ourselves and the dark parts we want to hide from the world."

A dramatic pause. Adrenaline pumping, Margolis scans the crowd to put an exclamation point on her lecture.

A hand shoots up in the crowd. It's Emma. She sits in a row with Brooke and a bunch of other sorority girls.

Margolis doesn't really want to stop to answer student questions—she's on a roll—but her helpful-professor nature gets the best of her, and she turns toward Emma's raised hand.

"Yes?"

"You keep saying noir is American, but isn't it an international phenomenon? There are British and Japanese film noirs, and the term itself comes from France."

"Yes, but the films themselves originated in Hollywood in the 1940s. The French critics in the 1960s weren't referring to Japan."

The audience snickers, sensing blood in the water.

Emma, bright and unsarcastic: "But their international appeal must mean they are about something more than the clichéd 'American Dream.'"

"You make a good point..." Margolis pauses and gestures questioningly for a name.

"Emma."

"Emma." Then a step. "This broad appeal shows that the genre of film noir cuts fundamentally to what it means to be human in a modern world." Now pacing away, talking at the whole class. "The individual and his (I use that term on purpose) aspirations are insignificant and even doomed up against the machinery of the capitalist State and its ruthless apparatus. An apparatus that turns out to be as evil as the criminals it seeks to apprehend."

She stops and stares sternly at Emma who has a smug look of victory on her face. Eyes aflame.

"That's all for today. Be sure to watch Stanley Kubrick's *The Killing* for next time. Screening is here, Thursday at 7:00 pm."

Lights go up and Margolis steps over to the podium. She closes her lecture notes and packs up her papers, while watching Emma scoot her way down the row of seats and out the door.

*   *   *   *

Back inside the president's office, it's day, the light inside is of that same glowing oak. Bill and Nancy Reinhart, Ford's parents, sit across the president's desk.

I've answered to blue bloods like this all my life, Lane thinks as he notices the finer points on Bill's suit—*French cuffs, tailored Alexander Kabbaz shirt...is that Glenurquhart check 200 count? Goddamn, I thought I'd be past this by now, but here I am on the bottomside of their boot soles.*

Lane tries to get his mind back on the conversation: "So what I'm hearing you saying is," he closes his eyes and puts a finger to his temple for concentration, "because of the U's involvement with the community college, you are concerned about the nature of Ford's relationship with Dr. Santos, am I correct?"

"That's right," Bill nods his head.

"But you do understand that Ford was not Dr. Santos's student, right?"

"Yes, but she was in *loco parentis*," Nancy pipes up. She was a schoolteacher for the first three years of her career, the years between Daddy's country club and Bill Reinhart's media fortune. So, she knows Latin phrases like *loco parentis*—"in the place of a parent"—from her Ed Theory classes at Wellesley.

"That's a position of power," Bill adds.

"And Ford is only 19, Art!"

Art's ears twitch at Nancy's voice, a kind of whine like she's talking to a kid who should know better. It makes the inferiority rise in his throat again.

"Yeah, but that means he's a grown up, right, Bill? I mean, he registered for the draft..."

"Inexcusable." Bill states from his seat. "And all we're hearin from you is—"

Nancy: "Excuses! Defending that, that—"

Lane tries to get a word in edgewise, but he can't because they start finishing each other's sentences.

Bill: "That woman professor. You're defending her! It's like you don't appreciate what I do for this school. This team..."

"Or the value of innocence."

"If you want a harassment suit, you'll get one!"

"And, with our friends, that would pretty much sink your Senate campaign, too."

Lane breathes, looks from one to the other. He sees how serious they are.

"Get it done, Art!"

They storm out of the office.

Calm until now, Lane balls his hand into fists while his face works into anger. He shakes and suddenly punches his fists in the air. He mouths to no one, "Fuck!" He looks around starting to panic, eyes searching for a solution to this dilemma. He picks up a gold fountain pen and rolls it around in his hands. After a few moments, his eyes fall on a picture of him and Frank. His face softens. He picks up the phone and presses a button.

"Gloria? It's Art." A beat. "Yeah. Listen, we got a situation. I need you to pull Margolis Santos's file." A pause. "Gather the Faculty Discipline Committee and get Marcia Stoddard on it. She can't stand Santos. I want a termination plan on my desk first thing in the morning." Longer pause. "No, this is not about the vote last year. Let's just say for now, 'conduct unbecoming.'"

He slams down the phone and calls out to his secretary: "Susie, would you call Dr. Santos? Tell her I want to see her!"

* * * *

Book bag slung over her arm, Margolis walks quickly with purpose down the hall of an elegant, old campus building, Hartley Hall. It's lined with office doors. This is the film department. A veritable gauntlet.

Marcia Stoddard, 50s, Margolis's faculty rival, stands outside her door, irreverently smoking a cigarette. She sees Margolis coming down the hall. She stares.

Mumbled nod, "Margolis."

"Marcia." Margolis doesn't even look at her, but quickens her pace. Then she thinks of something to say, so she turns and announces over her shoulder, "I got that grant!"

"Great. Just great." Marcia grumbles, as she steps back into her office. *That shut her up*, Margolis thinks.

Smiling at Stoddard's expected reaction, Margolis turns through an open doorway and into the department office reception area. She goes to her mailbox marked with a little white, typed sign saying 'SANTOS' stuffed with a pile of letters and papers. It all falls out when Margolis tries to retrieve it. Clearly, it's been awhile since she has been in the office.

Mail stowed away, Margolis walks up to Sandy, the middle-aged androgynous secretary, who is seated at a desk typing at a computer screen.

Margolis waits for Sandy to acknowledge her. A few beats. Margolis puts down her bag. Another beat.

Sandy, without looking up: "Yes?"

Forced reply, "Hi, Sandy. I need you to submit these production receipts for reimbursement." Margolis pulls a literal wad of paper receipts out of her bag and piles them on Sandy's desk.

Sandy looks incredulously at the mess and sifts fingers

futilely through it. She now looks up blankly at Margolis then back at the receipts: "Are all these for the off-site filming location with Farrah Maines from ACC?" Sandy turns back to the screen, then in lower voice: "Please would be nice."

"Yes. Please." Margolis pulls another sheet of paper from her bag. "And I'd like to set up a conference call with this list of producers. For next Monday. Late morning if possible."

Sandy stares up at her, frozen, waiting.

"Please?"

Sandy resumes and takes the list from Margolis's hand.

Margolis charmingly: "And thank you! With brown sugar on top."

"Done."

Margolis hams it up like Shirley Temple: "Sandy, you're the bestest Sandy ever!"

Sandy turns blasély back to the computer. Margolis again turns to leave.

Sandy spurts, "Wait, I almost forgot!"

Margolis turns back, face now impatient, suppressing a sigh.

"Did you get the message from Susie Adams, President Lane's secretary?"

"Well, no. I haven't checked since—"

"You better check. Says it's urgent."

Margolis finally gets out of there. But a worried look shadows her face. She stops at an office door with her name on it. She pulls out keys, unlocks, and enters.

As she flips through some envelopes, Margolis feels her way around her desk and sits down. Ah, a moment to herself.

Suddenly, there's a knock on the door. Annoyed look. Before Margolis can say "come in," it opens.

In pops the head of Mark Goldberg, mid-30s, her junior colleague in film. Like a puppy with a Brooklyn accent, he blurts out, "How was your summer?"

Margolis looks up.

When he sees that he has her, he slides his entire body into the doorway.

"Well, it's been over now for two weeks," Margolis snipes. "Where've you been?"

"Not writing my book, that's where."

"We never get done over summer break all the writing we thought we'd do, Goldberg. Happens to all of us."

"Said smugly and confidently by someone with tenure."

Margolis smiles and shrugs her shoulders, puts her feet on the desk.

He steps fully into the office and shuts the door. "How'd the date go?"

Margolis scrunches her face up, "What date?"

Mark points and widens his eyes, looking at her sideways.

"I know, I know!" She nods guiltily. We never went out. I just couldn't make it work schedule-wise. Anyway, you know how I feel about dating guys from school."

"Yeah, yeah. And you know that you eventually have to start living again after Frank, right?"

"Yeah. Maybe." A beat. "Can we talk about this later? And I'm *not* making a film, so don't even say—"

There's a knock on the door.

Mark ignores it and continues, epiphanic: "A movie! You keep talking about making a movie. Why don't you? A rigorous shoot is what you need, Glee! You'll meet new men—"

While he talks, there's a second knock. Margolis looks impatiently at the door. "Mark," she points. "Office hours?"

He looks back at the door and becomes aware of the knocking. He raises his hands in surrender. "Oh, yeah. Duty calls." He opens the door and steps out in front of Emma Barnes, who is standing there patiently with books in her arms.

Emma: "Sorry! Didn't mean to interrupt."

Margolis motions to her to enter. "No, no. Not a problem. Professor Goldberg was just leaving," Margolis hints. Then, back to Emma: "Do come in."

As Mark leaves, he makes the gesture of holding a movie camera, cranking an imaginary handle and focusing an imaginary lens. He exaggeratedly mouths "MOVIE!" Margolis shakes her head.

Emma enters the office and stands awkwardly looking around.

"Have a seat anywhere," Margolis gestures. "Emma, was it?"

"Yes. Emma Barnes."

Margolis shuffles some papers around on her desk as if she's busy, then looks up at Emma. "Well, Emma Barnes, that was quite a precocious display you put on today in my class."

"Yeah." She crinkles her nose. "That's what I came to talk to you about. I'm sorry if I was—"

"No, no. By all means, that course needs some lively debate. Film history. Most students just suffer through it."

"Suffer? Hardly. Everybody I talk to loves that class."

"Now you're just sucking up," Margolis smiles knowingly at Emma who smiles back, unashamed. Margolis continues, "I know you didn't just come to apologize. What else is on your mind?"

"Well, to be honest, I'm an English major but wanna go to grad school in screenwriting. Film studies, maybe. Like you."

They have a moment and eyes lock. Emma breaks the eye contact first and looks shyly at her books in her lap.

Margolis gets up and closes the door. "Well, you certainly seem to know your stuff. At least, film noir."

"I read your book."

Margolis looks surprised. Her dark eyebrows rise.

Emma continues, "You know, *Femmes Natales*."

Margolis covers in a fake southern accent, "Oh, that little ol' thang?" She gestures toward the copy sitting conveniently on her desk between them. The subtitle reads, *The Women of Hollywood and the Birth of Film Noir*. Both reach for it, and, as in some cheesy rom-com, their fingers grab the book awkwardly at the same time. They look up at each other, not really surprised at the crisp shock of the other's tug. Margolis regains her wits and is first to break contact, but Emma's eyes follow Margolis as she leans back. *Golden wolf-eyes*, Margolis thinks.

"It really is nothing."

"No, seriously, it was great to read about how women have contributed to the industry since the beginning. Made me see myself in their place."

"Well, I hope when you graduate and go to Hollywood that you'll do more than fetch coffee and scribble on someone else's script!"

Emma, unsure: "That's a joke, right?" Then, confidently, "I get it. That's a joke."

There's another knock on the office door. Margolis can't help but look annoyed.

"Yes?"

The door opens. It's Ford Reinhart. Margolis's face falls, but she gathers herself, smiles, and turns to Emma.

"I forgot that I have a scheduled appointment now with another student. I'm sorry."

"No, no. It's OK. I just waylaid you with my insignificant problems. I'll come back another time."

"Please do." A beat. Then politely to Ford as if she doesn't know him, "How can I help you?"

Emma gets up and walks out past Ford who watches her and waits for her to leave. He then steps in and shuts the door behind him.

His face looks uneasy and a bit frantic. "I just wanted you to know. It's my parents. They're pissed. No, way more than pissed. They've met with the president about us. You and me. They want to sue."

Margolis eases as coolly as possible back in her chair and tries to look calmly at Ford. Her eyes fall down to her desk where lies the message from the president's secretary.

IV.

Chet Orchard and Lucille Bontemps stand facing each other over a counter in the Theta house kitchen. The only light in the room streams in from the window over the sink. A million motes dance in the air between them. Lucille's arms are folded and shoulders slumped. She has a dish towel over one shoulder. Chet stands close, leaning forward. A bowl of fruit on the counter next to them: oranges, bananas, mangos, and grapes.

Chet, all Cheshire cat: "Oh, Lucille, come now. It's not like I'm asking to hire assassins!" He chuckles and smiles, raising both hands innocently in the air.

"But it does sound an awful lot like you're asking me to—" She stops short, doesn't say the word. She sighs and then raises herself up. "Demand far too much out of these young girls."

"What are you talkin 'bout? It'll give 'em a chance to show their school spirit. It'll be like a mixer. You have those all the time, right?" He tosses a grape into his mouth.

"Yes, but not under such bald-face, unseemly pretenses. I feel like the house madam, not the housemom."

"Well perhaps you should have thought about that before. I didn't hear you complain none about horse-tradin and sausage-makin when you got the new Great Hall addition with my $200 grand. Made you the envy of every housemom on sorority row. And your own parkin space out front." Chet waves at her like a comma. "Bill's come due, hon."

Lucille frowns, puts her hands on her hips, and looks defeated down at the floor.

Chet raises a finger. "You just make sure there are four girls in a limo outside the hotel tonight before the banquet. Good-lookin ones too. No pooches, for God's sake."

He grabs another grape out of the bowl, pops it in his mouth, and crunches it between his teeth. He walks smiling out the kitchen's back door.

Turning away in a huff, Lucille sees Emma sitting in the dining room studying at a table. Emma strokes a cat standing on her books. It gives Lucille an idea.

Lucille walks through, toward Emma. The cat jumps down at her approach. Lucille stands menacingly over Emma who looks up and jumps, frightened for a moment. Emma relaxes.

"Geez, you scared me."

"I just thought of a way you can make your dues disappear. Tuition, room and board, too. Everything. All in one fell swoop."

Emma, innocently encouraged: "Really! How?" She looks toward the kitchen where Chet was standing.

"You'll have to promise me right now that you'll trust me and do what I ask."

"Sure. Just as long as you don't tell my parents. I'm trying to help them out as much as possible."

"Of course. I'm sure your parents would hate for it to get out that you're on the charity wagon. It will just be our little secret."

"OK." Emma takes a breath. "What do I have to do?"

*   *   *   *

Emma lounges blithely on a couch in the Great Hall, the common room where the Theta girls watch TV and have parties. Her knee is up, and the hem of her long silver dress has slid down to reveal her smooth brown thighs. She plays unselfconsciously with the shoulder strap.

Brooke pokes her head in the doorway and holds up a full bottle of Stoli. "Ready to pre-game?"

Emma looks up quickly and then back lazily at her feet, stilettos on the coffee table. "Nah." The brush-off. "I don't even want to go to this fucking banquet. Bunch of dumb jocks."

"Come on, Barnes. Don't be such a stiffy. A drink or two will put hair on your back." Brooke plops down two red plastic

Dixie cups full of ice. She pours in the vodka. And pours. And pours, until the clear liquid is three-fourths of the way to the top. She then splashes in a dash or two of Hawaiian Punch.

Emma drinks, then wipes her mouth with the back of her hand. "What the hell are we even doing tonight? With football players—new recruits. Lucille didn't really tell me anything—kinda weird."

"We go to the club. We party. You know the drill."

"Not really."

"You go to the banquet, look pretty. After, we take boys out on the town. Dance around, party, take 'em home. Easy." Brooke takes a drink, as if building up to this next line but make it seem nonchalant. "If you help make these boys choose the U, you get paid and can stay in school as a Theta. Win, win."

Satisfied with her speech, Brooke throws herself back against the back of the couch and slings an arm over the top, leaning into it.

"So, somebody is going to pay my tuition. And dues?" Emma inquires. "Who is this person?" The strap of her silver dress falls off her shoulder again.

"Some fucking rich booster named Chet Orchard. But who cares?"

"You on the dole too?"

"Fuck right, I am!"

Emma reluctantly chuckles and nods, admitting that Brooke may be on to something with her sexual realpolitik. *After all,* she thinks, *if you've got it, why not use it. Someone else will.*

Emma slips the strap back on her shoulder. "You know what? Fuck it. I'm at least going to enjoy myself while I'm still here."

Brooke holds her cup up to Emma's. "Live for the now!"

"Live for the now!" Emma chimes.

They toast with the dull clink of plastic, and a little red stuff sloshes out on Emma's leg.

38

"Watch it, bitch!" Emma looks serious for a second, "You fuck up my dress, how will I ever get laid?"

Then a laugh hisses out of her closed mouth. Brooke almost spits out her drink and laughs right along with her.

*   *   *   *

A gauche hotel ballroom is set up like a freaking wedding reception with many round tables draped in white tablecloths. In front, a podium flanked by two tables on a dais. The room is crowded. Mostly white people shuffle around the bars at either end. There're a few black young men. Mostly players, of course.

Margolis and Frank enter the ballroom amid the garbled small talk of a huge crowd. Behind them is a sign with balloons that reads, "Football Kick-Off Banquet. Brought to you by The Raven Foundation."

They are dressed to the nines: Margolis in a slinky black cocktail dress and heels, Frank in a dark, dapper tux, even though all the other men in the room sport suits.

Frank smiles and waves briefly at people he knows. Margolis looks dour. She grabs a glass of champagne off a tray and immediately drains it. Then grabs another.

"At least try to look like you're not the evil stepmother at the ball."

"Screw you."

"Nice." He looks away. "Love you too, Glee."

She glances daggers at him then drinks. Puts the empty glass on a tray and grabs a full one. Margolis, under her breath: "No, you don't."

Not paying attention, Frank sees Chet and walks toward him, glad to get away.

Left alone, Margolis sulks for a second then looks around the ballroom. The first person she spies is Emma in her sparkling silver gown. Stunning.

Margolis eavesdrops from a distance, unable to turn away.

Emma talks and charms everyone around her.

"Emma, this is Reynaldo." Mickey's deep voice resonates from the middle of the crowd. He's going through introductions. Promptly, Emma smiles and shakes hands with Reynaldo, a tall, young black recruit in a crowd of athletes and sorority girls. One is named Stephanie Rogers, skinny brunette, a junior, about 20. Another, from what Margolis can gather, is named Aria Anderson. Brooke is with them. She has her own white recruit on her arm. It isn't long before Reynaldo has his hand on Emma's bare back.

Mickey looks up and notices Margolis standing alone by the entrance. He bids his pardon and leaves the young'uns alone to mingle.

As he approaches, he extends his hand. "Dr. Santos? I wanted to introduce myself. I'm Mickey Andouille, the new Director of Player Relations."

Margolis's face brightens a bit, by force. "Oh, hi. Sorry. I kinda spaced out." She takes his hand and is taken by how warm it is. "Nice to meet you."

"Another year, another banquet, huh?" He finally lets go of her hand.

She turns to him, gauging how serious he is. Not very. She scoffs in agreement, "I mean, yeah. And it never seems like there's enough booze." She grabs a flute of champagne from a passing tray. Mickey follows suit.

He raises his glass, "To the never-ending parade of self-congratulations in athletics." He clinks her glass.

"Here, here," Margolis replies, both simultaneously bemused and amused. She drinks, watching him the whole time. "How do you like your new job, 'player relations manager' or whatever?"

Mickey chuckles, knowing he's being fucked with a little. "Let's just say that it's testing my people skills. That's why I'm over here hiding with you." He smiles at her, gives a slight wink.

She doesn't know how to respond exactly, but she likes his face, smooth and trusting. And not bad to look at either.

On the other side of the room, Frank is standing with Chet Orchard and a thuggish looking Ronnie, a security guard—early 30s, dressed in a suit—who surveys the room.

Frank and Chet watch Mickey talking to Margolis.

"That doesn't bother you, seeing magnificent Mickey talking to your woman?" Chet goads.

"Naw," Frank takes a drink. "We're a...we're—"

"What? Don't tell me you two are a couple o' swingers..."

"No, no," Frank corrects. He sighs, "We're separated. I don't really want anyone to know yet, so..."

"My lips are sealed," Chet oozes in his southern drawl, making a locking gesture at his mouth.

Mickey sees Frank and Chet talking and is suddenly distracted.

"Well, duty calls," Mickey breaks the spell. "It was good to talk with you, Dr. Santos."

"Margolis."

"Margolis," Mickey smiles. "I hope you have a great time tonight."

She watches him weave through the crowd and out of sight.

Back to Frank and Chet, who talk in hushed tones.

"Why you got your petticoat all in a ruffle, Frank? I told you I'd take care of the details."

"I just want to know what my players are up to, that's all. How they're entertaining themselves."

"Those aren't your players. Not yet. Not until they sign on the dotted line with you smiling in front of the cameras." After a beat, "Let us soften them up for you!"

"Us?"

"Me and my lovely young assistants."

Smiling widely, teeth crooked, Chet gestures over to Emma and her group.

Radiant, Emma laughs and talks to Brooke's white recruit.

Emma doesn't notice Brooke in the background giving her the evil eye.

Emma pauses for a slight moment when Reynaldo puts his hand too low on her back, touching her butt, but she regains composure. She moves his hand off.

"Boys will be boys!" Chet chuckles.

Frank gives him a look and shakes his head.

"What?" Chet looks fake-hurt. "I know with political correctness and all you can't say that anymore, but that don't make it untrue," Chet winks.

Frank turns away and heads into the crowded middle of the room. Chet chuckles to himself, as Mickey steps up next to him. They both watch Frank talking with some of his players, where he seems most comfortable.

"Frank doesn't have the stomach for this," Chet announces, taking a swig of scotch.

"No, I guess not," Mickey agrees.

"We need a middleman to take him out of the equation altogether."

"I could keep an eye on him."

Chet turns to Mickey for a second. "No. No, I need you to be the face of the team in public, not the wise guy greasing the wheels behind the scene."

Mickey stands patiently waiting for Chet to come up with the answer because it looks like he's got one, and Mickey already knows what it's going to be.

"You know who I'm thinking would be the perfect person?"

"Egglebert?" Mickey asks innocently.

"Good old Eggy, owes me for that recruiting payout he turned down as a freshman." Chet shakes his head with a smile. "The perfect cover. Our ear on the inside."

"I'll set up Eggy an interview with Frank."

Loud feedback wails from a microphone at the front of the ballroom, and dinner is announced. Everyone turns and makes their way to the tables.

After the meal, Frank and Margolis sit next to each other near the podium with other coaches and wives. President Lane stands smiling at the podium on the dais while the crowd laughs. He's in the middle of his speech.

"Then Frank says to me, 'Art, that's not a lineman. That's our quarterback!'" There's more laughter, and he waits for it to subside. He's a master at milking a crowd. "'Well,' I says, 'I guess they *don't* grow them like they used to!'"

The crowd laughs again and then some applause. Frank is beaming, looking proudly at his players at tables in the crowd.

Emma smiles and looks over at Reynaldo, her recruit. She glances down at his body. He's huge!

A coach leans over to Margolis and says something in her ear. She smiles and nods. She looks over lovingly at Frank. She can't help it.

"In all seriousness," Lane continues, "our new coach has put us in a position to dominate recruiting in this state. With our network of high school coaches and Frank's new conditioning regime that starts in middle school, the U is bound to keep getting top-rated recruits for years to come."

Lane pauses. The audience applauds. He raises a glass of water. Since he's a teetotaler.

"Here's to a grand and glorious season and a grand and glorious future! Go U!"

The crowd responds instantly in unison, "Go U!"

He tips his glass to Frank and gives him a deadly serious look. He then smiles and toasts to the table where the recruits, Emma, and Brooke sit. They join the entire room in clapping for the president.

Margolis takes her purse and excuses herself from the table. Nearby, Nancy Reinhart watches her and follows her out of the ballroom.

Chet sees the ladies leave and leans over to Ronnie. "I want you to keep an eye on Santos. Find out where she goes."

Ronnie nods and gets up to follow.

*   *   *   *

In the ladies' room, Margolis stands looking at herself in the mirror. She takes out lipstick and puts it on. A coach's wife comes up next to her and stands at the next sink.

"Margolis, I'm just so glad that Frank brought us here. Luke's so proud to be coaching for him."

Coach's wife puts her hand on Margolis's shoulder. Margolis smiles weakly and nods in welcome.

"Really, we are truly grateful." Coach's wife squeezes Margolis's arm and leaves the bathroom.

Margolis turns back to the mirror and pauses, dissatisfied. She sighs and slumps her shoulders before lifting lipstick to her mouth.

Nancy Reinhart comes out of a stall and stands next to Margolis looking at her in the mirror. "So, you're Margolis Santos?"

"Yes."

Nancy turns to Margolis, and her voice takes a steely tone: "You stay the hell away from Ford, do you hear me? Some in this town may mistake the advancement of mediocrity for success, but Affirmative Action can't hide the fact that you people still don't know how to control yourselves. You damn—!" Nancy apparently cannot bring herself to say "hussie" or "slut" or even "wetback." She grits her teeth, stomps her foot, and in a turn she's out the door.

Margolis stands there with her mouth open, shocked. She touches her hand to her face. Fights back tears. Looks at herself in the mirror.

Within minutes, Margolis pushes herself out of the hotel front door into the crisp air. She is breathing heavily and looking around for which way to go. Anxiety attack coming on. Finally, she catches her breath, looks forward, and tilts toward the parking lot. She gets in her Mercedes and pulls out, tires squealing.

44

Ronnie turns on his lights and eases out behind her into traffic.

*   *   *   *

Through strobe lights, dance music blares. The banquet has long ended. Emma, Brooke, Stephanie and Aria dance awkwardly with the recruits in a chic nightclub. The girls face each other in a circle with the four boys ringed around the outside.

One of the dates gets close behind Aria and freaks on her, gyrating his ungainly hips and bending her over with his beefy arms. Shocked, she stands, turns, and pushes him back. Angry look on her face.

Brooke grabs Aria, turns her back around, and shakes her by both arms. Aria stops dancing and stares down at her feet. On the verge of tears, she relents, and the boy returns and freaks her.

Emma watches, then looks over at Brooke who raises her eyebrows at Emma, as if "you better play along or you're next." Emma turns, puts her arms around Reynaldo, and dances close and sensually. She looks up into his face. He looks down on hers, hungrily.

Drugs and alcohol make time skip. Beats pumping loud. The floor is absolutely packed, jumping. Strobes. Lasers slice through fog machines.

The four girls move their bodies, now much more in tune with the music. Eyes are closed. They spin and bounce as if in a trance. They caress each other's bodies, enamored with their own youth. Lips. Necks. Ankles. Breasts.

The boys are not on the floor. They drink beers at the bar looking around for the girls, but it's hard to see in this light and faux smoke. One recruit elbows another in the ribs. They talk, laugh, thinking they're going to get lucky. They sway slightly, drunk.

The four girls drift apart, involved in their own rhythms.

Emma dances by herself, eyes closed. It's a huge fucking club and Emma is swallowed in a sea of strangers. She notices Brooke by the bar making out with her recruit who pulls away and says something to the others. They all gather and head for the door, recruits pulling their girls behind them by the hands.

Emma's eyes follow her friends as they make their way across the crowded, thumping room.

Reynaldo lingers for a moment, looks around, but can't find Emma. She steps back, hiding behind a big dude, obscured from Reynaldo. From between bobbing heads in the flashing lights, Emma can see everything going on. The big dude looks down on her and smiles, so she moves to another part of the floor.

Reynaldo then steams out the door pushing past another lump of people who scowl and cuss at him. He meets up with the football crowd and stomps toward the limo.

As her friends walk out, Emma's professor walks in. Still in her black cocktail dress, Margolis stops and looks around. Emma can't help but think how fucking sexy she looks. She moves through the crowd toward Margolis.

Ronnie enters the club and follows Margolis, keeping his distance.

Margolis catches sight of Emma. Eyes lock. Margolis's view dominates the scene. Emma stares at her. Emma's eyes, wolf eyes. Emma returns to dancing. This time, slower, more sensually. Margolis moves through the crowd but Emma stays centered in her view. Emma looks again. Smoldering.

The beat from inside can be heard through the doors out to the portico where the group shelters from the rain. A limo pulls up, and three couples plus Reynaldo get in. As they drive away, Reynaldo has a pissed expression on his face. He looks out the window while Brooke and her white recruit dry hump next to him.

Margolis is now next to Emma on the floor. Emma does not

look at her but continues to dance. None of her friends or their dates is around anymore, so it doesn't matter. No one in the crowd notices. It's too packed.

Except Ronnie. He notices.

Margolis dances and moves closer. Emma does not seem to mind. Their bodies fall together in rhythm. Margolis slips her hand behind the small of Emma's back. Pulls her closer. Their eyes lock.

Crosscut to the limo, which stops in front of the Delta Delta Theta house. Three couples disembark, arm in arm, and we follow them up the path to the door. Inside, each girl takes a smiling boy into her room. Doors close.

Outside, the limo door also closes, and we see a lone Reynaldo headed back to his hotel. The tires hiss on the rain-wet streets.

Back in the pulsating club, Emma wraps her arms around Margolis's neck. They press together and look down at their bodies in tune: Margolis's thigh between Emma's legs at the crotch.

They kiss. It's long and deep, getting more passionate with every moment.

They spin.

Kiss. Out of control.

*   *   *   *

Margolis lies asleep in her bed. Pillow over her head. Her cell phone is on the nightstand. The phone rings, vibrates. She wakes with a start. Eyes squinted, she looks around the bright room in a daze. *Did we? Last night? No...* She reaches for the phone, answers it.

Groggily, "Hello?"

Sandy's tinny voice pierces the receiver. "Hi, it's me."

"Sandy?" Margolis looks around for a non-existent clock. "What time is it?"

"9:00 a.m. On a Saturday. I know. But the dean called me at home."

"What?" A little more awake now. "The dean? Why?"

"She wanted your home phone number, but I told her I didn't have it with me. I'd have to go in to the office to get my Rolodex."

"Who still has a Rolodex?"

Sandy ignores the question, "She wants to meet with you today in her office. Told her I'd tell you."

"Today? But it's—"

"I know." A beat. "Margolis, it's none of my business, but..."

"Yes?"

"She said it was about a student."

Margolis hangs up the phone, looks out the window for a moment. On the stand next to the bed is a note. She remembers Emma slipping it to her when Margolis left the club. Alone.

Margolis picks it up and reads it again: "Come see me at the Theta house sometime. Take the back stairs." There's an address.

She lays back on her pillow. Next to her, the bed is empty. Margolis breathes relieved.

V.

Margolis slumps hungover in a chair in the dean's office suite. She's wearing sunglasses, and we can't tell if she's asleep or not. Motionless.

"Do you know why I called you here today?" Dean Concord, late 50s, Hispanic, peers from behind her desk. She appears regal in her comportment and no-nonsense pantsuit. Her brown face is dry and tight, barely suppressing some silent rage.

"No, not really. Does it have to do with the message from President Lane—"

"I wanted to speak with you before you met with him," Dean Concord pauses. "Do you know Ford Reinhart, a student over at Athens Community College? I believe he was part of the film production you were involved in recently."

"Yes. So?" Margolis's body suddenly charges with fear, but she beats it back. Breathes.

"His parents called." She pauses dramatically and looks over her glasses at Margolis. "They're concerned about your relationship with their son."

Margolis looks back as dispassionately as possible. *Don't show anything.*

So Concord continues: "They claim that he spent the night with you in a hotel room after the shoot. They didn't know where he was and even called the police."

"I can see how they'd be worried," Margolis mumbles, with more than a hint of sarcasm. "Their fully-grown, adult son is away leading his own life, and—"

The dean interrupts: "Did you have a sexual relationship with this student?"

"He wasn't my student."

"So, your relationship *was* sexual."

"I didn't say that. He's not my student. And he had nothing to do with Athens University."

"Did you not work with him on Professor Farragut Manes's film production in July?"

"Farrah? Yes, but—"

"Then it involves this university." After a beat, she repeats: "Did you have sex with Ford Reinhart?"

Margolis pauses, weighing her answer. She knew this moment could come, but she's confident in her position.

"I prefer not to answer that. My personal life is none of the University's business."

"The concern is, however, that you were representing the University at the location, in a responsible supervisory role over those students."

"No, I had no power over those students in terms of grades or any other evaluative capacity."

"University funds contributed to the production of the movie, Margolis. My job as dean is to investigate any allegations concerning faculty involved in University-sponsored activities."

Margolis, suddenly now awake, sits up with a quick intake of air.

Concord cuts her off: "Once I finish my preliminary inquiry, I'll report my findings to the president and then let you know the next step. But I must inform you that you are officially under investigation. You may continue to teach until otherwise notified."

"Is that it?" Margolis puts her sunglasses back on, stands up, and reaches toward the dean. Margolis extends her hand. "Thank you, Gloria. I appreciate your time and effort. It's not an easy job."

"Listen," Concord leans back in her seat. "I know it seems unfair—you're the only woman but not the only professor on this campus having dalliances—but that's exactly why you need to keep your nose clean—everyone is going to come down on you like a ton of bricks. Especially when you're Latina. Trust me, I know."

Dean Concord smiles that weak smile again and shakes Margolis's hand. Margolis turns to leave and reaches for the doorknob.

"Oh, Margolis," Concord calls out.

Margolis pauses.

"If there is anything that occurs to you about this case over the weekend, please do give me a call at home. Anything."

Margolis smirks, nods, and slinks out the door.

*   *   *   *

"As much as I'd like to," Lane continues, "I can't just fire the head football coach's wife. In the middle of the season."

Lane leans back in his leather chair and holds a phone to his ear.

We can hear Chet's voice, tinny and muffled, through the mouthpiece: "But they're finished."

"What?"

"I practically heard it from the horse's mouth, Art," Chet insists. Suddenly, there's a loud bang. "He and Santos. They're splitsville." Bang! And another bang.

"Divorce?" Lane strains to hear over the noise. Cut to:

Interior. Shooting range – Day.

"Not yet, but separated." Chet stands at the line holding a pistol out in front of him with both hands. He squints, takes aim, and pulls the trigger. Bang!

Lane's voice comes through: "How are you talking and shooting at the same time, Chet?"

Chet chuckles, "I got the headphones up under my ear muffs." Bang, bang! Thin white cords hang down from each side of his head.

"Just in case, I'll have Ronnie follow her, maybe get some dirt. If we have photos, it'll be easier to find witnesses to go along with them."

"We'll only need it if she decides to appeal. For now, we

don't want to create unnecessary bad press for our head coach."

"Hell, get 'em both outta here, for all I care."

"Chet, we can't do that—you know what we had to do to get that boy here?"

Chet remembers and is silent, then he answers quietly, "Hell, I had to foot the bill."

"And I took the heat!" Lane exclaims before taking a calming breath. "Then we're agreed. When they split, we keep the coach, and ditch the bitch."

*   *   *   *

Margolis gets out of her Mercedes and walks towards her house, which, she suddenly notices, looks eerily like the exterior they used for *The Brady Bunch*. She's on her cell phone with Mark. She pauses outside the front door next to a window looking into the garage.

"I know, right? On a Saturday!" She takes a drag on a ciggy. "It was some bullshit about fraternizing with students."

Mark sounds metallic, typical movie off-screen voice-over, "Did you fuck him?"

A beat. "Well, yeah, I fucked him. But this kid wasn't my student!"

"Did you tell the dean you fucked him?"

"No."

"Well maybe you should."

Margolis shakes her head as if he could see it, "No."

"You didn't do anything wrong, so why not tell her?" Mark asks, while Margolis keeps shaking her head, listening. "You're separated. Single. He's a grown-up. You don't have anything to hide."

"Well, they don't know about me and Frank yet."

"Hmm. That could be trouble."

"What is that to them?"

"Oh, you're right. It's nothing," Mark responds, with more than a streak of sarcasm. "Football season is about to start, and Frank is just their next golden goose who stands to make them millions, unless there's something wrong with him, like he's *divorced*. Why would the president care about that?"

Margolis stops and turns toward the sunset, considering. "I hadn't thought of that."

A montage of images flickers in her mind's eye of Ford laughing uncontrollably as Margolis tickles him in the back lot, hidden by trunks of lighting stands—a naked pink-hard shoulder muscle, Ford sliding into her so easily, despite his girth, feeling like it did before she'd had a baby—Ford's face, looking quizzical, then smiling at her, stadium scoreboard in background, the smell of mown grass and popcorn—then she's back to reality.

"I think you need to tell them you made an error in judgment, Margolis," Mark counsels. "Come clean."

Five feet from Margolis, behind the window inside the dark garage, Brie sits on a large orange paint bucket smoking a cigarette. She listens to her mother's voice. Through the window, she sees Margolis talking on the phone, but Margolis does not see her.

"We'll see about that, Mark." A breath. "I don't know what I'm going to do next. I just want to keep my job." A long listening pause, then: "Yeah. OK." A beat. Exasperation: "I said OK! Jesus. Bye!"

Brie overhears everything her mother said. Surprise changes to anger as Brie thinks about it for a sec. She puts out the cigarette on the windowsill and gets up. She doesn't see her mother make the same gesture of crushing a butt on the same wall just outside.

Inside, Margolis puts her purse and keys down on the kitchen counter as Brie stomps in from the garage.

"So, you've been fucking a student?" Brie cringes. "That's just so cliché."

53

"What? You were listening to my conversation." A quick smell of smoke, beat of realization. "Brie, have you been smoking?"

Feeling entitled to her own inquisition, Brie ignores the question: "Why didn't I realize it was you who destroyed the marriage? Fucking boys half Dad's age. Hell, almost my age!

"Would you stop saying 'fucking'?"

"No wonder he left you. You just couldn't say 'no' to those young, stiff cocks—"

"Brie Rose!"

"That's it," a snide laugh. "You fucked a student and Daddy found out."

"You better watch yourself, young lady," Margolis raises a finger. "He wasn't my student."

"Still, he was young." A beat. Brie drops her arms in exasperation. "This is all your fault. You always lilting around like some big slu—"

"Brie! I am still your mother and I deserve your respect!"

"Sluts don't deserve respect!"

Margolis slaps Brie, almost involuntarily like a reflex. They look at each other, surprised, frozen for one unretractable moment.

"I'm moving in with Dad!" Brie runs out of the kitchen through the garage door and shuts it.

Margolis crumples on the kitchen counter with her head under her arms.

*   *   *   *

It's day, but the lecture hall is dark. Although rows and rows of rapt faces glow in the light from the projector, Emma's usual seat is empty.

Margolis speaks from the podium on stage. On screen behind her are stills of Marie Windsor from Stanley Kubrick's *The Killing*. Margolis looks at it and points briefly with her laser as she starts talking: "She's all business. Objective, ruthless, promiscuous, and impassive. Just like the men. Only she's not supposed to be."

As she lectures, the world goes on outside the classroom in a stream of moving images:

Emma sits on the grass of the quad with Brie, Aria, and Stephanie. They check out two guys in shorts with backpacks and whisper to each other. They laugh and talk while Brie idolizes Emma with rapt attention. Brie is just happy to be in her presence.

We don't see her, but we hear Margolis's voiceover everything: "She's supposed to be at home, preening for her man. Waiting for him to come back."

Nearby on the practice field, Frank blows a whistle and yells at a group of players at blocking dummies. He gesticulates wildly with his arms.

Chet Orchard stands across the field watching Frank. Chet's arms are folded. He raises one hand to his mouth. Concern.

"But she can't sit still."

At the club, Emma dances mindlessly amid a huge crowd on the dance floor. Strobes. Arms in the air. Spotlights and bodies gyrating.

"She has to act, though no one sees her as the hero of the movie."

Over students' shoulders, we see the clip from *The Killing* of Marie Windsor getting shot by Elisha Cook.

"But she's the heart of the film. In fact, there would be no film noir without her, our so-called 'femme fatale.' A catalyst. She's smarter than everyone else, and she has to pay for it."

Margolis emphatically closes the folder holding her lecture notes.

"The femme fatale resembles a woman of the 21st century, more than one from the mid-20th. In other words, she doesn't give a flip about social definitions of female propriety—she acts like a man: she takes risks, she has sex with whoever she wants, she uses power to get what she wants, she lives for the moment, she makes mistakes. She's unfettered by a double-standard. Just like many of you." Cut to:

In the club bathroom, Emma pushes a tall, older dark-haired guy into a stall and up against the wall. She jumps into his arms and wraps her legs around him. She kisses him hard and grinds her pelvis into him—he starts to kiss her neck. She lowers her head back.

Lecture hall. Close on Margolis's face, half in shadow. "There's no pity for a pretty face in this man's world. But she'll take a few of them down with her. She puts the 'fatal' in femme fatale."

*   *   *   *

Margolis stares up at the soaring tower of the main building, her hand pausing a little too long on the door handle. She looks up. A lens flare off her dark glasses blinds her. You can tell by the way she raises her hand. For mercy almost.

Margolis suddenly finds herself up many stories in the tower. Out a nearby window, the near-gold of the autumn green stretches to horizon. In the foreground, a secretary sits pecking out paperwork on an outdated computer at a large oak desk in an ornate office. She picks the phone up. Listens to phone. Hangs up phone.

"The president will see you now."

Margolis shakes it off. Pushes through.

The light changes from brown to red as she enters the office where Dean Concord and President Lane sit together at a conference table.

"Please take a seat." He gestures toward the empty chair across from them at the table.

"Thank you," Margolis moves toward the chair with as much poise as she can muster. Time slows down now, and

Margolis breaks them down like she's doing a character study for a film script.

She notes a large man in his early 60s, President Lane, who sports an expensive dark suit complemented by his grey, conservative haircut, a thin veneer of his Machiavellian brain. His face is large and friendly but the flab pinched in the collar at his neck shows he's hiding the coil of ambition. She hears President Lane talk with a southern accent, though he affects impeccable grammar.

"We appreciate your coming this early in the semester" blah, blah, blah...

Clearly, he is one of those "new" southerners who believe that tradition should snuggle up to progress, that Nocona cowboy boots go perfectly fine with $5000 Armani suits, and that power entitles the bearer to whatever he wants. His worst fear, Margolis bets, is being thought of as stupid or inferior. She didn't know this back when she voted to remove him as university president. What a dumb move that was.

"You know Dean Concord, of course."

Margolis turns to Concord, late 50s, Hispanic, who appears regal in her comportment and no-nonsense pantsuit. Her brown face is dry and tight, barely suppressing some silent rage. Margolis senses that this hard-assed dean is pragmatic, ethical, and politically naïve. You can see it in the way her lidded eyes shift back and forth between her and Lane. As a fellow minority, Concord holds Margolis to a higher standard and is itching to punish her for "betraying" and "embarrassing" their race.

Lane points. "Now, Margoliss—"

"It's Margo-*lee*, by the way. Rhymes with *glee*."

The power couple look sternly at Margolis who slumps, slowly shrinking, in her seat.

"You know the reason why we've asked you here." The president slides a paper over to her. "This letter contains the results of our investigation. And the ensuing punishment."

Margolis puts a hand on the letter, but she doesn't want to turn it over—she has a feeling it's going to be bad...but she doesn't know how bad.

Lane's voice booms, unreasonably loud: "It's all there in the letter, but the administrative faculty disciplinary committee met yesterday, including myself and Dean Concord here, and we have reached a determination. As of now, Margolis, you are stripped of University privileges and will be terminated at the end of the semester."

Several beats. Margolis looks desperately to Dean Concord for support, but the dean, face a hard glare, silently spurns Margolis's pleading glance. *Dean Pilate,* Margolis thinks, *washing her hands.*

Margolis switches to sarcasm; it's the only way she can think of to save face, "Well, if I'm such a threat to students, why not fire me now?"

"Your classes have already begun, and we don't want to disrupt—"

Lane breaks in, "You showed bad judgment taking students to establishments that serve alcohol where they could slip and fall..."

"Slip and fall?"

The dean: "Or be put in compromising situations."

"Compromising..." Beat. Margolis can't help but grin, a gallows grin.

"You have exposed the University to potential liability, and we must protect our customers."

"Potential liability? What does that mean? I simply met with students—not even my students, by the way—for dinner after a shoot—"

Lane: "It's all in the university's by-laws—your choices have made you no longer fit for having close ties with students."

"But the future of the film program—"

"Is no longer in your hands."

In stunned silence, Margolis rises from the table and walks

out of the office. On the way out, she manages a milquetoast "thank you."

Margolis exits the administration building and stands there in the grey field of her ghost-father's disbelief. His face appears before her, his voice echoes in her ears: "You've always gone your own way, Glee. You could have been your own boss. Not having to rely on anyone else. Now this. Look where your trust for institutions has gotten you. Failure. Dismal failure."

The sound transports her again to that desolate fallow field somewhere in the Midwest. It's a bright winter day. The wind blows. The fields remain grey and lifeless.

"Daddy, why did you leave me?" she cries aloud. "I can't do this on my own."

The world begins to spin for her, and she seems as if she's about to pass out. But she shakes it off and regains her wits. She heads for her car.

Margolis drives fast through the tree-lined streets of a bucolic, seemingly innocuous college town. Music blaring. The top on the convertible is down, and her black hair flows in the wind. She reaches into her book bag and takes out the folder of lecture notes. She throws it out into the road. Papers flutter to the ground. A photo of Sharon Stone.

In her bedroom later: Margolis is in black bra, underwear, and stockings. She sits at her vanity putting on heavy lip liner; her eyes are already darkly lined in black. She's getting ready to go out on the town.

She tries on various outfits and decides on one that is chic but revealing. Her makeup and outfit make her look 15 years younger.

When fully clothed, Margolis grabs a black clutch, takes $400 out of her dresser, and puts it into the purse. Margolis marches out of her room and through the house. Without looking, she tromps past Brie's room, which is bare of its posters and paintings, bows and knick-knacks. Just the bed and dresser are left.

Outside in his car, Ronnie watches the house. When Margolis backs out of the garage, he follows her.

Margolis drives her Mercedes convertible through campus. No one is around because it's late. She drives by the administration tower, the president's office. A fountain. Water splashes blue in lights.

Margolis pulls out the slip of paper with Emma's address. She stands at a back door of the Theta house. It's up a fire escape to a private room just like the one Brie stood on before. She waits and looks around nervously. Through Margolis's point of view we see: The quad. Trees now dark and ominous. Nobody around. Tower lit up in orange light. Menacing statues stare down.

Margolis raises her hand to knock, but her fist stays suspended in the air, like a misplaced power gesture, for a long moment.

I can't do this anymore. Margolis frowns at herself, lowers her hand, and turns to go.

We see her walk down the fire escape steps. She wonders how she'll ever get her life back and feels like the only person in the world.

Pull back from Theta house to quad to campus to city.

Fade to black.

*   *   *   *

The next morning, pre-class, Margolis sits in her office, head in hand, over her computer. The slight bow in her back says that she's not that excited about prepping for her next lecture, on gangster movies, which may be one of her last. The vacant stare at the floor underscores that fact. She's watching Benny nap carelessly at the foot of her desk.

Across the room, *Scarface* plays on a second screen. It's the scene where the sidekick wise guy hangs by his wrists in the bathtub; the tall thug moves across the shot with a chainsaw.

They force Pacino to watch the bloody gang-style assassination.

But Margolis isn't watching.

Despite her love of the synthesized violence, Margolis is focused on nothing. Motivation is but a mere fly *brrzing* in the corner of the large plate-glass window. Outside, students sit on green grass reading books, sketching campus buildings, and throwing footballs.

Margolis's mouth makes a duck-squawk. Benny's ears prick. He lifts his head at her.

Then she turns her head toward the desk. Eyes move down across it.

The surface is littered with papers of all kinds—books, scholarly and otherwise, magazines, student papers, journal articles, movie reviews, book and film catalogues, interoffice memos, unfinished letters of recommendation, half-filled legal pads, notes jotted on meeting agendas—layers on layers accruing over months.

She happens to spot a faded copy of the university's handbook and suddenly remembers what Lane said: *It's all in the by-laws.* As she picks it up and flips through it, the guitar intro to "Back on the Chain Gang" by The Pretenders jangles through the computer speakers.

Margolis sits for a moment with a thumb between her teeth, then pulls herself resolutely up to her keyboard. She clicks the mouse and a blank window opens with its blinking cursor. She begins to type rapidly; a look of determination tightens her face.

Close on the screen as the words appear: "The University, having violated these several articles of its by-laws, has overstepped its bounds, ignored its own procedures, and violated my academic freedom. Therefore, I appeal my dismissal to the mercy of the Faculty Senate and ask for a hearing to adjudicate the matter..."

Part 2: A Fall

I.

We open on the long, slender arm of Margolis draped desperately over her olive face in a vain attempt to keep the surging sunlight out of melancholic brown eyes.

Suddenly, they open. The icy grip of fear tightens her chest—she'd forgotten to set her alarm. It's Monday—she teaches in 15 minutes.

"Fuck!" Margolis bounds out of bed with the energy of the young and scrabbles around shoes and purses to get through the door to the bathroom for the proverbial 'whore's bath.'

Standing in a slip before the mirror, Margolis raises her arm and sloshes a stubbly armpit with a cold washcloth. First one, then the other.

Benny sits, watching her expectantly with his golden-red coat.

"I don't have time to walk you now, love." He wags and pants in response. "But I will when I get home. I promise."

Slip off, now in a bra, she spritzes her hair with finger-flicked tap water, while occasionally scrunching her dark curls.

Blouse now on, slathery toothpaste mouth, she simultaneously texts asking Sandy to warn her class she'll be late but not to leave, regardless of that ubiquitous, unwritten, yet completely mistaken rule that class is automatically canceled after a prof is tardy 15 minutes. Her phone vibrates. It's a reply from Sandy: "Not your servant..." Margolis, audibly desperate, thumbs a quick "PLEASE?!!" back and waits. After a long minute, Sandy responds: "Fine...."

Next, we see a fully assembled Margolis Santos looking at herself in the mirror: a little lipstick and blush, no-nonsense navy pant ensemble—unflattering, but the last decent and unwrinkled outfit in the closet. She looks pleased with herself, not even gonna be late.

*   *   *   *

We hear the TV sportscaster: "Five-star recruit and Savannah Central High tailback, Reynaldo Livingston, has stunningly announced that he has switched his intent from Athens and committed to play for Alabama next season."

"Analysts had long thought that Livingston was a lock for Athens U, which recruited him heavily last month with an official weekend-long campus visit for the school's annual Football Banquet..."

A pull-back reveals the boy's mother, father, grandmother, aunts, uncles, cousins, and entourage as they clap and celebrate at his side.

Cut to the next clip of Reynaldo arm-in-arm and furiously shaking the hand of Alabama football coach, Nick Sabin, and decidedly not Frank Sinoro.

Chet sees the story on Livingston and tightens up like a retriever ready to move its bowels.

"Fucking Alabama! How could we let this kid slip through our goddamned fingers like this!" Face red, he then drinks from his double scotch. Face drains back to a wrinkled paste.

It's only 1:00 p.m., but Chet and Mickey Andouille sit at the bar of the Raven's Rook, a hoity-toity steak joint near campus where bluebloods go to drink Bloody Marys on game days. Five televisions flit and flash above their heads, each man watching a different one, then switch.

Mickey plays idly with the straw in his virgin seabreeze. "Livingston?"

"Reynaldo Livingston. Best running back this state, maybe the country, has ever seen."

"It's a shame." Mickey just starts shaking his head.

"Didn't the boy Livingston have a night to remember with some of the best-looking women the South has to offer?" Chet throws back the last bit of Johnny Walker Black and plunks the glass smack on the bar.

"Actually, Chet..." Mickey's voice trails off.

"Actually what?"

"One of the boys told me Reynaldo went back to the hotel alone that night after the banquet."

"What in tarnation are you saying?"

"His dark-haired date disappeared. At the club or some shit." A beat, a quizzical look on Mickey's face, as he asks, "'Tarnation?' Really? Who says that anymore?"

"I don't think she's getting the message. I'm going to have talk to Lucille. What else am I paying these women for?"

Chet gets up and puts his sport coat on to leave.

"That's why we need Eggy, sir. I'm telling ya..."

"Alright, bring Eggy in already." Chet waves as he hits the door.

*   *   *   *

Emma and Brooke stand in the Theta kitchen under the vent-a-hood smoking cigarettes.

"That guy you were with? Reynaldo? He's a big-time running back, and he dumped the U and signed with Alabama."

"All because I didn't sleep with him?"

Cocked head, blank stare, Brooke speaks, "Jesus, Emma. I thought you were smart." She snubs out her cig on the sink. "Your membership dues aren't going to pay for themselves." She strides righteously into the main hall of the sorority house, which is crowded with girls.

"Listen up, all you Theta Bitches!" Her voice is loud, way loud. "I've got something to say to all of you who think you're so 'all that,' so little-miss-campus-angel, goody-two-shoes spirit-queens."

She turns back toward Emma and gives her a sharp look. Emma shifts her weight, flushed at the attention.

"I've been getting text upon text about girls being fucking dildos about sports. They say some bitches are actually cheering for the opposing team. The. Opposing. Fucking. Team. What, are you fucking stupid?!"

A long beat.

"I don't give a shit about sportsmanship—this week is Homecoming—you cheer for the goddamn U and not the other team. Are you fucking retarded?

"I would rather have four sisters that are fun, talk to boys, and know how to party than eighty girls who are fucking faggots. With that in mind, don't fucking show up unless you're going to stop being a goddamn cock-block for our chapter. Seriously. I will fucking *cunt-punt* the next person I hear doing something like that—do you understand me!"

A long pause and glare. The gaggle of stunned white girls is deathly quiet.

"Now," Brooke pounds her fist, "at the next mixer with the football team," (pound), "we are going to go out," (pound), "show those boys how we do it at the U," (pound), "and give them a night they will never forget," (pound). "That means dancing, talking, drinking, and *whatever else these guys want to do.* They are going to be superstars. Do you understand that? So, if you are not down with the goddamned program of making money for having fun and, I might add, for making this school less of a dipshit, second-rate, pussy-wuss fuck-hole, then tip your ass out the door!"

She stands there, looking around wild-eyed and breathing heavily.

And with that, President Brooke tips herself out the fucking door.

*   *   *   *

In the classroom, Margolis has not skipped a professorial beat despite her late start. She looks completely normal, with the exception of the white, nylon tag on the back of her neck sticking out of the top of the blouse. Students, all students, always notice every detail in what their professors are wearing. Sixty percent of class time, Margolis knows, and maybe more, their eyes are on boobs, crotch, or hair. In that order.

"Every character, particularly the protagonist, needs motivation to follow his or her desire, and drive the conflict and, thus, the story forward. Of course, this is not rocket science. Motivations are ancient, primal, and universal. What motivates people to do anything, in real life?"

A moment of silence—there's always that silence in American classrooms, as if people who are paying $50,000 a year for their education are trying to decide if it's okay to be smart.

"That wasn't a rhetorical question, people. What motivates you?" More silence, but Margolis is a Zen master at waiting them out. She could stand there for hours.

"We've got love, greed, hunger, fear, safety, survival. That can't be every human motivation, can it?" Margolis looks askance at every corner of the room, "What is Michael Corleone's motivation in *The Godfather* after his father gets shot?" She waits tantalizingly longer through dumbfounded stillness, and just as she's about to say the word and drop the mic, she hears it from the crowd:

"Revenge." An older mature voice from out of nowhere cuts the tension and reads Margolis's mind.

Margolis puts her hand to her brow for shade from the spotlights and is stunned to see, at the back of the auditorium, Dean Gloria Concord.

II.

Margolis sucks in the stomach-dropping jolt of shame and fear that hits her hard. Just in time to appear composed. "Dean Concord! Welcome to our humble class. Would you like to come up to the front?" A challenge almost, Margolis holds the questioning look with beseeching arms.

"Oh no, Dr. Santos. Don't mind me, I'm just a fly on the wall. Please do continue."

Margolis lowers eyebrows and pivots on feet to hide the deep intake of breath. Suddenly, nerves have overtaken her.

"Revenge. Restitution for slights and wrongs done to one, whether real or perceived, for real or trumped-up reasons." She purposely does not look toward the dean. "In *The Godfather*, Michael quote 'settles all family business' end-quote, by killing all of his enemies." She pauses again for effect. "Isn't that why we see everyone bowing at the end of the movie to kiss his ring?"

The rustle of books and papers being gathered.

Louder: "So watch *Godfather II*, perhaps the only sequel ever made that could be better than the original."

Margolis pretends to organize her lecture notes and pays no attention to the dean, who stands waiting for students to pass before moving down to the stage. Margolis doesn't look up until Concord is standing at her feet.

"A nice speech. I can see why your students give you such high ratings. Very entertaining and motivating."

"Thank you, though I guess that's past tense now." A beat. "To what do I owe the honor of your visit, Gloria?"

"I've come by to try to talk you out of appealing."

Concord hands Margolis an envelope as if to emphasize her point.

"Why?"

Concord pauses, and Margolis can't tell if that is sympathy or relief in the dean's eyes when she answers: "I just want you to think this through. Lane is not a forgiving man."

It crosses Margolis's mind that Lane may have an axe to grind because she voted no confidence in him. "Do I have any recourse, Gloria?"

"I've recommended you to my counterpart at Athens Community College for a job. I strongly suggest you take it. And forget about taking on Lane." Concord wheels around and climbs the steps. Margolis watches her go up and out of the auditorium.

Margolis turns back to the envelope, which has Lane's address and presidential seal. She opens it and reads that her appeal hearing is scheduled for next week.

*   *   *   *

"Are you sure you want to go through with it?" Mark Goldberg scratches his bald head. He sits across from Margolis in her office; he holds the letter from Lane announcing the date of her appeal hearing.

"Yes, I'm appealing." Margolis sounds steadfast.

"It's a very conservative place, Glee. Maybe Concord is right."

"Lane only fired me because I stood up against his policies in the first place."

"Oh, God, don't bring up the vote of no confidence, whatever you do. Stick to the issue at hand and don't try to say he fired you out of retribution."

"I am sticking to the issues! There's nothing in the by-laws against teacher-student romances, you know. In fact, it says almost the opposite." Margolis starts reading from the handbook: "'The University is dedicated to fostering an environment of free thought, open-mindedness, and respect that encourages close interaction between faculty and students.'" She looks at Mark. "I respected Ford Reinhart." Beat. "But he's not even my student!"

"I thought you said you didn't read the by-laws."

"Just the dirty parts." She smiles.

"Of course."

Margolis pauses for a moment and considers her dog, a regular visitor to the office. With head down on his paws, he appears oblivious, carefree. Margolis is jealous.

"So even if Ford was my student, which he decidedly was not, I haven't even broken any rules. They're punishing me for nothing, and making it public—or threatening, at least—may be the only way to make them stop."

"But they will make it seem like you did!" Mark cries. "They'll make it seem as unseemly and indecent as possible: middle-aged woman with a 19-year-old boy?"

"Wait. Middle-aged woman?"

"Sure, it's legal, but there are lots of people in this place who'd think that's unbecomingly creepy in the very least and salaciously scandalous at worst."

"Let's go back to the phrase 'middle-aged.'"

"I'm being serious, Glee."

"Yeah, I guess I really underestimated that." Margolis frowns. "I know getting with Ford wasn't the smartest thing I've ever done."

"Yeah, I'd say. Their top and only priority is to protect the reputation of the University." Now in a Yoda voice: "Knowledge? Creativity? Innovation? A University cares not for these things." He laughs, then back to his Brooklyn swag: "Reputation. That's our product."

Benny rolls over on his back. Margolis reaches down to rub his belly. Her face goes serious. "You're right." She straightens up in her chair and sighs, "I can't win."

*   *   *   *

In the Theta house kitchen, Chet scolds Lucille in quieter tones: "This one little Chiquita slipped through your fingers,

Lucille."

"Again, what was I supposed to do?" she hisses.

"You were supposed to make sure she was properly motivated."

"I paid her chapter dues. What other motivation does she need?"

"Well that's what I pay you for. Obviously, money isn't enough."

"I don't know why, her father is done, broke. Can't even pay her bills."

He perks up suddenly. "Who's her daddy?"

"Charles Barnes."

"Charles Barnes, of Chicago, really?"

"Yeah, so what?"

"It just so happens I have some business with Mr. Barnes." Chet practically licks his chops. "OK, here's how we'll play it. She needs to know her daddy could get hurt if she avoids this deal."

Lucille exhales deeply—glad for this mess to be out of her hands—but her relief comes too soon. On his way out, Chet turns and adds, last-minute: "Oh, and since you can't seem to handle this responsibility on your own, I'm bringing in some help. Prepare for a new resident in the Theta house."

He walks out, leaving Lucille staring after in confusion.

*   *   *   *

Margolis plops down on the sectional in her living room, trying to act casual. "Can I get you a glass of wine?"

"No. That's all right. Thanks." Frank stands near the door. He's crouching, petting Benny. The dog's tail wags like he's missed the man. "I just stopped by for a quick few things."

"Oh." She freezes. "I thought you were going to move-move. Like all your stuff. I mean, half of this furniture is yours."

"I don't have time." Frank stands there silently looking at

her.

"Of course, football season." Margolis's tone doesn't hide disappointment. "Well, I guess I should let you get to it." She gestures broadly around the house. "Your stuff."

"Yep." He walks towards the stairs while keeping his eyes on her.

While Frank is upstairs, she follows his every move with her ears. When there is a heavy bump, Benny lifts his head to look up the stairs, then back down.

Margolis gets up to look at the various frames and knick-knacks on the shelves lining the other side of the room. Her stomach starts to sink, and she's suddenly struck by that same feeling she had when her dad left, before her mother died and she had to move in with him. It was like someone had removed a wall from their house, where every passerby could gaze in and gawk at their grief. When Frank finally emerges from upstairs, the bottle of wine is empty.

He is carrying two medium suitcases and a backpack slung over one shoulder. Benny trots up to him and sniffs the bags.

Margolis glances up from her wine. "Is that it?" She tries to mask any bitterness in her voice.

"No, I got a few more things to grab." Frank sets down the cases and heads over to where Margolis is standing by the bookshelves. He reaches up. Close on his hand: It pauses ever so slightly between his Pac-12 football championship trophy and their wedding album.

He grabs the trophy. Puts it on the coffee table.

Margolis looks at it, her lip curling up almost imperceptibly.

Frank scans across the family photos lined along the middle shelf. He comes to one photo of them windblown yet giddy on the Giant's Causeway coast of Ireland.

Margolis stares at that album for a moment, then says, "I remember that trip. It seems so recent." Pause. "Do you remember the day we spent out on the Aran Islands?"

"Inishmore or Inisheer. I can't remember which is which. The big one."

"Inishmore." Margolis states with certainty, as if to prove her memory is better. "The weather was perfect, although it rained most of the rest of the trip. Cycling around those dirt lanes walled with stone, I actually got hot. In Ireland!"

In fake Irish accent: "Ah but the pubs and the beer were cool, lass."

"What a time to choose for your confession."

Frank looks down at his hands. "It was killing me to carry it around."

Frank pauses wishfully, as if there is a time-travel machine that could take them back to before it was bad, before he made the mistake. He didn't intend to have sex with that team trainer, but with long nights at the office alone, it just happened.

After a bit, he suddenly goes into motion, trying to pick up everything he got off the shelves. "Do you have a box or something?"

Margolis is lost in thought, and for a moment she doesn't react.

Frank looks at her expectantly.

Margolis finally comes to: "Yes. Is that all you want?"

A pause, then Frank answers, "I think that's it."

"No Benny?"

The dog's ears pique at the sound of his name. He jumps up from next to Margolis and wags up to Frank. Frank bends to pet him.

"He's always been more your dog than mine, Glee."

"Sure, but I thought you might at least ask for him. He's meant something to you, too."

"I don't want to take anything more from you."

He stands, helpless, clueless, and looks at her, sad and serious in his eyes.

Margolis shudders, the pain of years pouring out of her.

"Anyway, I've got to go. Got a meeting." He hefts his armful and heads out the door.

It takes two awkward trips for him to get his stuff out to his truck, but Margolis can't stop. It's been a long time coming for her to cry like this.

*   *   *   *

"Come on now, Eggy. You know exactly why you was hired." Chet grins as he grabs a seat, swings around the empty desktop and thunks the chair beside one Egglebert "Eggy" Compson. Mid- to late 20s, tall. A little too skinny, light-skinned African-American.

Mickey looks at them from across his desk. They're in his Burden Hall office.

"No, not really, Mr. Orchard." Eggy sports straight hair, a boyish Bieber cut with a long swath swept across brown eyes. Eggy looks like a masculine version of Rhianna or Alicia Keys. Although dwarfed by a white, knit golf shirt two sizes too big, the khaki athletic shorts visible at the bottom are tight, shapely. Nike runners, grey with pink swoosh.

"We want what you can do with that dual threat of yours." Chet gestures with his finger up and down Eggy's body. "Your decision to become a girly-man."

Mickey looks down at his desk, tries to fiddle with something. "Transgender," he says, muffled, to Chet.

"Nope, I didn't become transgender. Now I'm just a girl," Eggy says proudly. "I was 'transgender' *before*, but now the operation is complete. The offending organ has been completely," Eggy rolls the *r*, "removed."

"Whatever. We need you to be able to switch from one to the other. Beard and boner one day, tits and tiara the next."

"Well, sir, it doesn't really work like that." Eggy pauses and notices how uncomfortable Mickey looks.

"Ah, come on—you're takin me too literal, boy." Chet waves

Eggy off. "All I mean is you know how both sides think and act. That's your power." He leans forward. "Here's how it'll go: Work in Frank's office during the day, live in the Delta Delta Theta house at night."

"No doubt that this is a 24/7 job," Mickey adds.

Chet finishes, "But at the rate I'm paying you, you're still making out like a bandit."

"Facilitating recruitment." Mickey pauses a beat. "You see, we've started a little sister organization. Unofficial. And this group helps us with recruiting."

"Unofficially."

"Yes, unofficially," Mickey answers. "When players make their official, or unofficial, visits to campus, they get the regular rigamarole during the days—tours of the facilities, sit-ins with the players during meetings, tickets to that weekend's game— all completely by the book."

"And at night," Eggy is putting it all together, "the little sisters provide the entertainment."

"Exactly. We'll move you into the Theta house as a kind of RA, resident assistant, to Lucille, the housemom. You are to monitor the girls' activities and to make sure that they are doing their job—being entertaining and fun."

"Like any red-blooded teenage recruit would want," Chet inserts.

Eggy shrugs, mouth corner raising slightly. The arrangement kind of makes sense to her, in an androgynous, egalitarian ideal sort of way. She considers for a moment, then says plainly: "I'll do it."

Mickey grins and stands, offering her his hand.

"On one condition."

Mickey sits back down, smile fading.

"That I get to coach. Assistant kicking coach, whatever. But none of this trainer-slave bullshit. I'm done with that. I want in Sinoro's inner circle." She lets out a long breath.

"Fine." Chet agrees. "Done."

Eggy stands up, brimming with joy, and offers her hand to Mickey then Chet. He takes it, and she shakes it violently. Chet wonders if he's being mocked.

Eggy is all smiles. "When do I start?"

*   *   *   *

Margolis lies in her bed, tossing restlessly. Her head suddenly thrashes to one side, as she heaves a guttural breath. "No! Daddy." Her head turns back the other way.

Margolis dreams of a place in shadow. Grey shapes, blurry, loom in the background. Sharp smell of burnt pine.

She dreams of her father smoking a cigar in a living room. Dark wood-paneled den. He yells: "THEY KILLED ME, GLEE. THEY KILLED ME!" He grabs her arm so hard it jolts tears to her eyes. A fierce hiss: "*And you let them.*"

Margolis shoots straight up in bed, arms back behind, supporting her. Dazed, she looks around and then just breathes heavily for a few moments.

The first thing that pops into her head is that, after all, she is going to appeal.

*   *   *   *

"So, you're Emma." Chet slides in next to her, perched atop the bleachers in the U's main gymnasium. Hundreds of people have gathered for the football team's big pep rally before their Homecoming game tomorrow with rival State. All of the Thetas are spread out on the rows below Emma, who sits alone next to parents and eager freshmen relishing their first college pep rally. It's late starting.

Emma glances at Chet dispassionately. She's used to ignoring older men who hit on her.

"Yeah? I'm Emma." She chews her gum loudly.

"Do you know who I am?"

She takes a moment to size him up, eyes sliding down to his Sansabelt slacks. "You're that old guy who's been hanging around the Theta house talking to Lucille in the kitchen."

Chet belly laughs and several fans turn around to look at him. "And that means you already know what it is I want, so let's talk straight."

Emma doesn't look at him, but from the expression on her face, you can tell that Chet's smarmy words are worming their way quickly under her skin. "I'm not interested in selling anything," she says dispassionately.

"That's what your gal, Brooke, used to think, too, before we came to a mutual understanding." Chet whistles loudly with his teeth, and Brooke, who sits a few rows in front of them looks back. When she sees Chet, she raises her red solo cup and smiles.

"So," Chet lifts his hand to spin a toothpick in his mouth, "you gonna make the right decision, like your friend Brooke?"

"I am making the right decision by saying *no*."

Chet reaches back and pulls from his back pocket some papers folded vertically. He hands them to Emma.

"What's this?"

"Your daddy made some bad investments before the recession—naked short sales, collateralized debt obligations—not all of it exactly legal."

"Why are you doing this? Why me?"

"Because all the little high school boys want to meet you." He points down to the floor of the gymnasium where a group of six or seven massive man-boys stand waving at the crowd.

Emma's eyes follow Chet's gnarled finger down to the tall, slender white boy with shaggy brown hair. He's not waving like the other fools, and he sports a dapper V-neck sweater, tie, and khakis.

"That there is Ryan Cavanaugh, 18-year-old from Tupelo. Best quarterback in the state."

"And you want me to..." She stops, leans in, and lowers her

voice

"I just want you to make sure these boys have a good time. That they get to do what they want while they're in town." He places a hand on her knee. "That's all. Otherwise, things might take a downturn for your old man."

Emma turns her eyes toward the festivities on the floor. She glances sideways at Chet and chews on her lip.

*　　*　　*　　*

Margolis looks for Benny on his blanket at the edge of the sectional—she needs a friend. He's not there. She calls. Nothing.

At the top of the stairs, she calls again, her ribcage squeezing harder for more air. Nothing. She turns to the right. On her way down the hall, Margolis ducks into Brie's room and scans. No Benny. Frank's old office, the same. She turns her head toward her bedroom; the light worries her face.

Her bedroom is dark, and light from the hall floods in when she opens the door. She steps in and turns on the light. The first place she looks is his usual spot at the foot of the bed. No Benny.

She switches on the bathroom light, then the closet. No sign of him.

She wanders around the cluttered room, wondering desperately, confused at this point.

When she gets around to the far side of her bed, she stubs her toe on something stiff. She looks down. There's Benny. Margolis pauses, smiles, and mouths his name, "Benny."

His eyes are open and unmoving. She touches him, but her hand recoils. She looks up and down his form for a moment, and then she crumbles down on top of him, tears soaking into fur.

In the darkness of her backyard, Margolis drags a large, bulging trash bag in one hand and a shovel in the other. She's struggling with the load and has to pause every few feet. Her face glistens in the moonlight. The mouth is open and chest is heaving. She takes a few more steps and stops. Sobs.

When she gets down to the bottom of the yard, past the pool to the flowerbeds, she starts shoveling, haphazardly at first. Soon, her brightly colored annuals, dull from the moonlight, fly left and right with each shovelful of dirt and rocks.

Before too long, Margolis is knee-deep in a hole, mud caked to her boots and fishnets. Moonlit, she reaches over for the bag, and drags it to her. In one violent scream, she rips the plastic and lifts it, but the hole in the bag is not big enough. A furry patch of dog lodges, stuck in the opening.

Using both hands, she tears with all her might, and Benny's body, free of the plastic, flops awkwardly out and down into the grave.

Margolis looks down in the hole for several minutes, her chest heaving. Slowly, she calms. Sucking in snot, she stands, grabs the shovel, and starts filling it in.

Margolis puts one boot out of the ditch and tries to heave herself up on the shovel, and she almost makes it before plunging chest-first into the muck. She rolls over onto her back, looks up at the stars, and lets the sorrow shudder her like a child.

*   *   *   *

It's Saturday. Game time. Picture an establishing shot of a packed football stadium, like that taken from a camera on a blimp.

Out of a tunnel from below steps Emma into this sea of black, grey, and pink school spirit. Her dark hair makes her stand out. Behind her emerges Ryan Cavanaugh, the long and lanky football recruit, looking a bit in awe of the place. He's wearing neutral colors: his tie is red, neither pink nor orange.

It's a subtle message that he hasn't decided yet which college he's going to.

Emma smiles at Ryan and puts her arm through his to lead him up the steps to their seats. He's carrying hotdogs and drinks—she thought a snack might get his mind off how poorly the Raven are playing.

"That why you gotta come to Athens, Ryan. You'll make us better," Emma says as they take their seats. She nuzzles in closer, face in his hair, and kisses his ear. He grins sheepishly, shyly.

After Athens manages to get back two touchdowns, the game bogs down into a slugfest, neither team able to move the ball much, "a battle of attrition," the commentator calls it. It goes on like this for almost an entire quarter.

Chet and Mickey exchange nervous looks.

Frank looks up at the scoreboard. "State 21, Raven 17."

With a little luck, the Raven offense begins to drive the ball methodically down the field, controlling the clock, mixing up runs and passes, keeping the opponents guessing at what they'll do next. Now, the ball is 25 yards away from the goal line, with 1:29 left on the clock.

Emma grips Ryan's bicep and grits her teeth at him in mock nervousness. He chuckles.

Announcer: "The Raven have worked their way inside the State 7-yard line. They'll have four tries to win this thing. But they have to score a touchdown—a field goal ain't gonna cut it."

President Lane rubs his spotted hands dryly. On the right ring finger is a fat, diamond-encrusted platinum slug, his championship ring from his Athens U senior year, almost 40 years ago. He wants another.

But with three plays, Athens can't do anything. Only one more try left.

Frank leans into the huddle and tells his offense, "Now, break on three and run Double-Y Cross 33." Frank looks over at Eggy. It's a play she designed. Then he yells, "One, two, three. Break!"

Announcer: "It all comes down to this. The Raven break huddle and set the play at the 7-yard line. Fourth down, seven seconds left on the clock. They snap the ball. Back to pass..."

The Raven quarterback scrambles to the right. He can't find anybody. He stops, looks across the field. He throws it to his tight end wide open on the other side of the field.

"Caught! Touchdown! Can you believe it?"

In unison, Lane, Chet, Mickey, Emma, and Ryan, along with virtually all the other 100,000 in the stadium, fly to their feet, arms raised.

"With only 3 seconds left on the clock, the Athens University Raven score on their final play and defeat the Auburn State Rattlers, 24–21."

Emma jumps into Ryan's arms. They kiss. Both pull back for a moment and look cautiously into each other's eyes, then they kiss again, full-on French.

Chet, looking through his binoculars, sees the kiss as it happens. He lowers them and nods in approval.

On the field, Frank shakes the hand of State's coach but can't help but reveal the glow of his come-from-behind victory. The entire crowd is still on its feet, so Frank slows, takes off his cap, and turns to acknowledge each end of the stadium before waving and trotting off to the locker room with his jubilant players.

*　　*　　*　　*

The faculty hearing chamber looks like a courtroom, with a bench faced by two tables. Margolis sits at one, Concord and Lane sit at another.

From the front of the chamber, at the center of the line of faculty making up the Appeals Committee, Marcia Stoddard begins to speak as a hush falls over the room.

"Professor Santos is appealing what she contends are

unfair and unjustified sanctions levied capriciously on her by the administration for alleged acts that violate no law or stated university policy. Is that correct?" Stoddard looks up at Margolis.

"Yes. Yes, Marcia." Margolis swallows. "That is correct."

"You will refer to the Chair and the other members of the committee," Stoddard gestures down the row of stern-looking faculty, "as 'Doctor' or 'Professor.'"

Margolis sees Gus Johnson, her colleague from the English Department, at the end of the dais. He smiles weakly back at her.

"In the absence of any written accusations against Professor Santos, the committee has requested from the administration an official statement that includes the charges against her. Dean Concord, will you please read them?"

Cicero whispers into Margolis's ear: "This is always the hardest part. It'll be over soon."

Nodding at Lane, the dean stands and begins reading: "'Professor Santos is accused of conduct unbecoming of faculty including sexual harassment, delinquency of a minor, and violations of liability clauses in the University's insurance coverage.'"

"Insurance coverage?" Farrah Maines mutters not inaudibly. A middle-aged, punky lesbian professor from Athens Community College, and Margolis's best friend, she's sitting in the gallery next to Mark Goldberg. He chuckles. Neither of them is taking this hearing very seriously. To them, this hearing is a circus of folly.

Stoddard looks out over her glasses. "Would those in the audience please refrain from comment?"

"Yes, Professor Marcia. Sorry." Farrah bites her lips to keep from laughing. Goldberg straightens the smirk out of his mouth. Like a couple of kids.

Margolis gives them the evil eye before she turns back to the committee.

Stoddard turns slightly to face the dean. "Would you please detail to the committee your evidence for these charges?"

"Of course." Dean Concord continues, "As the first exhibit in our case, the administration would like to submit the following documentation." She hands the file to a young assistant who then passes it up to Stoddard.

"And how is her marital status relevant to this case?" Gus Johnson leans forward as he asks the question.

"Professor Johnson, the administration is endeavoring to show that Professor Santos's behavior, pursuing a relationship outside of her marriage, has deviated outside the bounds of normal and honorable expectations of any member of this community."

"Deviated?" Johnson laughs. "And exactly what kind of behaviors are considered acceptable in the eyes—"

Stoddard interjects. "The committee will allow it, Dean Concord, but we do insist that you justify the relevance of this expectation."

"To do so, the administration would like to call its first witness." She pauses and turns around toward the gallery. "Ford Reinhart."

Margolis turns around, quite in shock. She looks, then her eyes meet Ford's. He smiles nervously. And in spite of her anger, Margolis flashes a weak grimace.

III.

Ford looks helplessly at Margolis. "She said she was separated and—"

"Did you have a sexual relationship with Professor Santos?"

"What?"

"Please answer the question, Mr. Reinhart."

Margolis pipes up wearily, "Is this necessary, Gloria? He's not even an Athens student."

"But he has clear ties to us." The dean smiles haughtily. "Now, the question: Did you two have a sexual relationship?"

"I mean," Ford stumbles. "I started all of it! It wasn't even her idea. She didn't want to at first."

"Is that a 'yes,' Mr. Reinhart? I need you to say the word."

Ford looks out into the gallery. His parents nod back at him to answer.

Softly: "Yes."

"I don't think the committee can hear you. Would you repeat that louder?"

"Yes."

"So, you had a sexual relationship with a person acting in the role of a teacher."

"Yes, but she wasn't my professor. Dr. Maines was."

Cut to Farrah seated in the witness box where Ford just was.

"Professor Maines, thank you for agreeing to testify, even though the U is not your home institution." Dean Concord flashes the snakish smile again, and in an instant, it's gone.

"You're welcome. Anything to help."

"I believe that you can clarify Professor Santos's professional role in your film project."

"I will if I can." Farrah rolls her eyes at Margolis, not trying to hide her contempt for the dean.

"Would you elaborate?"

86

"I invited Margolis to consult on my film as a professional courtesy. It was all quite informal. I just wanted her on the set for moral support, really."

"Moral support? Did Professor Santos not bring with her $3,000 in funding from Athens U and," Dean Concord looks through her bifocals at a paper in her hand, "serve as Producer and Assistant Director on the film?"

"Well, that's what the credits say, but it's mostly ceremonial."

"$3000 is 'mostly ceremonial?'" The dean chuckles, the laughter sounding artificial in her throat. Now facing the audience, the dean resumes: "The administration submits to the committee this documentation that shows that I approved funding for Professor Santos's role in the project, not to pay for informal hanging out with her friends or her personal liaisons with young students."

"And what is the point of this testimony, Dean Concord?" Gus Johnson shrugs. "Relationships with students are what professors have every day. Sometimes they get personal. It's not against University policy."

"The administration has a compelling interest to protect students from the immoral and perhaps illegal behaviors of its faculty on and off campus."

Concord stops, takes a breath, and lets all of that sink in before she starts again.

"Incidentally, let it be noted that by her own admission, Professor Santos had off-campus meals with the student in question at establishments where they serve alcoholic beverages and where the student could have slipped and fallen. Such activities are not covered by our liability insurance." The dean ends to the sound of triumphant silence.

Then, Margolis bursts out laughing. Her loud chest-heaves echo through the chamber. Even after a breath, she doesn't stop. She keeps laughing like she's lost it. Suddenly, it's contagious. A titter here and there, and then suddenly the entire gallery is gripped in a fit of guffaws.

"Order. Order!" Stoddard bangs the gavel down on the sound block like a mad judge.

The laughter doesn't stop. Even Gus Johnson has caught it.

One more crack. "This hearing is in recess for lunch. Dear God..."

Lane looks over and gives Concord a worried look.

*   *   *   *

In the full, morning light, we see a typical office conference room. At the table sit a dozen businessmen—they look ordinary, but they aren't. Each one counts himself a billionaire for whom college football is not just a hobby but a blood sport. Every Division I university football program has an unofficial booster organization like this one, comprised of rich men vying for bragging rights at the country club or yacht club or church or wherever rich folks congregate. The success on the field of a team of downy-faced twenty-somethings determines the ability of these men to shove their rivals' noses at other schools in humiliation and defeat.

Huntley McBride, white, late 50s, rotund, with glasses left over from the 1980s that make him look like a computer engineer, not an oil magnate. His voice is calm, collected in a menacing sort of way, like a man used to being in charge.

"How are things coming together?" He looks around the table where no one is eager to start. "Ted. Donations. How's the fundraising going?"

Ted sits up and leans in. "It's okay." Ted Morris is the only black man in the room. He's graying but still in great shape from his playing days. He shrugs and slowly shakes his head. "It's just that..."

"Just that what?" asks Jack Wilson, early 60s.

A balding white man in his 50s named Tag Robertson to Ted's right picks up the slack. "What Ted is saying is that we're running into a little donor fatigue."

"Donor fatigue," Chet hocks out of his chest. "Why, y'all sound like some sissies from the U.N.!"

A smattering of chuckles.

"Then," Huntley raises his hands, "we will just have to give them more reasons to be excited about giving money to the Raven Foundation. Ted, Tag, you two need to double your efforts, you hear?"

The two men look around weakly, then nod down at their folded hands.

Huntley turns. "Chet, what about you—what are your folks in recruiting doing to raise excitement?"

"Well, we got several things in the works that I feel will raise our commitment, financially and otherwise, from the majority of boosters," Chet announces, really selling it. "But signing exciting players—that's what's going to put butts in the seats and get us to our ultimate goal."

"And losing Reynaldo Livingston to Alabama?" Tag asks facetiously. "Is that how you're helping us get to our ultimate goal, Chet?"

"Now listen, Reynaldo was..."

Ted piles on: "We're hemorrhaging players to other schools left and right. It's a goddamned clusterfuck."

"Yeah, we gotta see results, Orchard, my friend," Huntley shrugs. "No more Reynaldo Livingstons."

"It won't happen again, Huntley." Chet blushes slightly as he looks defiantly around the room.

"How can you guarantee that?"

"I've got my ways."

"What could it be besides paying them?" Ted wonders.

"Well that's for me to know and you to find out. But when I tell you about it, you're never gonna stop thanking me." Chet ends discussion with a shit-eating grin.

*   *   *   *

After Concord and Lane finish making their case, the committee has reassembled in the chamber to hear Margolis's defense.

"Professor Santos," Stoddard commences. "Are you ready to begin?"

"I guess." A long beat. She takes another breath and projects: "Dr. Ingersoll." Margolis turns toward the Chair of the Film Department, black, early 60s, who has taken the stand. "Would you please tell the committee about my performance reviews?"

"Yes." He turns toward the row of his colleagues, "According to Professor Santos's last three bi-annual reviews, she's a pillar of our department."

Margolis looks hard at Concord, who turns away.

"As my next witness," Margolis stumbles, grins, then regains her composure, "I'd like to call Professor Maritain Schomberg, president of the Faculty Senate."

A small, European-looking man in a tweed blazer and bushy white mustache takes a seat on the stand.

"Professor Schomberg, you have served on the Faculty Senate representing the Mechanical Engineering Department for some years, have you not?"

"Yes, Margolis. Twenty-five, as a matter of fact."

"Are you familiar with the sections regarding due process for faculty terminations or sanctions?"

"Yes, of course. Section Eight, I believe."

"It is indeed Section Eight."

"I remember because I have been through many appeals with this administration, particularly since the vote of no confidence in Lane failed. I believe you were a part of that, as well."

"I was." Margolis redirects, "Can you remind the committee what Section Eight says?"

"I believe it says something like, '*If the dean considers a faculty member's misconduct sufficiently grave to justify suspension or probation for a stated period or other severe sanction, the dean shall institute a proceeding to impose such a severe sanction."*

"That's almost exactly verbatim, Professor. Very impressive."

"Thank you."

"Must the dean inform the faculty member of such a proceeding before imposing sanctions?"

"Yes."

"In writing?"

"Yes."

"And yet in my case, the dean did not." Margolis turns to Gus Johnson and makes eye contact. She then turns to Concord and continues: "Let the committee note that no such proceeding or written notice of was given by the dean. In short, I was denied due process by the administration."

There's commotion in the chamber, as the members of the committee whisper to each other in consultation. Margolis looks back to Farrah who subtly pumps her fist. Yes! Margolis breathes out and relaxes tentatively.

Margolis turns back to the stand. "Thank you, Professor Schomberg, that will be all." But then she stops and turns back. "Oh, one other thing, Professor Schomberg." A beat. "Are there any rules, in the by-laws or elsewhere, that prohibit a faculty member from having a romantic relationship with a student of Athens or even a student-aged person who wasn't a student of Athens?"

"No, there is not. Not that we encourage such liaisons, mind you. But to protect free association and the exchange of knowledge..." A pause. "Anyway, we are all adults here on campus, are we not? And who can prevent love between consenting adults?" He casts a flirtatious glance at Stoddard. She blushes, looks down.

Some giggles from the audience.

"Thank you, Professor. That will be all. For real this time." Margolis stares down the dean, as she takes her seat.

* * * *

Margolis sits in her bedroom getting ready for class that afternoon, when a sudden clatter from downstairs shatters the quiet. Her dark head lifts, eyes trained across bed and through door. *Someone's here.*

Margolis freezes and listens intently, her heart pounding.

Adrenaline spurs Margolis, and she slips out of her bed, tying the robe around her hips.

We follow Margolis as she goes step by slow step, cautiously down the stairs. It's brighter down here, but not much—it's still very gloomy.

"Brie?" Margolis's voice reverberates in the other rooms. "Brie, is that you?"

Margolis stops in the kitchen. She can't see but she can hear someone rifling through drawers and cabinets.

Margolis pads into the kitchen, and someone pops out from behind the counter holding a knife.

"Ah!" Margolis jumps back, reflexively raising arms, then relaxes. Hands go to hips. "Brie! You scared me! Why didn't you answer when I called?"

"I'm just getting some stuff for my Halloween costume."

"Well, be careful, that's sharp."

Brie looks down at the filet knife, long and serrated. She turns it in her hand, face out of focus in the background. She stops, looks up at her mom, and slips it back into the drawer. "Where's my drama stuff? I need my green tights."

"Out over the garage, I think. Up in the attic. Why?"

"I'm going to be Peter Pan for the party." Brie turns and bangs out the laundry room door to the garage.

"What party?"

No answer.

Brie bangs her way back into the kitchen. "Jesus, this place is a mess." She looks around at the counters crowded with dishes, half-cooked food, and junk mail.

"What party?" Margolis repeats.

"The Theta party." Brie doesn't pause, "Where is my green top? And my skinny jeans?"

"I don't keep tabs on your outfits, Brie." Margolis shifts, "And did I say you could go to the Theta party on Halloween? It's going to be at a frat house. So, no." Margolis puts her hands on her hips.

"But Mom!"

"There will be drinking and older boys, and I don't want you there."

Brie stomps her foot.

"Just forget it."

Brie stands there fuming and looking daggers at Margolis. Then she speaks, "Dad already said I could go."

Margolis didn't expect this; she's shocked. She turns away to try to gather some response.

"I don't care. I said 'no.' And your dad has an out-of-town game, so you're spending Halloween night here. Just get used to the idea."

Brie storms out in a huff.

*   *   *   *

The Great Hall in the Kappa Phi Alpha fraternity house is covered with orange and black. The Thetas have to have their fete there because parties aren't allowed at sororities. It's a long-standing rule of the Panhellenic Council that clearly has roots in a bygone, lady-like past. Oh, sororities still host parties, just at frat houses. This has always been the loophole.

Theta sisters sit on the floor in little cliques, cutting construction paper, untangling lights, stringing cobwebs, or drawing big capital letters on poster board. Big beefy guys stand on ladders tacking up crepe paper and cobwebs. It's the run-up to the first-annual Theta Haunted House and Gore-fest. It wasn't the Theta's idea—the football team captains, all Kappas, came to them about collaborating. The houses, after all, are next-door neighbors. "Our house is perfect," they said. At Brooke's urging, the Thetas are going along with it. Brooke told them, "just as long as it's scary as your mom's face and there's lots of trashcan punch."

Emma and Brie sit together in one corner. Sisters and players keep coming up to them, saying 'hi' to Brie and how *awesome* it is that she's getting to check out Greek life even though she's still in high school. They say things like: "*Oh my god, I would have totally done that when I was a senior. All those college guys?*"

Brie smiles forcedly and nods and listens. Emma is a little less patient, though she introduces Brie to everyone who comes up and glazes them with her patented superficial smile.

"Nice fake smile," Brie observes when the girls walk away.

"What's up your crack, dude," Emma teases.

Brie tries to smile, but it's clear she's bummed out. "My mom's being a bitch. Says I can't come to the party."

"What? That sucks." Emma hides her relief that Brie is not going—that way she can bring Ryan and Brie will never know.

"I might go anyway. I have my ways," Brie smirks.

"Are you sure you want to tempt fate?" Emma warns. "Your mom's a hard-ass, and it seems like she'd bust you bad if you get caught."

"Yeah. You may be right." Suddenly blue again, Brie watches Stephanie and two other sisters working across the room on a welcome banner. They're laughing uncontrollably and touching each other's arms and thighs. Brie notices; she wants that.

Brie scoots just a little closer to Emma. Both of their laps are blanketed with construction, crepe, and printer paper. Brie reaches surreptitiously between Emma's crossed legs, slides her palm down Emma's thighs, and presses firmly on Emma's crotch. She can feel Emma's outlines through her stretch pants.

"Don't." Emma doesn't look up from her scissors. "Someone's going to see."

Brie's hand freezes. She quickly retrieves it and folds it with the other in her own lap. She looks down at them. She's glowing a little red. The thought suddenly terrifies her that maybe she's losing Emma.

At that moment, the front door of the fraternity swings open. All heads turn. In walks their illustrious leader, Brooke, and a new person. Eyes scan her up and down. Tallish, skinny. She wears a light grey dress, tight against her narrow hips, low scoop but totally professional. A matching blazer, buttoned, with sleeves pushed up to the elbow. Emma notices the square jawline and full lips.

Brie glances at Emma to gauge what's going on. "Who's that?"

Emma stays riveted and just shakes her head.

The pair walk through the commons toward the kitchen. Housemom Lucille emerges and meets them halfway. "Girls?" The whisper has grown to a murmur and won't stop. "Girls, please. Girls? May I have your attention." The girls stop, heads turn towards their housemom.

"I have an announcement." She puts her hands together daintily. "I'd like to introduce your new R.A., Eggy Compson." The murmur starts again, heads coming together around the commons. Lucille has a small red book in her hand, and she smacks it loudly against her hand, crack! That shuts the girls up. "Thank you. Now, this is Eggy. She's come to us all the way from Atlanta, and she has just been hired as Assistant Quarterbacks Coach for the football team." The players in the room break out in broad grins and pat each other on the back. The girls all look at them.

Lucille continues, "Isn't that delightful? A woman coach! Let's hear a warm Raven welcome for—"

"Why do we need an R.A?" Emma insists loudly.

"Well, my dear," Lucille says diplomatically, "*you* don't need an R.A. But I do. Miss Compson is here primarily to help me. Like getting y'all ready for a night out, or to be an experienced ear to talk to when you need it. Think of her as your Theta big sister."

"Big Sister is watching," Emma mumbles.

Brooke lingers for a moment until her eyes catch Emma's. An ominous look exchanged, Brooke follows Eggy out the door back to the Theta house.

*   *   *   *

"So, she gave you a hard time, huh?" Chet scratches the stubble on his chin. "I don't trust that Emma girl. We've got to make sure she hooks him. So, there's no way he'll sign somewhere else."

"Are you sure full-on bangin is necessary for that?" Eggy wonders.

"Listen, you may not have been able to stand being in a boy's body for longer than you had to, but I know them. Boys follow their peckers. Always have, always will."

"That's not how—whatever. Maybe Ryan is just a good boy."

"Nonsense. But just in case." He opens a desk drawer and pulls a prescription vial and dumps a few white pills on the desk.

"Roofies? Whoa. I'm not comfortable with that at all."

"Cool your heels, Egg. It's only in case of emergencies. A fail-safe. If you see Emma Precious playing coy, you can just slip one into her drink." He holds up the small pill. "This is the good, old stuff—dissolves quickly—not like that new shit that sits there in the glass and turns blue. Can't get these very easy anymore. So, no one will know. Not even young, upstanding Ryan. She'll get uninhibited, compliant, and eventually black out. She'll never even remember what happened."

Eggy smiles, then doesn't. "But I ain't roofying nobody."

"I think you'll do what it takes to keep this coaching job, Egg, my dear."

Eggy bites her lip and looks away. Out the glass, the thriving college town surges energetically beneath her. She thinks about her father again, those Saturdays watching games. She's so close to what he wanted for her. What she wants.

"That's what I thought," Chet mumbles. "Morals go out the window when ambition's at play."

*   *   *   *

In her bedroom, Margolis reads. She's been a homebody since Benny's death.

Next door, Brie is in her own room. She's dressed as Peter Pan, checking her hat in the mirror. She turns up some music to make it seem like she's still at home but then steps cagily into her closet. Pushing aside her hanging clothes, Brie reveals a small door in the back wall. She bends down and opens it.

As Margolis reads, blithely unaware of what's going on in the next room, Brie tiptoes diligently through the rafters of the attic, trying not to step through the pink insulation between the wooden slats. She comes to a trap door, bends down, and opens it. Like a cat, she deftly slips through the opening and lowers herself down on top of Margolis's Mercedes parked in the middle of the garage. Brie climbs down the car, looks one last time back at the kitchen door and then slips out the side into the night.

*   *   *   *

Cut to an exterior shot of the Kappa fraternity house. It's night, and droves of couples and gaggles of girls migrating toward the front door. A two-story mansion like the Theta house, the Kappa house sits dark and foreboding, closer to the heart of campus.

The yard and front of the house are lit up with white and orange lights, a graveyard of Styrofoam gravestones painted to resemble slate, and an elaborate choreography of witches and ghosts fly between the porch columns on complex wire rigging. The canned sound of eerie cackling and scary organ music rises out of the shrubs and barely covers the sound of dance music coming from inside. The walk and porch are packed with people dressed in costumes and holding the ubiquitous red Solo cups.

Emma and Ryan move through the crowd and into the building. She doesn't want to go into the TV room where there's dancing just yet—she jerks her head toward the Great Hall where the trash cans full of punch stand guarded by Thetas in skimpy costumes sipping red-colored moonshine.

Meanwhile, back outside, Brie stands in the eye of a flurry of girls in heels and bunny/vampire/angel costumes trying to act older. Brie is dressed as Peter Pan, and the green androgyny of her tunic and cap makes her stand out.

"Look, it's fucking Peter Pan," Brooke says, drunk-loud.

Stephanie laughs. "That's perfect, Brie. Good job."

Brooke sighs and grabs Brie by the arm. She pulls her past the ID check and into the Kappa yard. "Let this one in. She's good." Brooke gives a smile. The Kappa at the check shrugs. Brie is relieved.

In the foyer, Brie notices Emma near the trash can. She's with some guy, and Brie's stomach drops through her tights to the floor.

*   *   *   *

Cut to the brighter, cheerier light of the Great Hall where Brooke and Eggy conspire over some punch. Brooke sports a sexy German barmaid get-up; Eggy is dressed like Rosie the Riveter. They're glancing around the crowd.

"Steph is in form tonight." Brooke takes a slurp from her Solo cup.

Eggy turns her head, and we get her point of view: Stephanie stands, back against the doorframe leading onto the side patio. One recruit—Tarzan—leans on his hand next to her head; he's bending over her, talking low. Another player—Superman—stands at her side, blocking the doorway; he's got his hand slipped behind the small of her back. Stephanie grins.

"She's not the only one in rare form. So are Lennox, Jaspers, and Johnson," quips Eggy into her cup. "They don't get rich girls like that down in Valdosta."

Then Eggy turns their attention to Emma and Ryan.

"They look like they're gonna do it," Eggy says, then considers for a moment, pursing her lips. "Right?"

"I don't know," Brooke purses her lips doubtfully. "Look, his eye is already wandering."

"Hard not to," Eggy admits. Their eyes follow a couple of Thetas dressed as various woodland animals, bushy-tailed squirrel and bunny, tops of thigh-highs showing under short skirts.

Emma and Ryan find a seat, but it's not one second before Emma has to pee.

"Hey, Ryan," she says, pushing off the couch, "I'll be right back."

Brooke and Eggy see Emma put her drink down, get up, and leave. Ryan sighs and distractedly rubs his thighs.

"Emma's already ignoring him." Eggy shakes her red, bandana-wrapped head. "This is not going well."

"You got Plan B, right?" Brooke asks resolutely.

Eggy hesitates then pats the pocket of her blue denim button-down where the roofie is.

"Fucking give that thing to me." Brooke reaches roughly into Eggy's boob pocket. Eggy reaches out to grab Brooke's arm but is too slow. White pill between finger and thumb, Brooke heads toward Ryan.

"Wait, Brooke. Wait!" she hisses, but Brooke doesn't stop. "God dammit." Eggy looks around, animated, and folds her arms. She knows she can't just go up to Brooke and say, "Give me my roofie back!" So, she watches and waits.

Brooke plops down next to Ryan on the couch. "I was just fucking with you earlier about your costume. It's cool—you're a big star and all. Anyway, your ass looks great in football pants." Brooke leans toward Ryan, and just as her left hand teases his thigh, her right hand stretches back unlooking and effortlessly drops the white pill into Emma's cup.

"Thanks. I think," Ryan replies.

"Have fun tonight, stud. I think you're gonna get lucky." Brooke crosses her fingers right in his face and then pops off the couch, and she's gone.

Ryan watches her go, ass swishing in her costume.

Someone bounces on the couch. Ryan turns back to say something to Emma but instead finds Stephanie.

She slurs, "Hey. This your drink?" Before Ryan can answer, she picks up the red cup and takes a long draw of punch.

Eggy cringes in the shadows.

"No, it's Emma's," Ryan answers blandly.

"Emma. Pshh. Does she even drink?" Stephanie giggles. "I'm sorry, if you two are, like, a thing."

"I don't know. Maybe. We're not. I'd like—"

"Don't worry, dude." Stephanie leans in like Brooke did before. "I'm not trying to hit on you and steal you away." She pouts her face innocently. "It would be so unsisterly of me." Then she busts out laughing and bounds away from Ryan, cup sloshing in her hand. She takes a slug on the go.

Eggy follows her.

A third bounce on the couch and Ryan turns warily back, but this time it is Emma. "Hey, where's my drink?"

Ryan goes in the other room and gets a new punch. When

he brings it back, Emma places a huge, lingering smooch on his lips.

From the shadows, Brie watches, stunned.

She wants to go yell at Emma but knows she's not even supposed to be here. So instead she turns, moves quickly back through the gauntlet of bodies.

At the doorway to the crowded TV room, Brie surveys the pulsating mass of bodies and sees a large group of Thetas dancing in a group. Brie moves to the center of them, where she's hidden, and they whoop and holler as Brie spins to the music, hands high in the air.

*   *   *   *

Track Eggy moving up the curving stairs in the upper reaches of the foyer. She holds a cup and steps gingerly into the hall, as if there is something there she knows she doesn't want to see. She lost Stephanie in the crowd but thinks she may have gone upstairs.

Eggy turns knowingly down the right wing of the house and moves steadily toward the end of the hall. It's dark, but light streams out of one of the open doors. She moves into a shadowy spot where she can see inside without being seen.

We see Eggy's face looking in the room. Her eyes widen. Her mouth opens helplessly.

In the center of the room on a disheveled bed lies the limp body of Stephanie. Her skirt is hiked up around her waist, exposing panty-less pelvis and bare pudendum. Her bra is pulled up exposing her breasts, which seem red and chapped. Her legs are spread and her head is turned toward the back wall.

There's the crescendo of boy laughter and chaotic banter energy. A tall skinny one, Jaspers, stands in the corner holding up his cell phone, recording the event.

A large one—Tarzan—Eggy recognizes him as one of the

visiting recruits but can't remember his name, Lemon, Landron maybe—falls to his knees on the bed between Stephanie's thighs. His pants are down and he is feverishly stroking his limp penis. Through laughter and mirth, the others goad him to get it up.

Another boy, older—Superman—Eggy knows him as Johnson, a current starter on the football team—moves toward the door with a cup in his hand. He turns his head toward the hall and Eggy, who instinctively moves back further into the shadows. But for some reason he does not see her.

As he starts to close the door, Eggy looks down at Stephanie. The head lolls back toward Eggy, as the recruit descends now upon her, large erection now straining from his fist. As he puts his weight on top of her, Stephanie does not move.

The door closes. Eggy gulps. Now in darkness.

*   *   *   *

Back in the TV room, Brie dances. She closes her eyes, trying to forget what she's seen and to let the music carry her frenzied mind away. She's so mad she just wants to let it go and get drunk. She opens her eyes and sees Emma grab Ryan's hand and pull him off the couch. She leads him through the foyer and up the stairs.

Brie follows them upstairs to a random room where they stand at the door.

Brie moves quickly towards them. "What the fuck is wrong with you, Emma!" Brie pushes Emma by the chest.

"Hey!" Emma snarls, a little drunk. Ryan raises his eyebrows and enters the room, leaving the two girls in the hall.

"Who is this guy?" Brie's voice rises as she points at Ryan.

Emma's face goes blank. "It isn't what you think. We're not—"

"Bullshit, Emma!" Brie interrupts. "Have you been fucking

him?"

"No!" Emma stares for a split second then turns toward Ryan who has a confused look on his face. "You know what? This is bullshit." She turns to go into the room.

In an attempt to stop her, Brie grabs Emma by the costume, ripping it at the sleeve.

Emma turns, looks at the sleeve, then at Brie. "I don't think you should hang out here anymore. You don't want to be a Theta, trust me." As she says it, her eyes go wide, glares.

Tears rise in Brie's. She looks in at Ryan and then back at Emma. Before Emma can say anything else, Brie turns and marches down the hall. At the bottom of the stairs, Brie strides toward the door. As she passes the center table, eyes forward, her hand extends nonchalantly and sends a vase of orange flowers crashing to the ground. From just above the shattered fragments and scattered petals, we see, framed through the open doorway, the image of Brie stomping down the walk receding to the street.

IV.

We push in through the hearing chamber door and crane above the crowd in the gallery and down to the front of the room where the Faculty Committee sits patiently waiting. Stoddard takes a sip from a coffee cup. Both parties are giving their final statements.

Dean Concord stands rigidly at her table as she speaks: "Parents send their children to the U with the understanding that they are going to be safe. That they don't have to worry that their children are going to be hurt or taken advantage of in any way. They trust us—our faculty—to deliver personal yet professional service that will help their young people grow and emerge prepared for their lives and careers.

"Margolis Santos's actions jeopardized that trust."

The dean smooths her skirt at the back of her legs as she sits down. She's feeling pretty good about the administration's position, so she smiles, ever so briefly. She feels like she's taught a wayward faculty a lesson—no more of this loose behavior, no more reinforcing Hispanic stereotypes.

From the other table, Margolis stands and begins to pace slowly in front of the committee as she speaks.

"Despite my clean and positive record as a faculty member at Athens, the administration suddenly claims that I am not fit for my job. What is more, these punishments *in toto* are unreasonable and inordinate with the alleged infractions. And by the University's own by-laws they have not established that I did anything wrong. Except maybe put someone in danger of slipping and falling."

Titters from the audience.

"The due process ascribed to faculty in the by-laws is the bulwark that protects all of our academic freedom." She gestures to all the faculty on the committee with a sweep of an arm.

"Due process and the rights therein are supposed to

prevent administrators, for whatever reason, from using sanctions or dismissal to silence, limit, marginalize, or discriminate against faculty members for unjust or capricious reasons, including fear of lawsuits by vindictive parents."

Margolis turns and looks at the Reinharts in the gallery. They fume.

"If we, as faculty, do not vigilantly guard these rights, then we can be summarily intimidated, punished, or fired for anything the administration does not like, including any legal activity in our personal lives. As faculty and citizens, we have the right to association and to free speech unhindered by administrators."

Margolis turns toward the committee: "I urge you to recommend that all of these specious charges be vacated and expunged from my record for the protection of our civil rights and academic freedom."

A smattering of applause from the audience prompts Stoddard to smack the gavel.

"The committee will recess to deliberate and will render a judgment on the case of Professor Santos in this chamber tomorrow morning."

As the noise of the crowd swells, Margolis turns to the back of the gallery where Farrah and Mark smile, giving the thumbs up.

Close on Margolis, whose face breaks, for the first time in a long time, into a smile.

*   *   *   *

Sitting alone in the deserted hearing chamber, Lane picks up the phone, hesitates, then dials anyway.

"Chet. It's Lane. Santos seems to be winning her appeal. I think it's time to bring in the cleaner."

Cut to Chet sitting at his office desk.

"Yeah." Beat. "Yep. I hear ya." Beat. "And I think I got just the person to take care of your problem."

Chet hangs up the phone, then dials and waits.

"Ronnie. It's Chet. Remember those pics you took of Santos a couple months back?..."

*   *   *   *

In the darkness, we hear two voices.

"Wait, wait. Slow down. What exactly did you hear?"

"I didn't hear nothing. I saw it myself, with my own two eyes."

Lights up on Mickey Andouille's office. Eggy sits across the desk from Mickey. She's got two fingers pointed right at her own two eyes. She bulges them widely for emphasis.

"Whatever." Mickey waves away the discrepancy. "What exactly do you think you *saw*?"

"A gang rape." Eggy exhales. "I saw our football players—and a recruit—rape a girl. Frank is worried about you taking care of the media frenzy over his wife's hearing, but I'm telling you there is something much bigger bearing down the track towards us."

Mickey breathes in sharply, like he's arming himself for something he doesn't want to do. "When was this?"

"Halloween."

"And you're just coming to me now? Almost two weeks later?!"

"I got busy!...And scared." She looks down at her folded hands. "I didn't know who to tell or if I even should."

All the air and allegro leaks out of Mickey's body. He puts his knuckles to his mouth and turns, slight fear in his eyes, to the window. After a moment of reflection, he turns back: "Who was it? The girl. Emma?"

"No." Eggy shakes her head. "You see—" A hesitation: "There was a mix-up." She braces herself against Mickey's reaction.

"A mix-up? Girl, what you mean there was a 'mix-up'?"

Eggy sits silently, a desperate grimace across her mouth. Then it all rushes out: She tells Mickey the whole ugly story, in detail.

Eggy sits slightly out of breath. Mickey just sits there breathing, too.

Then Mickey: "So she wasn't being paid—I mean, she wasn't assigned to—"

"No, I don't think so. Not with three guys..."

"Three—who were the others?"

"The recruit—Lennox, I think—and two other players, Jaspers and Johnson."

"Were they witnesses or participants?"

"Witnesses, I think. I don't know for sure. Is there a difference? They shut me out."

Mickey is stumped for a moment, just staring back at Eggy.

Eggy: "What are we going to do?"

Mickey is suddenly animated. "You just leave the rest to me and forget that any of this happened."

"Forget?" Eggy asks incredulously.

Mickey realizes he may lose her if he doesn't say this right. "All I meant was, you did the right thing telling me. You protected the team. Now let me protect you."

*   *   *   *

Margolis sits in her office—what she's pretty confident will continue to be her office. She reaches down to pet Benny, but he's not there. Oh, yeah.

There's a knock on the door; she tells whoever it is to come in.

It's a nondescript dude in a Member's Only jacket. He hands her a manila envelope, and she instinctively takes it.

"You've been served," he says, as he turns to go.

Margolis is a bit stunned, but not enough to not open the

package.

A divorce decree. Signed by Frank.

So, this is how it ends, Margolis thinks, *with a whimper.*

After a moment of flipping through the papers, Margolis tosses it down. She doesn't even care anymore—she grabs a pen and signs it.

Done.

*   *   *   *

"Halloween? Oh my God, Steph." Emma reaches out and squeezes Stephanie's shoulder. "It must have been hell going through this all alone."

Emma and Stephanie face each other, leaning shoulders on piles of pillows and stuffed animals on Stephanie's daybed.

Brooke stands in the center of the room. "What's the point now? She didn't get a rape kit. All the evidence has been destroyed." Her arms are folded and she chews her index fingernail.

Emma turns, her face twisted in disgust. "Jesus, Brooke. Blame the victim much? She needs our support right now."

Brooke softens her arms and sits down on the other side of Stephanie. "I'm sorry, Steph. I didn't mean it like that. I just. I just want to get the fucking bastards, you know?"

Stephanie nods and sobs once into a tissue. Her face is streaked and red.

"She's right, Steph. You still gotta report it. We'll all testify that we saw you with those guys. Football players, right? They were pawing you in public all night."

Brooke: "They probably fucking roofied you, man." Emma glances at Brooke who stares back. "What? It happens!"

"But did you see it? Did you see someone put something in Stephanie's drink?"

A beat. Brooke straightens herself, wondering if Emma is suspicious. "I didn't see anything, y'all."

Emma is about to press the issue.

"You're so lucky, Emma." Stephanie's low voice interrupts. "You have Ryan. He'd never do anything like this."

Brooke: "Not all football players are bad. It's just a few assholes."

"Don't worry, Steph. We'll figure this thing out and help you bring these guys down."

Stephanie: "I don't even know where to start. It seems hopeless."

Emma takes Stephanie's face in her hands. "Steph, listen to me. We are going to find you help. We are here for you."

*   *   *   *

"I thought you'd want to know about it right away, sir. Some of the Thetas tell me that Stephanie is going to file a complaint." Mickey stands in front of President Lane's huge, oak desk.

Lane stands for a few beats chewing on a cuticle. "Has she reported it to the cops?"

"No, sir. Not that I'm aware of."

Lane thinks for a moment. "I want this handled in-house. No leaks to the press."

"How should I—"

"Get your Thetas to keep her quiet, convince her to let the system work its course. Then, we need to start recasting."

"Recasting?"

"Here's how the story goes: The two were budding lovebirds. One visit to campus and he was in love. He even sent flowers afterwards. That means it must have been consensual, right?"

Mickey waits silently for several moments. "Flowers. Check. Anything else?"

"Just make this go away."

"Like everything else," Mickey mumbles under his breath.

"What was that?" Lane raises his eyes.

"Nothing, sir. I'll get right on it." Mickey turns for the door, kicking himself for backing down. Everyone making a mess then saying, *Let Mickey fix it.* What he wanted to say, right to Lane's fat face was, *"There's some things that can't be wiped away..."*

But he didn't. He chickened out.

*　　*　　*　　*

"Although most courtroom dramas are a lie we tell ourselves to feel good about our system of justice, there are some exceptions." Margolis pauses and looks out over the lecture hall for effect. "There are some films that challenge our system and even our biases that shape how we understand justice.

"For today, I asked you to watch *The Accused*, the 1988 film that demands discussion in the context of the genre of courtroom dramas because it turns the tables on the very system it applauds. It stars Kelly McGillis of *Witness* and *Top Gun* fame and also Jodie Foster, who won an Oscar for Best Actress for her role as Sarah Tobias, a working-class woman who is brutally gang raped in a bar. But what made this film so important then is that never before had people been witness to what a rape may actually look like, how conditions can suddenly turn horrible, and little choices—the choice by the rapists to ignore the victim's 'no' and pleas to stop, the choices of the spectators to incite the crime by cheering—can turn into the huge, terrible, life-altering choice to sexually assault and rape a woman. This film, perhaps for the first time in popular culture, challenged the widely-held view (which some still hold, mind you) that women are responsible for their rapes by wearing the wrong clothes, saying the wrong things, and acting in a promiscuous manner. Of course, the same standards do not apply to men—only women victims must prove their own innocence before proving the guilt of a rapist."

Margolis looks down and notices that her hand is shaking. She pauses and puts her hand on her hip to steady it. Despite the nerves, she is emboldened.

"I was almost raped once. And I've never told anyone that."

She looks around the room and finds Emma, who puts her hand to her mouth in sympathy. "I was taking a shower in my college dorm bathroom. No one on the entire floor was around—they had all gone out—and I was kinda glad to have the whole place to myself. Lots of hot water. Anyway, with my eyes full of suds, I feel this body up against me. Scared the fuck out of me, but I knew right away that it was a boy because of the hair and his huge, swollen penis."

The faces of students around the room—shock, sadness, even tears. Margolis can feel Emma looking at her—it makes her want to go on.

"He grabbed my arm," Margolis swallows hard, "but I was soapy and slipped away. I just blew past the curtain without even rinsing my hair, and there I am, running nude down the halls of the dorm, my eyes streaming with tears from the shampoo and the fear. I must have looked like a mad lady."

Margolis takes a deep breath. "Anyway, I'm telling you this because I needed to. People need to hear these stories. I was lucky, I got away; but there are so many women who don't."

*　　*　　*　　*

Brie sits on the couch in the Great Hall with a bunch of Thetas that she met at Halloween. The huge, flat-screen TV blares the Raven's game. Her stomach is all tight. She wonders if she's going to boot.

The game is close, late in the final quarter, with the Raven down four and needing a touchdown to win. The Thetas all lean forward in their seats, chew on pillows, or bite their nails—everyone knows that their quest for a championship will end if they lose.

Brie drinks compulsively from a red Solo cup. She's pretending it's beer, but it's not—that would really make her sick—it's just ginger ale. She notices Brooke, who's drinking more than usual for some reason. Brie wonders what it is, trying to ease the midterm stress.

"Your dad better win this." Brooke sways a little between gulps—her eyes are blinking slowly, unfocused.

Another one of the Thetas reaches out and puts a hand on her shoulder. She mouths, "I know your dad can do it!" and points at the television. She watches Brooke stagger to the side of the room where Emma is standing.

Brooke whispers in Emma's ear. "Ryan is waffling about coming to the U. Better change your Thanksgiving plans, stay here and make sure he signs on the line."

Emma is about to get pissed at Brooke, but out of the corner of her eye she sees Brie watching.

Brie's head turns toward the TV, where Frank paces the sidelines nervously. Brie feels a pang of guilt—she doesn't want to blame her dad if they lose—but a lot is on the line for her: all the girls are watching, and sometimes Brie fears that the only reason they let her hang out with them is because her dad's the head coach.

This is it, the last play of the game, and the Thetas all hold hands or brace themselves against each other. Some put their hands together, as if in prayer. They look at Brie sympathetically, and she looks back, a little prayer really going through her head now. The ball is snapped and everyone holds her breath. Eyes widen. The ball is thrown.

As it sails through the air, Brie prepares for the worst. *I'll just say goodbyes and then leave with a little dignity. I could start hanging out again with the theater kids after school. It wouldn't be that bad.*

The receiver catches the ball. Touchdown, another come-from-behind win for the Ravens.

The Thetas explode off the couch and jump into each other's arms. Hopping and screaming, the group mobs around Brie. They rub her head, hug her neck, and kiss her cheek.

Suddenly, it's like someone has untangled her gut—now that the game is over, she has to pee really bad, all that ginger ale built up—and she leans into the group hug, bodies of Thetas surrounding her. This is her moment—her father did that for her—she feels a wave of gratitude—she's so proud of him.

The TV shows a mass of huge boys in bulging pads dancing on the green football field like children on Christmas morning. The title at the bottom of the screen reads, "Raven Stay Perfect at 10-0 with a victory. Only Rival Alabama Remains in Cinderella Season."

One of the Thetas yells and points at the TV, "Look! There's Eggy!"

In the middle of the mass, the camera cuts to Eggy and Frank, arm in arm and smiling at each other. They hug and Frank lifts Eggy off the ground. When he puts her down, a wave of orange Gatorade washes over them both.

"Could this signal a budding romance for newly-single Coach Sinoro?" the announcer jokes.

Commentator: "On top of a potential berth to the national title game? He's having some night!"

Cut back to Brie staring at the TV in disbelief, eyebrows wide. For a moment, there is dead silence, and then in unison all of the girls break into raucous laughter. "A romance!" one of them yells. Another: "With Eggy!" "That's hilarious." "Whatever." Catcalls. Brie is doubled over at the absurd thought of her dad with Eggy Compson, the big sis of Theta house.

Brie basks in the attention. Girls are swirling around her, whooping and hollering. They touch her, kiss her, tell her she's awesome. She's never felt so a part of something before, not even theater. She doesn't even have to pee anymore. But something catches her out of the corner of her eye.

Across the hall, Brie sees Emma standing in the doorway to the dining room. Their eyes meet.

Emma smiles weakly and nods.

Back to Brie, who doesn't even care anymore about Emma's boyfriend, about the kiss, about Emma. She just turns back to the adoring Thetas and lets their joy wash over her.

*　　*　　*　　*

Emma pulls open the door to Margolis's classroom, and we follow her inside.

The volume of Margolis's voice greets her like a northerly gust. She finds a seat near the back and waits. When the lecture is over, Emma hurries down the stairs, against the flow of students shuffling out of the hall.

Margolis disappears through a door, and Emma jogs to catch up, slipping through just behind her. When she gets in range of about ten feet, Emma speaks.

"Professor Santos?" She does not stop walking, so Emma says, louder, "Professor Santos!"

Margolis halts, turns. She sighs with a frown, "Ah, Emma, you finally decided to grace us with your presence."

Emma holds up the paper with the bright, pink "A" at the top.

"So? You got an A."

"There's hardly anything on it. No comments, nothing. And this was a shit exam. I didn't even study, and my essay is crap. And yet you gave me an A. Why?"

Margolis closes her mouth.

Awkward silence. Emma breaks it.

"Okay. I get it. I understand. I just want you to know that I respect you. Despite what happened at the club, I still want your respect."

"You have to earn it, Emma." Margolis takes a step toward her, softens her tone. "Look," Margolis turns and starts walking but keeps talking: "Be at my office first thing Monday after New Year's. Before classes start."

"Why?"

Margolis, who still has her back to Emma, shifts her weight. "We're going to talk about making a movie."

Emma watches Margolis recede down the hall.

V.

Lane sits motionless staring at his computer screen. He notices the dust all over the keyboard and wipes it off, the powdery cloud wafting slowly through the air to the ground. He thinks about how he hasn't written a letter himself in a coon's age—not since he addressed Margolis Santos and the LGBTQ protestors last year when they threatened to occupy his office. Didn't work, they took it over anyway—that woman has been a pain in his ass ever since she got to Athens. No head coach is worth that, but now he doesn't have to worry about that. She loses her appeal, she's out.

But with potential media attention over this rape allegation looming, he wants to take on the task himself, a delicate operation. Write the wrong thing, and it could go viral, the hounds of social media all over your ass. Then, kiss the Senate campaign goodbye.

Lane leans forward, thoughts flitting across his face. To whom should he address it? Stephanie? No, Ms. Rogers? Miss? Then, he sets his fingers to the keyboard and starts typing:

"...in reality, you did indeed wear something—a French Maid's costume with short skirt, fishnet stockings, and low-cut blouse—the committee wondered at the appropriateness...

"...you could not remember if Mr. Lennox had penetrated you with his penis or any other member or object. You failed to seek immediate assistance, so no physical evidence to support your claim...

"The committee believes that you were more interested in protecting your reputation after making the decision to have sexual relationship with Mr. Lennox...

"...based on the inconsistencies in your testimony, I have determined that there is insufficient evidence that Mr. Lennox violated the Student Honor Code...five days in which to appeal..."

He types the closing and bangs the 'enter' button. There,

done.

*   *   *   *

"We reconvene this Appeals Committee because new evidence has come to light in the case of Margolis Santos."

Caught off guard by these words, Margolis jerks her head back around toward Stoddard.

"Very recently, it has come to our attention that photos of Professor Santos have surfaced on the internet that may corroborate the administration's charges. Is this indeed the case, Dean Concord?"

"Yes, Dr. Stoddard, we submit the following photographs into evidence."

The lights dim, and a projector shines larger-than-life the photos of Margolis from Brooke's Facebook page. They're the ones Ronnie took: Margolis in the club dancing with a man. Then getting freaked by a younger man. Then she's dangerously close to a young woman who looks like she could be a student. As they flash across the giant screen, Margolis watches helplessly with horror and shock.

"Where...where did these come from?" Margolis turns back to look at Brooke, who swallows self-consciously but does not look at Margolis.

"And how did you procure these photos, Dean Concord?" Stoddard asks.

"An anonymous source alerted us to them, your Honor," Concord stiffens.

"And you can confirm that this is indeed Professor Santos in these pictures?"

"We can indeed. We have the person who took them here in the room today."

"Can you point her out to the committee?"

"Yes, ma'am." The dean turns around and points. "This is Brooke Golindy, president of the Delta Delta Theta sorority and

117

former student body vice-president."

"Ms. Golindy," Stoddard shifts her line of questioning, "did you take these pictures yourself and can you confirm that they are authentic? That Professor Santos was actually there when you took them?"

"I can. And she was," Brooke states calmly without moving from her bench.

"Thank you, Ms. Golindy."

"And we have other witnesses that can testify that such behavior—these images can only be said to depict that of a sexual predator—"

"Where did these witnesses suddenly come from?" Gus Johnson interrupts.

"I can answer that." Lane rises to his full, impressive height and smooths his suit coat. "These three, including Ms. Golindy," he gestures toward the bench behind him and the other administrators, "showed up at my office with the fear that Professor Margolis might somehow get away with sexual assault. I listened to their stories, was adequately convinced by them, and immediately got into contact with the committee to share the new evidence."

Margolis deflates and silently accepts the horror show happening before her. She wants to scream that she's innocent. That those photos are fake. That she's being framed. But she doesn't. She sits still, like a good girl.

The second witness begins to tell the story of how Margolis accosted her in the bathroom at the club and how the professor pushed her into the stall and kissed her and touched her breasts. Another explains how Margolis asked her for her number in a coffee shop.

"Did you give it to her?" Lane asks.

"Well, yeah. Look at her. She's frickin gorgeous."

With titters all around her in the audience, Margolis puts her head in her hands. At the back of the room, Farrah shakes her head and looks at Goldberg. His eyes are disappointed, perhaps the image he's held of his film mentor has tarnished slightly. Maybe more than slightly.

"If you have no further witnesses, President Lane," Stoddard announces, "then the committee will adjourn and reconvene after Thanksgiving to render a verdict." She bangs the gavel and Margolis starts slightly.

Margolis looks over at Lane who is smiling smugly right back into her face. She grits her teeth; he doesn't change his expression until he reaches up and shakes Concord's hand. She smiles confidently, glowing in her boss's praise. Brooke stands and scoots by the two other young witnesses. The sound of controversy and scandal hisses through the chamber. Chet turns on the ball of his foot and slips out the door.

Close on Margolis, her face blank in a state of shock as "Primadonna" by Marina and the Diamonds begins to play. *Primadonna girl? Yeah.*

Emma strides purposefully down the walk from the house toward the street. She's dressed up in a little black strapless and heels. At the curb, she stops, and within minutes a black limousine pulls up right in front of her.

The window glides down to reveal Chet, who smiles broadly at Emma. He looks her up and down approvingly. *Primadonna girl. All I ever wanted was the world.*

The door opens and there sits Ryan Cavanaugh. He's giddy with excitement as Chet exits the car. After searching Chet's eyes and finding no relief, Emma bends into the innards of the limo. With a dispassionate face, she sits next to Ryan and looks up at Chet. The door closes, and Chet watches the limo pull away.

Frank's office, where the conference table is crowded with assistant coaches all talking over each other: they're animated, arguing about a proposed strategy for beating their rival Alabama team tomorrow here in Athens.

Eggy pushes back her chair in frustration and walks over to the whiteboard. She begins writing.

Close on her hand as she scrawls out the following: STRATEGY TO BEAT ALABAMA—PLAY ACTION ON FIRST DOWN. COUNTER THEIR SECOND HALF DEFENSIVE ADJUSTMENTS WITH THE RUNNING GAME.

Below this line of bold print, Eggy begins writing the cryptic names of some of the football plays she has in mind: 1) PA Y-crosses, 2) PA FB flat, 3) Red Dogz 38 counter slant, etc.

Frank puts down his pen, takes off his reading glasses, and nods in approval. Instantly, the other coaches burst into a fit of activity, combing the playbook to flesh out Eggy's strategy.

While Ryan sits on Emma's daybed in his underwear, she straddles him in panties and a bra. She wraps her arms around his neck, as he strains up to kiss her mouth. Behind her back, he struggles with the clasp, so without stopping her sensuous kiss, Emma reaches back and unclasps it with one smooth motion. He gazes at her breasts, pale in the faint light from the desk lamp.

Emma reaches down between her legs and pulls Ryan's penis out of his boxers. She slides her panties to the side and eases down on top of him. His eyes darken with pleasure.

She begins to slowly move up and down. He runs his hands down her back. Emma's motion gets faster and faster, and Ryan's head lolls back, his eyes closed.

Frank opens his front door, and the light from inside streams out onto Eggy Compson. With a sheepish grin, she holds up the playbook and a huge thermos of coffee.

Frank stares at her for a minute before he relents. Somewhat annoyed but unavoidably fascinated, he steps aside and motions for her to come inside. She kisses him on the mouth, then walks confidently, with even a little wiggle, past Frank and into his apartment. He looks around vigilantly before he shuts the door.

Thursday morning, Margolis sets the table in the breakfast nook of her kitchen. She's waiting for Brie. The centerpiece features a festive fall tableau, featuring a ceramic turkey, fake leaves, and a miniature cornucopia. After 2 hours, she gets up and starts putting things away. Brie's not going to show.

Lane has called a press conference for a special announcement before the football team's rivalry game Friday with Alabama. The seats are filled with reporters eager for any news about the top-ranked Raven. Everyone perks up as Coach Sinoro, Ryan Cavanaugh, and his parents file into the room. They take a seat at a table in front of microphones.

Frank hugs Ryan with one arm, and with the other places a grey, black, and pink Raven's hat on Ryan's head. At the bottom of the screen, a TITLE appears in all-caps: "BREAKING NEWS: STAR QB RYAN CAVANAUGH SIGNS WITH ATHENS UNIVERSITY."

The next day, we see Frank standing on the sideline during the rivalry game. He's watching a play unfold, one of Eggy's, his head moving slowly from left to right tracking the player with the ball. Suddenly, a runner in grey and pink streaks past the coach and towards the opposite end zone. We see Frank cheering him on, pumping his fists in encouragement.

We know the ball carrier has reached the end zone when Frank—and all the rest of the Raven sideline—jumps as one unit into the air and explodes into a roar.

The Raven have done it—the scoreboard shows their victory over rival Alabama—they've gone undefeated for a perfect regular season and will face Texas in the national title game.

At the Theta house, the girls again mob Brie when the team wins.

The committee enters the hearing room; Dean Concord rises to her feet. Margolis follows, a bit slowly. She's suddenly very worried about the outcome because Gus Johnson won't look at her.

"After further deliberation, the committee has come to a verdict," Stoddard announces. "In light of the new evidence presented this week, we had no choice but to deny your appeal and uphold President Lane's decision to fire you. This committee's decision is final. Do you understand this ruling, Margolis?" The look on her face seems almost gleeful.

Margolis nods assent without the need to say anything. All the years of study and struggle flash before her face.

The poppy music of "Primadonna Girl" crescendos.

We see the back of Frank, who sits at the head of a happy dining room table stuffed with appetizing dishes, sparkling glasses of wine, and ornate decorations. A hand reaches in from his right and slaps him on the shoulder in congratulations.

The camera begins to move that way and reveals the back of Chet Orchard, his face turned toward Frank and chewing a huge mouthful of turkey. His face is so happy, he could be eating dog food for all he cares. With that grin, he continues to slap Frank's shoulder.

As the camera circles around the table, we see everyone— Mickey Andouille, the rest of Frank's coaching staff, Ryan sitting next to Emma, Brie at her other side—Brie casts a quick look at Emma, sees that she has Ryan's hand in her lap. Brie swallows her sadness, her pride and takes a bite of turkey.

The rest are eating and being merry. They lift glasses and toast each other in revelry. And, as the camera comes a full 180 around to the front of Frank, we see that seated next to him, in a place of honor, is Eggy Compson. Close up on Frank's hand, under the table, stroking Eggy's skin.

Eggy stops dead for a moment, looks at Frank, and then turns back the other way with a shy grin on her face.

Primadonna girl.
Music fades.

*   *   *   *

Margolis sits at her kitchen table again, lit only by a single candle in front of her. Next to the candle is a bottle of Bushmills Black Irish whiskey, a single tumbler full with a double serving in Margolis's hand.

In front of her, papers are spread out on the table: her termination letter and divorce decree.

Margolis is talking to someone we can't see. "I just don't know what happened, how all those kids came out of the woodwork. I didn't even know any of them. They were complete strangers."

Voice: "You mean, you don't remember any of them."

Margolis stops and stares at the person across the table from her.

"You were probably drunk. Again."

Margolis takes a slog from her drink. "So what?"

"So what? You've always been a sucker. Weak for the drink. And weak for the young piece of ass. And it's cost you this time. Big."

As the camera comes around completely behind Margolis, we see that her dinner guest is none other than her father, Cicero Santos, framed by the window out to the backyard.

"Fuck you, Dad." Margolis sways just a little but steadies herself for retort. "You never had anything for me but useless advice. I didn't need it then, and I don't need it now."

"Look at you. You lost to the assholes you trusted to protect your rights. What does that make you? A sucker." Cicero palms a hand down definitively and leans back for punctuation to his point.

"God, you must really hate me." Margolis stares at him and takes another drink.

Cicero looks back hard, but then he relents, his voice softens: "You're at rock bottom, darling. And I hate to see you like this."

At the note of even bare sympathy, Margolis begins to lose it, she slouches her tear-streaming face down into her sweatered arms. She's sobbing uncontrollably.

"I didn't raise you to be this way." A hand appears on her shoulder. "I know you are stronger than this, Glee. And I know that you will figure this out. They won't keep my girl down for long."

At these words, Margolis raises her head, eyes hopeful and expectant—but as she looks across the table, all she sees is her reflection in the darkened window.

Part 3: A Championship

I.

It's a Monday, a day or two past New Year's, and the sound of electric piano music fills the void of a very dark room. Light and music from the TV flicker faintly over the mess as we track across it, a veritable slacker's landscape of laziness and depression: empty beer bottles, food-caked dishes, and grey-greasy pizza boxes strewn over tables, chairs, and couches. It looks like a frat house after a long weekend of football on TV. The song becomes recognizable as "Goodbye Love" from the film version of the musical, *Rent*. The deep baritone of Jesse L. Martin croons desperately.

As the piano fades, Margolis buries her head between her knees. Margolis watches *Rent* when she needs to feel something, anything—happy, sad, excited, elated, nostalgic—she watches it to think about Frank, she watches it to forget about Frank, she watches to salve herself over the Ford scandal, she watches it not to feel lonely, she watches it to forget she got fired, and she watches it to cut through all the bullshit depression of the ordinary. Other musicals make her feel good or remember certain times in her life, but only *Rent* seeps into every corner of her being.

There's a knock at the door, but Margolis doesn't move.

Knock. Louder this time.

Margolis presses pause on the remote, uncorks her legs, and hauls herself with obvious struggle off the couch. She slinks to the door half hoping that the persistent son-of-a-bitch at the door will have already given up.

No such luck. When she opens the door, there stands Emma, fresh as a fucking daisy.

II.

"I thought we had a meeting today." Emma thumbs over her shoulder in the abstract direction of the U. Outside, it looks like the killjoy of winter break at a southern university—instead of snow and ice, there's green trees spreading out in the lowered sun, a warm southerly breeze, and kids lying out by the blue of a pool at the Theta house.

By the look on her face, Emma is clearly starting to feel smugly proud that she wasn't the one to forget the appointment. She likes having something on her professor.

Margolis looks back at Emma blankly for a moment.

"You know. You said meet first Monday of the new year. We're going to talk about making a movie? You were all dramatic."

"I just forgot all about it, and you should too, okay?" Margolis slumps with a grimace and walks back inside. Emma follows her.

"Why? What movie did you mean?"

"There isn't any movie."

"But you sounded so cocky about it."

"Well, I'm not. I wouldn't even know where to start or how to pay for it." Margolis slumps back on the sofa and points the remote at the TV. The movie starts playing again.

"Ooh! I love this movie," Emma looks elatedly at the screen. "*Rent* is my favorite musical!" She sings along in duet with Margolis on "Will I?"

"You have a nice voice." Through bloodshot eyes, Margolis finally really looks at Emma. She's so young, with so much ahead of her, triumphs and tribulations.

"Thanks." Emma looks back, then smiles weakly. "Really, what movie were you thinking of? To make."

Margolis looks at Emma, a little too long. "There never really was any movie." A longish pause. "I thought I'd figure something out before we met. It's just..." A beat. "Things got crazy."

Emma nods. "I see." A moment. "At least I'm not your student anymore."

Margolis snorts smilingly in spite of herself but doesn't look up. She's picking at an afghan, and the sinking feeling is coming over her that she may have lost any authority, power, or respect that she may have had with this young woman, student or no student.

Emma turns back to the television. "Hey, you could make a movie like the Mark character does in *Rent*. About friends and family."

"What family? My husband left me." Margolis looks around at the empty house, as if making her point. "Even my daughter hates me."

"She doesn't hate you." It just comes out so fast that Emma doesn't have a chance to stop the statement.

"How do you know? Do you know Brie?"

"Oh, she hangs out at the Theta house sometimes." Emma waits for Margolis to explode but it doesn't come. Emma is relieved she doesn't know about her and Brie.

Margolis shakes her head. "That girl. Thinks the U is her own personal playground. I don't know where she is half the time, but I know she's somewhere on campus. Makes me worry less." A pause. "I should make a doc about life inside the Theta house. That'd sell to the *Girls Gone Crazy* crowd."

Emma chuckles, then her face gets serious. "Actually, there is something you could make a movie about in the Theta house."

Margolis looks up at Emma, amused, waiting for this great idea.

"There's been something going on." Emma looks away. "Something happened."

Margolis shakes her head impatiently and smiles, as if, "Well?"

"Sexual assault. You know, a doc on sexual assault on

campus."

Margolis: "Well, there have been a few other good documentaries on the topic: *It Happened Here* and *The Hunting Ground*. Stuff like that. So, it's already been done." Margolis is suddenly concerned, "Emma, did something happen to you? Are you okay?" Margolis leans forward toward her.

"No, no. I'm fine. It's," a hesitation, "someone else. The case was dismissed. By President Lane. He told the student there was nothing he could do. In a letter."

"Typical. What can I do about it?" Margolis flops back on the couch. "Nothing."

"Please? Just come talk to her."

"To whom?"

"I'm not going to tell you yet. I don't know if she'll even do it."

"Then what is there new to say about it?"

"There's stuff she wouldn't tell. Things the U swept under the rug."

Margolis considers for a moment, then dismisses, "Yeah, but the whole *Rolling Stone* fiasco with the lacrosse players. It kinda poisoned the well on campus exposés. No one will give that kind of story any credibility now. Especially coming from me."

Emma talks fast: "But that's exactly why you need to make it. To set things straight. Tell the truth. Do real, rigorous reporting."

"What. You aren't going to break into song, are you?" Margolis chuckles.

Emma ignores the smart remark and cuts to the quick: "Remember, it almost happened to you. In the dorm shower."

Margolis looks up suddenly at Emma and knows that she's right, but she wants to take her time. "I'll think about it. While you're checking things out."

"But I get to ask the questions." Emma smiles slyly.

"Look at the graduating senior, making the executive

decisions!" Margolis smiles.

"It's settled then." Emma gets to her feet and lifts her bag. Over her shoulder on the way out: "I'll be in touch."

*   *   *   *

Art Lane, dressed in muted golfing shirt and slacks, sits on a lounge chair in his lush backyard. Even though it's January, it looks verdant with winter blossoms and evergreens.

He's staring off into the blue sky over the pine trees. He's not much of a religious man, but the thought of John Calvin has crossed his mind. Predestination. His followers had faith that history was set from the dawn of time—so much so that some of them went so far as to sin on purpose just to prove their favor with God. Simply the fact that they were not struck down on the spot demonstrated that they were chosen. Those elect had a kind of confidence, knew they were saved. Made their ambition righteous in reverse. All becomes God's will.

Holding a newspaper, Lane suddenly snaps out of his philosophizing. He straightens out the pages with both hands when he spies the story he was looking for. He brings it closer to his face.

Close on a headline that reads, "ATHENS PROFESSOR FIRED AFTER RAUCOUS HEARING." There's a photograph of Margolis. Lane reads the article intently, and after a few moments, he chuckles to himself and shakes his head. It's the schadenfreude gesture of satisfaction that comes from vanquishing one's enemies. No more Santos to deal with. No more slutty female professors sullying the U's reputation. No more pesky feminist film activists agitating against his hiring or firing or whatever the hell else he wants to do on his campus. He could feel a new sense of freedom rise up in him.

*   *   *   *

Tuesday. It's Margolis's last day in Hartley Hall on the Athens U campus. She packs stuff from her desk into a box. All her movie posters are stacked, leaning against the wall next to the door. There's a knock.

"Come in."

The door pushes open a bit, and Sandy pokes her head in. "I just stopped by to see how you were getting along." The voice is as even and flat as always.

"Oh, I'm fine. Fine. Come in, Sandy."

Sandy fully steps into the room and shuts the door, looking awkwardly around at the boxes everywhere. "My, but you have quite a bit of stuff to move."

"Yeah, mostly books. The doctorate may be the sails that take my academic ship to new and distant places, but all the books you have to read end up being the anchor."

"I see." Sandy peruses a box or two aimlessly, not really seeing what she's looking at. She's waiting for the right moment to speak. Margolis continues to pack.

"Listen, Dr. Santos."

"Margolis, please, Sandy. We don't have to uphold any institutional pretense anymore."

"OK, Margolis. I just wanted to wish you well and to say that if you need anything from me—after you're gone—to please let me know." Margolis raises an eyebrow, and Sandy responds, "I know we haven't always been, uh, you know, chums, but I respect you and appreciate you reaching out to me after my mother died."

"And I have too, Sandy." Margolis is heartened at Sandy's revelation. "You always made my job easier around here, despite me giving you a hard time."

Sandy smiles sadly.

"Well, goodbye then." Sandy edges toward the door and pauses before opening it. "One more thing: It's an occupational hazard of my job that exposes me to almost everything that's going on in this department. And for what it's worth, I don't think you did anything wrong." Sandy opens the door and is about to leave.

"Hey, Sandy?"

Sandy stops, turns.

"You wanna join me and my daughter to watch the Athens football game next Monday?" Margolis asks hopefully. "My house."

"Sure." She smiles and steps out the door.

Off Margolis, feeling a small burst of good will.

$$* \quad * \quad * \quad *$$

"I can't fucking believe I'm in here." Standing in the middle of a bright, sterile room, Eggy hugs a phone between her cheek and shoulder while she stuffs towels into the cubby holes of football player lockers.

Frank's voice replies even and steady through the tinny speaker: "It's just for the month—I need all hands on-deck making sure everything goes smoothly."

"But it's the week before the championship game. I should be with the coaches."

A pause and then a sigh. "Egg, we talked about this." A beat. "Ever since the Ross rape investigation—"

"But President Lane dismissed that case," Eggy reassures herself. She must have *thought* she saw something Halloween at the Theta party, but she's relieved she was wrong.

"And with the way things are between us," Frank hesitates. "I can't be seen playing favorites. Not now."

"But if banging the coach doesn't get you a place on the sideline, what will?" she teases, but her face is sad and serious. She closes her eyes, as if remembering.

Flashback to: The image from TV of her jumping into Frank's arms after the Alabama game. Plastered all over social media, that simple pic has been a headache. She's not used to the exposure.

Frank laughs softly. "Look, I know. You'll be standing next to me again out there real soon. Just give it time." Another beat. "You know I want you, right? As a lover and a coach."

Eggy keeps putting towels, making him wait. "Yeah yeah," she begrudges.

"So, what do you say?"

Monotone: "Go get 'em, Coach."

"That's right, baby. Talk to you soon." Click.

Eggy puts one more towel away before she lets the phone slide off her chest. She hangs up and slumps, all the vinegar draining out of her person. Standing silently in the back corner of the room, she stares straight forward into a random locker. A stinging feeling of unfairness shudders through her—she should be coaching, not this trainer bullshit—but she beats it back. With a sigh, she looks down at her hands as she grabs the laundry cart. Part of her wonders if getting involved with Frank was a mistake. But it's been a thrill, getting this taste of the limelight. Part of her knows she'd do it all over again.

*   *   *   *

Brie walks by herself across the front of her high school. She has a distant look in her eyes, like she's prepared to walk for a while. It's a fair distance to her dad's apartment. She thinks about maybe going to the Theta house instead, but she knows Emma might be there, back from break.

Suddenly, a voice startles her.

"Need a lift, stranger?"

Brie turns towards the voice but can't find it.

"Brie. Over here!"

Brie finally spots her mom in the Mercedes convertible, top up. Brie's expression doesn't change, but she changes course and heads towards Margolis.

Margolis shifts uncomfortably in her seat; she's slightly disappointed in Brie's reaction to her surprise visit, but she bucks up and smiles anyway.

Brie leans down to the car window. "What are you doing here?"

"I thought I would save you the walk. I know your dad's busy with the game. Maybe we could go get lattes or something. I'm still on vacation, remember?"

"God, what a hard life you have," Brie exasperates as she pulls open the car door. Flopping down in the passenger seat, she continues in the same disaffected teenage tone: "I wish I were a big shot college professor who got 5 months off a year. Oh wait, you're not a big shot college professor anymore. Community college instructor." She shoots Margolis a sarcastic look, but Mom doesn't take the bait.

"Just wait until you're in college. You'll get all those months off too."

"I can't wait."

Pulling out of the school drive, Margolis shoots Brie an inquisitive glance to gauge the level of irony in that statement before turning eyes back to the road.

"No, really. I can't wait." Brie rivets a serious face in her mom's direction.

"Don't be in too big of a hurry to grow up, Brie. You may think my breaks are full of fun and games, but that's when I have to get my own work done."

"What work could you have to do now that you're fired?"

"Well, as a matter of fact, I'm thinking of making a movie." She looks quickly at Brie for a reaction.

Brie seems genuinely surprised. "Really?" Then she sags back toward the cynical. "When was the last time you made one? Grad school?"

"Yeah. In the last century." After a brief pause, Margolis looks over and catches Brie's eye, which softens, seeming mollified by the joking but honest reply. "It was the one about illegal immigrant sex-workers in LA. Remember?"

"Yeah. You only told me a thousand times." Brie bows her

head back toward her lap where she is fiddling with a strap on her backpack. Margolis smiles to herself, the sarcasm means that things are getting back to normal. Little by little. She promised herself she would not ask Brie whether she had decided to move back home or not. It's hard. So hard not to. But Margolis bites her lip.

They ride in silence for a while, Margolis just biding her time, as patiently as possible, until Brie instigates the conversation. Keeping her eyes on the road the rest of the way, Margolis swings the car into the coffeeshop parking lot.

Inside the eclectic-hip campus café, Brie sits and watches her mom standing at the condiment stand, stirring her coffee with a wooden twizzle. Brie glances up and down, taking in Margolis's long, muted beige cardigan. It's thick, knitted cotton, tied at the waist and covering her hips. It looks soft. She can't remember when her mother seemed so soft, maybe even subdued. Like a regular mom. No trace of the hard-edged, type-A, go-getter that usually inhabits the smoothed-slick fabrics of lecturing and meetings and conferences. She suddenly has an urge to touch her mom. Hug her. Something. But she shakes it off.

When Margolis finally joins her at the table, Brie's curiosity gets the best of her: "So what's the film about?"

An inquisitive look. "What film?"

"The film. The one you're going to make. Duh."

"Oh." Margolis is confused then suddenly pleased by Brie's interest. "Oh, yeah. My film." She takes a sip of coffee, bracing, as if in preparation. "It's about sexual assault on campus. Athens."

"Oh, so you're going to try to tear down the U again, is that it? Just like the speech last year against the president over LGBT stuff."

"Hey, you agreed with me on that issue!"

Brie backs down and takes a sip. Then under her breath, "You just don't want me to go to school here."

"Brie, honey, that's not it at all. I want you to go wherever you want. Really." Margolis pauses.

Brie looks up from her mocha with angry eyes not believing that her mother wants her to actually be happy, but wanting it to be true. She waits.

"That's just it. I want you to be able to go anywhere, to places better than Athens. With better theater programs so that you can have more opportunity—"

"Sounds like you just want to get rid of me."

Sternly, "Brie, you know that's not true. You're just being sil—"

Margolis stops midsentence, forcing herself into patience: "I can see how you might feel that way, honey. I've been completely self-involved, out of it for a long time now. I've not been a great mom at all."

"That's for sure."

"I was going through a lot of stuff last semester, but I'm over it now. Things have settled down. Please believe me when I say I want what you want."

Brie frowns her disbelief as she takes a drink.

Margolis waits, picks her moment, and continues undeterred: "As a matter of fact, I thought you might want to help."

"With what?"

"My film."

"Need or want?"

"Both actually." Margolis skips a beat. "You're good on sound, and I could use a hand with the equipment. Plus, I think you might have some insider information about my first location."

Curiosity piqued: "Yeah? Where's that?"

"Before I tell you, let's just be clear: I am not trying to tear down the U. I repeat. I'm not trying to tear down the U. I know you love it and want to marry it." She winks, Brie begrudgingly smiles. "But it's just like any other college campus, and stuff happens here. Bad stuff. We shine a light on the bad stuff and the place will just get better, right?"

Reluctantly, "OK. Sure."

"And there are certain places on campus where assaults tend to happen more often than not. Usually not in official university buildings."

"You mean frat houses."

"Yes. But not exactly." Margolis pauses in wait for another guess, but Brie just stares back at her expectantly. "Also, sorority houses. Namely, the Thetas."

Brie bows her head, subdued. "I guess maybe some bad things happen there."

"Yeah." Margolis frowns, sensitive to how Brie might be disappointed and scared. "I think you should go with me to find out what happened last Halloween. For your own sake as well as the sisters. Plus." She pauses, readying herself for the ask: "You hang out there and must know those girls pretty well." Margolis glances quickly at Brie. "With you around, it'll make them trust me more."

Brie seems, at first, a bit chafed at feeling used by her mom, but she has to admit it makes a lot of sense. Anyway, she doesn't want that kind of bullshit happening at *her* house, to the Thetas, especially since she's dead-set on pledging there next year. "Yeah, I'll do it. Just tell me what you want me to do."

Margolis smiles all big; she can't help it. She's such a nerd: "That's right, you and me. Ruling the galaxy as daughter and mom."

*   *   *   *

A TV sportscaster's voice runs smoothly over a clip from the Raven's comeback win to end their regular season: "Do the Raven have any chance of winning the title game this week, Len, and if so, what do they have to do?"

Cut to a shot of two men in suits sitting at a desk in front of a busy background of football-esque colors: deep crimson, burnt orange, deep grass-green, the browns of wood grain and pig skin, and, of course, the black, grey, and pink of Athens's logo.

Len: "Well, John, this is going to be a very difficult game for this Athens team. They stumbled a bit early in the season and then got the signature win against Alabama in their big matchup on national TV."

John: "Yeah, Len, everyone remembers that famous photo of the female trainer jumping into Coach Sinoro's arms at the end."

Len: "Yes. Exactly, John. Eggy Compson. One of the first female coaches at the college ranks, recently demoted to trainer after rumors surfaced of their romance. But that's just a distraction. Coach Sinoro better keep his mind, as well as the mind of his players, on this game. Athens has no room for error against this very talented and dominating Texas team. The Raven are going to have to run the ball consistently, and get big plays from their passing game..."

*   *   *   *

Frank sits in his office, watching the sports news on TV.

"To be honest, Mickey. I'm not doing too fucking good." Holding the phone, he shuffles the other hand desperately around his desk groping for a pen, a highlighter, a printout—god knows—but he's distracted, and his desk piled with playbooks, stat binders, and DVD cases reflects his frazzled state.

"Preparations for the game aren't going well?" Mickey's voice thin through the phone.

"Preparations? Hell, this team isn't ready for a championship game on any level. Half a dozen of them didn't pass finals and are academically ineligible—"

"And we're appealing those cases. That's my issue to worry about, not yours."

"And on the field, everyone looks like they've forgotten everything they've learned all season."

"You've just got the big-show jitters, man. Don't worry. Things will come together."

"Jitters my ass. We are going to lay a frickin turd on national TV and embarrass ourselves, that is what is going to happen."

"It ain't all that bad, Frank. You kicked Alabama's ass. Made you a permanent hero around these parts." Mickey pauses before he teases: "We thought your divorce was going to be a big story, but it wasn't. And that pic of Eggy jumping in your arms has made you a social media darling."

"It was a great idea you had, to demote her," Frank says. "Stopped the talk." He feels a little jolt in his stomach, like the world has confirmed him being with Eggy or something. Approval.

Cut to Mickey sitting erect at his desk, knit shirt pressed and tight across his chest. "That's my job, taking care of all the circus side-shows," Mickey smiles even though Frank can't see him. No response. "Come on, Frank. I thought you'd be reveling in this situation—X's and O's, extra workouts, the TV interviews, all the hype without the personal stories as distractions—it's what you've prepared for your whole career!"

"You're right, Mick. It is," Frank hesitates. "I guess I'm just worried about screwing it all up."

"I feel you, man. I feel you." Mickey sees an opening to change the subject. "Uh, that's something I've been meaning to talk to you about," Mickey puts gingerly.

"What, something else come up?" Frank anxiously. "Is it the Rogers case—did she go public?"

"Ah nah, nah. It's all good." Mickey pauses.

"Then what?"

"I was just wondering if you'd mind if I asked Margolis

out."

"Oh!" The tone more of surprise. Frank is completely taken off guard. "Um, yeah. Why not." He says before he's totally sure. "We've been separated for almost a year now. And it was over way before that."

"You sure?"

"Yeah, man. I'm sure."

Mickey doesn't know if he should take Frank at face-value, but he goes with it anyway. "Okay, great. Thanks, Frank." Then quickly, "You do have great taste in women." He cringes that he let those words out of his mouth.

"Sure. Bye, Mick." Click.

Mickey hangs up the phone and leans back in his chair. He stares out the window, seemingly musing on the possibilities. Then he reaches down and pulls his phone out of his pocket. He swipes to his address book, pulls up a contact. It's Margolis.

III.

"Alright, alright. Settle down," Margolis's voice fades in over a din of student chatter. She stands at the front of her new Athens Community College classroom.

"I know we start back earlier than Athens U—and every other college in the civilized world—but here we are. We got a lot to cover, and it's going to be a struggle to get to everything you need to know before the end of the term. So, let's get started."

Dressed in her usually flowy gowns of silk and chiffon, bracelets a-clinkle on her wrists, Margolis seems out of place in the small space. No lecture hall, it looks instead like a high school classroom, and she's hemmed in on all sides by single-seat desks arranged in a prison-like grid. Students are packed in to the gills—35 to 40—standing room only. There's no expanse, no stage, where Margolis can roam as usual.

"We begin this semester-long course on film genres with one of the oldest genres of film, the musical."

A groan from half of the class.

"I know, I know. I'm sure most of you hate musicals—they're certainly an acquired taste—what with people spontaneously bursting into song—I used to hate them too.

"But then I started watching film versions of more recent musicals, mostly after 1970, that changed my mind. And I'm here to convert you, too. When you leave this course, I'm betting you will love musicals as much as I do."

"Yeah, right." A voice from an indistinguishable location in the middle of the crowd.

"I'm serious and willing to take bets. Who wants to put a twenty spot on it?" Palm out, Margolis looks searchingly around the room for exaggerated effect, and she gets her first laugh of the class period.

"Now," Margolis continues. "Musicals. Here's my pitch: Musicals are, and always have been, a kind of *strip-tease*."

She pauses and looks around the room for eye-contact. Everyone is so close to her, she fights off the feeling of claustrophobia. They are waiting. Tough crowd.

"Musicals always take us to the edge of showing us something titillating and then they pull back, never fully showing what they promise. Everyone knows they show us something we never see in real life—people singing to each other as if it were normal. But people love that about musicals because we can sing things that we would never say out loud like, 'singing in the rain'? 'Oh, what a wonderful feeling?' 'The hills are alive?' 'I'm gonna wash that man right outta my hair?' Who says such things in real life?"

"Nobody," a husky male voice, deadpan from the back of the room. Everyone laughs, made ready by mounting nervous energy. The class is starting to warm up.

"So, by definition, musicals show us things that we don't usually see—or maybe even don't want to see—in real life. We may want to sing our love aloud to the world, but because of social embarrassment, we don't. So, we go see musicals to live vicariously through characters who act sappy and sentimental through song and dance."

Margolis twirls halfway around in her small space, a little dance.

"Starting in the late 1950s with shows like *Gypsy*—one of the most famous book-musicals of all time, with lyrics by the great Steven Sondheim—Broadway (and by extension, Hollywood, since it was adapted to film) begins to actualize the notion of the musical as strip-tease. *Gypsy* is literally about a budding dancer pushed into stripper-stardom by her overbearing stagemom, Rose.

"Since then, musicals have been increasingly about peeking over the edge of social acceptability and giving us a brief glance at all sorts of profane and sexually aberrant human behavior. In *Cabaret,* for example, the taboo topics include ménage-a-trois, abortion, and free love."

Margolis presses a button on a remote and a screen comes to life showing a still shot of Michael York from *Cabaret* frozen in some palm fronds.

The clip won't start—it takes her a while to get it rolling—makes her feel awkward, embarrassed. The setup here in the classrooms at ACC is a lot clunkier than at the U. She doesn't even know how to turn off the lights.

After some awkward silence, Michael York finally stumbles into motion, hiding behind the plants watching Liza Minnelli dance blissfully with a dashing Helmut Griem. Michael stops and half-heartedly gives a Tarzan call, "King of the Jungle," before going to drunkenly refill his champagne glass at the piano. While Liza and Helmut continue dancing, Michael watches jealously before walking over to them where Helmut puts an arm around him and smilingly brings him into the dance. They spin around together, grinning and putting their faces close together. But when the song ends and the record player hisses, the spell is broken. A defeated and completely snookered Michael York stumbles to a sofa where he passes out.

When the clip ends, the ruffled students look around cautiously at each other, wondering what they just witnessed and if it's okay to show something like that in college.

"This scene comes right after the silly and suggestive song where the cabaret characters jokingly portray a polyamorous living arrangement featuring regular threesomes: 'Two Ladies' is the title of the song that Joel Grey humorously sings."

While pointing to the three characters using her laser, Margolis bursts into song, bragging about how great it is to be the only man living with two ladies.

The students laugh uproariously at the melodious sounds of their professor actually singing. She waits for them to calm down a bit. She's smiling the whole time, right along with them. When it quiets down, she continues the lecture:

"In *Hair*, the taboos are psychedelic drug use and anarchy.

In *Rocky Horror Picture Show*, it's cross-dressing and S&M. More recently, in *Hedwig and the Angry Inch*, we see the results of a sex-change operation. In *South Park: Bigger, Longer, and Uncut*, we see a gay character's penis (oh, and Saddam Hussein's too), and in *Book of Mormon* we get to hear characters blasphemously say 'fuck you' to God as they mime anal sex and bestiality.

"All of these musicals take us to the edge of these perverse topics, rarely spoken of in polite company, but never really show us the actual *act*, the full monty, as it were. For example, we never see the three main characters of *Cabaret* in bed together despite the innuendo in the scene I just showed you. In *Hair*, social order is restored when a hippie is sent to die in Vietnam (which we also don't see on stage). In *Hedwig*, we never seen the 'angry inch,' and in *South Park* we don't see actual penises because it's an animated film. We never get to go 'all the way.'

"And musicals can't ever really take us all the way, right? Because it's fiction. Actors playing pretend in the dark. If people actually had sex or whipped each other on stage, suddenly we'd be in a totally different world: the world of actual strip clubs, dominatrix dungeons, and opium dens. Hence, the musical is really never more than a strip-tease, promising a full-access behind-the-scenes but only giving a glimpse before pulling the curtain."

Margolis pauses and looks around at the blank faces, which she can't tell are from boredom or shock. "Well? Don't you want to watch these movies already?" A beat, then suddenly everyone is nodding yes! "Well okay, then, get to watching!"

The classroom erupts with motion. Students muttering to each other as they put their materials away in backpacks and bags. The clock shows the period is over.

"OK. Watch *The Rocky Horror Picture Show* for next time and be prepared to talk about explicit stuff! 'Cause this course ain't no strip-tease. It's real!"

As fleeing students turn to stream out the door, Margolis's shoulders slump, as she is left alone at the front staring at their backs.

Suddenly her phone vibrates on the desk.

Margolis draws her head back in pleasant surprise. It takes a second before she decides to reach for the phone and answer it.

"Hello?"

"Margolis. It's me, Mickey. You remember, from athletics?"

"Of course, of course! Mickey." Margolis nods even though there's no one else in the room. "Hi."

"How you doin?"

"I'm good, good. I just got through teaching class."

"Oops. I'm sorry, I didn't mean to interrupt. I'll let you—"

"No, no. You didn't interrupt me. All my students are gone—they couldn't wait to get out of here," Margolis chuckles nervously.

"Well, I won't take much of your time. I just wanted to know, actually, if you had plans for the game? I've been invited to a swanky game-watch party at the President's house, and I was thinking you might come along and save me from the attack of the billionaires." A ring of hopefulness in his voice, and Margolis doesn't want to snuff it out, but the sound of Lane's name—and the idea of being in his house—turns her stomach.

"Well, unfortunately," her mind spinning fast for an excuse, "I do have plans. Watching it with the coach's daughter." She pauses, her face contrite, hoping the humor will soften the rejection.

"Oh, yeah. Ha ha. Of course. I'm sure she'll be rooting big-time for her dad."

"Yes, she will," Margolis takes a breath. Holds it for a second. "Listen, Mickey, I thought you did a great job with the divorce thing. Allowed both Frank and me to save face. I really appreciate it."

"Sure. It was nothing." Mickey slows down. "Divorce is a difficult thing. For everybody. I'm just sorry that you had to go through it."

"Don't be. It was a long time coming, I guess." Margolis unavoidably a little sad, can't keep it out of her voice.

"I've been to that barbeque," Mickey snorts.

To Margolis's relief, he's keeping it light. There's a brief moment of silence between them.

"Well," he adds, "maybe we can see each other some other time then."

"Yes, I'd like that, Mickey." She says his name, hoping that it will encourage him to call again.

*   *   *   *

Frank sits motionless at his desk. He has on reading glasses, the half-kind that old ladies wear. He's studying a playbook.

There's a knock at the door.

Frank looks up to see Eggy's blurry head poked through the doorway. He talks off the glasses and smiles. "Hi, you."

"Hi, Frank—I mean," Eggy turns her head back out toward the hall to see if anyone heard. "I mean, 'Hello, Coach Sinoro,'" she mocks in a fake deep voice.

"Would you just come in already?" He motions. "And shut the door."

With another glance over her shoulder, Eggy steps in, shuts the door, and takes a seat opposite her lover, who seems so distant and unreachable now.

Eggy starts anxiously, "Frank, I—"

But he cuts her off: "Listen, Egg, I know you're not happy working behind the scenes, and I just want to say—"

"It's okay, I get it. Moving slowly. Gotta come up through the ranks. Avoid any whiff of nepotism, but..."

"Yeah," Frank rushes in, "but I'm serious about making it

up to you. Next year. There should be a couple of coaching positions opening up, especially if we win this damn game. Coaches always get poached off championship teams, you know this."

"Yeah, but what I don't know—"

"What you don't know," Frank anticipates, "is if you'll get the job because of us," Frank motions back-and-forth between them, "or because you deserve it."

Eggy just looks back at him, plainly understood.

"But I have to say that you've done a fine job this year, what with the other duties the U has placed on you in terms of recruiting and all. You goldamn deserve a promotion. Starting spring training."

The thought flits through Eggy's mind that spring is too late, but she doesn't want to forget about what she has to say. "Good. Thanks, doll. But I—"

"I appreciate your patience, you've been such a trouper, biding your time, keeping your head down, working hard. And I promise—"

"Frank," Eggy interrupts. "I know that. I didn't come for your promises. I came for another reason."

Frank shrugs slightly, having no idea what this could possibly be about. He puts everything down and gives Eggy full attention.

"It's Stephanie Rogers." She pauses.

"Look," Frank rationalizes, "Lane said he'd investigate, so I'm just going to let—"

"But he didn't. Not really."

"Well, what am I supposed to do about it, huh, Egg? I've got enough to do in my own job. I can't be doing everyone else's!" The words come out harsh, harsher than Frank meant them.

Eggy looks shocked, a bit frightened.

Frank's face slowly softens until it sinks unto his hands. He sits covering his eyes for several moments—so long that Eggy wonders if she should leave now.

"I'm sorry." Frank says, muffled, into his hands. "It's just. I'm so wigged out already. It's almost one week until the championship. I just..."

"I know," Eggy loosens. "It's bad timing, but this is fucked up." She looks at his covered face for some reaction.

Suddenly he straightens up and pulls his hands away from his face. His eyes look like they've been asleep, looking around his desk in a daze, as if for the answer. "You're right. I'll take care of it."

Eggy leans forward eagerly for clarity. "You mean, 'take care of it,'" she air quotes, "or take care of it?"

Losing his cool, "I will take care of it." Frank's eyes pierce— then he sees his anger reflected in Eggy's shocked face. "I will. I promise. Just keep a lid on it until I can figure out how. OK?"

"OK," she searches his face before she weakly smiles back. She doesn't believe him. He doesn't believe himself.

A moment later, Eggy finds herself, unsure, huddling outside Frank's office leaning back on the closed door.

A couple of assistant coaches turn the corner and head toward her so she straightens up, like nothing has happened. Putting on her boy-game, she nods, they pass, and she just stands there, wondering what in the hell she's going to do now.

*　　*　　*　　*

Margolis sits in her new office at the community college. It's sterile and bare, but there's a window at the far end. Still, it's a far cry from her cushy office overlooking the quad at the U. Her desk now faces a blank white wall. She's leaning back in her chair, legs straight out. Sitting across from her is Farrah. With an office right down the hall, she can pop down any old time she wants.

"It's just not fair, Farrah," Margolis complains.

"Get it? Fair-ah?" Farrah chuckles at her own bad pun. She's also leaning back, feet extended towards Margolis's so that they form a V-shape.

Margolis ignores the weak joke; her mind is on a million other things. "If what my former student says is true, about the rape at the Theta party being covered up—I can't even wrap my head around it—it's so fucked up."

"What in heaven's name are you blathering about?"

"The rape. The one *not* in the news. It may have been a football player, so the university covered it up."

"What the hell."

"Either way, it means Lane was protecting a rapist the whole time he was busting my balls for having legal, consensual sex with a non-student."

"Barely legal." Farrah purses her lips comically. "It's what makes it kinda hot..."

"Would you be serious. For, like, one second?"

"Sorry." Farrah pauses. "But, Margolis, you don't know for sure this incident involved a student, an athlete, or a recruit. Hell, you don't even know if it was a rape."

"What kind of administrative mumbo jumbo is that? You're starting to sound like Lane now."

"Maybe your former student, Emily—"

"Emma."

"Emma. Maybe she made a mistake. Or doesn't know what she's talking about. There's still a chance you could get your job back, so why blow it by going snooping around?"

"Because some girl got raped, Farrah," Margolis fumes, then backs off. "Most likely." She pauses and then suddenly wonders, "Why am I having to make this argument to you, of all people, that the only side that has something to gain by covering things up in a rape case is the University? You know this!"

"Yeah, you're right. Most likely." She looks down at her hands, a splosh of shame, and takes a breath. "I'm just worried about you, Glee. I know how much your career means to you. Teaching at the U."

"Yeah, but it isn't worth teaching there if it means staying quiet while people conspire to cover up sexual assault on campus. And over an athlete. Jesus Christ!"

"I just think you should take it slow, Glee. Go talk to the girl, but be careful. All I'm saying is that it's in your best interest to make sure you got the story straight..." She pauses.

"What?" Margolis asks, looking Farrah in the eye. "No, really. What is it? Spit it out, if you have something to say."

"It's just." A beat, then the damn bursts: "I'm worried that your anger over Lane may be clouding your judgment. That you're confusing justice with vengeance. I'm not certain you can be objective right now, after what you've been through. It may make you see what you want to see in this case so you can craft a personal vendetta against the U."

Margolis stares, her mouth a bit open in disbelief. "You must have an awful high opinion of my character, then, to think I'd use some young girl to sharpen my personal ax-grinding."

"No, you've never used a young person to salve your personal needs before, Margolis." Farrah looks up sharply at her best friend, "Never at all." Dart hits the mark.

Thinking of Ford, Margolis rolls her head back, part in anger, part in surrender.

"Fuck you for being right."

*   *   *   *

Sportscaster's voice: "In just a few days, the Athens U Ravens will face off with the Texas Longhorns in one of the most hyped championship football games in recent memory. Can Athens Coach Frank Sinoro, who took over just last year and went 4-7 in his first season, complete a miraculous turn-around and win it all? Today, we go inside the success of the Athens football program, which many attribute to the man behind the coach, Athens President and Athletics Director, Art

"Lightning" Lane...

*　　　*　　　*　　　*

Lane stands at the edge of his lush backyard where's he's been playing with grandkids and neighbor kids the entire afternoon. The scene before him looks like a fairy show out of Shakespeare: colorful pink and red streamers flying as kids chase each other, stuffed animal heads, bubbles everywhere, loud squeals of joy—they must be playing some sort of kiss-me-not pantomime of love.

Lane is winded from running, one hand on hip, the other holding the phone to his head. He looks like a teapot dressed in golfing plaid.

From his phone, a loud southern voice, "...and signing day may not be as good as the boys expect—" It's Chet.

Lane interrupts, distracted, yelling at the kids: "Come on, Deek! Boys! Stop playing that sissy stuff and play some ball!"

"Would you listen to me for a minute?" Chet exasperated over the phone until he knows he has Lane's attention again. "Just because we landed that Louisiana boy at quarterback doesn't mean that the rest of the entire fucking forest isn't a raging inferno. The emergency is far from over, my friend."

"What are you telling me, Chet. Or did you just call on this lovely Sunday afternoon to interrupt my family time to bust my agates about recruiting?"

"Goddamn your Sunday afternoon, Lightning!"

"There's no need to get so riled up, Chet. We're about to play for a national title. Tomorrow night, as a matter of fact. Can't you just enjoy it?"

"I gotta raise hell and make sausage so everyone else can enjoy it. I'm way past Monday's game. I'm thinking three years down the line. Somebody has to. I mean, would you be satisfied if this was our last chance to win it all for another decade? Or do you want to be a dynasty? A juggernaut of football brilliance that keeps your name in the press and greases the skids for your political future?"

Lane grits hit teeth. "You've made your point, Chet. Now what exactly is the problem?"

"The money's dried up."

"What, donations for athletics, for football? I find that beyond the pale. We're about to win a title for the first time in years!"

"*Play* for a title. We haven't won nothing yet. Folks is taking a wait-and-see attitude about the U. No one's convinced that Frank Sinoro is the guy to keep us winning. So, they're keeping their wallets in their pockets."

"Well, when we do win, maybe the coffers will open up again."

"That was what you said last time, Art. They're tired of paying and paying and not seeing consistent results in recruiting and on the field. We need something that's going to wake up the echoes, get these old boys excited about the U again! Know what I mean?" For Chet, it's a rhetorical question, so he keeps rolling: "And that's why I pay you the big bucks—to make the excitement, to raise the dough. So, now's the time for all your big ideas, son."

Over the phone, Lane hears something coming from the background, and it sounds like music. "Where the hell are you?" Cut to:

"The Delta Delta Theta house. Their housemom, Lucille Bontemps, is an old friend of mine. Invited me to watch the girls rehearsing for their Valentine's Day variety show. Fundraiser."

Chet glances over to where Lucille stands. She's holding open her red diary making notes and looking up at the girls and then back down at the book. Then he looks back to the girls dancing on stage. "They are all so goldamned cute. Mm-hmm!"

Chet is standing in the exact same posture as Art—hand on hip, other hand to ear. His blazer is spread open revealing his large belt buckle, and he's smiling like a bobcat, a jarring incongruity with the tone he was conveying through the phone. We circle around his back to see what he's looking at.

There, on a set of risers for a stage, stand all the Thetas. Brooke, Emma, Stephanie—all of them dressed in precious cowgirl get-ups—boots, straw hats, red handkerchiefs, tight plaid blouses tied between their boobs, some prodigious and prominently displayed. They're back early from Christmas vacation to practice.

Chet: "Just listen to this, Old Man!" On the other end of the line, Lane is silent as they sing "I'm Just a Girl Who Can't Say No" from *Oklahoma!* and Chet knows it well, his own booted toes tapping in time. The girls hoedown across the stage, swinging elbows and knees.

Chet focuses on Emma. Under her straw hat, she's sporting a blue checked shirt, long black pig-tails, and has penciled little freckles all over her face. Her beauty sends a warm wash of pride over him. That's his girl! His eyes close on her mouth as it sings.

Cut back to all the girls, in a chorus line, with arms thrust high, palms out and fingers spread. They hold the pose for just a moment before bending over into a vamp where half the girls move up, half move back, in synchronized choreography. Brooke steps to the front, centerstage to sing her solo on "I Cain't Say No," lines that seem a little too on the nose, to be honest.

The piano slides us back into the chorus as we cut to Lane still outside. Suddenly, his eyes brighten and he moves the phone up closer to his mouth, "Hey, Chet."

No response.

Louder: "Hey, Chet!"

Chet's voice, distracted, through the phone: "Yeah?"

"You think some of the big boys would also like to be invited to the Theta house variety show? You know, just some of the bigger donors."

"You know, they just might."

Lane's mind is working while he watches his own grandchildren play. "Seems a shame that the attentions of these young women be wasted only on high school football recruits. As they say, youth is wasted on the young."

"That's for damned sure."

"And a display of spirit like this might just be what people need to feel excited again about the U."

"I like where you're going with this, Lightning. The performance could showcase the variety of talents among these ladies, and spectators could just, say, pick the ones they liked best."

"And make a bid."

"Not unlike a silent auction," Chet points out.

"Precisely. Make it happen," Lane instructs. "See if they need anything, to make this a memorable spectacle. Maybe a sexier musical, for starters. Just write a check. Same account."

"Got it."

Lane pauses a beat. "You coming over tomorrow night to watch the game?"

"Wouldn't miss it for the world." Chet hangs up and puts his phone back in his front pocket.

Brooke barks loudly, "Let's take the ending again, Jesus you guys suck!"

Cut back to the stage, where we are now surrounded by the Thetas who swirl and stomp, belting out the song's grand finale: *"I can't say no!"*

As the girls hold their final position, arms out wide, we swing around to the back of the stage and can see them in silhouette, like a Western tableau from a swanky saloon.

Cut back to the floor of the Great Hall. Chet's gone. But where he was just standing, now stands Brie. And next to her, Margolis, arms akimbo.

*   *   *   *

"Can I help you?" Eggy's voice fills the silence when the music and dancing stop.

Margolis starts a bit and turns her head—she had not noticed Eggy come up—the music was too loud, the fascination at the spectacle too deep.

Margolis lowers her arms. "We were just watching," she says in a far-away voice, while turning her head back toward the stage. The troupe of sorority singers are milling around, back toward their starting positions, to take it again from the top. Many adjusting hats, and skirts, and boobs.

Margolis folds her arms but can't stop looking.

Brie is also fascinated with the activity on stage, but when she spots Emma, her interest is dampened.

"Hi, girl." Eggy leans around to wave at Brie.

"Hey," is all she can manage.

Eggy stands awkwardly smiling for a moment, watching the pair. "Something I can do for you?" She looks Margolis up and down and notices they are almost eye-to-eye. Tall.

"Yeah, we were just—" Suddenly the music starts again, loudly, so voice raises: "We were just," louder, "trying to talk to—"

Eggy grimaces and, after a second, takes Margolis by the elbow and leads her out of the Great Hall and into the foyer as the music fades. Brie notices and follows. They stop, face each other. "That's better. It's a little quieter in here."

"Yes, we were just wanting to talk to Emma."

"Emma Barnes," Brie clarifies.

Eggy gives her a side glance, as if to say, *I thought you two broke up.*

"We're making a movie," Brie adds, as an answer.

Margolis's head jerks toward Brie a bit. A signal to zip it.

Eggy's face changes from welcome to surprise. "Oh?"

Margolis's explainer voice: "Emma is—was—in my film class. She's volunteering."

"As am I," Brie crows.

156

"What's it about?"

Before Brie can get anything out of her open mouth, Margolis jumps in: "We're not sure yet. That's why we're here. To talk about it."

"With Emma," Brie adds.

"With Emma," echoes Margolis.

"OK, well. As you can see she's busy," Eggy stalls, but still in a friendly way, as if she's wondering what this is all about. At that moment, the music stops and almost instantly girls burst through the hallway laughing and joking. Some humming or singing the tune, obviously stuck in their heads.

"Well, I guess she's not busy anymore. Emm!" Eggy rises on tip-toes, waving at Emma through the crowd. "Emm!"

Emma hears and her eyes open a little wider, as if she's got to change gears back to her role as student since her professor is here. She pas-marchés a little quicker, hurrying over, while Margolis and Brie both watch, marveling at the grace she shows through her feet. Emma looks up, seeing, for the first time, that Brie is also there. Emma stops and stands among the three pairs of eyes looking at her; she searches Brie's for a moment. Then she looks at Margolis. A slight blush crosses her face. "Professor Santos."

"Emma," Margolis nods. "You have a sec to talk about—"

"Oh yeah, of course. I'll go get Stephanie." Emma evades. "I'll meet you guys upstairs. Brie, you know where my room is." Emma jogs quickly down the hall toward the kitchen in the background, where Stephanie stands with a bunch of other girls.

Brie: "Yeah."

Margolis looks at Brie with mild surprise.

Then Eggy intervenes, with interest, before Margolis can comment. "Stephanie?" Eggy asks, "She helping with the movie, too?"

"Yeah, Stephanie may run camera." Margolis lies with a squint, purposely patronizing in an attempt to stem any nosiness. She knows that subjects in documentaries always film better when they are anonymous, or at least *think* they are anonymous, so she's learned how to keep prying from curious parties to a minimum. Especially when the identity of a rape victim might be compromised.

"Camera. Or sound." Margolis heads up the staircase, leaving Eggy below.

"I thought that was *my* job," Brie frowns, not getting any of this.

"Are you going to show me where Emma's room is or not?" Margolis climbing.

"I can do it," Eggy interjects.

"I got it," Brie says, already heading up after her mom.

"OK." Eggy deflates, then watches them go up and around over her head. Then her eyes narrow, looking suspiciously after Margolis.

*   *   *   *

"Tell her," Emma taps Stephanie slightly with a foot, "so that it won't happen to anyone else." She's getting impatient at Stephanie's resistance. They are both sitting on Stephanie's bed, knees making a triangle, not fully facing each other.

"It's okay," Margolis puts a hand up to Emma, then turns toward Stephanie. "You don't have to tell me anything, Stephanie. And you certainly don't have to go on camera—you are not responsible for stopping all bad things in the world. No one is." She looks emphatically at Emma, who softens.

Margolis puts a hand on Stephanie's knee. "I understand how hard it is to talk about these things, so there is absolutely no pressure."

Margolis keeps her hand and eyes steadily on Stephanie. We can feel the waves of anticipation streaming off of Brie and Emma. All focused on Stephanie. But, like some sort of empathic counselor, Margolis is prepared to sit quietly there for days if she has to. The Reporter's Trick. She knows that most people will talk if you just shut up and wait: Liars will tell the truth. Lovers will admit infidelities. Murderers will confess their crimes. Because people really do want to tell their stories—all they need is time and an eager audience. And this group certainly was that.

Stephanie looks tentatively around the room, like she's looking for a hole she can slip through and disappear. She then looks at Emma, then Brie, then Margolis.

She takes a breath, and then lets it all out.

IV.

"I'm not doing it." Margolis strides quickly down the walk away from the Theta house.

At her side, Emma struggles to keep up and implores, "Why not?"

"I'm just not. I'm not making a movie about this...gang rape. Nor am I ever letting Brie back in that fucking house, I'll tell you that. Three goddamned dudes? Jesus, that must have been horrible."

"Then why not make the film?" Emma stops, watching Margolis recede.

"Because there's no story there—" Margolis stops too, rewinds, and gets closer to Emma. With voice lowered: "I mean, there's a story there. This girl has a story. Something horrible happened to her, and I believe it. But that's just it. It can't be a movie just because I believe it."

"Why not?"

"You can't just make a movie parading rape victims in front of a camera making unsubstantiated accusations."

"Why not?"

"Would you please quit saying 'why not'? Because we could get sued for libel. That's why not."

"Even if they didn't name names or reveal victim identities?"

"Then we really have no movie because it's just blurred faces and garbled voices. That's no movie. And I already don't want to make one. It's expensive, a pain in the ass of work, and for very little recognition, usually. Since I'm not at the U, all I want to do is teach my four classes, go home, and put my feet up. I don't need this kind of trouble in my life."

Emma's mouth freezes in disbelief, then: "Oh, that's great. Yeah, you just go relax. We may have a campus full of serial rapists, but, you know, you should just put your feet up!"

Margolis stops and takes a breath. Her eyes are closed. She

doesn't want to look at the anger in Emma's eyes. Shut it all out.

Margolis, after a breath: "There's just not enough for a movie here, okay? Girls get raped all the time. On campus. In rooms. Here. At home. In India. In the street. By their friends, by their dates, by their families. It's so common that it doesn't even shock anyone anymore. So what difference is a documentary film going to make, huh?"

Margolis is just letting it all loose; she's a woman at the end of a proverbial rope: "All these powerful assholes always get what they want anyway. They know the general public doesn't really give a fuck when girls get raped especially by football players or rich guys. It's not even a thing. Everyone thinks, 'oh, boys will be boys,' so there's a big excuse. Or 'girls really want it secretly anyway.' Shit. Nobody is going to care. Get that through your thick, highly-producted coif of yours. Geez."

"Then tell me what's missing!" Emma pleads. "What do you need to make this film? Because Stephanie is my friend, okay? I don't want this fucking shit happening to her or to anyone else. Nobody signs up for this when they apply to college. And you know what, Glee?" Emma asks expectantly.

At the use of her nickname, Margolis turns towards Emma—all Margolis can do is look in those golden eyes.

Emma: "That coulda been me."

Margolis shakes her head in disbelief, just because she doesn't want to think about that happening to anyone. She keeps shaking.

"Yes." Emma continues. "You know it could have been. I was there. A roofie could have easily been slipped into my drink. I could be the one sitting up in that room now wanting to die. It could have been me. Or your daughter."

Margolis considers for a minute, looking around the neighborhood of finely manicured lawns and sorority mansions. She takes a breath, then: "We need a voice from the inside—a rogue administrator willing to tell-all, an exculpatory document, a smoking gun—God, anything that we can *show*, more than just shots of talking—in this case, crying—heads. And more than anything? We need an angle that people are going to care about. Hell, if this was a movie about football, you know people would fucking watch then."

"Leave that to me." Emma suddenly jogs off in the opposite direction. Over her shoulder: "You'll see!" She's on a mission.

*   *   *   *

Stephanie's room is laid out just like Emma's, but instead of candles and theater posters, it's way more froo-froo: pink stuffed bears, posters of One Direction, a Hello Kitty comforter. Stephanie sits on the bed, both arms huddled around her. Emma stands over her, leaning on the dorm-room desk-chair.

"I understand why you didn't show her the letter, Stephanie," Emma implores, "but why won't you let me show it to her?" As if it were a winning lottery ticket, she holds up the letter that President Lane wrote to Stephanie explaining he dismissed her rape accusation.

"Because."

"You keep saying that. But *why* exactly?" Emma slaps the envelope back on the desk in frustration.

Stephanie's eyes follow it, protective, not wanting it out of her sight.

"Explain it so I'll understand," Emma folds her arms and stares down at her. Both girls, arms folded, stubborn.

As if electrocuted, Stephanie unwraps her arms and slams her fists down on the bed. "Because I don't want to, okay? Would you just get out of my face! Unless you've been raped, you don't get to tell me what to do!"

Emma sits down, stunned for a moment, looking back into the face of someone she thought she knew well. Now the distance seems so great. Unbridgeable. Emma feels lucky and guilty at the same time. No one has ever done anything to her unless she'd said it was alright. She is always the one in control and can't really even imagine that power being taken away from her, like a thief stealing family heirlooms in the night. Even this bullshit for the football team—escorting the recruits—had been her choice. She fucks them and gets something for it. She doesn't love it, but at least she's paying for college and protecting the people she loves the most. And, most of all, she is in charge.

Emma looks away, a moment of remorse. "I'm sorry, Steph. I've pushed you too hard." Then she moves to Stephanie's side and puts an arm around her shoulder. "You're right, I don't get to tell you what to do. I don't know what you're feeling. That's why I want to help. I just want what's best for you."

"Then leave it alone, okay? I want to forget all about it and just move on!" Stephanie buries her head in Emma's neck and just starts to bawl uncontrollably in the warm semi-circle of Emma's embrace.

"Okay." Emma lays her head on Stephanie's and strokes her hair with the free hand. Her hair spills over onto Stephanie's, black on brown, threads intertwine. "Okay."

They sit there for a long time in silence, mostly because it seems that Emma doesn't know what to do. All she can think of is to hold Stephanie, to not think of anything else. But over the course of a long hug, we see Emma's face go from worry to serenity.

Time passes and Emma tucks Stephanie into bed—the girl looks beat, the sleepiness of stress and need for escape. Emma pulls herself erect and just looks at Stephanie for a moment, head cocked in sympathy. Then Emma turns for the door.

Something white on the desk catches Emma's eye. It's the letter from Lane. Still in the envelope.

Emma glances back at Stephanie and then slips the letter into her sweatshirt. In a second, she's slipped out the door.

* * * *

An overhead shot of Lane sleeping in his bed next to his wife. It's like he's in a movie. The soft sound of strings begins an overture that crescendos into a cascade of horns that sounds like a bell tower. A bright sunrise streams through the windows and illuminates Lane's face as his eyes open to the light.

Excitement wells up in him when he realizes it's gameday—the day the Ravens finally play for the national football championship is here. He swings out of bed and, as the music rises, he bursts forth in a clear baritone about a golden haze in some meadow.

Cut to Lane in a steamy shower. We see him belting away at the song as he soaps up his armpits. His singing continues through the following montage of images:

Now dressed in his best grey suit and deep magenta silk tie, Lane stands in the pew of a packed country church—it's a prayer service for the football team—some of the parishioners have on Raven's jerseys and sweatshirts. Even though it's Monday, his grandkids standing next to him down the row have on their Sunday best bordered and ornamented with pink, black, and grey. As he sings, Lane turns his head out the paned-glass window across a field.

Cut to a deep green football field bathed in sunlight, as the camera tracks across the yard lines and hashmarks, the sun glints off the lens. Panning up, we see the yellow goalposts rise like high corn into the effervescent blue above the empty stadium.

Suddenly, we find Lane in his office, sitting at his desk. He serenades, then shakes Dean Concord's hand as she silently nods, smiles, and then marches out of the office.

Still singing, Lane happily shuffles then signs papers in a repeated pattern from one place on his desk to another, as if he were in a line of synchronized swimmers passing beach balls. He signs the last one, stands up, and walks through his office to the reception area. *I've got a wonderful feeling.*

In the reception area, he strolls by the trophy cases,

glancing at all the many statuettes, plaques, and awards behind the glass. He stops in the very center of the case where a spotlight shines down. Lane's had a space cleared to make room for one more trophy. A little sign under the empty pedestal reads "National Title—Football." He smiles at it as he sings: *"Everything's going my way."*

Next, Lane strides proudly down the main quad of the Athens campus. A group of students stands on the grass by the walk, incredulously watching the president of their university walk by in a business suit singing.

He stops to shake each of their unbelieving hands before he continues on his merry way.

He passes a female student in a Raven's jersey; she smiles at him.

Lane looks at the camera and winks at us before he walks away.

Cut to Lane now sashaying through his massive house. He's wearing a pink Ravens golf shirt and grey slacks with black wingtips. He belts out the tune. There's Athens U paraphernalia and decorations everywhere, which he marvels at. *Oh, what a beautiful day.*

Throughout his mansion, he strides among domestic servants dusting furniture and polishing brass; between caterers bringing in trays of food and laying out fruit, cheese, crackers, chips, heavy hors d'oeuvres; among bartenders carrying cases of liquor and beer, setting them up on his wet bar. *Everything's going my way.*

On the last note, Lane ends up seated in his recliner in front of a huge, high-def television screen. He leans forward, grabs an intricate remote, and pushes a button. The song ends as the TV comes on to the quick guitar riff of ESPN's SportsCenter, which Lane hums, "Na na na, na na na."

A sportscaster's voice blares out of the box: "Good afternoon, and welcome to Sports Center on this championship edition of College Football Game Day, where the Athens

University Raven will face the University of Texas Longhorns for their first NCAA title since 1990.

"We begin, though, with a report on this year's college recruiting class, where the Raven also seem to be cleaning up. After signing New Orleans High star quarterback, Ryan Cavanaugh, last month, the Raven have committed five more ESPN top 100 players, giving them by far the best recruiting class in the nation..."

Lane smirks proudly to himself, dismissing Chet's worries. "See Chet," he says out loud to no one in particular. "Told you. No need to panic at all..."

Lane then looks once again at the camera and croons softly: *Everything's going my way.*

*   *   *   *

It's the day of the big game, and the team is conducting last-minute, no-contact run-throughs of their plays. Coaches watch, then yell. The occasional whistle. The players are just in helmets and jerseys, no pads, and it makes them look like little kids in oversized gear.

Eggy Compson stands at a far corner of the huge, cavernous building, a cloth-like dome over a regulation sized football field, 100 yards by 50. It's the Raven indoor practice field that was a donation by the Uncle Jim Food Corporation and Orchard Oil. A sign over the far end zone reads, "The Maybelle and Chet Orchard Practice Facility." The players and coaches just call it "The Bubble." An apt moniker, Eggy thinks— thin, oily, and full of hot air.

No one can see her, standing in the shadows cast by the bright spotlights at the end of the field where the Bubble meets the ground in huge bands of riveted steel, which hold down the thousands of pounds of air pressure needed to keep the thing inflated.

She watches the coaches running back and forth, hunching

over and peering at players going through drills. She's jealous of the coaches—their concentration, their full attention to the plays, their polyester shorts, and even the whistles in their mouths. They seem so far away; she might as well be on the outside of the Bubble.

After a long time, when the players break up to run their final laps around the field before practice ends, Eggy steps out a side door, the force of the air rushing out pushes her ten yards from the building before she can stop herself. She looks back at the dome and then surveys the rest of the university campus. Through Eggy's point of view, we see Burden Hall not too far from where she stands.

She stares at it for a moment, then heads that way. As she walks, hands buried in her jacket pockets even though it's 70 degrees, she starts humming a tune. Pretty soon, she's singing "Somewhere over the Rainbow."

Eggy stops and turns her head toward Burden Hall, now closer, rising up before her.

She hesitates, looking behind her like it's not too late to run away. *Why, oh why, can't I?* She turns toward the rest of campus towering over her.

She continues towards Burden Hall, now with renewed purpose. She stops at the front door and projects that last aching line of the song out toward an empty quad.

Cut to:

"He says he's going to take care of it, but he hasn't." Eggy is now sitting across the desk from a very concerned Mickey. "I'm going to leave him and Athens if he doesn't do anything about it."

"Now, let's not do anything rash," Mickey cautions smoothly. "Does he know that you know?"

"About the video?" Eggy knits her brows. "No, I haven't said anything about the night of the rape."

"Good. Just keep it that way." Mickey relaxes. "Let me have a talk with him."

*　　　*　　　*　　　*

"Taboo subjects." Margolis repeats the words of a student as she strolls slowly across the front of her crowded community college classroom. "Yes, good." A dull January light diffuses through the grimy windows. The muted tones of navy, rust, and black color the sweaters, plaids, and coats of the students. A far cry from the gaudy pink and grey of Athens U.

"Sex, drugs, rock and roll, free love, homosexuality, transgender identity. But what else do contemporary musical films sing about?"

Fewer students are present today—no one standing against the walls—but the seats are full. The thing about students at two-year schools is that they sign up for a bunch of classes, sit in on the first day, and try to determine if the course is going to be too hard or not relevant to their career goals. If it will take too much of their time, they'll drop. Hence the fewer numbers in Margolis's class. Most of these students work for a living, have a family, and are paying for college themselves. They demand to know why a course is relevant and why they need to know anything and everything. Margolis is ready for that— she feeds on that, and it's why so many have stayed—because she was like that herself as a student. Hungry. Practical. Demanding. She almost seems more at home here, among people like she is, than at the U.

Margolis looks around and shrugs. "How else are today's musicals different than the classics like *The Sound of Music* or *The Music Man*?"

"They're cheesy as hell," a black man, about 20, from the back pipes up. "I mean, Jesus made up like a clown, a dude dressed in a bustier? That's wack."

Laughter.

"Yes, *Godspell* does seem a bit dated. I think you're saying that these musicals are *campy*." She looks at the guy seriously but with a smile.

168

"Whatever. I don't even know what that means."

"*Camp* refers to the self-aware exaggeration of theatrical conventions—loud costumes, heavy make-up, large gestures, extravagant song and dance numbers, purposely bad or over-acting, et cetera. It also refers to a sort of carnivalesque bending of boundaries, such as gender. Hence, Dr. Frank-N-Furter dressed as a woman in *The Rocky Horror Picture Show*.

"You may have noticed the red triangle he was wearing on his green lab gown-slash-cocktail-party-dress. Anyone know what that means?"

"Isn't it like a gay-pride thing?" a thin, young white boy responds pertly.

"Yes, and no. The gay-pride symbol is a triangle, yes, but it is often upside down and usually pink. Frank-N-Furter's triangle is right-side up and, to me, it looks red. Still, it could be a reference to his sexual orientation, which is clearly omnivorous in the film. But does anyone know where the upside-down pink triangle came from?"

A sea of blank faces stares back at Margolis. She's happy that she can at least teach them something today.

"From the Nazis," she continues. "Just as they put yellow Stars of David on the uniforms of Jews in concentration camps, they put the pink triangles on homosexuals, who were also put in death camps. Remember that the Nazis not only exterminated 6 million Jews—they killed 6 million other undesirables, including homosexuals, political dissidents, Poles, and, in their view, other degenerate or imperfect people. The use of the pink triangle as a symbol of gay pride is a re-appropriation of a negative symbol in order to make it a positive."

"So, what does the red triangle mean?"

"Glad you asked—even though I would prefer you to look it up yourselves—but I did, thank you very much." Margolis smiles playfully. "The red triangles were put on prisoners-of-war, spies, and deserters. Remember when the hippies in *Hair* burned their draft cards? Perhaps the red triangle on Frank-N-Furter suggests that he was also a draft-dodger. Or perhaps it's a tribute to missing POWs. Either way, it could be reference to the war in Vietnam. Keep in mind the musical debuted in 1973 and the film was 1975, the year the United States pulled out of the war.

"All in all, the triangle on Frank-N-Furter's costume invokes the prisoner and death camps of war, thus giving a whole new layer of meaning to the word 'camp.' Can you see how complex these otherwise silly and irreverent musicals can be?"

Margolis looks around at the faces, they seem genuinely impressed. Satisfied. But she's not: "What else? What other themes do these films tackle?"

A young Hispanic woman raises her hand. Margolis points to her.

"Death? It seems like somebody has died in all the films we've watched so far."

"Yes. Right!" Margolis suddenly straightens with excitement, almost jumping off the ground in a little hop of joy. "And not just ordinary, run-of-the-mill, natural-causes death either. We're talking violent deaths on a massive scale: cannibalism, genocide, mass killings, assassinations, crucifixions, and the fatalities of war. Jesus is crucified in both *Godspell* and *Jesus Christ Superstar*. The Nazis at the end of *Cabaret* suggest that most of the main characters, who include Jews and homosexuals, as well as all the people on stage, will soon be exterminated in concentration camps. And even good ol' Frank-N-Furter is executed by his alien underlings who want to go back to their native planet of Transsexual in the galaxy of Transylvania."

The class laughs at that last line.

"While posing as campy send-ups of old vaudeville acts or pastiches of classics from the Golden Age of Broadway, these contemporary, postmodern musicals almost always take on the ultimate subject of human existence, Death. It's this ultimate theme that makes these plays—usually considered fluffy entertainment—true works of art that make serious social and existential commentary on the state of humanity.

"Now, let's see if this artistic merit continues in the musical films of the 1980s, like *Little Shop of Horrors* and *A Chorus Line*. The Reagan Era! Watch those for next time. Because we are having class Wednesday despite the Athens game tonight."

A groan from the students.

"Dismissed!"

*   *   *   *

"Look, Frank, I've been trying to keep the heat off, but word on the street is that it's going to come out, one way or another."

"God dammit, Mickey. You know how busy I am. I told you. Lane said that he—"

"Lane ain't gonna do shit because it's not his ass twisting on the line. When this thing comes out, who do you think they are going to blame?"

Frank sits there, rubbing a finger back and forth across his lip. Then he bursts—stands up with a huge playbook in his hands and heaves it, shotput-style, across the room. It crashes into the white board and lands with a *whoom* on the conference table. Cups break, old coffee splashes all over the plays.

While Frank lowers himself down into his seat, Mickey leans back in his, his mouth tense and tight.

"You know we gotta get ahead of this thing," Mickey grits through teeth. "It's the right thing to do."

Frank closes his eyes and sighs, knowing Mickey is right.

"As soon as the game is over. I'll come up with something."

V.

All the boys from the cabal are here at President Lane's house tonight for the big championship game watch party: Chet Orchard, Huntley McBride, Jack Wilson, Ted Morris, Tag Robinson, all of them. There's enough knit fabric and Sansabelt in the room to stock an entire men's outlet store. The classy kind, though. For Raven fans only, of course.

Chet sits next to Lane in the middle of the room, in front of the massive flatscreen TV. Mickey hovers around the outside of the donors' circle.

Caterers and bartenders circulate the room with trays of hors d'oeuvres and bottles, freshening drinks.

Tag: "Looks like your recruiting class is really shaping up, Chet."

Jack: "All 25 scholarships spoken for. 16 of them to ESPN's top 300."

Huntley: "That's good enough for a top five class nationally."

Ted: "Anyone remember that we're playing Texas for a championship tonight? It's not all about the future recruits."

Chet: "Ted, you just don't like the taste of crow. What was that at our last meeting about 'hemorrhaging players' to Alabama?" He chortles.

Mickey: "We're beating them on the field and off."

Huntley chuckles: "Musta been using some deep, dark magic, huh Chet?

Ted: "Yeah. What's your secret?"

Chet: "Nah, nah. Ancient *Chinese* secret. A gentleman never tells."

Ted: "Come on, ya old racist bastard."

Chet: "Why you offended, Ted? I didn't say, 'ancient African secret.'"

Ted laughs hard. Mickey shifts ever so slightly in his stance.

Jack: "Come on, Chet. Spill."

"I guess it won't hurt now that we got almost all of the players inked for next year." Chet leans in to the center of the space, pulling them in closer somehow too.

Lane: "Is this going to take long? Y'all do know the game's about to come on."

"No, no. It's quick." Chet pauses to watch the last of the help leave the room. When they're out of earshot, Chet resumes: "Remember I said there was things in the works to up recruiting?"

They all nod.

"Well, they's working. The lovely, young ladies down at the Theta house have graciously agreed to court many of our gentlemen callers when they come to town on campus visits. And they all are encouraged, shall we say, to enjoy each other."

Huntley: "What are you saying, Chet?"

Jack: "Yeah. My daughter's a tri-Gamma. I would not want her fraternizing with—" He shudders.

Chet: "Cool your jets, Jack. It's just the Thetas. These girls aren't exactly the upper layers of the sororal ecosystem. They're the troubled ones, so to speak. Debts and parents of lower stock and such. I mean, they are being handsomely remunerated and all, for their efforts," Chet continues in this room of CEOs and tycoons, where such a statement of product for profit makes total sense, "but none of your daughters, let me jus' say, fit the profile."

It's only slightly tense in the room for a moment until Huntley chimes back in. "Damn, I wished they'd had that back when I was recruited at the U!"

Damn right's and *hell yeah*'s echo around the room. Some laughter sprinkled in.

Mickey wonders to himself, *This is just locker room talk, right?*

Tag reaches out with his glass. "Well, hats off, Chet. It really worked. It seems like we locked up every player we wanted."

"But I may have outdone myself, haven't I, Mickey?"

"What's that?"

"Oh, I didn't tell you, did I."

Mickey shrugs, "Tell me what?"

"Ol' Lightning and I here came up with the master plan. The coup de grâce!" He turns to the room: "Christmas has come extra early this year, boys."

"Hell, it's only January," Jack exclaims.

"See what I mean, extra early," Chet laughs. "No, seriously. Y'all gonna want to make me Man of the Year for this shit."

"Just cut the crap, and come out with it, Chet!" Ted needles.

"Well, the Thetas have a Valentine's Day variety show every year. Did you know that?"

Vacant stares.

"You know, where they do songs and dances from musicals and the radio and such. I think they're doing something from *Oklahoma* this year. Or *Moulin* something."

"So, what's so masterful about that?'

"Well, we gets to thinking, Lane and me, what if the variety show were also an auction?" Chet looks around the room into every eye. "Ain't that right, Lightning?" He slaps Lane on the thigh.

Lane chuckles. "I still don't think they get it."

"No, we don't."

"You mean, like they sell cakes and cookies and stuff too?"

Chet stares around in open-mouthed disbelief. Lane shakes his head and smiles. Mickey reacts, forcing himself to pay attention for what comes next.

"Y'all are unbelievable," Chet scolds. "No, you frickin eejits, the girls. The *girls* are available to auction. To the highest bidder. You watch the show, pick the one you like the best, and bid. The winner gets some special time later on with the lady of his choice."

"Wait, you're saying we just go to the show and get our pick of the litter?"

"Proceeds go straight to the foundation's fund for next

year's recruiting class. Donor fatigue be damned!"

"It's not on Valentine's Day, is it, Chet? 'Cause we got spend that day with our wives."

"No—I mean, come on—do I look like a fool? Of course it's not on Valentine's Day. It's after. A weekday night. A Wednesday. Business travel time. You take care of your wives the weekend before, and then take care of yourselves the week after. They won't even know you're gone."

Mickey looks around the room at the men's faces coming to life with this news. There's handshaking and backslapping, and Mickey feels a little sick.

Lane grabs the remote and points it to the TV. Sound flares to life with the Raven team pouring onto the stadium field in a swirl of black, grey, and pink. "Here we go, boys!"

Cut from Lane and the boys to living rooms, dens, and bars all across the city:

A huge crowd is gathered at Rooster Racoon's Chickenshack, with girls in tight Raven tees standing on the wooden picnic benches. We see on the televisions around the room that a Raven running back has broken a long gainer up the field. The fans at the Chickenshack go crazy.

At Dennehey's Irish pub, even the tweedy academic crowd is glued to the game. Farrah Maines and Mark Goldberg sit at the bar almost engulfed by colleagues and plus-ones from all across the departments of the university. The short-sleeved, khaki types from the business school have bogarted the best corner of the room where you can see 5 TVs at once. They cheer the loudest when Athens takes the lead for the first time in the game somewhere toward the end of the second quarter.

Farrah looks down and sees Gus Johnson and Stoddard are at the other end of the bar, doing their best to show school spirit. Farrah raises a glass to them and mouths the words, "fuck you, Stoddard," with a smile on her face. Stoddard smiles back thinking it's a kind greeting.

Back on campus, the Thetas crowd around the TV in the

Kappa fraternity, everyone leaning on pillows or biting nails. Brooke holds the remote with a laser focus on the announcer's commentary; it's a key moment in the contest. A frat boy comes into the room to ask where the keg is and gets shushed. Brooke turns back to the screen with an annoyed look on her face—how could he, doesn't he know the *game* is on?—but the expression melts into concern as she watches her football team struggle on the field.

From a back corner, Emma silently watches, not the game, but the girls. *Who are they? What do they want to do with their lives?* She honestly wonders. Even though she's making the same choices they are, she feels outside herself.

At the Sinoro-Santos home, Brie sits on the edge of the couch; she's nervous as hell. The Raven are losing. Margolis rubs her daughter's back comfortingly, but Brie doesn't even acknowledge the attention. Margolis looks over at Sandy, sitting on the other side of Brie. Sandy shrugs as if to say, *she'll be alright. Let her fret.* Margolis turns back, wondering what's going on in Brie's mind.

When the Raven start to make a comeback, as they have all season, Brie allows herself to wonder how it would feel to watch her father on the edge of glory and universal admiration, and maybe just maybe she's a little jealous. Margolis jumps, startled, when Brie explodes off the couch into a roar—the Raven have scored again and lead the game going into the fourth and final quarter. Brie's face is ecstatic, and Margolis is happy for her. And happy for Frank.

Upstairs at the Theta house, Eggy sits alone in her room. She's got the game on her little computer monitor, but she can hardly watch it. She tries to focus on doing her nails instead, the slow, short strokes of the polish brush take her mind as much as possible off what's happening on the field, where she is not but should be. There's a knock on the door. Eggy acknowledges it without moving. Lucille pops her head in, asks if Eggy is alright. Eggy nods. Lucille just watches her sadly for a moment. She offers for Eggy to come downstairs with some other girls. Eggy shakes her head and smiles. She points to the monitor. She'll be fine here. Lucille closes the door, and Eggy watches as the Raven offense grinds out another first down.

Looks like they will be able to kill the clock and bring home the first football championship to Athens in 25 years.

Back at the presidential ranch, all the cabal boys are drunk, standing around the room arm-in-arm. There's grey, white, and pink confetti and streamers everywhere—the party has shifted into post-victory gear now. Chet and Lightning stand shoulder-to-shoulder, glasses held high, and belt out the chorus of "I Did It My Way." It's rough, drunken, and loud.

When the boys get to the "regrets, I've had a few" line, Tag yells over the music, "Lightning, you gotta run for Senate now!" He stumbles backward over the chaise lounge.

Moving his legs to dodge Tag's fall, Mickey sits in a chair off to the side. He checks his watch. He feels dirty. He shoves the chaise lounge out of his way and bolts to his feet. Nobody notices. They're too busy singing and swaying. With one last glance and a gritting of teeth, Mickey turns, and leaves.

*   *   *   *

It's pitch dark, but we can hear someone grunting, regularly, in a rhythm of pleasure. Track up the legs of a bedside table and stop, for a moment, on a plastic bottle labeled *BlastoGlide Xtreme—Personal Lubricant.*

As the bottle goes fuzzy in the foreground, we focus on the motion in the background. It seems to be the body of a man, hips covered with a sheet and humping more and more quickly back and forth. The knees of another person are visible through the covers.

In the dim light of a nearby window, Eggy looks up at the ceiling. From the hairy back, strong shoulders, and well-coiffed head, we can tell that the other is Frank, grunting away as he buries his face in Eggy's neck, kissing it passionately.

Close up on Eggy's face. It's expressionless, her eyes focused on something past the roof.

We see her moving with Frank's rhythms and then hear him groan in climax.

Eggy's eyes do not change at all, and although she doesn't move, from her jostling we can tell that Frank has rolled off her to his side of the bed.

Cut back to overhead shot of them lying next to each other, both looking up. "God, that was so fucking hot," Frank sighs, still breathing hard. "What a perfect ending to the best night of my fucking life!" He puts his hands behind his head, arms and elbows forming triangles like big bat ears behind his face.

"It still doesn't seem real," he muses to himself for a moment. "A fucking national championship!"

They lay there in silence for a long moment.

Frank turns his head toward Eggy. "You're awful quiet. What's on your mind?"

Eggy snaps her eyes back to focus. "Nothing," she lies. "Just thinking about the last time I felt that feeling. Of winning."

"Fucking great, isn't it? Like meth! Or coke. Something. Some addictive metaphor."

Frank looks to Eggy for a response—she can feel his eyes on her, so she nods in agreement—then under her breath: "And just as much cost."

"What was that?" Frank asks, sincerely.

"Nothing, I was just saying I felt that much the most when I won the state high school title."

"When you were QB Boy Wonder?"

"Yeah. That." Eggy suddenly moves out of the frame and reaches for something beside the bed. We see the smooth skin of her back shining along lithe muscle and bone, slender and dappled. She moves back into the frame holding a glass of water to her mouth. She's drinking.

"Can I ask you something?" Frank changes tack.

Eggy can't answer because she's taking a deep swig so she just shrugs.

Frank takes it as a signal to ask, "Were you gay or something when you were a kid, you know, before the operation?" Swig, swig. "Did you like boys then?"

The regular rhythm of Eggy's swallowing hitches for a moment, but she continues her draught.

"That's a legitimate question, right?" Frank pleads, suddenly unsure. "I mean, I'm sorry if I—don't know the right way to ask..."

"Yes, in a way, I guess. But I didn't *feel* gay. Still don't. I felt—I *feel* like a girl. I liked boys in high school. I just didn't want any of them touching me until I was right, you know, down there."

On that phrase, Frank moves toward her and grins. "And, boy howdy, are you right down there!" He reaches between her legs still covered by the sheet and rubs her.

"Stop it, Frank," she retorts abruptly, powerfully moving his hand away. Then, seeing the disappointment on his face, she relents a bit. "Please. I'm a little sore. From, you know."

Cut to an angle from the foot of the bed: Eggy swings her legs over the side of the bed and sits up, facing away.

Frank suddenly starts and pops up to his knees behind her. "Too much for you, huh?" He chuckles and digs two claw-hands into her side. She jumps in ticklish horror and can't help but laugh with him.

"Stop, Frank," she cries amid breaths of laughter. He keeps tickling her as she squirms, then firmer but quieter as he moves his hands to cup her breasts. "I mean it. Stop."

Eggy's full figure now sits erect on the bed and pressing back against Frank. He hugs her from behind and rests his chin on her shoulder.

"You know," he says, "I think I'm falling for you."

Frank can't see it, but Eggy's eyes go suddenly troubled. She puts her arms on his, wrapped around her chest.

"Yeah," she replies. But she can't get the conversation they had about Stephanie out of her head, *"I'll take care of it."* He seems to have totally forgotten.

After a moment, she unwraps his arms and stands, walking herself out of the shot, leaving Frank alone in child's pose.

*   *   *   *

Wrapped in a bathrobe, hair somewhat wild, Margolis stands in front of the TV and watches a clip on Sport Center of Frank celebrating the previous night on the field. He's covered with Gatorade and being carried off the field on the shoulders of his players. She's happy for him, but his success just exposes her failure in high contrast.

She clicks the remote and the room turns dark—all the shades are pulled on this otherwise sunny day. Margolis turns and looks around in the dark. After a few minutes standing there, she mopes aimlessly around the house. She's totally alone. She passes from the living room, through the hall, by the bar, and into the kitchen. Everything is bland, grey, black and white. She seems distracted, and we can't tell if this lack of color is real or just her imagination. She hums "Going through the Motions" from the musical episode of *Buffy the Vampire Slayer*.

Margolis finishes the final note in her foyer and opens the door to the outside.

Suddenly, the color returns to the world with a vengeance. As if in Panavision, people walk, dance, and sing through the neighborhood. There's music everywhere. Margolis looks on in amazement: A couple sings a romantic duet while walking the dog. A trio of men jig in unison, miming doing yard work, while a woman stands on a moving lawnmower and belts out that she's "Queen of the World!"

Margolis walks down her driveway towards the street and watches all the performances as if they were perfectly normal.

When she reaches the end of the drive, she opens the mailbox. She looks inside. There's a single envelope.

The music stops. The color returns to normal.

Margolis, face slightly puzzled, reaches in and pulls out the envelope. It's addressed to her, but there is no stamp. She turns it over, no return address, so she turns it back again. Someone must have put it in there by hand. She looks at it for a couple of moments, as if in a daze, thinking she recognizes the handwriting, but she's not sure. *Stephanie? Mickey?* She speaks aloud:

"Emma?"

Attentiveness returns, and she looks up, around the neighborhood. The neighbor across the street rides her mower earnestly, no singing, and the couple conspires in hushed voices, looking warily at Margolis as they pass. Their dog sniffs Margolis's ankles briefly considering taking it for a hydrant. No dancing. No pantomime. Life is not a song.

She turns and lumbers resignedly towards the house, disappearing into its darkened door.

*   *   *   *

It's evening now and Margolis is slumped on the couch, still in her bathrobe. The TV is on and Margolis is mindlessly flipping through the channels. She comes across the press conference with President Lane. She stops. Frank is sitting next to him at the table. Headlines read, "President of Athens to Announce 4-year Extension for Head Coach."

Suddenly, the front door opens, and light floods over Margolis sitting on the couch. In silhouette, a figure with long hair stands with a backpack over the shoulder.

"Hi, Mom." Brie shuts the door and comes into focus. She walks over and stands next to the television. "Dad on TV again?" She watches for a moment.

Margolis looking up from the couch in awed surprise:

"Yeah. Got his contract renewed."

Brie nods matter-of-factly, then turns to face her mother. "I'm moving back in, okay?"

Margolis just looks at Brie for a moment. "Yeah, sure."

Brie starts for the stairs. "Thanks."

Margolis watches gratefully as her daughter disappears upstairs, taking two at a time. She's been doing that since the age of eight, when her legs got long and she discovered the power in them.

Unexpectedly, Margolis's phone vibrates muffled but loudly on the couch next to her. Distracted, she reaches for it. On the lock screen, there's a text from Mickey. Margolis perks up a bit and opens the message app.

Mickey: *How bout we grab that coffee next week when school starts?*

Margolis stares at the text for a second before she replies. A little butterfly zags faintly through her stomach. Her thumbs start to move quickly.

Margolis: *You know I'm not at the U anymore, right?* Angel emoticon.

No bigs. We can meet off campus.

Splendid. Maybe Tuesday? Text when you're free.

Mickey: *Will do. Looking forward...*

She considers that last text and its ellipsis, promising and asking at the same time. She can tell he's trying not to come across as too eager, but he's not hiding it well. She smiles faintly to herself, then locks her phone.

Margolis's attention is suddenly drawn to Frank's press conference on the television by the word "rape." A reporter has just asked Lane about Stephanie's rape case, and the president shifts gears coolly, explaining slowly and methodically that no wrong-doing was found in the investigation and that all the recruits and players involved—Lennox, Jaspers, and Johnson—had been cleared. We owe them an apology, he said, and reported that they would attend training camp in the spring.

Margolis looks down at the letter in her hand. She has an impulse to open it, but Frank's voice stops her.

"I also want to report on an investigation recently held at Athens that involved the Athletics Department."

A murmur ripples through the crowd.

Frank does not look over at Lane, who shifts uncomfortably in his seat. Lane doesn't know what's coming.

"It very recently came to my attention that three prospective recruits may have sexually assaulted a female student here at Athens." Frank looks around the room, frozen with anticipation. "So, it is with regret that I must retract the offers I made to these three men."

Frank holds up their signed letters of intent to play football at the U and rips them in half.

The room erupts into chaos. Bulbs flashing, reporters shouting out questions over each other. Lane tries to keep calm, but shock clearly grips his face.

"I take full responsibility." Frank ignores tugging at his sleeve and reporters yelling. He has the mic. "President Lane didn't even know about it until now because we had to act quickly."

Frank looks over at Lane who is stunned.

Frank: "This behavior, real or alleged, will not be tolerated in our program. Athens does not stand for even a whiff of sexual assault. Period."

An uproar bursts through the room.

As Frank tries to stand, Lane grabs him by the sleeve. "You better win another championship," he spits, "or I'll have your head for this!" Lane grits his teeth at his head coach.

Frank pulls away, unshaken. He walks off the stage and is swarmed by reporters. Some corner Lane and are demanding answers.

In the wings, Eggy waits for Frank and, as he walks up, steps in front of him. She looks into his eyes, hers filled with admiration. She smiles and puts her arms around him.

"That was amazing," Eggy whispers.

Frank takes off his hat, hugs her back hard.

Back at home, Margolis is stunned, her face in the half darkness of the TV glow. She stares for a moment and considers texting Mickey back to see what he knows, when something white on the coffee table catches her eye.

It's the letter.

Considering the envelope for a moment, she does not hesitate this time to rip into it. She unfolds the paper and starts to read. It's Lane's letter to Stephanie telling her the results of his investigation. It was not released to the public, as far as Margolis knows, and now she sees why. Its logic makes no sense—it doesn't deny that the football players had sex with her—it just says she wanted it.

The more Margolis reads, the angrier she gets. Her face twists up in a hot flush. *Blame the victim.* That is how she reads this letter, its words engorging her with righteous indignation. She looks over at the TV. There's a shot of President Lane standing right next to Chet Orchard. Trying to talk their way out of this mess, they stare sternly at the camera. And, through the TV, at Margolis.

Then she realizes she's having the exact reaction Emma wanted her to have when they visited the Theta house. It's so obvious now to Margolis that Emma is the one who slipped the letter in her mailbox. The thought gives her pause, and she pulls back, knowing she has to be careful with this. The letter is reprehensible, but it is not enough to even convict Lane in the court of public opinion, let alone a federal jury. She needs something else. She needs to learn more about what happened that night in the Theta house. That Halloween night.

Margolis stops herself. Closing her eyes, she takes a deep breath. *This has to be done right. Considering these new allegations*, she thinks to herself, *the situation could be explosive. An exploitative culture as pervasive as this has to be approached objectively, with clear eyes for evidence and fact.*

But Margolis also knows a good documentary has to be motivated by passion, even when trying to stay as objective as possible. *Let emotion motivate but not rule me. Find the evidence. Let these girls tell their stories.* That way, she doesn't have to be at the mercy of her own anger. In the film, she can let the facts speak for themselves.

She reaches instinctively for the phone and has Emma's number ringing before she can think otherwise.

"Yeah, I'm in. Let's make this movie."

Part 4: A Show

I.

Margolis is leaning down behind a camera, her eye in the viewfinder. It's a nice piece of equipment, along with the lights, stands, and software to use it, but since she no longer has access to Athens, she had to sell her Mercedes to get it.

Through Margolis's point of view, we see Stephanie, sitting on a chair in the middle of her dorm room; her head hangs down so that we can't see her face. Behind her, we can see posters for Athens U and other signs of school spirit—plush toys, fluffy comforter, frilly pillows, cut out flowers, ribbons, and smiley faces—all in the Raven's football team color palette of gray, black, and pink. Lots of pink. It's one of the reasons Athens's sports merchandise—tank tops, jerseys, shorts, even shoes—are such big sellers with women around the country. Doubles your reach. Brilliant marketing. Margolis can't help think about the irony of the moment.

Margolis pulls back from the camera, hands on hips, and presses stop. The recording light on the view screen blinks off. She looks up: "Well done, Stephanie. That was just fine."

Emma gets up from her seat next to the tripod and goes over to Stephanie and hugs her. "Yeah, you did great, Steph. I'm sorry about some of the questions, but you know I had to go there. For the truth."

Stephanie sniffles, wipes an eye. She nods weakly.

Margolis can read in their faces the damage that going back over that story had done not just to Stephanie but to Emma as well—asking the tough questions, pressing a witness just hard enough to elicit the gruesome facts, knowing when to back off and give space—Emma had done well, better than Margolis would have done, even in graduate school. But if it were up to her, she'd go back at it after a break—Margolis wasn't sure if Stephanie had gone deep enough to make her testimony truly damning. She wouldn't say her rapist's name—Emma had to prompt her—and Margolis thought that a direct accusation would be most effective. Emma turns back to Margolis, "Are we done here?"

At Emma's look, almost pleading, Margolis nods assent—it's over. All in all—lighting, sound, Stephanie's raw emotion coming across—it was a pretty good shoot.

Suddenly, a fart rips loudly through the room. A beat of silence, then: "Excuse me."

Margolis and Emma turn with shock to Stephanie who raises her tear-stained face with an innocent look. "What? I've been sitting here, like, for an hour!"

Immediately, the three women burst into laughter, a relieved laughter that comes like a wave. Margolis puts her hands on her hips and chuckles. Stephanie wipes her eye, but now even Emma is in tears.

Margolis's back pocket vibrates; she reaches for her phone and presses to answer. Before she talks, she ducks out of Stephanie's room and onto the back fire escape. She looks around to see if Lucille, the housemom, or any of the Thetas sees her out there. But the coast is clear.

"Hello?"

"Margolis, it's Mickey."

Margolis pauses for a second, processing. It seemed like a jarring dissonance of contexts, to go from the gut-wrenching atmosphere of Stephanie's story to now, suddenly, excitement flitting in her stomach. "Hi, Mickey."

"Everything alright? You got a second?"

Margolis giggles in spite of herself. "Yes. Yes, of course. It's just I was in the middle of something. Had to switch gears."

"You want me to call you back? I wasn't going to take long."

"No, no. It's fine. I'm here."

"Well, I was just seeing if you'd like to go out, maybe Friday. Get a drink."

"You know that's Valentine's Day weekend, right?"

Mickey *ums* and *ers* over himself for a moment. Obviously, he forgot or didn't think about it at all.

Margolis decides to help him out, keep it light: "If you want to ask me out, I'll be expecting a little fold-over Mutant Ninja Turtle Valentine and a candy heart that says 'Be mine.'"

Mickey chuckles. "I only got ones that say 'Super Fly' on them."

Margolis laughs too. There's a brief moment of awkward silence, neither knowing how to top that little exchange of flirty wit. So Mickey steps up: "So, great. Why don't we meet at 8. Dennehey's?"

Margolis is quick to reply, "As long as you can deal with the throng of young couples ordering fettuccine alfredo."

"Don't you worry, I think I'll be able to hack it. See you there."

"Bye." Margolis hangs up. She bites the thumb of the hand holding the phone. Things really may be looking up.

II.

It's Monday, Feb. 10, and Margolis and Frank begin their very different days.

At the front of her ACC classroom, Margolis begins: "Since it's almost Valentine's Day, it's only fitting that we discuss comedy."

A student pipes up: "What does comedy have to do with Valentine's Day?"

"Well, if you let me explain..." She raises her eyebrows at the student, and he smiles back, *you got me.*

"Classically, comedies are stories that, in the words of the great poet Sir Philip Sidney, 'imitate our errors in life.' Think about that for a second. Comedies imitate our errors in life." A beat. "Because, let's face it, humans are pretty absurd creatures who bungle through the world doing crazy stuff. And it's hilarious. We love laughing about the foibles of other people—think about how we love to laugh at videos of people falling down, getting hit by something, or saying something stupid—and we laugh because those shenanigans make us feel better about our own shortcomings and mistakes."

Outside, we cut to Frank who strolls leisurely down the quad at Athens U. Students wave to him, pat him on the back, and offer high fives, which he returns with glee and pride. A champion. He continues on, and we see him stop in front of the administration building. He looks up at the tower and shades his eyes from the glare. The window shades up and down the tower are lowered and raised in such a way to form a huge, 10-story number "1." Frank soaks that in for a moment before he continues on toward the athletics facilities.

Margolis continues: "And, because comedies 'imitate our errors in life,' they unsurprisingly often end with at least one marriage."

The classroom chuckles in response. They are riveted to Margolis's lecture, nodding their heads in agreement, writing down pertinent points, but most eyes are on her, following her moves.

"Of course, these stories have to end with the wedding ceremony because once the honeymoon is over the comedy of a marriage usually turns to tragedy, am I right?" A few more titters, and then Margolis changes her tone. "No, seriously, marriage provides a convenient way to temporarily, at least, resolve conflicts in a comedic narrative. Films that end in marriage, we now call 'romantic comedies,' but essentially they are the same kind of comedies that Shakespeare wrote, all ending in marriage. Hence, the relevance to love and Valentine's Day."

Inside the Boom Fisher Athletics Facility, Frank puts his stuff down in his office before venturing out. He walks by offices with his assistant coaches on the phone with what he knows to be the parents of prized recruits. They are already working on next year's class, even though this year's has yet to be completed. Tomorrow is National Signing Day, when all high school senior players announce where they intend to play college ball, and Frank is confident that he'll have one of the top classes in the nation—all of his recruits are already signed, sealed, and delivered. In fact, he's just looking forward to the hot spotlights of the television cameras at the press conference, where he will put the exclamation point on a championship season with a new crop of future star players. He's thinking 'dynasty' as he peeks in a few doors, looking for someone.

Back in her classroom, Margolis paces around, talking casually: "Usually comedies involve a protagonist who is first presented as a normal person, like us, before his or her life goes off the rails. Love, in particular, makes a normal person act crazy, and we love to see the effects love can have on others because in our minds we ourselves are immune to its effects. We think we are too rational and self-possessed to succumb to the absurdities of infatuation. All of these movies show characters doing ridiculous things, against their better judgment no less, all for love."

Frank has to venture to the locker room before he finds Eggy, working alone, holding a clipboard and focusing on her writing. She's taking inventory of player gear for end-of-season reports. After looking around to make sure they are by themselves, Frank sneaks up behind her, puts his arms around her waist, and buries his face in her neck for a huge strawberry. Eggy jumps, turns, and shows a defensive, frightened scowl. That scared the crap out of her. When she sees that it's only Frank, she raises the clipboard and smacks him on the chest, only a little playfully. Frank grins and mimes a defensive pose, raising his arms to block her harmless blows. Breaking through her arms, he bear-hugs and lifts her off the ground spinning.

"Somehow," Margolis continues, "in all this ridiculous behavior, the characters find love and happiness. How? Because we are all flawed creatures who need to belong and feel love. And we're lucky to get it."

Margolis stops and claps once. "That's all for now, everyone. For next time, be sure and watch our group of romantic comedies, including *Moulin Rouge*. We'll pick up there."

*　　*　　*　　*

Chet stands behind his desk and closes a safe. Then he swings a large, framed portrait over the safe, to cover it.

Chet stands looking up at the painting, which depicts an older, white man in a suit. Mickey sits silently on the other side of the desk.

"You know, when my father built this company, he didn't do it alone. He had friends and employees that stayed loyal for years, working their asses off. All because the old man treated them right.

"I've tried to do the same building the Raven Foundation, Mickey. It's all that's really ever mattered to me. I've tried to maintain my daddy's business, but I put my passion into making the U a better place."

He takes a deep breath, eyes still on his father's likeness.

"College was the time of my life," he continues wistfully. "Good friends. Great times. *Great* times, if you know what I mean. Football glory. All the lovely ladies. This campus was my fucking oyster. It was for all the boys back then and today, especially after winning a championship. I just want to see that pearls are passed on to future generations."

He savors the moment.

"Ah fuck it, I guess I'm feeling sentimental today."

Snapping out of his reverie, Chet turns and passes a check across his office desk.

"Mickey, my boy. You've earned it. A bonus." Chet smiles. "I couldn't have done it without you."

Slightly taken aback, Mickey isn't sure what to do exactly, but after a moment's hesitation, he reaches for the piece of paper. When he tries to pull it away, Chet holds it fast.

"Of course," Chet lowers his voice slightly, "this isn't just payment for services rendered. It's also an investment in the future. You protect this system we got going, flying low under the radar, keeping everyone happy, and the checks will just keep coming. But, take your hand off the wheel," Chet pauses ominously, "and there will be hell to pay. For both of us. We understood?"

"Completely," Mickey says, face serious.

Chet lets go of the check but Mickey keeps it hanging there, over the desk, like a surrender flag in the field of battle. *Does this mean he's locked in to this whole sorority scheme long-term?* Mickey wonders. For a moment, he thinks about letting it drop, leaving this racket and Chet far behind, but he quickly folds it and puts it in his pocket without even reading the amount.

Out on the street, Mickey stops and pulls the check out of his pocket. He unfolds it and stands just staring at the amount as if he can't comprehend what he's seeing. There, on the paper, in the messy chicken scratch of Chet's handwriting, are the words, "Pay to the order of Mickey Andouille, One Hundred Thousand and no 1/100 dollars." He looks up, looks down again because maybe he misread it or maybe it was a mirage. He looks down again, but there's no mistaking that one and those five trailing zeroes.

Mickey looks around, puts the check back in his pocket, and hurries down the street.

*   *   *   *

Under a banner that reads "National Signing Day," Frank Sinoro sits at the center of a long table stretching across the front of a hall filled with dignitaries, fans, and reporters. It's a press conference. Cameras whir and lights swell brightly from TV crews. With multiple microphones in front of him from different networks, Frank is flanked by a dozen or so large and muscular recruits, all holding pens and signing letters of their intent to play football for Athens U. Their parents stand in clumps proudly behind most of them. We recognize some of these recruits from earlier scenes at bars, clubs, and, of course, the Theta house.

As the thunder of applause fills the room, the twelve boys pick up black-and-grey baseball hats with the Raven logo and put them on their heads simultaneously. As Frank leans towards the microphones in front of him, his voice cuts through the ovation: "Your new Raven football recruiting class!"

A glowing Frank stretches one arm down the length of the table one way, acknowledging the recruits, before he turns and gestures to the other side—he's spreading the spotlight of the moment with his new players, but he knows that his Caesar-esque magnanimity and humility will play well with the fans at home. He finally raises his hands, as if to silence the crowd. It takes them a few moments.

When it begins to fade, he leans in again toward the mics. "We've had an amazing year in this program. Not only the top recruiting class in the nation—we've won a national title." More uproar, a quick laugh from Frank. "Yeah!"

"But it's been a long road," Frank pauses as the room settles down. "My dedicated coaches and I have spent countless hours on the road, on the phone, on social media, trying our best to get the word out to these guys and their families how great a place Athens is to play. We all know how close-knit this program is—players and coaches support each other, build each other's characters—not just win football games. And I think that is why the U prevailed for many of these players and their parents." Frank looks over as many of the recruits and parents nod their heads. "So, let's hear it for the great families, coaching staff, and returning players for the Athens University Raven!"

The group of coaches, players, and their parents stand; they raise their hands to acknowledge the applause.

"But last and not least—more than anyone—I have to thank President Art 'Lightning' Lane for all the help and support he's given me through thick and thin during my two years here at Athens. None of this would be possible without him. President Lane!"

To more applause, Frank gestures grandly toward the back of the hall, where Lane stands, arms folded, unmoved.

Next to him is Chet. Chet claps slowly and firmly. He mutters under his breath, "Looks like he's making up for that spectacle last month."

"Lucky for him," Lane says through his teeth, "those three recruits were small potatoes."

Lane raises his hand in acknowledgement and gives a winking thumbs-up across the room to Frank.

When the crowd calms, Frank takes a breath. "Before I go— and let these guys get to their steak dinner, which is what I know they've really been waiting for," the recruits chuckle joyfully back at Frank. "I have one more announcement to make." He pauses a beat. "Starting today, I am promoting athletic trainer and assistant quarterbacks' coach, Eggy Compson, to assistant head football coach—the first black woman to hold such a position in all of college football—Ms. Compson!"

Zoom to the side of the stage where Eggy stands, stunned. The TV cameras pan toward her, shining spotlights on her startled face. One of the other coaches nudges her toward the podium. She climbs the steps and shuffles, bewildered, toward Frank and the microphone.

"With coaches like Eggy at my side, we're going to win another national title next year. And you can quote me on that!"

Margolis stands in the hall outside her classroom at the community college. She watches a monitor where Frank puts one arm around Eggy and waves to the cheering crowd with another. Margolis recognizes her from the Theta house and has a hunch that Brie might even know her pretty well. She also has a feeling Frank knows her very well—boyish, slender, young assistant—she's his type. The old pang of their breakup flashes through her stomach. They've been split for almost a year, but it still gets her.

Margolis picks up her phone and dials, still looking at the monitor. The call goes to voice mail. "Frank, it's Margolis. Just watched the press conference and wanted to leave a message. It seems like congratulations are in order..."

*   *   *   *

"I think that's the last of them." Frank unburdens himself of a box on a small credenza in Eggy's new Boom Fisher office.

"I don't know how I'm gonna fill even half this office with my shit. It's huge!" Eggy looks around and then turns to the window where she takes in the view.

Frank comes up behind Eggy and puts his arms around her. "Oh, you're not going to have any problem filling it." He chuckles into her neck as he kisses it.

"I'm serious!" she says, pulling away from him slightly.

"I am too! Assistant head coaches have hella paperwork. Soon you'll be up to your eyeballs. It's not all bright lights and tickertape parades, you know." Frank recalls the parade, *an actual parade*, celebrating the championship, just a few days before, where Eggy rode next to him on the back of the pink convertible, Raven-colored confetti falling all around them to the cheers of adoring fans lining the streets of Athens. He felt like he was going to burst. He was so proud. Finally, his life-long goal met, finally happy.

"Not to mention all the trophies we're going win together. Accolades, awards. You're going to kill it, Egg."

"You know," Eggy stiffens, "I wasn't too sure I could work with you. After the Stephanie situation. I had my doubts that you'd handle it right." She looks up into his eyes. "But you did."

"What, you didn't trust me?"

"I just wasn't sure—"

"I'm teasing," Frank says. "I had to keep you out of the loop if I wanted you to be my new first mate."

Eggy's body softens and she turns to Frank, putting her palms on his face. "Frank, I want you to know how much I appreciate this. I'm gonna do my best to live up to your confidence in me."

Frank takes her wrists in his hands. "Of that, I have no doubt. You worked your ass off this year, on the field, in the locker room—"

"At the Theta house?" Eggy frowns, mockingly. "Shit, those girls are up to my last inch of anus!"

Frank laughs heartily. "And at the Theta house. You've really gone above and beyond the call of duty. But you won't have to live at the Theta house anymore." He pauses, puts his hands on her hips. "I want you to move in with me." He kisses her nose.

"But what about Brie?"

"Brie won't care," Frank dismisses. "She's back living with her mom now and has her own room at my place for when she visits. Anyway, Brie loves you, doesn't she?"

Eggy nods. "We get along."

"Well it's settled then. See? Your time in the Theta house did triple duty—you won the heart of my daughter, navigated desperate sorority girls through girly crises, and saved the football team." Frank smiles and shrugs as if to say, *am I right?*

Eggy nods again, then a concerned look. "Shouldn't we tell Brie we're a thing. And when?"

"You're right." Frank puzzles for a moment, then eureka. "I know, we'll have a fancy dinner. I'll make reservations. Alright?"

Eggy is unconvinced but she gives Frank a she's-your-daughter shrug and says, unsurely, "OK..."

"Great, I'm on it." Frank strides, pleased as punch, out Eggy's door, leaving her surveying the mess on her desk.

*   *   *   *

Margolis leans out of the elevator and looks both ways down the hall—everyone knows she's the coach's ex-wife and will wonder what she's doing there. She wants to stay undetected. When she sees nobody else, she slides toward the opposite wall, hugging it as she strides quickly down the corridor.

She comes to some sort of gymnasium with a glass wall facing the corridor. Inside, she sees a black-robed Mickey Andouille standing in front of rows of girls in white, martial arts gees. He's teaching a self-defense class to female athletes and makes the fierce gesture of taking a gun away from an armed assailant. The girls follow his moves in sync, screaming "hye" each time they take the imaginary gun.

Mickey looks up and sees Margolis. His face breaks into a huge grin, as he keeps going through the motion.

Margolis waves weakly before she hurries on down the hall.

She checks numbers as she passes offices and stops abruptly when she comes to the one she's looking for. She quickly knocks, low but firm. Margolis tilts her head a bit closer to the doorjamb and hears, "Come in!" She slips inside.

Margolis stops just inside the office. "Hi, I know you're just settling in, but I was hoping to get a word with you."

Standing at her desk reading a mess of papers, Eggy raises her head. A look of surprise flits across her face, then recognition. "I know you, you're Brie's mom. The professor making the movie with Emma." Eggy knows exactly who Margolis is—she's the Woman Before. With Frank. She braces for a nasty scene with the ex, about the new woman blah blah blah.

"Yeah, we met last month at the Theta house."

Eggy pauses for a decisive moment. "Yes, right. To what do I owe—"

"Oh, I'm sorry," Margolis interrupts. "I'm just here to talk about Stephanie Rogers. You know, the Theta. Who was raped."

Eggy is thrown for a loop. "Who—I mean, what are you—"

"I'm just wondering if you know anything about Stephanie's case or any like it."

"I know President Lane dismissed it, and Frank tore up the letters—"

"I know, but perhaps maybe you know of other girls who have been—"

"I've only been in the house a few months, Ms..."

"Dr. Santos."

"Yes, I know. But didn't you get—"

"Fired. Yes, but I still teach. Now over at ACC." Margolis

jerks her head in the imaginary direction of her new college. "But do you?"

"Do I what?"

"Know of any girls who have been assaulted. At the Theta house. Or anywhere else on campus."

"Dr. Santos, I have a duty to protect the privacy of the girls at Theta." Eggy sounds like a real coach now, a natural at fielding nosey questions. "HIPAA laws prevent me from—"

"Yes, but I'm also a concerned mom, so you can imagine why I would worry and want to know. Brie does spend an awful lot of time there."

"Yes, she's a sweet girl; the others call her their 'mascot.' Kind of a good luck charm." Eggy smiles sweetly, sincerely, having regained some of her southern composure. "I can assure you that she's perfectly safe at Theta. I, the girls, adore her and watch out for her."

"I really appreciate that Coach Compson."

"Eggy, please."

"Eggy, would you please do me a favor and just let me know if you hear of—or remember—anything about assaults at Theta?"

After a beat, Eggy replies, "Yes. Of course."

"Thanks." Margolis steps forward and extends her hand to Eggy, who takes it, shakes slowly.

Margolis turns for the door, to Eggy's relief, so she looks down at her playbook.

"Oh, one more thing." Margolis turns back and plonks her phone right on top of Eggy's papers. "I want you to see this."

Margolis pushes the triangular play button on the screen. The image of Stephanie, sitting in her Raven-decored dorm room, rolls across the screen, and her voice begins: "He was on top of me, so heavy. He's big. I couldn't move, but I could feel him between my legs, grunting."

Emma's voice: "And were there other people there, someone who could have stopped it?"

Stephanie: "Yes, a few. And I think there was someone at the door because a couple of them moved toward it and slammed it."

Margolis reaches over and stops the video. "Like I said, if you hear anything. Please let me know."

Eggy stands there, stunned for a moment, then nods. She watches Margolis leave. When the door shuts, Eggy plops down in her chair and stares out the window, biting her nails. Now her assurance that she didn't see anything that night is shaken. *But the President said there was evidence it was consensual.* But maybe it wasn't. *Shit!* She pictures Stephanie's head lolling back and forth on the bed.

She knows she should say something, but, goddamn it, she just got here—the opportunity of a lifetime—assistant head coach at a championship-winning football program. First black female assistant. And this position could open future doors for her—big ol' doors—to other jobs. History-making jobs. The first Division I black female head football coach in a program that cares, at least according to its head coach, about sexual assault.

"Fuck!" Eggy slams her fist down on her knee and turns back to her nail-biting. After a long moment, she pulls her phone out of her pocket and dials. "Hey, Mickey. I think we might have another problem. A movie."

*   *   *   *

Margolis and Mickey sit at a table in the middle of a crowded Dennehey's Pub. Through Mickey's eyes, we look around and see many young couples of different races chowing on creamy noodles and munching cheesecake. He's more than a little impressed with Margolis's brown eyes in this candlelight.

"Well, I must admit you were right—this place is packed—full of little lovebirds."

Margolis wryly lifts her wine glass. "What does that make

us?"

"By comparison? Wise, old hoot owls, I think."

"Here's to that!" Margolis holds her glass out to Mickey who clinks his against it.

"Cheers." Mickey holds Margolis's eyes over their glasses as they drink. "How's your movie going?"

"Huh?" Margolis says, into her glass, a little surprised. She swallows hard.

"A couple weeks ago, when we had coffee, you said you were making a movie about the university." Mickey takes a bite of salad.

"Um, I may have said I was making a movie, but not what it was about."

"Yeah, yeah, you know, life behind the ivy-covered walls, et cetera et cetera." Mickey tries to look innocent, but Margolis narrows her eyes, and he sees he's not going to fool her. "OK, OK. I heard it through the grapevine that you were filming around campus, at places like the Theta house, so I just assumed it had to do with the U."

Margolis doesn't say anything but the word *Eggy* jets across her mind. Eggy told Mickey. Maybe this whole investigation has been compromised, but that won't stop her from making her movie, *con dios*.

Mickey continues his explanation: "I'm not gonna bust your chops, Margolis. I actually want to encourage you."

"Why thank you, Mickey Andouille," Margolis quips sarcastically. "I'm so glad that I have your encouragement. You know, this has nothing to do with athletics—"

"Whoa, whoa, Annie Oakley, put away the big guns." Mickey raises his hands. He is walking a thin line, and he knows it. But this is a chance to stick it to those rich fucks and still protect the football program. "I actually have a tip for you because I know that it *is* about athletics."

Suddenly, Margolis stops. This might be the break she's needed to get inside. Her heart begins to pound, she can feel it in her neck, and she wonders if Mickey can see her jugular pulsing slightly faster.

Mickey looks around and leans in. "All I can tell you is, don't overlook the variety show."

But Margolis is a bit disappointed at the riddle. "What? What variety—"

Slow, low, and steady: "Every year. The Thetas. Have. A variety show. Around Valentine's Day. I think this time they're doing a revue of *Moulin Rouge*."

"Really? I was just lecturing about it," Margolis muses. "I love that movie."

"Me too."

"You? Big football player guy—a chick flick?"

"Yeah, why not?" He chuckles. He catches her eye for a long moment.

"Guess we'll have to catch one sometime," she answers. "A chick flick, I mean."

Mickey breaks the spell nervously. "Aw man, look at all these amazing entrées. They have much more than fettuccine...this menu's like a book!"

Margolis moves to ask more about the variety show, but she sees it would be pointless—Mickey has turned his attention to the menu now covering his face—she supposes that she should not look a gift-horse, but she wonders why he's telling her about a sorority music revue.

She looks up the front of his dapper wool suit, admiring his build. Hearing Goldberg's voice in her head—"remember, you're on a date!"—she relaxes back into her seat and picks up her own menu. Cut to:

A shot of the two of them through the front windows of Dennehey's, as if someone may be watching.

III.

"Girls, girls!" Lucille, leaning over the edge of the stage in the Great Hall, claps her hands. All the Thetas mill around the floor and stage in costumes. They laugh and chatter away. "May I have your attention? Girls, please!"

Chet whistles loudly. Suddenly, the girls quiet down and turn toward Lucille. She's holding a little red diary in her hand as if it were a Bible. She gesticulates with it for emphasis.

"Thank you, ladies. Now, as some of you know, this fine gentleman is Chet Orchard. He's the patron saint of Delta Delta Theta and was the one who graciously funded this Great Hall expansion," Lucille gestures around her, "as well as the new kitchen and the parking lot. He'd like to say a few words about this year's variety show, for which he tells me he has big plans. Mr. Orchard?" Lucille claps but only a few scattered hands join her.

Chet takes center stage and projects loudly. "The Thetas are renowned far and wide around the South for this variety show. Every year, y'all deliver beauty, hilarity, and spectacle that none soon forget." Chet waves his arm to encompass everyone in the room. They all beam proudly. He sees Emma out in the middle of the floor looking up at him—he searches her eyes for anger and finds none. He tastes a little satisfaction at that—but he's not sure. He makes a mental note to circle back around with her. "So, this year, with your biggest show yet—yes, yes, I've seen rehearsals, I know what y'all have cooked up [laughs]—and what with Athens being the," Chet builds on each word, "new...reigning...national...football champions!"

All the girls cheer wildly. They're jumping now. Chet marvels to himself, with just a little flattery, how easy it is to get a crowd riled up. "With this best show yet at the best university yet [whoops and cheers], it's only fitting that we open the Valentine's Day variety show to a new audience, our illustrious Raven Booster Foundation." Blank looks, but Chet explains: "The men of the foundation are the wealthiest, most successful alums and fans of Athens. They are pillars of the community and cornerstones of the college. They have influence on campus and around the world. You want to break into the entertainment industry? We have boosters who are Hollywood decision-makers and can get you a role. You want a position in a big New York accounting firm? We've got the CEO. These men can help you realize your dreams. Ask and ye shall receive. They love Athens U that much. With their success, they are not only positioned to help you after college, they are also in the perfect position to help our school now. In fact, these guys provide the facilities, equipment, and financial support to build the biggest, best, and most-storied football franchise in college sports!" The girls get it now, they cheer. "Now don't you think they deserve a little gratitude?" More cheers. "We want to show them how much we appreciate what they do for us. With your beauty and talent and their resources, it's a match made in heaven! So, you think we could show them our thanks?" Cheers. "You think we could get them to open their wallets to keep making the Raven the best football program in the country?!"

"Yeah!"

"Now, here's how it's going to work." His audience is captive now. "During the show, each one of you will be wearing a number." Chet holds up a plastic card with a "1" on it, like the ones you find on marathon runners. "I think we all know who this first number goes to." Chet tosses the card to Brooke, who catches it, grinning. "Your illustrious president!" All the girls laugh, and Chet waits for them to pitter out. "You'll wear the numbers, and while you're performing, the foundation members will bid on you to spend a little time with you backstage after the show. The highest bidder wins your time, as much as you're willing to commit."

Someone from the crowd: "You mean like a date?"

Another voice: "Is this a joke?"

"No, ma'am. No, I'm afraid it's deadly serious." Chet pauses, looking ominously over the crowd that suddenly has become uneasy. "Deadly serious about securing your future and making you rich!" Chet breaks into a huge grin and swings his fist into the air.

The crowd releases its tension in a flood of high, tittering laughter.

When it starts to fade, Chet continues. "Not only will you raise money for the foundation, but you'll also be making a small fortune for yourselves. In a little bit, Miss Lucille and I are going to come around to each of you and talk to you individually about the reward levels you can achieve during your time with your winner. You can pledge your time at any level, but the higher your level, the bigger your bonus today and reward after the show."

Chet holds up a wad of $100 bills.

At this, Emma slowly starts to make her way to the back of the room—she knows what's coming.

Chet: "As a little advance, you can walk out of here with a nice little bankroll for your Valentine's date tonight. Might even want to surprise your beau by paying for dinner yourself! That'd be very feminist of you, right?" Laughs. "Of course, I'm kidding. This cash today is only a down payment for your pledge—the real reward will come after the show, when you've won your bid and before spending time with your booster. Get paid, then play. That's all there is to it."

The Thetas remain silent, but their eyes sparkle with thoughts of that kind of dough.

"Now I won't lie—these men will expect to be entertained—but the higher your commitment to your bidder, the higher the bid to the Raven Foundation, *and* the higher your earning potential. And I am certain that you will give each and every one of them, especially your sponsor, the warmest of Theta hospitality. For the sake of the U!"

The Thetas turn to each other and debate the merits of

Chet's offer. Some turn their noses up in disgust, and a few even leave. But most of them stay. Chet knows that once they've tasted the sauce—payments they've already received for escorting young football recruits—they won't have any reason to say no to the bigger game.

He strolls over to a group of Thetas in glittering costumes still standing near him on the stage. Lucille fans out among the crowd on the floor. She goes up to a Theta and takes out her little red book and starts writing in it as she takes commitments from the girls.

Emma stands now at the back of the Hall near the doorway into the foyer. She watches Chet talk animatedly to a group of first-years. He never takes his eyes off theirs even while his hands are slipping hundred-dollar bills into the girls' suspenders, pockets, and lapels. She turns to Lucille, and through Emma's eyes we see the housemom counting bills out into upturned palms, then making notes.

A voice brings Emma out of her focus. She overhears Brooke talking to some juniors nearby, and she turns her attention to them.

Brooke: "I know I'm in. You kidding? That's easy money. They say it could be as much as ten grand!"

Junior #1: "But what if these guys are skeezy?"

Junior #2: "Yeah, hooking up with young football players is one thing, but these old dudes? Eww."

Junior #3: "Gross."

Brooke: "You mean sugar daddies who can bathe you in opulence? So what? Pound their old puds, take their money, and film it with your phone. For evidence. When you show up at their office in your business suit after graduation, they won't be able to say no or you'll show their wives. You'll have them by the balls for real!"

Two juniors have to concede to Brooke's reasoning and nod, convinced. The third one is like, "Whatever. I just want to get outta here so I can meet my boyfriend. It's fucking

Valentine's Day."

Emma shudders and feels her stomach turn a little. She can't help but think about the recruits everyone has slept with for the team. She thinks about Ryan Cavanaugh, whom she considered her boyfriend, at least for a while, but she couldn't keep him strung along and fulfill her...obligation. So, after he signed with Athens, she just stopped texting him.

But there were the others, the new boys, about one a week; she had gotten good at tuning them out. When she closed her eyes, they all felt pretty much the same.

Naturally, Emma thinks of Stephanie and guilt rises up in her face. How could she worry about vanity when Stephanie didn't choose her fate? That helplessness of being drugged. *Say what you will about Chet*, she thinks, *but at least he's giving everyone a choice. That's more than Stephanie had.*

Suddenly, there's a voice at Emma's ear. It's Chet: "Just in case you were thinking of sitting this one out, remember, your daddy could still get tangled in litigation. We wouldn't want the prosecution to suddenly get some damning evidence, now would we?"

Emma turns to say something, but Chet is already smiling and talking loudly with another group of girls.

*   *   *   *

"You're what?" Brie has to swallow hard to keep the water from coming out through her nose and all over the soiled dinner plates on the tablecloth. She puts her finger to a nostril to catch a drop.

"Eggy and I are seeing each other." Frank turns to look at Eggy sitting next to him. "Well, more than seeing each other. I'm in love with her. And we want you to know we are together."

On tenterhooks, Eggy watches Brie's reaction closely, but Brie has turned away slightly to hide her smirk.

"How long?" Brie turns back to them. "How long have you two...been together?"

Eggy looks at Frank but doesn't answer. She's unsure of his line and wants to leave wiggle room.

Frank answers, "Since before Thanksgiving." He takes Eggy's hand and looks back at Brie waiting for her wrath.

It all starts to come together for Brie. She remembers the shot of them on TV after the game jumping into each other's arms, the Gatorade bath.

"Oh my god," Brie laughs and turns to Eggy. "Congratulations!" Brie puts her hand to her mouth to stifle her rising laughter, but she can't. She starts to giggle uncontrollably.

Eggy visibly relaxes—she's off the hook—and the relief shows on her face.

Frank, on the other hand, cocks his head, annoyed. "What's so funny, Brie?"

But Brie can't stop laughing. Frank watches for a little bit, hoping that she'll stop. But she can't.

"Brie," Frank insists, looking around, embarrassed.

Eggy puts her hand to her mouth to stifle a smile, but Frank sees that too. Now he's pissed. He throws down his napkin and stands up. "I'm glad this is all so funny to you. Maybe I'll see you later when you can keep it together. Happy Valentine's Day." Frank huffs off.

Eggy stands and goes to follow him. "I'm sorry, Brie. I've got to go." She smiles worriedly and hurries after her man.

Soon, Brie has reached that point where the laughter hurts her face, the tears already falling. At her father's words, though, she feels a tinge of guilt for not taking him more seriously. But, then, she's mad at herself for feeling guilty. Why should she feel bad? She is tired of feeling guilty for what is beyond her control. Despite her indignation, hiccups of laughter keep bubbling up through her throat.

Brie looks across the restaurant, and in her field of vision, we see couples, lots of couples celebrating Valentine's Day. There're mixed couples, same-sex couples, some holding hands. Some drinking champagne. Suddenly Brie feels alone. The old longing for Emma wells up in her chest a bit, and it trips within her some sort of sympathy for her father. For Eggy. *Why shouldn't they have each other?* More than anything, Brie is shocked that she didn't see this coming—that she's been so blind to her father's personal life, just as she was with her mother's. And Eggy? Brie thought the Theta house was Eggy's personal life.

The next involuntary giggle feels more like a sob, and soon Brie's sitting alone at a fancy table with empty plates, feeling mixed up and miserable, laughter turning to tears.

*　　*　　*　　*

"Are you out of the house?" Margolis's voice sounds distant and small coming from Emma's cell phone.

"Yeah." Emma fidgets a little with her jacket zipper. From her point of view we see the Theta house across the street, far out of earshot.

"Good. Now, tell me about this variety show. I got a tip to check it out. Is something fishy going on?"

Emma pauses for a moment before answering, her voice a little too loud and clear: "No." She lies. "I don't think so. Why?"

"That's the thing. I don't know. But my source is pretty reliable. I think I should be there."

"Wait, no—I mean, um. Let me find out about it a little more, before you make any plans, okay?"

On the other end of the line, Margolis is suspicious that something is up; Emma can sense it.

Margolis finally relents. "Alright, have it your way." She's sitting in her classroom.

Emma's voice through the phone: "Thanks. I promise I'll get back to you if there's reason."

As Margolis hangs up, there is a knock on the door. "Come in!"

Eggy steps inside and closes the door behind her. Margolis is surprised, frozen with her phone still in her hand like she's about to dial. She waits for Eggy to speak.

Eggy inhales. "I have some information. About Stephanie." When Margolis opens her mouth to respond, Eggy raises her hand to silence her. "But, if I cooperate, I need some protections of some kind."

"Okay," Margolis says cautiously. "What kind of protections?"

"I want to remain anonymous."

"That's fine. We can just shoot in shadow, blur your image, and alter your voice."

"Wait, whoa whoa whoa. I didn't say nothing about going on camera."

"But Eggy, what did you think I was asking for?"

"Confirmation. You already have that vid of Stephanie talking. I can tell you that it's true."

"You were there?" Margolis is surprised.

"They shut the door on me."

"Look, Eggy, that makes it all the more important that you go on the record. I need your testimony to corroborate Stephanie's story. If I don't have it, people could just say that she made it up! I mean, this could lead to another investigation, maybe a trial—"

"Nope, no cameras. I mean, Dr. Santos, I just got this new promotion. I want to help, but I also want to keep my job." She pauses briefly. "And there's Frank."

"Yes, Frank," Margolis sighs.

"He had nothing to do with this, and I really don't want to hurt his career. He's doing such good things at Athens."

"And I understand that. But, Eggy, if people don't come forward, others will continue to be victimized. Do you want that on your conscience?"

Eggy stands there, her hands unconsciously wringing her knit shirt. Suddenly, her face flushes resolute. "That's what I'm offering. Deep background. Take it or leave it." She turns and walks out of Margolis's room flinging the door open wide. It bangs on the stop. Eggy stomps off.

Margolis listens until her footsteps are gone before she opens her phone. She dials. She knows she doesn't have enough to take this to the police yet, but Eggy, even blurred, will make it more than "he said, she said." Maybe a little pressure on Frank will shake some things loose.

"Frank? It's Margolis. Listen, I have Stephanie Rogers on camera saying she was raped by a recruit of yours, and I now have an eyewitness who can corroborate it." Margolis listens. "Yes, I'm working on a documentary on the case." A beat. "No, Frank. I'm not trying to tear you down—you said yourself not a whiff—" She listens for a moment. "Listen, this is just a courtesy call to give you a heads-up that something's coming down the pike. But it's coming. Do what you want with it."

She hangs up.

* * * *

"I don't think this rape allegation is going away, Art."

"Well, it might have if you hadn't called attention to it by ripping up those letters on live TV!"

Frank's eyes are closed and he's rubbing his temples with one hand and holding the phone with the other. "There's apparently an eyewitness that can corroborate Rogers's story. And Rogers has filmed her story for some sort of exposé. We should really get in front of this—"

Lane's voice sounds alien through the telephone receiver. "Who told you there was an eyewitness? There was none during the investigation..."

Frank pauses for a moment, then lies, "An anonymous source. I just got off the phone with...them."

"Could be a bluff. Maybe a goldbricker wanting a piece. You win a championship and all the bloodsuckers come out of—"

"I don't think so, sir. This source sounded quite reliable. And seasoned."

"What the hell does 'seasoned' sound like?" Lane chuckles. "No offense, Frank, but you should stick to coaching pubescent boys. Leave the cloak and dagger to the *real* seasoned veterans." Lane pauses and Frank doesn't say anything, which worries Lane that he may have gone too far. He doesn't want Frank to turn coat, so he shifts tack: "Look, Frank. I just don't want you to worry about any of this public relations stuff. I appreciate you bringing it to my attention, but it's most likely nothing. You let me and my office take care of it from here. You just focus on getting that team ready for next year, okay?"

"I got it, sir."

"Alright then. And you send my regards to that talented daughter of yours. I hear from Dean Concord and Admissions that her application for fall is climbing up the rankings. May even be a scholarship in it for her, if she chooses the U, hear?"

"I will, sir." A beat, then: "And thank you."

Lane presses the hook of the phone and keeps his finger there for a second. Then he dials. Waits for the beep.

"Chet, it's Lane. We might have a snitch inside the Theta house. Frank got a call—could be nothing—but I think it would be best to get your people on the inside to lock it down, just in case..."

Cut to Chet: "Understood. I'll put Ronnie on it." Chet ends the call and then looks up from his desk. Standing across from him is Ronnie, the huge, bulking former Athens football player-turned-security-chief.

"What's up, boss?" Ronnie asks.

"We need to secure the Theta house. Up to and including the variety show. Get on it."

Ronnie nods and pulls his phone out as he heads for the door.

IV.

"So, Emm." Brooke looks at her slyly. "Someone's been sneaking around the house filming girls talking about rape and stuff. You wouldn't know anything about this, would you?"

Distractedly, "No." Emma is studying at her desk and continues to take notes from a large literature anthology.

"Are you sure?" Brooke moves into Emma's personal space.

"Yeah, I'm sure, what?" Emma turns towards Brooke, as if to ward her off.

"You know how it goes at Theta. Snitches get fucked up."

"Of course they do." Emma swallows."

"Then who's interviewing Stephanie?"

"I don't know. Why are you asking me?" Emma doesn't like being pressed. "Do you think it's me?"

"I didn't say that." Brooke raises both hands. "It's because you're all buddy-buddy with the film professor, that's why. And she's been over here a couple of times."

"Yeah, for her daughter, our so-called 'mascot,'" she makes scare quotes with her fingers, "who is always around. I think she's even here right now. Anyway, Santos doesn't even teach here anymore."

"Exactly, she doesn't have anything to lose by running her old employer up the shaft."

"That doesn't mean she's filming around campus, doofus."

"Alright, alright." Brooke raises her hands in retreat. "It's just we can't really afford to have people snooping around. Theta business is Theta business, nobody else's."

"What about Stephanie then, huh, Brooke? Who's going to take care of her business? That shithead Colby Lennox signed with Auburn—he sat up there and smiled for the world on camera like a hero—he's a rapist!"

"Listen, I want to fuck those bastards up as much as you do, but we have to do it our way. On our time. That's why I need to know if you're bringing someone in from outside. All you have to do is stop it, so we can take care of this ourselves."

"Outside? Why don't you talk to Eggy? She's the outsider—she's the one who knows everyone's business—all this has gone down since she joined the house as our 'mentor.' I mean, what the hell is that?"

"I've thought about that, and I'll handle Eggy, believe me. If she had anything to do with this, her ass is grass."

Emma turns back to her work, confident she's thrown Brooke off her trail.

Brooke saunters to the door and stops. "Remember, Miss High-and-Mighty, you're in this just like everybody else, so I'd watch yourself. It'd be a shame if your parents found out what you've been doing with our young visitors. It might burst their bubble knowing their precious daughter is a little slut."

Brooke leaves her with a dirty look.

Emma stares vacantly down at her papers. She puts the pen tip nervously into her mouth.

$$* \quad * \quad * \quad *$$

Emma lays on her bed with a stuffed animal under her chest. "We can't bring cameras into the variety show. Someone will see." Now she's biting her nails.

"No, they won't." Margolis's voice is firm and confident.

"Do you know what the Thetas will do to me if they find out?"

"Listen, Emma. Stop worrying. They won't see. I've got micro cameras and snakes with wireless receivers. Or, at least Athens has them. I've asked Goldberg to get them for me. At any rate, we'll put them inside your costume, bra, my purse...they'll be invisible."

"What about Brie?"

"We won't need her. You and me. We'll have it covered." Margolis takes a breath. "Plus, I don't want Brie anywhere near that place when this goes down."

"Makes sense."

"Come on, Emma, you said you wanted to become a filmmaker. This is what it means. Are you in or not?"

"I don't know..."

"I thought you'd be totally down for this spy mission," Margolis fusses, "but you're all wet-blanket. What's going on?" Emma doesn't respond. "I can tell there's something else. Tell me."

Emma considers telling Margolis about the escorting, everything. "I just don't want to get any of my friends in trouble."

"This is to *stop* them from getting into trouble, Emma. To expose the bastards coercing you and paying for sex."

Emma sees that Margolis has no clue how deep this thing goes—she doesn't know about the recruits. Emma takes a defensive tone: "But they're not coercing anyone. That's the thing. It's totally voluntary, and most of the girls are doing it. For a *lot* of money. Can't that make them guilty of, like, prostitution?"

"No, they're not prostitutes because these guys are predators." Margolis sighs. "Come on, Emma. You were so gung-ho to blow the lid off these scum in the Theta house, and now that we have a chance to really nail some assholes and make the house safer, you're balking." Margolis pauses. "What is it? Really..."

Emma exhales and stutters, like she's about to cry. "It's my dad. This booster, the ringleader—"

"This Chet guy?"

"Yeah. He has some dirt on my dad and can make his trial go bad. And...there's other stuff."

Margolis pauses—she didn't expect this complication. Then, suddenly, her voice carries a new resolve. "You know what, fuck that bastard. He won't be able to do anything to your dad when he's behind bars for felony pandering. After what you told me he said at rehearsal, I know my contact was right about the variety show. Plus, Stephanie. There's a lot of bad shit happening at the Theta house."

After a few moments, Emma retorts: "But some of the girls said they are going to video themselves having sex with these rich guys. For blackmail. Couldn't we just use their footage?"

"Ugh, that's disturbing on so many levels—and though tempting for embarrassment's sake—we'll have to keep that in our back pocket—it doesn't really serve our purposes. Having sex is not illegal. These girls are adults. Instead, we need to catch these bastards in the act of exchanging money for services. Do you understand?"

"Yes."

"So, you'll help me."

A long pause. "Yes. I'll help."

"Good. Let's take these fuckers down."

*　　*　　*　　*

"Your dad is still pretty sore at you. About our Valentine's dinner." Eggy leans empathetically towards Brie, who is sitting cross-legged on the bed, in a posture of penance. Eggy's room, the confessional.

"I know, and I'm sorry." Brie plays with her shoelace.

"You should go talk to him."

"I will," Brie continues. "But I wanted to apologize to you first. I know I ruined your Valentine's Day, and I'm sorry. I want you guys to be happy. I really do."

"Thanks, Brie. That means a lot."

"I'm super pumped at the idea that you might be a part of my family."

"Whoa, Bee," Eggy laughs, "one step at a time!"

"I know. I'm just excited. In a big-sister-I've-never-had kinda way, you know?"

"I understand." Eggy chuckles and puts her hand on Brie's long hair. Looking at Brie's youthful face for a few moments,

Eggy decides that this is the right moment to share. She has a deep urge for a confidant, a sympathetic ear, and Brie's not in athletics, but she's related and won't tell. "And now that we may be family..." Eggy smiles, the irony contagious to Brie who also grins, "I could use your advice."

Brie perks up, "About what?"

"I know something, and I'm wondering if I should tell someone."

"Who and what?"

"I'm not sure I should say. But here's the thing: telling it might hurt your dad or, at least, put him in a really tight spot." Eggy watches Brie carefully, as they search each other's eyes.

"What is it? What do you know?" Brie asks, breathy and low. She suddenly feels special, an insider—it makes her feel needed, powerful even.

"You know Stephanie Rogers, the Theta?"

"Of course," Brie nods.

"It's about her rape. The president's investigation?"

"He threw out the case, right? Not enough evidence..."

"Well, I know that's bullshit." A beat. "Because I saw it."

Eggy pauses and watches Brie carefully.

"But my dad, he tore up those—"

The gravity of the situation dawns quickly on Brie, as Eggy knew it would. She's young, but not dumb. "Holy fuck. And it was on my dad's watch..." Cut to:

Frank and Mickey sit across a coffee table from two parents and a son who is obviously an athlete that Frank is trying to recruit for the U. Frank is sitting forward, pointing out pictures of Athens University on glossy pamphlets. Like the family, Mickey watches Frank in action, and even he's impressed. Frank makes a big gesture, and the parents smile. He looks at the kid, then takes off his huge, gold championship ring that he just won. He hands it to the kid who is obviously wowed as he tries it on himself.

Back to Eggy's bedroom: Eggy replies to Brie in an I-told-you-so tone: "Yeah, Stephanie's rape happened on your dad's watch."

Brie considers all the implications for a moment. "That must be why my mom wanted to interview her—she knew Stephanie was telling the truth."

"Yeah. And your mom wants me to go on camera. Tell what I saw." Cut to:

Frank and Mickey ride together in silence; they both are obviously exhausted. Frank drives, his head on his hand. Mickey slumps in his seat, his feet surrounded by fast-food garbage. Back to the girls:

"So, go tell Dad first," Brie says quickly. "He'll understand. Maybe there's something he can do."

"No, Brie. It'll kill him, make him think I'm betraying him. Plus, it puts him in the position of knowledge, after the fact, which means he's toast. It's better for him if everyone just thinks he's ignorant."

Brie inhales, as if to speak, then stops, knowing Eggy is right. Cut to:

Frank and Mickey sit in the stands watching a high school football team's spring practice. It's cold—we can see their breath—and they look miserable. Mickey stares down at some notes on a clipboard. The quarterback takes the hike, drops back, and launches a long pass down the field. Frank nudges Mickey's arm, and Mickey looks up just in time to see the ball land perfectly into the arms of a sprinting receiver who makes a diving catch. Mickey looks at Frank, both nod, and Mickey makes a note on his clipboard.

Later, Frank and Mickey walk up to a coach and the receiver and shake their hands. Mickey makes a gesture to the boy that mimics how he caught that pass. The boy nods, and they both laugh. Frank talks to the coach and thumbs toward the boy; the coach nods, as if saying, "Yeah, he's that good." Back to the Theta house:

Eggy continues, hoping Brie will have the answer, "Your

mom says she can blur me out, keep me anonymous. And I'm thinking I can tell the story in a way that insulates Frank."

Brie thinks for a moment. "Then do it. It's the right thing to do, Egg. Poor Stephanie. And knowing that will make it worth the risk."

"I hope you're right..."

*　　　*　　　*　　　*

Brie is leaving Eggy's room and runs into Emma.

Emma: "Hey. What are you doing?" She glances over Brie's shoulder at Eggy's door.

"Oh nothing, just talking with Eggy about something." Brie changes the subject. "You excited about the show tomorrow? I can't wait."

Emma: "Brie, you can't go to the show."

"What?" She's incredulous. "Why not?"

Emma looks both ways to clear the coast, then pulls Brie to the side of the hall. "There's going to be some bad stuff going down."

"Like what?" Brie asks, curiosity heightened.

"I can't tell you. But you don't want to be involved. Trust me."

"Why should I?" Brie bristles. "I'm not your girl anymore."

A pang shoots through Emma's gut. "I know. But I still care about you and don't want you getting mixed up in any of this." Emma pauses and looks into Brie's eyes. "Plus, your mom's gonna be there, filming it."

"Emma. You can't keep this from me. After all you've done? You owe this to me."

Emma stares at Brie for a moment, thinking. "OK." She pulls Brie down the hall and into her room. "But you have to promise not to tell your mom."

Through the door, we see Emma telling Brie everything that's gonna go down at the variety show.

*   *   *   *

"Look, I just got back from a long recruiting trip, and I'm wrecked." Mickey leans back in his office chair for emphasis. He's glad that Margolis is here, in front of him, but a little annoyed that she's poking around, especially now when he's so beat. Really beat. If it were any other time, he might play ball.

"I know, I know. And I'm sorry. I hate to ask, but you teased me with the tidbit about the variety show. And I don't like to be teased." Margolis smiles coyly, a little seductively even. She likes Mickey and doesn't want to take advantage of his attraction to her, but she's getting a little desperate. She hopes he doesn't notice.

"Seriously, Mickey, I need to know more."

"I really can't tell anything else, Margolis. I shouldn't even be talking to you right now, let alone have the knowledge that you are making a movie about my program."

"Alright, alright. I won't press." Margolis holds her hands up in surrender. "But you can't blame a girl for trying. I'll just go back to the house one more time to see if someone might finally talk to me."

"What about Eggy Compson—do you know her? He, I mean, she—works part-time at the Theta house. Maybe she'll give you something. She's a good kid. You know, transgendered. Used to play college ball, if you can believe it."

"No, I didn't know." Margolis considers, even though she's already talked to Eggy—it confirms that Mickey doesn't know how far her investigation has gone—in other words, he's not going after Eggy. Margolis smiles. "I'll be sure to talk to Eggy."

"Yeah, good. And I'm sorry. I wish I could help you more." Mickey waits a beat. "Does this mean you won't go out with me again?"

"Well, if you play your cards right..."

"Ahh. I see how it is." Mickey chuckles. "Gonna keep my feet to the fire, huh?"

"If I can." Margolis raises her eyebrows and turns on her heels toward the door.

"Oh, and Margolis."

Margolis stops, turns back.

Mickey smiles. "Keep the faith. It's a good thing you're doing."

"Yeah, you too." Margolis smiles back. "I really appreciate your help. Thank you."

As Margolis walks out, Mickey's phone rings.

"Mickey!" It's Chet's voice on the other end. "You haven't cashed your check yet. What gives?"

"I've just been busy, sir. Recruiting trips with Frank, you know. I just haven't had time." Mickey smiles hard, even though Chet can't see him, to make the words sound convincing.

"Alrighty then. Be sure you do it soon. Wouldn't want it to expire on ya."

"No, sir. Thank you. I'll get on it ASAP." Mickey is just glad to be getting off this call.

"Oh, and Mickey."

Mickey pauses, his finger on the phone screen ready to hang up.

"Don't make me question whether you're going soft, like a little bitch."

*   *   *   *

"In a romantic comedy, the lovers cannot couple right away—no—there must be obstacles to their desire—obstacles that raise our own suspense, like a kind of foreplay." Margolis, used to traditional, younger Athens students, expects a snigger at these words, but these older community college students don't giggle. "A dramatic tease that builds our audience expectations up so much, that when they do get together, it's more pleasurable. But, rest assured, some dastardly antagonist—be it a rival or merely fate—stands between the lovers and their bliss."

In the Great Hall, the Thetas are rehearsing. The members of the Raven Foundation have been invited to watch, as a kind of preview.

Chet stands off to the side next to Eggy. He puts his hands to her ear. As he whispers, Eggy zooms in on Stephanie who dances in lock-step with the others. Eggy hardly hears what he's saying—something about shutting her up. Eggy pictures Stephanie on the bed that Halloween night—the image clangs so dissonantly with how innocent she looks now. When Chet is finished, he straightens up and lowers his hand to Eggy's chest. He pokes her twice firmly in the pecs. He says something menacing and then without looking back returns to his pack.

"Sometimes, a lover's own shortcomings, foibles or deceits are what threatens true love. She must decide if being with the man she loves is worth the trouble it will require. Because it is a rare comedy indeed, where the girl foregoes the advantages of marriage for the sake of her own freedom."

Eggy has not moved. She stands watching the men. She folds her arms—she can't believe the audacity of these motherfuckers coming in here like they own these girls; well, maybe they do, and the girls have handed their asses right to them. The men? Eggy thinks they should know better. Her face hardens into resolve.

Eggy hadn't even noticed that the music had stopped. She breaks her brooding to see that the girls are taking five, wiping their faces with towels, drinking water.

Eggy now knows her next move—talk to the professor.

V.

"You were right, Emma. It's no use." Margolis is driving her new car, a beat-up old Subaru, but she's trying not to worry about money. Even renting equipment from Athens isn't cheap. She's talking over the hands-free. "Without a smoking gun, this film is dead in the water."

Doubts are creeping into Margolis's mind, as they do in any major project like this. Even though she's aware of that dynamic, it happens to her anyway.

Emma senses it. "But, wait, why have you changed your mind? You talked me into this thing; now let's follow it through." Emma thinks for a second. "We have Stephanie's account, don't we? That's good."

"But it's not enough. And our eyewitness isn't willing to corroborate unless it's anonymous." Margolis thinks about Eggy. Disappointed. "And that isn't good enough."

"Surely there's somebody else who will come forward."

"But nobody else is talking either. I've been trying for days, since we interviewed Stephanie, to get other Thetas on camera. It's like they've all sworn *omerta* against any outsiders."

"*Omerta?*" Emma puzzles.

"You know, the mafia code of silence. Not one word from any of your sorority sisters. Boy, your pledge hazing must be some serious-ass shit."

"No comment." Emma pauses. She knows that she has more information to share that might help Margolis, but Emma is too ashamed to say it. Escorting recruits—sleeping with them? It implicates her. It would ruin Margolis's respect for her. So, she can't. She's too afraid. There has to be another way.

"There's no way," Margolis says, "that the Thetas will let me in to film the show. Not now that they know I'm snooping around."

"What if," Emma's idea is dawning, "we filmed the show without you there?"

"What with just one camera on you? It'd be too isolated a point of view. We'd need views from all around the room. And with me not there—"

"No, not just me. I could get Stephanie. She'd obviously be down."

"Okay, that's two. Still not enough."

"I could fix a camera backstage—Chet said something about winners meeting their bidders back there."

"Great. Three. We could do sound there too."

"I bet Eggy would—"

"Nope. Said she didn't want to be on camera." Margolis turns the wheel and makes a right.

"But maybe she'd agree to wear a camera," Emma points out.

"I doubt it. Plus, why would she want to expose the boosters? That foundation helps pay her salary. And the coach is her new boyfriend..."

"Coach Sinoro, your ex?" Emma sympathizes.

"It's nothing." Margolis straightens up, shakes it off: "It would be against her own interests to tear down the football program in any way."

"You're right." Emma thinks for a moment. "How about some of your friends at Athens—Professor Goldberg, maybe?"

Margolis's mind starts to move—she thinks of Farrah, too, and Sandy. "They won't be able to get into the show, but they can work remotely with me."

"But then there's always...Brie." Emma pauses a beat. "She can easily get inside the Theta house."

"No. No way. Emma—"

"Margolis, they were handing hundred-dollar bills out at rehearsal this week. Just as an appetizer, to get the girls locked in so they'd go fuck the guys after the show. This is some serious sick shit. Anyway, these guys aren't worried about being seen—they think they're immune."

"And that makes them vulnerable." Margolis nods. "Wise

beyond your years, Barnes. But no Brie."

"She can stay anonymous in the audience, pretty much hidden."

"I said 'no.' What if one of those creeps approaches her?" Margolis stops herself and looks out across the road. She considers the risk of letting Brie participate in this cabaret of charlatans, this burlesque brothel of hubris and manipulation. The thought makes her ill.

"These assholes only want what they paid for," Emma reassures her. "So, Brie will be fine. Anyway, I'll keep an eye on her."

"I don't know..."

"Margolis, she'll want to do this. Just give her the choice. She's a big girl now. You have to let her help clean this place up. For her future."

Margolis pulls into her driveway and throws the shifter into park. She sits for a moment staring at the garage door going up.

And there, standing, hand on hip, looking very grown up, is Brie.

She taps a toe, her arms akimbo. When Margolis doesn't move, Brie comes up to the car window. She motions to her mother to role the window down.

"I heard about the variety show operation," Brie deadpans. "Strap me up, I want to go in. For Stephanie."

Margolis searches deeply into her daughter's eyes. Hers dart back and forth between Brie's, trying to gauge how stubborn and sincere Brie is about this. What she sees there is not girlish curiosity, but womanly determination.

"Alright." Margolis sighs. Into the phone: "Brie's in." Then sternly: "Emma, you better keep an eye on her. She's my baby."

"Not anymore," Brie butts in. "At least I won't be then. It's my birthday."

"Oh yeah, the big 1-8."

"Like I said," brags Emma, "a grown up."

"Not a great way to spend your birthday, Brie-Brie."

"Are you kidding? It's gonna be so dope!"

She turns and heads into the house. Margolis watches after her, marveling.

*　　*　　*　　*

In the Theta house, it's Variety Show Night.

Chet flits around the Great Hall like a black butterfly, dressed in his tux, as are many of the groups of men he chats with. Lucille follows him around like a puppy; she has her red diary open, pen at the ready. The room is packed with formally dressed patrons, mostly co-eds from other sororities and fraternities, but we recognize the regulars from our booster club clumped in small groups scattered around the room.

"That's right, Tag." Chet chooses his words very carefully. "The *bid* is for the Foundation—aiding our recruiting efforts not just in the state, but across the country—so that money comes to me. And the *gratuity*—tipped by the winner backstage before the date—is for the girl's *time*."

A little later, we see Chet standing with another group of men. "Oh my, yes, there will be opportunities for privacy. There's an entire floor of rooms above us, man. It's like a dad-gum dormitory!" The men nod their heads, satisfied. One pulls what looks like a check out of his inside coat pocket and slides it smoothly into Chet's vest-front pocket. Lucille makes note of it.

"Why thank ya, Chester. That's mighty white of you!" The men all guffaw and slap each other on the back. A fanfare sounds, and the men turn their pasty faces towards the stage. "Oh, the show's about to start."

The stage is decorated to look like the famous Moulin Rouge in Paris—elephant, windmill, and ornate, baroque décor rich with velvet reds and golden yellows. Across the top of the proscenium is a banner that reads, in 19th-century font: "It's a

Little Bit Funny—A Moulin Rouge Spectacular Spectacular Review!"

The strains of "Diamonds Are a Girl's Best Friend," a retro-rendition—more Marilyn Monroe than Nicole Kidman—accompanies Brooke as she is lowered from the ceiling in a swing. Brooke's vamping croon is surprisingly good.

Chet looks over grinning at Huntley—*isn't this something?*—and winks. Huntley shrugs coolly, but in spite of himself his face admits that he is impressed.

Emma dances in the chorus. Her face is blank as she spins and leaps around the stage with the other girls in the number, all wearing gold sequined leotards, their legs in fishnets, and, as promised, numbered placards on their chests.

Cut to: The video feed from Emma's camera on a screen. The room spins around and we can occasionally see the audience and lights, as well as the other girls in formation as they move around. From the frame of the feed, we can guess that it's coming from a camera placed in a sequin somewhere on Emma's left breast.

Margolis watches the footage at a console in a control center, which is in the back of a van—Goldberg's—parked just outside the Theta house. He and Farrah sit at their own screens next to Margolis, who has a headset on.

"Emma's feed is jarring, but it's coming in."

Farrah: "And Stephanie?"

Goldberg clicks a mouse, and his screen cuts to Stephanie's feed: she's in front of a mirror making last minute touches to her make-up. She's dressed like the Duke, the wealthy antagonist of the film, tailored in an expensive tux.

"Got it," Goldberg replies.

"And backstage?" Margolis adds.

Farrah clicks, and up pops the feed from a fixed camera backstage. It has audio and is transmitting the applause coming from the Great Hall out front. But in this view, we see the girls from the "Diamonds Are a Girl's Best Friend" number rushing around. The music has ended, and they are preparing for the next scene. We can see in the foreground Emma doing a quick change with the help of Lucille—she peels off the sequined costume (Farrah to Goldberg: "Avert your eyes, you perv.") and steps into a tux—she's Ewan McGregor—a poor poet in a shabby suit. We see her adjust her bow tie.

Margolis: "Cut to Emma's feed."

The camera moves like it's being adjusted in Emma's tie. Through it, we see the stage where two lines of Thetas kick up their legs under ruffled skirts to music of *The Can-Can.*

Margolis: "And finally, Brie."

Farrah clicks and up comes a shot of the full stage from Brie's point of view, and we see a frontal view of the can-can dancers. Only a bit of the corners of the feed is blocked by girls in evening gowns and men in tuxes.

Brie herself stands anonymously in the crowd. Dressed in a long sparkly gown, she looks quite a bit older than 18, with a bag strapped over her shoulder. Unafraid that people will know she has a camera in there, Brie is watching the show with a look of childlike glee on her face. To her mind, this situation is perfect: watching an amazing revue of one of her favorite movies, all while playing spy games. *This is so awesome!* But wait, she remembers she has to play it cool, so she suppresses the smile on her face and looks around.

From backstage, we see Emma waiting for her next bit. She's peeking through the curtain, and from her point of view, we see Brie out in the audience surrounded by men in tuxes like the one Emma's wearing. A twinge of anxiety rises up in her chest, but she soothes it down. *Don't worry—Brie's a big girl, just like you said.* The music has ended, and the can-can girls stream past Emma's face; she can feel the rush of air from each. She smooths the front of her suit, turns, and prepares to go on stage.

We switch to Brie, watching the scene change from out in the audience—the backdrop is a huge elephant that frames the entire stage. When the girls come back on, Brie's eye is immediately drawn to a be-tuxed Emma, whom we watch for a moment.

We then watch through Brie's feed, as the Thetas act out a fake musical extravaganza set in India that they make up by the seat of their pants as they go along: they pantomime playing sitars, riding horses, sword fighting maharajas, and swooning at courting lovers—all in a silly vaudevillian slapstick. The audience laughs heartily as the players switch between acting like they are acting, and singing: *Spectacular spectacular*, so delightful, one might say, it will run for fifty years.

In the middle, Stephanie's character interrupts, asking if in the end of the play someone should die.

Everyone looks at each other with ridiculous questioning expressions. The shortest Theta, playing the sitar itself, lifts her tux-tails and breaks wind right in Emma's face.

"Just like Rabelais said," comments Farrah sitting at her computer, watching Emma's on-stage feed, "the best comedy is all about the lower bodily strata."

"Dick and fart jokes," Goldberg adds. "They always work. Too bad none of this scene is funny to anyone but these skeezes."

"Would you cut your lecturing, you lame academics? Jeez, such nerds," Sandy retorts.

Margolis interjects. "Would everyone just keep their eyes on the skeezes, please? We're looking for any exchanges, like a drug deal."

More laughter from the crowd—and then the players suddenly break back into song with "*Spectacular, Spectacular!*"

After, there's applause.

In the middle of the audience's delight, on the opposite side of the room, Eggy circles around the outside of the crowd. She looks different—her hair is slicked back flapper style—and she's wearing a tux like many of the men. For a moment, she wonders if this is what it would have been like if she'd stayed a guy: being served and entertained by young ladies, having the pick of the litter, receiving job offers from older, more accomplished men sealed by a game of golf or a hunting trip. But she beats back the thought. That's a road untraveled. Here she is, one of *them*—she looks on stage and sees two Thetas dancing the tango together to "Roxanne" by the Police—not one of *us*—she glances around at the men in the crowd—mostly white, finely appointed.

In the corners of the room, she starts to notice larger, beefier guys in tuxes. They're not boosters, more like thugs. *They have earpieces, so they must be security. Former Athens players? Probably. The ones who didn't make it in the pros.* Eggy counts six, maybe seven of them, in view. Then she recognizes Chet's man, Ronnie, head of security.

Suddenly, Chet cuts across her field of vision. She shrinks back into shadows, hoping he didn't see her. She watches him weave through the crowd and stop next to Ted—oh, there *is* one black guy, at least—it figures—and next to him Eggy spots Brie. Her heart races a bit—is Chet going to talk to her? Coach's daughter, surely he knows that.

Brie notices Chet move into the group next to her. She twists her upper body so that her purse swings around. She stops where she thinks they will be squarely in the frame.

Margolis watches Brie's feed. On it, we see Ted take out a wad of cash and hand it to Chet. Ted mouths "number six." Lucille makes a note of it in her red book.

"Bingo." Margolis turns smiling to Farrah who replies, "Caught red-handed, bitches!"

Goldberg giggles.

Back in the Hall, a version of "Like a Virgin" comes to a comedic stop, and the audience roars. Intermission.

"OK, it's halftime—let's cut to the backstage camera," Margolis orders. Up comes the feed: girls swirl around and all drain into the dressing room (really the Theta dining room) so that the backstage area is fairly empty. Into the frame walks

Chet, trailed by Ted who looks kind of nervous. Chet catches the arm of the girl wearing #6, and turns her toward Ted. He introduces her, and they shake hands. The girl pulls her hand away, now clearly holding something green that she stuffs into her low costume neckline.

"Can we get a close-up?" Margolis asks.

"No," Goldberg responds. "These cameras aren't that fancy."

"Fucking cheap-ass Athens U.," Margolis laments. "Always investing in shit."

"Yeah, evil bastards and their poor-ass equipment," Farrah smiles sarcastically. "But at least they have it."

They all turn back to the screen just in time to see the girl peck Ted on the cheek. Chet and Ted wave as she turns to follow the other girls back to the dressing rooms.

All through the second half of the show, the cameras capture transactions like this: money exchanged, Chet moving from crowd to backstage with a different booster every time. Another exchange backstage, and a girl takes it, sometimes joyfully, sometimes uneasily. But they all take it. Some take their bidder off toward the kitchen or upstairs, away from the cameras at least. In a stroke of good luck, Emma's camera captures a clear handoff of cash from Huntley to the freshman he had his eye on, and Margolis keeps waiting for someone to tap Emma's #2, but it hasn't happened yet.

"It's hard for me to keep in mind that we're just watching these girls reenact scenes from a film." Goldberg rubs his eyes and then some sweat off his brow.

"Yeah," Farrah observes, "pretend courtesans, true love, a show—it's a little creepy how true to life this is."

Cut back to the house: it's time for the final number of the revue, and all hands are backstage furiously changing clothes and sets. Emma finds herself next to Brooke for the last costume change for the finale—the wedding between Brooke's courtesan and Stephanie's duke.

The girls work quickly and in silence, hands zipping zippers and buttoning buttons: Brooke, the intricate wedding dress of the maharaja's bride; Emma, who is supposed to interrupt the wedding, dons the shabby poet's tunic hidden under a long Indian coat. As Emma puts on the coat, the camera snake falls out of the buttonhole and flaps down over the lapel, the camera conspicuously black against the white fabric.

Bent over buckling her shoe, Brooke sees the dangling camera—it's right in her face. She looks up at Emma and grits her teeth, *why you fucking bitch.* "You're the snitch!"

Emma looks away, re-secures the camera, and darts away to the stage, where she takes her place at center stage behind the curtain. She's breathing hard but dares not look around at Brooke, who remains in the wings, whispering to Lucille and looking at Emma. Through the crack in the curtain, Emma can see that Stephanie has taken her place as the Duke, who sits out in the audience during this number.

Unaware of what just happened backstage, Brie watches breathlessly as the curtain rises. When it does, we see Emma the poet standing over a tearful courtesan Brooke. Emma holds a wad of stage money and throws it into Brooke's face.

"This woman is yours now," Emma says to the crowd. "I've paid my slut." She turns to Brooke and gnarls, "I owe you nothing, and you know you are nothing to me. At least you've disgorged me of my silly infatuation with love."

Brie's eyes are welling with tears. She's forgotten why she is there. With her hands to her face, she's covering her camera on the bag's strap.

"We've lost Brie's feed," Goldberg announces. "We've been caught!"

"No, she's just got her hands in the way," Margolis assures him. "She's wiping her eyes—she always cries at this part. Her arm is just covering the lens."

Goldberg sighs relief.

Emma passes Stephanie and walks through the crowd,

which parts for her. The spotlight follows Emma, and she stops right in front of Chet and Brie, who stand in the light's bright ring. Emma gives Chet a dirty look, then turns to Brie and winks.

Chet turns to see who Emma is looking at and double-takes when he sees Brie. His confused look at first morphs soon into recognition as Chet's mind progresses from 'coach's daughter' to 'coach's ex-wife' to 'Margolis Santos.'

Softly, Brooke starts to sing to Emma the opening strains of "Come What May."

Chet is distracted for a moment by the sound but then frantically looks around to see if he can find that sneaky, lying film professor lurking anywhere. He can't, so he turns back to Brie.

Brooke's lovely courtesan voice fills the hall with lyrics of undying love for Emma's poet. Stephanie the wealthy duke sits fuming in the spotlight.

Chet looks Brie up and down. He sees the bag, and then he suddenly understands. He rips it off her shoulder and opens it. Reaching in, he pulls out the camera's memory unit and transmitter. He holds it up like a snake he's hunted and then smashes it to the ground, the music now swelling over the sound of the crash.

When Chet crushes the camera under his boot, Brie steps back, scared, her hand to her face.

In an instant, Eggy is beside Brie sweeping her out of the spotlight and through the crowd toward the doorway away from a fuming Chet. They hurry through the Great Hall and out of sight into the foyer.

Still blinded by the spotlight, Chet searches for his security guards. He sees Ronnie and hurries over to him, pushing his way through the crowd that is too entranced with Brooke and Emma's duet to notice.

Emma sings lovingly back to Brooke, "Come what may." They kiss a final kiss.

The tune ends, and the audience erupts into applause.

Chet whispers in Ronnie's ear and points backstage. The guard talks into his sleeve and suddenly all the men positioned around the room jump into action. Ronnie heads the other direction and pushes through the curtain at the side of the stage, and like the bald thug from the movie, he sneaks around backstage, gun drawn. He looks around and spots the camera. When he comes to the place where it is mounted, he raises his gun, and brings it down on the bug. He picks up the pieces and looks closely. He sees the wireless transmitter and then yells over the applause into the mic on his sleeve: "The receiver can't be far away—maybe outside. Go check."

Back in the van, Farrah notices, "We've lost the backstage feed."

Margolis: "What—how?"

Goldberg: "Check the receiver."

Busy fiddling with the offline camera, the three don't notice Emma's feed that shows four of the guards pushing through the crowd, into the foyer, and out the door.

Suddenly, there's a loud banging on the side of the van. Margolis looks at Farrah, and Goldberg lunges for the lock, but he's too late. The door slides violently open and there stands Ronnie, along with four guards. They look around for a second, and then Ronnie nods. Instantly the other four jump inside, pushing the professors out of the way. The thugs rip out consoles, sparks flying, and smash monitors and harddrives onto the pavement.

"What the fuck, man!" Goldberg yells, a hand running through his hair. He's freaking out that all the Athens equipment is toast.

Margolis stumbles out of the back of the van and looks toward the house. There, on the porch, stands Chet smiling smugly back.

The four thugs, job complete, head up the yard toward him. After a gloating moment, Chet turns and heads back inside.

Past him runs Brie, out into the yard. Brie and Chet pause briefly when they see each other, exchanging an indicting stare. Then Brie sees her mom and runs to her: "Mom, Mom. Are you okay?"

"I'm fine. You okay?" She takes a frightened Brie into her arms. "But we lost all the footage. All of it." They look for a few, long moments at the wreckage of electronics scattered around their feet. Margolis takes Brie's face in her palm and pulls it up toward her: "But you did great, Brie. Just great."

"Yeah, you did." Emma has run up, still dressed as Ewan McGregor, and put her hand on Brie's shoulder. "Happy birthday, by the way."

Brie blushes. "Thanks."

"Not everything was lost." From out of nowhere, Eggy steps into the circle. "The house is chaos inside. Girls are calling home, leaving in their cars." Eggy looks at Margolis. "Our disruption may just have prevented any of the Thetas from having to pay their bidders on their backs tonight. And then there's this."

Eggy holds out a mini camera with snake attached to a small black box.

"A simple nanny-cam," she explains. "With memory unit. I couldn't afford much more, but I got a few good shots. Happy birthday, B."

Brie smiles.

"You had this on you?" Margolis wonders at the camera, then looks at Eggy. "I bet that Orchard guy isn't too happy with you right now."

"Oh, he has no idea I was wearing it."

"But I thought—"

"Wearing a camera isn't the same as being in front of one, someone once told me." Eggy looks over at Emma and winks.

"Nicely done, Barnes." Margolis nods. "You may make executive producer yet."

Emma chuckles. "Ain't that hard." She and Margolis share

a moment of respect. "But Brie really is the one who talked Eggy into wearing it."

Margolis looks over at Brie, who glows. Margolis is suddenly taken by pride for her daughter and gives her an *attagirl*.

"But about that..." Eggy inserts.

"About what?" Margolis returns.

"Testifying on camera. Tonight may have changed my mind."

"Great," Margolis points, feeling new wind in the sails of her project. "Why don't you come see me in my office tomorrow? We'll shoot you."

"Okay," Eggy nods.

"Let's go home." Margolis walks away, arm in arm with Brie. "Happy birthday, big girl."

"Thanks, mom," Brie replies. They hug.

"Oh, and Goldberg," Margolis calls out. "Sorry about your van. Athens has insurance. They'll pay for it..."

Farrah laughs *ha ha!* and punches Goldberg in the arm. "Ouch!"

Brie muses, as they stroll down the street toward campus: "I guess the only thing that's missing from this romantic ending is a marriage, huh Mom?"

"And any ounce of humor whatsoever..."

"True."

*   *   *   *

Margolis puts a hand on the camcorder sitting on her desk. "Are you ready to put an end to this madness, maybe help Frank in the process?"

Eggy nods her head.

She sits in a chair in front of the camera. Margolis fiddles with some lighting behind Eggy and then goes around the other side of the tripod, where she adjusts something on the camera.

"Are you ready?"
   "Yes."
   "Then let's roll."

Part 5: A Break

I.

Emma sits at a computer with a large monitor, while Margolis paces back and forth behind her, drinking coffee. The elder blurts out: "I wonder what's keeping their mouths so shut. A sister gets raped, all of them get asked to fuck old guys, and they still clam up. Don't they see it could be them next? What gives?"

"Well, it's spring break..."

"That just started! It can't be the reason they've been avoiding us for a month."

Emma bites her lip. She knows exactly why—The Slut Diary. This seems like a perfect time to tell Margolis, but the older woman changes the subject.

"Okay, we've got some good stuff, stuff we can work with. But there's something missing." Margolis thinks for a moment, and Emma is about to speak, when Margolis continues: "All of these are separate incidents, disconnected, and we want to show what they have in common."

"What do they have in common?"

"The person who gave the order. We need the big fish. We need a way to connect all of this stuff on the ground—the rape, the pandering at the variety show—to the top."

"You mean Chet Orchard?"

"Yes, but even higher." Margolis taps her mug. "I mean President Lane."

"Jesus, Margolis." Emma is a little stunned. "That could bring down the entire university." All at once, the magnitude of what's happening all around her—the web of corruption, lies, and exploitation—hits Emma like a great blow. She's never been involved in something that's had this much impact on her world.

"No, I don't want to bring down the school; just its crooked leaders." Margolis backs off. "But we need more Thetas to come forward—what's holding them back?"

This time, Emma just blurts it out: "I know what it is."

Margolis turns to her expectantly.

Emma's face flushes red: "It's really bad."

"Then why haven't you told me before?"

"Because I'm really, really ashamed of myself. That's why."

"What could be so bad that you wouldn't tell me?" No answer. "Emma?"

Emma's mind races—*it's not too late to hush up—no, Santos won't let it go—cat's out of the bag.* So she lets spill. "The Thetas, most of them, slept with football recruits when they were in town on visits. For money."

Margolis's face bespeaks her utter shock. She can barely get out, "What?"

"Yeah. Pretty bad, isn't it?" Emma sets her jaw. "My guess is they don't want to come forward out of fear that they'll be found out."

"You mean to tell me that the Thetas have been serving as escorts for the football program, exchanging sexual favors for payment?"

"Yeah. Just so star recruits would sign with Athens."

"Wow, this changes everything." Margolis is stultified; then quickly she turns to Emma: "You too?"

Emma doesn't answer; she just puts her hands in the lap and lowers her head, face beet red.

"Oh my god, Emma..." Margolis thinks for a moment. "I think it's time to involve the police."

II.

Margolis turns towards angry students. "Think of it this way: if you take the midterm exam on Friday before spring break, you won't have to worry about film class while you're chilling on the beach. You'll be done and carefree. Am I right?"

The students mutter and roll their eyes, but they clearly see that she has a point.

"OK, let us continue with class, can we?"

Some rustling. Students are shifting gears, getting out notebooks and settling into their seats.

"Today, we are talking about the action/adventure film. This genre includes spy thrillers, superhero tent-poles, war pictures, heist movies, or any other film that contains guns, explosions, chases, fast machines, fights, and lots of plot twists. Often, this category overlaps with the other genres we've talked about, especially science fiction and fantasy, because they all share an epic scope, apocalyptic implications, or the stakes of saving the people, the city, the nation, the planet, and/or the galaxy from certain doom. Now..."

Margolis turns and pauses for effect.

"...over the past several decades, particularly with the rise of special and digital effects, these movies have tended to dominate the industry. Hollywood has invested more in the action/adventure film than most countries spend on their defense budgets. Why?"

"Because they make a lot of money."

"Correct! Give a fuzzy teddy bear to the girl with the fringe!"

"But just because they are big-budget, crowd-pleasers, does that make them bad films?" The jock in the back asks.

Another student pipes up, "Kinda..."

"Why do you say that, Rolanda?" Margolis asks genuinely. It's all a set-up anyway. "Why are action flicks bad films?"

"Because most of the time they're just mindless

entertainment."

"Yeah," another girl chimes in, "people don't watch these films in order to have deep discussions about meaning." She puts the last word in sardonic air-quotes.

"And I bet now," a young male student predicts, "you're about to tell us why these movies all have some profound cultural significance, aren't you, Dr. Santos?"

"Oh, Felipe," Margolis hams it up, putting her hands on her heart. "How would you ever have guessed that?" The class cracks up in spite of itself, and Margolis gestures with joy: "You see? You *are* learning."

"No, really, Professor Santos, what symbolism could these movies have? They're just for fun."

"Alright," Margolis concedes, "what if we say, just for the sake of argument, that these movies are *only* entertainment. That they are *just* for fun and escape." The class waits for the twist—Margolis loves this part, where she turns the academic lever and gets their brains turning—and then she brings it: "The question is *why* do we find action pictures so entertaining? After all, these movies often involve death, destruction, murder, war, crime, rape, and holocaust. If we *ourselves* were actually put in such life-or-death situations, we wouldn't think it was much fun anymore. So..." A beat. "What does it say about us that we love to watch other people risk their lives? After all, films may not have any 'deep meaning,' but they do reflect the culture that made them and the people who watch them. We reveal ourselves in our choices, including the films we watch."

"We watch people risk their lives because it's amazing!"

"Yes!" Margolis points emphatically. She then reflects back to the students what she heard, amplifying and fine-tuning the response, ever so slightly pushing what they already know into the zone of what they don't yet know: "We are amazed by heroes who can do daring things—rescue the princess from the dragon, fight the evil lord with a sabre, jump across a chasm full of man-eating crocodiles—because they are very difficult."

"And that's stuff you don't see every day," a new voice pipes up.

"Yeah, it's badass," still another student talks. The class is starting to warm up for Margolis.

"Yes, 'badass.' Often times—and this is mostly true for spy thrillers or war flicks—we admire the protagonist and other heroes because they are experts in things we will never master, like ninja throwing stars, or hacking computers, or blowing up bridges."

"Well," a girl speaks tentatively, "sometimes the hero isn't an expert. They're ordinary, like us."

"Right, you read my mind." Margolis flashes up on screen a picture of Mark Hamill in *Star Wars*. She points to him with her laser.

"Farm boy Luke Skywalker is propelled by random events into the reluctant role of savior of the galaxy. But he's just like us—with the right guidance and training, we all could become Jedi. I mean, at least that's why I loved *Star Wars* so much when I was nine."

Smiles from the students, particularly the girls.

"It's her choices, not her skills that make her a hero."

Margolis tracks a knowing look around the room.

"Is anyone else getting tired of the little red dot?" Felipe asks. The class laughs.

"Better watch out, Felipe, I can put an eye out with this thing," Margolis jokes. More laughter.

*   *   *   *

We see a shot of a sunny beach—there are lots of bare-chested boys and bikini-clad girls dancing in the foreground—all of them holding Solo cups full of some red liquor concoction. A DJ speaks into a mic and the crowd raises glasses and gives a cheer. Their bleached white teeth gleam in the sunshine.

Pull back to reveal that the images are only on the large, flat-screen TV on the wall of the Theta house TV room. A pale hand reaches in to turn off the set. It goes blank.

"Alright, alright, everyone settle down! This isn't Daytona Beach," Chet hollers to a room full of Thetas and meaty, young football players. Then softer, "Jesus."

Emma tries to fade into the back of the room as others turn toward Chet. They've gathered on the first Monday of spring break for an afternoon mixer and barbeque, sponsored by the Raven Foundation. It doesn't quiet down much.

Chet turns to Mickey and mutters an aside: "You'd think we'd just injected them all with some Spanish flies—are you sure you don't want to handle this introduction, Mick?"

Mickey demurs, raising his hands. He retreats next to Eggy, who gives him a silent nod hello.

Chet turns back to the crowd, as if he's speaking through a bullhorn: "Now," Chet claps. "These boys are all here on unofficial visits to the U., all thinking about choosing the Athens football team for their next step, and I'm sure that all y'all Thetas will do your best to help them become familiar with the campus, the social life, and the way we do things in these parts." He pauses. "Let's hear it, gentlemen for our beautiful and gracious Theta hosts!"

The recruits hoot and holler rambunctiously, tickling and teasing the girls standing around them. Emma shirks from this, moving away from any boy near her.

It takes Chet a few moments to calm them down. "And last but not least, boys, let's hear it for our lovely and talented housemom, Lucille Bontemp, for wrangling this whole mess and fixin up a meal fit for kings!" They all applaud politely for Lucille, who blushes with delight.

"Let's eat!"

As the crowd disperses for various parts of the Theta house, Mickey watches Lucille from across the room. Mickey leans over to Eggy and asks real low, "What's she doing?"

"Oh," Eggy smacks her lips, "that old bitch is writing in her slut diary again."

"Slut diary?" Mickey follows Eggy's look and sees Lucille, standing in the middle of the room and writing in a hardcover notebook, like a diary. "Oh..."

Emma lingers long enough to see it too—Lucille writing in a little red book.

Working against the flow of traffic, Chet weaves his way over to Lucille. "You got the pairings yet?"

"I'm working on it. I kinda wait to see." Lucille follows the different groups of girls and guys quickly with her eyes.

"You mean, like who naturally pairs up with whom?"

"Exactly," Lucille replies. "It's usually pretty obvious, and pretty quick." She points out a couple standing over by the TV, standing close and talking low. "The only one I haven't seen is Miss Barnes. She's not in my book yet."

The two adults look across the room at Emma who, for a moment, returns their glare.

Chet, low, to Lucille: "Don't worry, she'll come around, just like last time."

"And when she does, I just jot it down in my notebook. To make sure the right girl gets credit for the right recruit and then when and how much."

"Just as long as we can keep things straight. This is costing me a fortune, no need to waste anything."

"If I need to make changes, I can just do it in the margin, right here." She shows him the notebook. "And then the payout amount goes over here. Easy peasy."

"Well, you better protect that fucking book. After the variety show debacle, some of the ol' Foundation boys got spooked. We gotta focus on getting the Thetas in front of recruits."

"Don't worry—it's in code. See? It looks like gibberish to anybody else." She holds the book up for Chet to see. "Plus, I keep it very close."

"Well done, my dear Miz Bontemp." Chet smiles. "What would I do without you?"

He kisses her on her hand and leaves her in stunned silence as he heads for the buffet line.

*   *   *   *

"A detective should be right with you, ma'am." A uniformed officer smiles and nods at Margolis and Emma, who sit in cold, fiberglass chairs in the waiting room. It's filled with grieving parents, loud children, and a woman with a black eye being comforted by a friend. Emma's never really been in a police station before—this is all new to her—the other side of the proverbial tracks.

Emma turns to Margolis, looking for conversation to relieve the stress—even facing her guilt is better than contemplating the withered masses around her.

"I thought you were going to hate me."

"Hate you?"

"Or, at least, lose respect for me."

"Listen to me, Emma. I'm not saying that what you did was okay—in fact, it was a really dumb choice—but I understand why you did it. Your father was in trouble, Orchard made threats; you did what you had to do to protect your family. So, I'm not judging you."

Emma searches Margolis's eyes for a second and finds sincerity. She believes her. "Okay. And I also hope you don't judge any of the other Thetas. They had reasons, too."

"Well, that's another story—" As Margolis starts to reply, two plain-clothes detectives walk up to them. "Dr. Santos?"

Margolis turns, "Yes."

"I'm Detective Pantucci." She's a white woman, pantsuit, firm handshake, hair back in a bun.

"And I'm Collins." Male, black, mid-thirties, narrow-faced, skinny.

They all shake hands, and Margolis points to Emma. "This is Emma. She's a student at Athens."

"Is she a victim of the alleged prostitution ring?" Pantucci asks hopefully.

Margolis looks furtively at Emma then back at Pantucci. "Um, no. She works with me, helping me with my film."

Pantucci nods, a bit disappointed. Emma looks relieved.

"Look, we've gone over your statement," Collins continues impatiently, "and we've decided to check out your claims because of your husband—"

"Ex-husband."

Pantucci continues, "But we're just telling you right now, without victims willing to testify, or documents, papers of some kind, you really don't have much here."

Emma is about to open her mouth when Margolis interjects, "That's fine, detective. We appreciate you looking into it. We're not even sure exactly what's going on, which is why I'm making the movie."

"So, you'll bring us anything new that you find," Pantucci states more than asks.

"Certainly." Margolis smiles. "Thanks again for your time." They shake hands and the detectives retreat to the innards of the station.

On their way out, Emma whispers emphatically to Margolis, "Why did you cut me off? I was going to tell them I was involved."

"And incriminate yourself on possible solicitation charges?" Margolis scoffs. "Never reveal all your info to sources when working on a documentary. We have to be careful, pick the right time. Once the police start poking around, we might be able to shake more girls' testimony out of the Theta tree. Then yours won't seem so incriminating. Got it?"

"Got it."

They stride out the door and into the brightening spring sun.

*   *   *   *

TV announcer: "In other news, Athens University student Stephanie Rogers has filed a criminal rape complaint with the Athens Police Department against former Raven football recruit, Colby Lennox. Afterwards, she addressed a crowd that had gathered outside the courtroom by reading from an open letter addressed to her alleged attacker."

Video rolls of Stephanie standing on the steps of the Theta house, surrounded by her sisters, Emma on the left, Brooke on her right. Clad in a blue spring dress, her hair up, the fresh skin of her neck. Stephanie reads from a spiral notebook.

"After you raped me, I wanted to step out of my body, take it off like a wetsuit, and let it swirl down the drain."

Stephanie pauses to brush a wisp of brown hair out of her eyes. Her blue floral dress flutters in a dry gust of wind.

"Then, I got angry. You don't have sex with a girl who can't say no, who can't even talk. And you don't invite your buddies to watch. That's sick and lacks any sense of human decency. I'm not sure this anger will ever go away."

Stephanie pauses to wipe her eye, but otherwise it doesn't look like she's crying.

"You say you've been falsely accused—you say your college experience has been ruined right as it has started. But you knocked down my ivory tower, too, not just your own. Here's the difference: you may still climb your tower, play football, make new friends, date someone, earn a degree—but this place is dead for me. And not only this place, this entire world—you've ruined the inside of me. I can't walk, sit, stand, lie down, sleep, or wake without wondering what you did to me and why. I can't restore the thing that is lost inside. You've taken it. Stomped it into the ground, smothered it in the sheets and pillow where you raped me. I have no confidence, no will, no reason, no value, no self. If it wasn't for my friends and sisters here, at Delta Delta Theta, I would be nothing. With their help,

I may recover, but I'll never be whole again."

She closes the notebook, turns, and walks up the steps into the house.

*　　*　　*　　*

It's evening. Margolis and Brie sit at the breakfast table eating in silence. Then Brie breaks it.

"Hey, Mom, I think another Theta is going to turn state's evidence," Brie says with suppressed exaggeration.

"Oh, yeah? Which one?"

"Her name is Betsy."

"Betsy—as in Betsy Ross? That's an old-fashioned name."

"Yeah, well, she's an old-fashioned girl, I guess. Probably the nerdiest in the house. She's not in the Slut Diary or anything, but she sure saw—and heard—a lot of the, um, activity in the house."

"Slut Diary?" Margolis raises an eyebrow.

"Oh yeah, ha ha. That's what Eggy calls it—the notebook that Lucille is always writing in when recruits come around."

Margolis starts pointing knowingly at Brie, who interrupts before her mom can say anything: "No, Mom. I'm not in the diary. I never—"

"That's not what I was going to ask, Brie." Margolis frowns. "I know you would never do that."

"Then what?"

Margolis can feel Brie's eyes piercing her. "It's nothing."

"Jeez, Mom, you still don't trust me, do you?"

"It's not that I don't trust you..."

"Then what?" Brie's voice is raised, more pleading than angry.

"I'm worried about you, Brie. Okay? We just keep uncovering layer after layer of repulsive scandal at this university, and I'm scared to death they might get you too."

Margolis raises her hand to her mouth, trying to keep it

together.

Brie is surprised by her mother's vulnerability—she's never this open or honest with her fears—so Brie lowers her proverbial weapons and takes a deep breath.

"Listen, mom. I know you don't want anything bad to happen to me. Despite being a huge flake," Brie jokes—it makes Margolis smile through her building tears—"you are an awesome Mom who has always kept me safe." Brie reaches her hand out. "But I'm 18 now. I can take care of myself." She pauses until Margolis meets her eye. "But I don't have to, right? Be alone? You'll be with me every step. So, ask me what you want to ask me."

After a long moment looking into the eyes of this young woman who used to be her baby girl, Margolis continues, voice softer: "This diary is exactly what we need, but I don't want you anywhere near there. Will you ask someone else to get it?"

*   *   *   *

"My mom wants to know if you can get your hands on Lucille's, you know, slut diary."

"Me?" Eggy is taken aback, then she starts shaking her head. "No, no. I've done my part. I got her the footage inside the variety show, and I've testified about Stephanie. I'm already in too deep."

Emma steps out of the room and into the Theta house hall where she sees two women talking.

"Oh, I see," Brie pipes up. "Big new assistant coach here is too worried about losing her precious job."

Eggy objects, "That's not what I meant."

"Yeah, but it's true." Brie pauses, checks her sarcasm.

Emma butts into the conversation: "What are you two talking about?"

"Nothing. Don't worry about it," Brie snips. She tries to hide the hurt blooming in her face.

Eggy to Emma: "Margolis wants me to steal Lucille's little red book."

"Look, I understand," Brie continues to Eggy. "You just got a new job and you've already risked a lot. But my dad's job is on the line, too. Or do you not care about that anymore either?"

Brie's eyes cut to Eggy's quick.

"Alright, alright," Eggy relents. "Just give me some time. And I'll get that diary."

"No, I got this," Emma insists. She knows that she's the best shot and that it'll save Eggy from any further trouble. They may need her still on the inside.

Before either of the others can say anything, Emma is halfway down the stairs.

*   *   *   *

Emma ducks quickly behind the doorjamb of the Theta house kitchen, just out of Lucille's sight. When Lucille goes back to the stove, Emma peeks her head back around.

To her left, Emma can see, off the kitchen, the door to the housemom's bedroom; it's open but dark inside. *Perfect*, she thinks to herself, *all I have to do is get in, get the diary, and get out before Lucille is done.* Watching Lucille for a bit, Emma can find no opportunity to sneak by, so she starts to panic. As each moment passes, Lucille is closer to finishing for bed and leaving Emma with less time. Plus, Lucille keeps coming to the island, which gives her a view of the kitchen, her bedroom door, and the dining room. *I could get caught—what am I going to say if she finds out.* Then Emma notices that the island is pretty high and must block Lucille's view of the floor, so Emma get down on her hands and knees.

At the end of the island, right before the gap between it and the door to Lucille's room, Emma pauses and listens for the sounds of Lucille at the stove, when her back will be to the door. When she hears the clatter of spatula against cast iron, she scoots quickly into Lucille's darkened bedroom.

Fuck, she thinks, *it's too dark to see in here.* As she stands up, Emma considers just waiting for her eyes to adjust, but the sound of water at the sink quickens her pulse. Just then, she remembers her phone in her back pocket, so she takes it out and turns on the flashlight. The circle dimly illuminates a modest bedroom with an old, musty bedspread, pictures of grown kids on the bedside table, and an old analog alarm clock. But no diary.

Shit.

Emma looks frantically around the room and can't see the notebook on any of the surfaces. She flails the light around, then suddenly realizes that the light may be visible from the kitchen. The sound of footsteps getting closer makes her freeze in her tracks—Lucille is coming—and Emma looks around for a place to hide. She dives down behind the desk off the foot of the bed, but the space is cramped and not really a good hiding place—*if Lucille comes in the room, she will see Emma right off.*

Lucille reaches out her hand—*to turn on the light*, Emma thinks—and, instead, opens a drawer at the end of the counter. The noise makes Emma jump. But she's instantly relieved when she hears Lucille back at the stove, stirring pots and turning sizzling meat. When Emma hears the oven open, she knows that Lucille will be tied up with baking long enough for her to get the hell out of there diary or no.

But just as Emma is about to crawl out of the room, her phone light catches a rosy glint off a rectangular object high up on the top of a wardrobe. Emma stops, stands, and, lifting the phone, shines the light closer to the object.

It's the diary.

She recognizes the gaudy red color. In a flash, Emma is up on her tiptoes, grabs the book, and has it under her arm. As she slips the phone back in her pocket, Emma stoops to the floor and shuffles on hands and knees to the doorway. She listens. *The sound of the oven closing.* Emma has to go now, so she quickly skitters across the floor and stops behind the island. She now needs just one more opening to slip into the dining room and out of sight. Emma can see the door—it's just a few feet away. But Lucille is now at the sink—sounds like she's washing her hands—and in a moment she's walking again, toward Emma's side of the island.

Emma thinks about dashing immediately into the dining room but realizes she won't make it. Instead, she goes around the other side of the island, opposite now of Lucille, deeper into the kitchen toward the oven. If Emma can just keep the island between her and Lucille...*but if she comes back around to the stove, I'm fucked.*

But she doesn't. The kitchen light goes off, and Emma hears Lucille walk into her bedroom and shut the door behind her.

Emma slumps back against the island, relieved. She pulls out the diary, looks at it for a second, then high-tails it out of the kitchen and up the stairs.

III.

"What do you mean, 'it's gone'?" Chet's voice comes in loud and clear through Lucille's phone.

"I mean, it's *gone*. It was in my room where I always keep it—she looks up at the top of her wardrobe—and when I woke up this morning to write checks to the girls, it was gone."

There's a long silence on the phone, as Lucille listens, feeling like she's made the case soundly that she's not culpable for its disappearance.

Then Chet finally speaks, "I betcha one of those little *bitches* got in your room and took it." Another pause.

"Now why would they do that—it's how they get paid?"

Chet's mind is racing, "Is there anybody else who was in that house last night?"

Lucille considers but shrugs her shoulders. "No, just a couple of the girls, Eggy, me, and Brie Sinoro-Santos, but she's always here—"

"God dammit!" Chet yells. "That film-cunt's daughter—you're still letting her have the run of the place, after what happened at the variety show? How fucking stupid could you be—"

"Now Chet, you don't have to—I mean, Brie is the coach's daughter, why would she ever want to do anything to hurt—" Then it suddenly dawns on her, the answer to her own question.

"Except she's in cahoots with her mom," Chet puts smugly. "Tried to film the show."

Lucille sits there, a sinking feeling dropping through her belly. If that book ever got into the wrong hands—if they could crack the code, that is—it could mean arrest or prison or worse.

Chet shakes her out of her thoughts. "You just search that house high and low—I'll take care of Professor Bitch. We've gotta get that diary back. Tear that place apart until you find it!"

$*$ $*$ $*$ $*$

Margolis sits at her classroom desk with her head in her hand; in the other, she holds her phone to her ear.

"Brie, honey? It's Mom. I'm going to be a little later still—I have some work to finish up. Go ahead and fix yourself a frozen pizza or something." A pause, Margolis listens. "Yes, a movie is fine. But bedtime at 9:30." Pause. "Because it's still a school night, okay?" Margolis pauses. "OK, love you too. See you. Bye."

Just as Margolis puts the phone down, the door flies open. Margolis wasn't expecting students, since it's not her office hours, so she's taken off guard when in walks Chet Orchard.

Margolis puts her hands down on the desk, as if to steady herself, and she instinctively reaches for her phone. But her purse, with the pepper spray, is on the floor too far away to grab quickly.

"Well, Ms. Sinoro-Santos," Chet snides.

"It's Dr. Santos."

"I know what your name is." Chet strides directly up to the desk and stops. "And I don't give a fuck."

Margolis takes a breath, tries to collect herself. "To what do I owe the pleasure, Mr. uhhh..."

"You know goddamn well why I'm here."

Margolis looks back at him blankly. She wants to run, move, lunge—anything to get out of there—she can even smell the garlic on his breath—but she fights her fear and waits.

"You have some property of mine, and I want it back."

"I don't know what you're talking—"

"And if you don't give it to me, I'm going to take it myself."

"Are you threatening me?" Margolis rears back in offense.

"Yes, yes, I believe I am. I am indeed threatening you."

Chet leans forward ever so slightly, his face looking down on hers, his stare hot and intense in contrast to his sardonic tone.

"Look, I don't mind you sneaking around or taking your little videos at the Theta house because they don't prove shit." A beat. "But when you steal something that belongs to me? Then you got trouble." He can feel himself losing his cool, even though he could see the fear in her eyes when he walked in. She's regained a bit of composure, but it just makes him want to clench down, pit-bull style.

"I haven't stolen anything that belongs to you."

"Don't play semantic games with me, professor. One of your little minions, then, took something from me, and I won't stop until I get it back."

"You know what, Mr. Orchard? It doesn't matter anyway. I've gone to the police with all the evidence I've gathered, and they are investigating claims made by me, students, and other witnesses. What's more, I can connect you to the prostitution ring being run out of the Theta house." She pauses, relishes the shock on Orchard's face. "Pandering, solicitation, and sexual assault of minors? That's 20-30 years minimum. Oh yeah, Mr. Orchard. I think you will stop now."

Chet stares back for a moment, a red rush now rising from his neck. "You think you're better than me, but you're not. Do you think anyone has forgotten about your teenage tryst?" He snorts. "You're a predator, just like the rest of us."

Margolis looks back at him. Just before she flinches, she manages, "You're right. But at some point, I had to do what's right."

He suddenly leans over on the desk, both of his meaty hands braced on its opposite corners. For a moment, his face glares pure hate down at Margolis.

Then his mouth breaks into a smile. "You wanna test me? Go ahead. Try. But I own the police. You know why? Because they love the Raven football team, that's why, and they won't do anything to hurt it—they love championships too much. And I bring them championships. And the judges, too. They're not going to issue a search warrant or give you a favorable rule on the admissibility of your footage. Why? Because I'm best friends with all of them; hell, they're donors to the Foundation, you beaner idiot!"

Chet pushes off the desk and straightens back into a standing position. He points at her, "Do you really think any of them will help you, a disgraced philanderer who sleeps with her students?"

Chet stares down at Margolis who is silent, her mouth shut tight.

Halfway to the door, Chet turns back. "And Ms. Santos—I would hate for anything to happen to that scholarship for Brie. Or something worse." He stares at Margolis for a moment, then turns his back and pulls the door firm. Then he's gone.

Margolis looks down at her hand, fingers white gripping the desk; then she lifts it and looks at it, shaking uncontrollably right in front of her face.

*　　*　　*　　*

Margolis pulls up into her driveway and cuts the lights. Her mind is grinding, trying to anticipate what Orchard might do next. It takes her a second to come around in the darkness.

But instead of opening the garage door as usual, she decides to go around back so that she can water her flowers before going inside—*maybe that will relax me a bit, give me a chance to think.* So she takes a hose and walks deeper into the yard. She thinks about Benny and sees the dog's grave.

Standing there, rather ridiculously, in the pale moonlight holding a hose, Margolis absently glances into the windows of the back of the house facing the back yard. For a moment, Margolis is unsure of what she is looking at—it strikes her at first like some sort of lightsaber duel—a band of white light waves up and down in a haphazard but regular pattern, as if parrying invisible blows.

Suddenly, Margolis realizes there is someone in her house

with a flashlight. Her first thought is, *What is Brie doing in there?!*

Then she sees the dark shape of a man. Margolis is suddenly gripped by fear. She looks up and sees the light on in Brie's bedroom window. *Oh god, Brie!* She tries to push away the involuntary thoughts of what they might be doing to her, whoever these intruders are.

Margolis gathers herself and instinctively crouches down, hoping whoever is inside hasn't seen her. She drops the hose and lurches up against the house, where she's frozen in indecision. *What should I do?* After a few moments, she begins sidling up a walk that leads to the back door.

At the door, she thinks about going in full-ass banshee, screaming and yelling, to do whatever she can to get these people away from Brie. She reaches for the door handle but stops, remembering the pepper spray in her purse. She reaches down, feels in the bag for what seems like agonizingly long minutes—*hurry up, they are going to see you*—and feels out the canister of spray. She takes a breath and steels herself before reaching for the door again.

With all her might, Margolis pushes on the door handle to barrel her way into the kitchen. But the weight of the door is not there as she expects and she stumbles forward, past someone in black who sidesteps her falling body.

As she hits the ground, Margolis turns, hand with the mace upraised, and lets loose. As the stream of potent liquid flies across the room, the man turns quickly as the spray glances him on the side of the face. One hand to his eye, he bolts through the door and out into the backyard. In an instant, the man has gone over the back fence and into the alley before Margolis even has a chance to breathe.

On the inhale, Margolis's lungs burn with the acrid fumes from the pepper. She covers her mouth and nose with a sleeve and turns away, stumbling to her feet and over to the sink. She turns on the water and rinses her hands before splashing it on her face. For a moment, after the water is turned off, Margolis stands there, dumbfounded. She can't really process what just happened, it all went down so fast, *boom boom boom, and he was gone.*

Suddenly, Margolis remembers Brie. She turns and runs through the kitchen into the living room and up the stairs. She makes it in a few bounds and turns down the hall towards Brie's room.

Margolis throws open the door, half expecting to barge in on a horrific scene, but the room is empty.

"Brie?" Margolis stands and listens for a moment. She turns and walks down the hall, calling a bit more loudly, "Brie!" She goes to the opposite end of the hall to her room and calls Brie's name again. A muffled sound freezes her in place, her skin crawling with fear. It's coming from Brie's bedroom. Margolis strides back into the hall and breaks into a jog.

"Mom?" Brie appears in the doorway and runs towards Margolis. They meet in the middle of the hall and wrap arms around each other. "I was so scared, Mommy. So scared. The man—he came into my room—I hid in the attic..."

"You hid in the attic?"

"Behind my closet. Over the garage."

"Oh, thank God." Margolis squeezes her daughter tightly in her arms and realizes suddenly how fragile Brie feels in her arms, like she's five again and just had a bad dream. "It's going to be okay, Brie-Brie. Mommy's here."

*　　*　　*　　*

The next morning, Margolis and Brie sit on a couch amidst the rubble of what was once their living room. Chairs are overturned with their bottoms ripped out. Books, photos, and knick-knacks scattered off of shelves and flung in random piles on the floor. Drawers pulled out and overturned. Completely ransacked by whoever broke in last night.

Across from them are detectives Pantucci and Collins of the Athens Police Department. They stand and survey the damage one last time.

"Well, our fingerprint crews have wrapped up their work, so the next step will be searching against the database." Pantucci pauses. "Most often these deals are burglaries, but we'll let you know if we find anything else."

"Anything related to the Athens investigation," Margolis clarifies.

"Yeah." Pantucci steps through the front door and out into the bright light.

"Again, I'm sorry about the mess." Collins says, as he tips a salute, looking sympathetically into the faces of both mother and daughter. They watch him follow Pantucci to their unmarked car.

Dismayed at the chaos, Margolis turns back into the living room,

Brie does not think her mother's obviousness is very funny. "Why didn't you tell them?"

"Tell them what?"

"Who you thought broke in. And why."

Margolis looks hard at her daughter—the fragile girl of last night seems to have aged years in the hours since they finally fell asleep together in Margolis's bed. Margolis can see the determination and grit in Brie's eyes—she's not going to let this go.

"I didn't want to tell the detectives this because I don't have proof yet, and I'm not sure they'd even believe me."

"You know it was someone from the football program—"

"Your father wouldn't do this," Margolis's voice goes up.

"Are you sure? Are you sure Dad didn't know about this and all the—you know—things going on at the Theta house?"

Margolis takes some time to consider so that she can say the right thing without making Brie's concern worse and without lying. With a breath, Margolis starts: "I think your father would be seriously pissed off if he knew—I mean, look at the way he reacted to Stephanie's rape investigation—he was completely beside himself that such a thing could happen under his nose." Margolis gets up from her chair and goes over to Brie, taking her by the shoulders. "No way your dad would allow any of this."

"Okay." Brie still seems a little dubious.

"And mark my words," Margolis says, bringing Brie's face up to hers. "I'll do everything I can to protect your father as this stuff about Athens starts to come out."

*   *   *   *

At her father's office door, Brie stops, knocks. "Excuse me, sir," she mocks in a deep voice. "I have a warrant for your arrest."

A sour Frank looks up seemingly startled for a moment, then he laughs, a total change over his face. "Brie-Brie!"

"Hi, Dah." Brie jogs over to him and gives him a hug as he rises.

"What brings you here, darling?"

"Oh, I just wanted to stop by and see how you were doing."

"And it's spring break and you're bored. All of the Thetas have gone to the beach."

"Well, yes. A few of the Thetas are at the beach. But most stayed for the football mixer for new recruits." Brie pauses, a bit puzzled. "You didn't know that?"

Distracted by his computer screen, Frank looks up, noting her inquisitive tone. "Why would I know that, honey?" He goes back to his keyboard, typing.

"I don't know, because it's football related?"

Frank continues to type, apparently not hearing the question. "Uh-huh," he says absently.

Brie is suddenly reassured by his vapid response. *Maybe Mom was right—he has no idea.* She decides to change the subject. "I also came by for another reason." Typing. "I'm worried about you."

Frank closes his eyes and drops his shoulders with a slight sigh before he recovers. "Brie, you don't have to worry about me. I'm fine."

"No, you're not. You spend all your time in your office. I hardly see you anymore."

"That's because you moved back in with your mom."

"Maybe. But we haven't had a daddy-daughter date in a while."

"I thought you said you were too old for that kinda stuff."

"I did. But now I miss it." Brie smiles. It melts Frank a little—sadness shadows across his face for a moment. She asks hopefully, "Want to do something next week?"

"You bet."

"Great." She hops up, pecks her dad on the cheek, and bounces toward the door. She stops, turns, a little ditzy, "Oh, Daddy, I almost forgot."

Frank stops what he's doing—slightly annoyed look on his face—and waits for her question.

"You haven't seen anyone carrying a little, red hardback book, have you? Like a diary."

Frank's face is blank. He shakes his head. "No." Of all the silly questions.

"Oh, okay. It's just one of the Thetas lost it. Thought one of the staff may have picked it up. You'll let me know if it turns up around here, won't you?"

"Sure, honey. Whatever you want." He's back to studying his screen. Brie watches him for a moment. And with a sudden burst of joy and relief, she walks out of his office, convinced of her father's ignorance.

* * * *

Margolis and Brie are working, packing up camera and

lighting equipment. Brie looks a little exhausted. Margolis turns to her. "If the cops aren't going to do it, then we have to." Brie nods her head and goes back to packing.

Margolis and Brie stand outside, just across the street from the Theta house. Margolis holds the camera, and Brie holds a mic, asking girl after girl if they will talk on camera. But everyone shakes their heads.

After a while, they give up and pack up. Margolis carries the camera as they walk down campus.

Brie: "There has to be someone we can talk to in athletics. Someone on the inside but not so invested in the money game. Do you know anybody, from your days as Coach's Wife?"

"Not really—I've stayed as far away from Boom Fisher as I could." Margolis gets a sudden thought. "But I know someone who would know someone in athletics!"

Margolis fishes her phone out of her purse and dials. She raises a finger for Brie to wait.

"Hello, Sandy? It's Margolis. Professor Santos." Beat. "Yeah, hi! I know it's been awhile. You been okay?" Margolis pauses to listen, intently.

Brie taps her foot, wondering when Margolis is going to cut to the chase.

"Yeah," Margolis's voice soothes, "I think about you and your mom every time I watch that show." Margolis listens some more. "I hope her loss hasn't been too hard on you." A beat. "Listen, I need to talk to someone in Athletics about finishing my film. Do you know anyone who might be willing to help?" As Margolis listens she looks at Brie; then her eyes open wide. "That's great, Sandy. Just perfect. Yeah, thanks for the offer." Beat. "Yeah, you too. Bye."

Margolis turns to Brie. "Got it. Let's go."

*　　*　　*　　*

Chet sits at the bar at *The Nickel Lady Saloon*. He's sipping on a scotch on the rocks. The two regular drunks sit on the other end, oblivious to anything going on until the door opens.

In walks Detective Pantucci. Suddenly, the drunks stiffen up, put their faces down sullenly into their beers. She walks past them and pulls out a bar stool next to Chet. She taps the bar and nods to the bartender. Within a few seconds, he puts down a shot glass and pours in a brown liquor. Probably bourbon. She lifts it and throws it back.

Chet doesn't look at her. He just reaches into his jacket and pulls out a fat envelope. As he drinks, he puts it down in front of her.

"Will this close it?"

Pantucci takes the envelope and puts it in her blazer. "It'll close it."

"Thanks. I owe ya."

"Anything for the team." Pantucci pushes the stool back and adjusts her pants at the belt. "Thanks for the drink." She saunters back toward the door.

Chet nods and then raises a finger. "Don't forget Edwards, the judge!"

Without stopping, Pantucci acknowledges with a wave, giving the drunks a wide smile as she passes.

*   *   *   *

Margolis emerges from the Athens Community College building where she teaches into the muggy early spring air of downtown Athens. The sun is almost completely down, but a few stragglers walk here and there down the building-lined streets. Margolis casually looks around but hardly takes note of the typical end-of-the-day scene.

As Margolis walks, we hear a voice-over; it's her voice from the lecture she just gave: "One of the most common and prominent elements of the spy thriller is 'the tail.'"

A few blocks from her car, Margolis takes out her keys. As

she does, she notices the echo of footsteps—someone has turned in behind her from a side street and their footfalls are matching hers almost completely, but not quite. It's the slight difference that makes Margolis's ears perk up. It's as if they are trying to hide their steps in the sound of hers.

"Sometimes, our main character, the spy, is the one doing the following, but usually, at some point in the film, the tables turn and the hunter becomes the hunted. In these scenes, our protagonist, or maybe a future victim, is being followed by an ominous presence."

Margolis glances back quickly over her shoulder—she's trying to be as casual as she can—and she catches the figure of a man, hands in his jacket pockets. She turns forward and is struck by a slight oddity: his coat. *Who wears a peacoat, in Athens?* It's mid-March and already up to almost 80 degrees during the day. She looks across the street—a few men in business suits—but no one else is wearing a jacket-jacket. The click of his shoes still echoes in synch with hers.

"But as an audience, we are often left to wonder if there's really someone there or if the character is just paranoid. Of course, since it's a spy movie, we know that 9 times out of 10, the person is not paranoid." Margolis pauses. "Like the saying goes, just because you're paranoid, doesn't mean they aren't out to get you..."

Margolis comes to a light and turns left toward the crosswalk. She's waiting for the light to turn, and the man in the peacoat approaches her, but he's facing the other way, as if he is continuing straight. Margolis lets out a short breath and chides herself for getting too wrapped up in the very movies she's spent the day analyzing. *This guy isn't following me, come on.*

"That's what spy stories do: they put you in the place of the spy—James Bond or whoever. They want you to be paranoid. They want you to feel what the spy feels. And that empathy puts your voyeurism at risk—you can't just sit back and watch—

you're in the game too."

As the light turns, the peacoat passes behind her and she steps into the street, crossing with the white walk sign. On the other side, she's just two blocks from her car, so she slackens her pace.

"When the hero, like the audience, is placed in the dark, not knowing what is going on, then the tension and suspense really surge. If this trained spy can't tell she's being followed, we think, then how are we to know? A clever film will set you up with a scene in which the protagonist is wrong before the real tail happens."

Margolis's mind wanders—to Brie who may be waiting at home, wondering if she's okay—or Mickey whom she hasn't seen for so long, it seems—he's on her mind, at least, which is a good sign, she'd like to see him again, maybe after the film is done—but he's a good one—he's unlike the others who just disappear right away to be replaced by the everyday business of her life.

By the time she realizes where she is, it's dark.

When she passes in front of a building, set back a little from the street, she hears reflected off its polished granite that same clicking again, almost in lock-step with her feet. He's back again, on the other side of the street, still following her. Suddenly, a cold chill grips her. *What if he follows me home, out of the public eye? I can't let that...*

"Once the tail has been 'made'—that's spy lingo for realizing one is being followed—" Margolis continues over student chuckling, "that's when the skills of the hero are put to the test."

Margolis doesn't turn her head this time—she imagines what she'll see—the man in the navy peacoat. She slightly picks up her pace and rattles her keys nonchalantly.

"Since secrecy is a spy's greatest weapon, the danger of the tail is that the secret will be exposed. Once a spy is known to be a spy, she can't work her trade anymore."

Margolis takes a sudden turn down an alley, leaving the street and fading into a shadow between streetlights.

"The best solution in every spy's mind is to elude a tail by simply slipping away. Any agent worth her salt is able to cunningly lose a tail without even appearing to be trying."

Down the alley, the man in the peacoat slows. He looks around behind him and then back ahead—along this alley are a long line of doorways, stoops, trashcans, parked cars, and a hundred other places for someone to hide. He goes down the row, checking under cars and in a few dumpsters. He tries a door here and there.

"But our hero can't panic—she has to make it look natural— so that the bad guys won't know if she knows she's being followed. At the same time, she has to make sure that her mind isn't playing tricks with her, so the double-back is the preferred move. Rule #1: Put eyes on the tail."

From out of a deep shadow, as if from Margolis's point of view, we see the man in the light of the alley, coming back the way he came, toward the street. In a last effort, he looks up at the tops of the buildings for a fire escape or maybe a ladder.

Reverse the point of view, and we see Margolis watching. She sees the man turn and there, on the other side of his face, is a huge red rash. Margolis's mind flashes back to the night her house was searched, when she sprayed her mace at the intruder.

So, it's true—the man just wasn't behind her randomly— now she knows that's she being followed by the same people who searched her house. They still think that she has the diary, and she knows they won't stop until they get it.

"That way, the hero can pretend to not be followed in order to trace the tail back to the person who gave the order."

Margolis exits the alley the other way, goes the long way around the block, and ends up back at her car. Before she unlocks it, she watches peacoat get into a car, so she quickly slips inside her own car and starts it. In a second, she pulls out and accelerates into traffic.

She follows him for a few miles, careful to stay inconspicuous, until he turns into a factory-looking building in the warehouse district. She looks up at the sign.

Orchard Industries.

*　　*　　*　　*

Margolis, looking through the living room blinds up and down the street, gets a call from Pantucci saying the investigation of Athens University is now closed.

"Yeah, I'm sorry, Dr. Santos." Pantucci pauses. "I think maybe you should turn on your TV." Click.

Margolis reflexively reaches for the remote and clicks it on, though she wonders why she followed Pantucci's orders so readily. She flips to a local channel.

TV announcer: "In a tragic turn of events, Stephanie Rogers, the Athens University junior from Atlanta, was found dead tonight in her room in the Delta Delta Theta house on the university campus. Police say the details are still sketchy, but it seems she died from a self-inflicted overdose of painkillers. This coming the same day a district judge, Billy John Edwards, threw out her case against former Raven football star recruit, Colby Lennox, for lack of evidence. In a statement from the bench, Judge Edwards, wrote, quote, 'We all made mistakes when we were 18, 19 years old. Throwing this kid in jail would have ruined his life.' Leaving some wondering if the ruling led incidentally to Ms. Rogers' death. The D.A. has ordered an autopsy..."

Margolis rears back and throws the TV remote across the living room. It smashes into a vase on the bookshelf, which shatters in a loud crash.

"God dammit!"

Brie runs into the room, half ready for bed: "Mom, what the hell?" She looks down at the broken porcelain, then glares back at her mom. There are tears in Margolis's eyes. Brie softens, goes to her mother's side.

"Mom, what happened?" Brie sits close and puts her hand on Margolis's shoulder.

Margolis has her hand to her mouth; she can't talk, just points to the TV.

Brie reads the headline on the news story about Stephanie's suicide.

Brie collapses on her mother's breast in shock. The two women hold each other, unable to say anything more.

*   *   *   *

PRESS RELEASE: "It is with great sadness that the Athens University community mourns the passing of junior Stephanie Rogers. A memorial service will be held for her at Athens North Cemetery next Friday. The family has asked that, in lieu of flowers, donations be given to the National Sexual Violence Resource Center in Stephanie's name. The University also announces that this concludes its investigation of Miss Rogers's case..."

The second item on the release reads:

"Athens University President, Art 'Lightning' Lane, announced his bid to run for the state's open U.S. Senate seat. He made the announcement at the monthly gathering of the Raven Foundation, which just announced its capital campaign for a new Athens stadium..."

*   *   *   *

Margolis opens the front door. It's Emma.

"I came over as soon as I heard." She walks in past Margolis without waiting for an invitation, "The Theta house is chaotic. I had to get out of there."

Emma stands in the middle of the room, not sure if she

wants to sit, stand, or cry.

Brie hears the door and comes into the living room. "Emma, oh my god I'm so sorr—" But Emma has enveloped her in a massive bear hug. Brie is a bit taken aback at first, but then returns the affection, as if clinging to the last petal on a bloom.

Emma hardens her face and grits her teeth: "I just want to finish this movie."

Margolis shakes her head. "The film is not as important as your safety or Brie's. Maybe we let the police do their—"

Emma reaches into her bag and pulls out a red, hardback journal and puts it in Margolis's hand.

"What's this?"

"The 'Slut Diary,'" Emma insists.

Both Margolis and Brie stare at it blankly for a second.

"But how—?"

"It's written in code but will be easy enough to figure out if you know what it's about." Emma opens the book and points to a listing. "See? These entries look like names, dates, amounts. There's more I don't understand, but we'll keep working on it."

Margolis looks in wonder at the document, flipping through the pages in disbelief. "This could be what we've been waiting for. It may at least prove transactions were made." After a minute, though, she comes to her senses. "But it only implicates the Theta organization. We still don't have anything to connect this to the top. If we go public with this now, it'll just seem like the Thetas were acting alone, running a sorority as a brothel."

"We have to try!" Brie insists.

"Yeah, I mean, we get one or two Thetas to admit that Orchard approached them, we can—"

"It's still the word of a billionaire against girls who sold their bodies for money, Emma!" Margolis exasperates. She puts a hand in her hair, lowers her voice: "Look, I was followed today, by some thug, and barely got away."

"What?" Brie is genuinely worried.

"I'm okay. I doubled back and traced the guy, and he led me right to Chet Orchard's office. So I know he's the one. But I can't prove he gave the order, okay? I can't prove anything right now. He's covered his tracks too well." Margolis sighs. "We have to face it, girls. Without that info, we've lost."

*   *   *   *

Walking through the cemetery, Margolis knows she's nervous, but knowing doesn't help. It's why she's standing in the back surveying the huge crowd who showed up for Stephanie's funeral. It was a big-profile case, so everyone in Athens is there to show their support for the university, for Stephanie.

She turns back to Emma who is giving the eulogy.

All that is going through Margolis's mind are thoughts like, *please don't say his name, don't mention athletics, don't blame, no revenge, play it cool, play it cool, play it cool.* Margolis doesn't even notice that she's biting her nails again.

"It's true," Emma continues in a bell-like and resolute voice, "the circumstances of Stephanie's death are unresolved." *No, no, no!* Margolis thinks, braces for what's next from Emma: "Depression, isolation, abuse, violence, perhaps even sexual assault—and we will all have to face these problems—in Stephanie's life and the lives of many college-aged women around the country."

Please, please, please. Emma, please don't.

"But the circumstances of Stephanie's life are not unresolved. They're exemplary. She lived a life of joy, devotion, love, and friendship."

Thank god. Thank you. Thank you. Margolis can barely listen to the rest of Emma's speech. It's a candid and heartfelt tribute from one best friend to another. It's detailed, eloquent, and moving.

As Margolis makes her way toward the grave, she realizes that her thoughts betray her—she cares about Emma's speech so much because she doesn't want the film project to be over.

There, right in the front, visible to God and everybody, stands Art Lane. His head is bowed, solemn face, black suit. *What balls*, Margolis thinks. She can't get over the thought of him stonewalling Stephanie's rape investigation and sweeping it under the rug, but if you want to be Senator I guess you have to do whatever it takes. *I have proof you lied, asshole!* She looks over and standing right next to Lane is Chet Orchard.

Lane is tight with Chet. Suddenly the tumblers in Margolis's head click into place. *Proof. That's it. And I know where to get it.*

A new urgency moves her through the crowd, looking for Emma and Brie.

*   *   *   *

"It was a brilliant tribute," Eggy glows, as Emma approaches her. "Steph would have loved it."

"Thanks, Egg." Emma demurs, uncomfortable with compliments, given the situation. "Listen," she continues, "I've seen the tapes. Your interview. And I want you to know. It wasn't your fault. Stephanie's rape."

Eggy cringes, can't answer right away. Instead, she fights back tears, looks up into the trees for a justification. The bright spring light imbuing the new-budded leaves with a radioactive green.

"I'm serious," Emma insists. "You weren't responsible."

"It's true, Eggy." Brie interjects. "You weren't."

Eggy looks from one white face to the other—she can't hold back anymore. "I'm tired of people saying that. It's killing me." She smiles disbelievingly at the girls. "You two are so naïve, do you know that?" She shakes her head.

Brie and Eggy stand stunned in shock.

"I'm responsible!"

Margolis interrupts, walking into the trio of women who seem rooted and stiffened into the ground. "None of you are responsible for what happened to Stephanie. Do you understand me? Rapists are responsible for rape. They are the only ones responsible for their actions." Margolis looks each in the eye in succession, like three exclamation points. "But, you can help stop it from happening again."

The three girls look questioningly at Margolis and then at each other.

"And that's why you're going to meet me tonight at my house. All of you."

V.

In Margolis's breakfast nook, a circle of light shines down on the table from the hooded chandelier, revealing the forearms, hands, and faces of five women: Margolis, Emma, Brie, Eggy, and Sandy.

"I'm glad you all decided to join me here tonight. You all know Sandy." Margolis raises a hand toward her former secretary who nods in greeting to the others.

"Stephanie's death had me feeling down, like we could never win, like this whole investigation has been for naught." Margolis pauses. "But when I started thinking about what Stephanie might want us to do, I settled down a little and started seeing things more clearly." She looks around the table at the group. "I've figured out how we can connect the dots and take down these assholes all the way at the top.

"I am going to explain the plan because each of you have given me, without knowing it, a different piece of the puzzle." A pause. "And it all revolves around breaking into a few offices, including the athletics department."

"What the hell?" Emma.

"Are you crazy?" Eggy.

"Sandy assures me it can work."

Everyone looks dubiously at Sandy, who smiles sheepishly.

"You trust me, right?" Margolis asks. Everyone nods. "And I trust her. We good?" More nods. "Here's how it all started." Flashback to:

Margolis is walking downtown, looking cautiously over her shoulders and down the street. She picks up her pace.

"Walking to my office one day last week, I got a call."

Margolis takes her phone out of her purse. Still walking fast.

"It was Mickey."

Margolis suddenly stops in the middle of the sidewalk, listening intently to her phone.

"Andouille?" Eggy asks, incredulously.

"Yeah," Margolis replies. Cut to:

Mickey's office. We hear Margolis's voice while we see Mickey on the phone, his lips moving with hers: "He said he'd been thinking hard about what I'd said—about needing to root this corruption out at the top—and when he heard about Stephanie, something snapped in him. It's all gone too far. Said he knew of some documents that might help us make the connections."

Back to the breakfast nook.

Eggy: "Dang. I thought he was bought-and-sold. Way to go, Mickey."

"What did he say?" Emma asks eagerly. "What are these documents or whatever?" Cut to:

Boom Fisher, the main athletics office, which is bustling with staff, coaches, players, and recruits. Toward the back, in a cubicle, a young athletics assistant with hair in small, tight buns takes out a CD labeled "RECRUIT FILES." She pops it into her computer's drive and begins uploading files onto the computer.

Margolis: "Credit card transactions for bar tabs for recruits, which is illegal since most of them are under 21. But paid for out of university accounts. Confiscated phone footage out on the town from a few recruits like Ryan Cavanaugh."

Brie looks furtively at Emma, who blushes.

"But none of that ties directly to Orchard," Eggy points out.

"That's true. But Mickey says that there are check stubs made out directly to Thetas. For what?" Margolis begs, "With testimony from you, Emma, and a few other Thetas, the link is stronger." Margolis gestures confidently. "And according to Mickey there are construction invoices from last year that tie Chet to the injury of a previous coach under Lane's administration. All of it together shows a pattern of deceit, cover-up, motive, intent, and commission of illegal activities, including solicitation and even attempted murder."

"Not to mention the fact that they broke into our house and knocked Mom over." Brie frowns.

"Is that true?" Sandy implores Margolis, who shrugs assent.

"Where is this treasure trove of files?" Emma wonders.

"Well, that's the tricky part." Margolis looks hard at everyone and wonders if this will crack their resolve. "Some of this stuff is in athletics."

"Boom Fisher?" Eggy cries. "That place has cameras and guards crawling all over it!"

"Yeah," Brie assures her, "but I know where they all are. I sneak around there all the time. Not a big deal." She smiles at Eggy.

"Anyway," Margolis reassures Eggy, "it's spring break. Hardly anyone will be there. Plus, you're a regular; nobody will think twice about you being on campus."

"Which office?" Eggy's getting uneasy.

"The main office."

"Jezuz! Why doesn't Mickey just give us the files?"

"Because he says he'd like to keep working in the business. Doesn't want to get caught. Wouldn't be able to work anywhere else, if it got out he was the leak. It was his one condition for helping us." Eggy seems dubious. Margolis continues: "The other files are at Chet's office downtown."

"Oh, no big deal," Sandy snipes. "Orchard Industries is only one of the most highly guarded buildings in Athens..."

"That's why we have this." Margolis holds up a key card ID with Orchard's face on it. "Get us in and right through Chet's door."

"How did you get Orchard's ID?"

"Just hold on, I'll get to that." Margolis raises her other hand. "Let's start at the beginning and go through the plan step by step."

"Wait," Brie interjects. "Is this like the part in those heist movies where the ring-leader explains how the job is going to go down?"

"Yeah," Emma piles on. "And the explanation back at the hideout is used as a voiceover to narrate the action of the actual heist?"

"No." Margolis laughs, faking defensiveness. Eggy snickers into her closed fist. She glances over at Emma who grins back. Margolis begins realizing she's being played: "You guys *do* listen to me talk about movies after all!"

Emma: "I guess all this useless movie knowledge is finally paying off." She smirks at Margolis who smiles back. Everyone laughs.

"Alright, alright. Here's how it's going to go down," Margolis continues, energized by the camaraderie. "First, it starts with Sandy and the keys. We already have a key to Boom Fisher's main doors because of Eggy, but we need one for the main office."

"Again, can't Mickey just give us his?"

"Nope. He wants complete deniability that he was ever there that night."

Frowns.

"As I was saying," Margolis injects, "it starts with Sandy. She's pals with the administrative assistant in athletics, so she'll ask to borrow the key. Make up some bullshit excuse."

Cut to Sandy scratching her short, blond hair. She's leaning on the desk of her counterpart in the athletics department, a heavy-set, crotchety secretary who's been working on campus since the Nixon administration.

Margolis's voice-over: "And everyone has a particular weakness that makes them give in to the desire to trust. Sandy knows this woman's desire...to belong."

Sandy (to Crotchety, her counterpart): "I couldn't believe that she'd say that. To the president!"

Crotchety: "Well, she is Keri Russell!"

Sandy: "True. That's why I love *The Americans*."

"Best show on TV!" Crotchety laughs in agreement.

"Oh, I almost forgot," Sandy says as she stands up to leave. "The film department is all out of copy paper. Mind if I take some of yours?"

Crotchety gives her a doubtful look.

"Don't worry, I'll restock you when we get a delivery next week. But we needed it, like, yesterday. You know Dean Concord. Slow on the uptake. We're always running out."

After a second thought, Crotchety relents. "Sure." She places her hands on her plump knees and with a groan starts to stand.

"Oh, don't bother. I'll fetch," Sandy insists. "Just give me your key."

Crotchety seems relieved, and without blinking an eye she hands her skeleton key to Sandy who takes it with a smile. Every secretary is given a skeleton key that opens every office, conference room, and closet in their building. Sandy reassures, "I'll return it after I've taken the paper to my office, if you don't mind."

Crotchety snorts in reply.

Cut back to the breakfast nook where Margolis continues: "Sandy pretends to head off to the supply closet on the next floor up, but instead goes down to the first where Brie is waiting to take the key to get copied at the hardware across the street."

"Wait," Eggy interjects. "Don't those kinds of keys say 'DO NOT DUPLICATE'?"

"Shhhh, whatever," Brie retorts. "You'd be surprised what you can get away with when you're young and cute." Cut to:

Hardware store.

Brie stands on one toe then the other twirling her hair while a pimply young clerk in an apron absentmindedly copies the key, glancing up at Brie every few seconds and smiling.

"And the coach's daughter," Emma teases, punching Brie softly on the arm.

"I know, that's right," Eggy laughs. Cut to:

Boom Fisher. Brie runs back into the foyer of the athletics building and comes right up to Sandy, who holds her palm up, halt. They both look at the guard who looks up from his YouTube; then he turns back to his screen. Sandy puts her hand down, and Brie brandishes the new key copy. Brie smiles, chewing gum. Sandy takes the key and the copy and slips them both in her pocket before she heads back upstairs to give the original back to Crochety. Cut back to:

The breakfast nook, where Margolis pushes on: "Then, we come to Brie's next job—getting her father off campus and away from any fallout. Plus, he usually works late and would probably notice somebody snooping around the main office next to his. That's why we need to get him out."

Brie and Margolis share a knowing look. Cut to:

Boom Fisher. Brie and Frank walk out of the front of the building laughing. Brie holds his hand and swings it. They walk leisurely down the quad as we pull back to see a wide shot of the campus. It's big, so they'll be gone a long time. Next, we see them sitting in the ice cream shop licking cones. Again laughing.

Back to the breakfast nook.

"Wow, double dips, huh? You got the real hard assignment, huh Brie?" Eggy teases. Brie playfully pushes Eggy's shoulder.

"That's right," Margolis imposes. "I don't want her anywhere near this cockamamie plot. Brie will not get embroiled."

"A little too late for that, Mom." Brie chuckles.

"Fair enough." Margolis smiles. "But no more. After that part, you're out." Brie frowns.

"Now, to Eggy." Margolis turns. Eggy straightens. "You'll walk in Boom Fisher like you own the place—new, sexy assistant coach of the football team coming in during break to burn the midnight oil for team and glory."

"But I usually don't go in late—that's when I'm at the Theta house. Anyway, spring break is not a busy time for football."

"Doesn't matter," Margolis shakes her locks. "Confidence. It should be enough to get you in the door." Cut to:

Boom Fisher. Eggy strides up to the security guard at the desk. She leans over and says, "Hey. I'm just going up to my office. Got a few things to finish up before the weekend."

"I'm sorry. I can't let you in without authorization."

"But," Eggy says patiently, "I'm the new assistant coach. I just need to do a few—"

"I can't let you in without—"

"Authorization. Yeah, I heard you." Eggy looks around nervously. "No worries. Thanks."

Eggy makes for the door, then doubles back behind a plant. She's improvising but knows she has to get upstairs.

She glances at the desk. The guard has turned his attention to Candy Crush on his phone. Perfect. She slips around the other side.

Once in the elevator, away from the spying eyes, Eggy pulls out the duplicate key and watches it glint in the light as she turns it.

Cut back to Margolis's breakfast nook.

Emma: "What do I do?"

"You're with me. We're hitting the Orchard building."

"Glad you always give me the easy stuff," Emma sighs sarcastically.

Then Eggy remembers. "But wait, how did you get the key from Orchard?"

"Well," Margolis leans in, confidentially. "The man actually came to visit me the other day in my office." Flashback to:

Margolis's classroom. Chet suddenly leans down, both of his meaty hands braced on its opposite corners, his face breathing down on Margolis.

(Margolis voice-over: "He wanted the Slut Diary.")

(Emma's voice-over, "But you didn't have it.")

(Margolis: "I didn't have it. And he was pissed.")

Then Chet's mouth breaks into a smile. "You wanna test

me? Go ahead. Try. But I own the police, you know why? Because they love the Raven football team, that's why, and they won't do anything to hurt it—they love championships too much..."

While Chet is diatribing about football, we slowly zoom in on Margolis's hand on the top of the desk. Without looking, she reaches up and pulls off a nametag clipped to Chet's outside blazer pocket. As he stands up, pointing at her, she quickly slides it to her lap under the desk. "You think any of them will help you," Chet spits, "a disgraced philanderer who sleeps with her students?" Cut back to breakfast nook.

"How did you know you'd need it?" Emma wonders.

"I didn't; I just took it."

"Lucky break."

"And he had no idea I swiped it," Margolis chuckles. "He was so blind with rage at my female insolence."

"Were you scared?" Brie bites a hangnail on her thumb.

"Of course I was." Margolis turns to her. "I couldn't stop shaking for like ten minutes after he left. But I got this!" She holds up the ID tag.

"OK," Emma impatiently urges, "now you got his key. What do I do?"

"Your job," Margolis points at Emma, "is to case the Orchard Building and assess the security situation. If there are cameras, then you've got to find me a way in. Look for blind spots, memorize the timing of the changes on the security feed."

Emma enters the two sets of double doors at the front of the Orchard building and walks into the foyer reception area. It's right before 5:00 pm, so the place is crawling with people trying their best to get the hell out of there. Suddenly, because Emma is looking for something, the building starts to impose on her. Like she's being watched. Like she's guilty. She sees the security guard sitting at a desk in front of her. He looks up casually, then back down. It takes Emma a minute to swallow her nerves.

She walks up to him and says "Hi."

He barely notices—he's watching videos on his phone.

In front of him, Emma notes, monitors are mounted showing a half-dozen, no eight, views from security cameras. She knows there are more cameras in the building than that. They rotate in succession, about ten seconds on each. Emma sees herself on one of the screens, so she looks up. There, on the ceiling of the atrium is a camera covered in a smoky plastic bubble. She looks around some more. There's another one on the wall near the elevators.

She looks back at the screen—the others seem to be on the upper floors, so that's where she has to go next—get their exact positions in the floorplan. She watches the scenes rotate through one more time, making sure her timing is right.

"Can I help you?" he asks impatiently.

"I'm here to see Mr. Orchard. He's expecting me."

The guard acknowledges with barely a grunt. Emma walks past him to the elevators. As she waits, she looks up at the camera. When the call light on the elevator dings, she sticks out her tongue and makes a funny face before slipping into the car. *Bet he didn't even notice*, she thinks.

On the second floor, she walks down the hall and locates the first camera. She notes its location on a small pad of paper and continues on. Taking the stairs, she does the same on each floor.

On the way back down, the guard stops her. "You didn't have to do that," he says firmly.

"What?" Emma flushes.

"Go to each floor. I could have told you Mr. Orchard's office was on the fourth."

Emma's face goes from fear to fun: "Oh yeah," she giggles. "I hate to ask for directions. Very guyish of me."

"I am about to go on my rounds—I could take you back up."

"Thanks, I found it, but he wasn't even there. Oh well,

guess I'll try again tomorrow," she says with a girlish flick of her hair and marches out the door, the guard shaking his head in the background.

Back in the nook, Margolis continues: "Once Emma gets that intel—"

"*Intel?* She's even using the spy lingo," Eggy teases, pointing at Margolis.

"Once you've got that info—is that better, Eggy?"

"Yes." She stifles a giggle. "Much less nerdy."

"Once you've got that info, Emma," I can break into the building."

"And how's that going to work, Ms. Professor, who's never broken into anywhere in her life?" Sandy pipes in after being silent this whole time.

"I'm going to slip in right before closing time and hide in the bathroom. Once the doors are locked, I'll make my move."

"I don't like it," Sandy shakes her head. "Too dangerous for you. Let me help."

"How can you help? You're only a—"

"What, a secretary?"

Margolis blushes—she didn't mean it that way, but she sits back, face flushed.

"You see," Sandy continues. "People don't appreciate what we mere underlings do for an office. Secretaries, janitors, maintenance crew. Hell, most of you don't even see us. Which means we can get away with a lot. Practically invisible." She looks at everyone around the table, then back at Margolis. "I'll be your distraction. Every movie has one, right?"

Sandy grins knowingly.

"Wow, check out badass here," Eggy clucks.

Sandy smiles. Cut to:

Orchard Building—night. We track down the halls of Chet's building and it's empty, with the exception of the security guard. He's a different one, but like the last, he sits at the front desk entertaining himself.

Down a side corridor, we see the women's bathroom door. We linger there for a moment, as if waiting for someone to come out. But the door stays shut.

Sandy's voice-over: "As Emma discovered, the building is equipped with multiple redundancy cameras on all floors. The views feed to the central guard station, but not all are shown at the same time. They rotate. We just need to confirm the timing of the cycle. I'll send you a signal when it starts over, and that'll give you your window, Santos, of how much time you have to get to the office."

Cut quickly to Margolis who shrugs to the other girls, *OK, Sandy is a badass*, then cut back to the Orchard Building.

Out of another door next to the women's room emerges a cleaning cart, replete with mop, broom, stacks of supplies, and a trash bag hanging in the front. Behind it steps Sandy. She's dressed in an apron like a housekeeping lady. From a crack in the women's bathroom door, we see Sandy steadily shuffle her way to the security desk and stop on the far side. She starts wiping the top of the counter vigorously. For a moment, the guard doesn't even notice her—we can see that he's watching two people doing it doggie-style on his phone—but after about half a minute he looks up, surprised. He quickly puts his phone away.

"Yeah? What do you want?"

"It's really dusty. I'll just start up here, so the dust sifts down to the floor *before* I mop."

"You're not the normal cleaning lady."

"Who, Hermedia?" Sandy snorts. "Nah, she's home sick. Company sent me." Sandy takes out her mop and starts running it across the top of the bar. Some water flicks down on top of the security desk.

"Hey, what'er ya doing? That's not how you're supposed to—"

"It's my technique. Gotta cut the grime." Another pass, and more soapy water flicks near the guard.

He hops up to try to keep it off his tie. "Jesus! Watch it!" He lifts his coffee out of the way and turns to face Sandy, his back toward the bathroom. For a moment, he's not looking.

Margolis holds her breath, peeking out from behind the bathroom door. She turns behind her as she whispers, "You ready?"

There stands Ford Reinhart.

"As ready as I'll ever be," he smiles nervously.

(Emma's voice-over: "Ford? What's he doing here, that traitor. He gave you up to Lane, Glee!")

(Margolis: "Would you be patient? All will be revealed...")

Margolis turns back to the crack in the door. When she sees the guard distracted, she sneaks out of the bathroom and tiptoes her way to a door marked "stairs." She opens the door, Fords slips into the stairwell, and she follows behind.

Back at the checkpoint, Sandy continues wiping around the top of the desk with her mop. At the end, she puts it back in her cart and grabs a rag.

"Alright," she announces, "gotta get back here. Excuse me."

She pushes her way past the guard, sits in his chair, and starts wiping furiously, lifting his things and knocking a few on the floor.

"Ah, come on!" he whines.

Sandy pays no mind to him but continues wiping.

Climbing the stairs, Margolis goes over the camera timing in her head. She knows that there will be one right on the door as she emerges from the stairwell on the top floor where Chet's office is. That means she can't go early, or she'll be caught. At the door, she stops, closes her eyes nervously, and waits. The sound of an exhaled breath. She can feel Ford standing next to her, hardly breathing at all.

"You know, it's not too late to pull out of this." Margolis turns her head to Ford. "Your parents would be so pissed if they found out you were involved in a robbery."

"I know," Ford smirks. "Kinda would make it worth getting

caught."

Margolis looks him hard in the eye and sees that he means it. For a minute, she had wondered if he'd only agreed to come along out of remorse, as a kind of make-up for his testimony against her at the hearing. But she sees his sincerity.

Back to Sandy downstairs at the desk. All the while she cleans, she has her eye on the security cameras on the computer monitors in front of her. First, she takes note of the timestamp. It reads 8:08:45...46...47. Then watches the camera feeds. The various camera views rotate clockwise around the screen, and it doesn't take Sandy long to get the pattern. When it starts over, she begins counting in her head. Feigning to be done with dusting, she gets up.

"Okay, thanks, all finished." She smiles at the guard as she walks around him to her cart. "I'm off to clean the john."

"Whatever," the guard mumbles under his breath as he sits back down in his seat. He picks up a chocolate donut topped with soapsuds like icing. He frowns and tries to brush them off before he takes a bite.

As Sandy pushes her cart toward the men's room, she takes out her phone and quickly thumbs out a text. She hits send and starts to whistle as she slides her phone into her back pocket.

Eyes still closed, Margolis raises her watch and puts her hand on the timer, waiting. Then she feels her phone vibrate in her pocket—it's the text from Sandy, the signal about the security camera pattern—Margolis starts her timer. It's her mark that the cameras on the guard's monitor have switched.

Margolis opens her phone and looks at the text from Sandy: "120 second rotation, start 8:14:45."

The building has 16 cameras, but only eight can show on the monitor at a time, so they rotate on each over about 80 seconds. That means she'll have about 40 seconds to get from the stairs to Chet's door before the camera in that hall comes back up on the guard's screen. Looking at her watch, she does the calculation in her head for the next opening. She waits and when the start rolls around, she pushes the stairwell door and slips out into the hall.

Margolis's feet flurry down the low-carpeted floors. She doesn't run, which might flag some motion sensor or be conspicuous if her camera happens to come up before she's out of the hall. But she doesn't walk either. She's hastened by the thumping of pulse in her neck.

At Chet's door, the two stop. Margolis takes the key card from around her neck and swipes it through the lock. Nothing. Ford looks nervously behind them. She does is again, quicker this time. But it buzzes a negative dee-dum and flashes a red light.

"Come on!" Margolis fights a swelling sense of panic rising in her face. She takes a breath, lines the card up, and drags it through, slow and steady. This time, it beeps up and turns green. She wrenches the knob and lunges into the opening.

Back at the desk, the guard glances over at the monitors. The camera in the hall outside Chet's office comes up. It's clean. He turns back to the video on his phone.

Inside the office, Margolis breathes heavily, leaning back against the door. Ford watches her. She knows that her pose is a movie cliché—the intrepid cat-burglar breathing against the door having narrowly escaped detection—but she has to take a moment to regain her wits, which is hard to do with the motor of her heart racketing like a washer out of balance.

Margolis opens her eyes knowing that she only has so much time to search for what she needs. But as she steps toward to the huge mahogany desk in the center of the office, she looks up at the painting of old man Orchard on the back wall. It stops her in her tracks.

Suddenly, she hears a voice: "This will never work."

It's Cicero. He's right up against her likes he's whispering a secret in her ear.

She waves him off petulantly. "Would you shut up?"

Ford halts. "But I didn't say anything."

Margolis glances at Ford. His words are loud and rouse her from her reverie. She puts her finger to her lips. Without saying anything, she goes to the desk. She glances across the top, which is almost perfectly clean and clear.

"Jeez, there's not even a computer," Ford notes.

"That's just one less thing we have to break into. Plus," Margolis points out, "Orchard does not strike me as a man who would leave electronic records of anything. Too old school. He's all about paper, which is good for us."

Margolis slides around the back of the desk, and sits. She pulls at the center drawer, but it's locked. She nods at Ford.

Ford hurries over as Margolis scoots back in Chet's massive leather chair. He kneels in front of her and pulls out what look like two dental instruments: long, thin metal blades with hooked or jagged ends. Inserting one and then another into the lock, Ford applies tension as he wriggles and turns the picks. Within moments, the lock turns and he slides open the drawer. He turns back and winks at Margolis. She gives him a sidelong look, impressed.

(Margolis's voice-over: "See Emma, that's why we bring Ford along.")

(Emma nods, *who knew?*)

With the center drawer open, Margolis can now look through the other drawers in the desk. She motions Ford to start with a filing cabinet against the back wall.

"What am I looking for?" he whispers.

"You know, anything that has to do with recruiting." She waves and turns back to the desk. "Itineraries, financials, budgets, meeting minutes...anything."

Ford turns to the cabinet and has the lock popped in a blink.

"Oh," suddenly, she turns back to Ford, "and keep an eye out for construction invoices for repairs at the U. Maybe 2-3 years ago."

He nods, pulls out the first drawer, and starts fingering through the files.

She doesn't find stuff at first but things start to emerge. Scripts for roofies, receipts for hotels and bar tabs in recruits' names.

Ford finds the construction invoices.

"I've gone through the filing cabinets," Ford announces. He starts looking around the back wall for more places to look.

"Good." Margolis closes the last door on the desk. "I'm done too. I'm just a little disappointed we didn't find more financials, you know, payment records, et cetera." Margolis looks around the desk one more time just to make sure she didn't miss something. "You know, maybe there's another place they keep these records. Some place more—"

"Safe?"

Margolis turns toward Ford, and there he stands, where the picture of old man Orchard is swung away from the wall to reveal a combination safe.

"Exactly!" Margolis jumps to her feet. "Can you crack it?"

"Pssh, no way! Lockpicking is one thing, but this tumbler is another." He reaches his hand for the latch. "But you know, I've heard half the time people hide these things because they are too lazy to..." Ford pulls up on the latch, just for shits and giggles, "...lock them."

It releases and the door swings open. He stands there agape at the open safe.

"Yes!" Margolis zips over to the safe and stares inside. Stacks of cash, a handgun, passports, and other papers—*just like you'd see in a fricking movie*, she thinks to herself.

"Just like in a friggin movie," Ford observes. Margolis glances at him wryly.

Atop the piles of bills, she sees some files and a black ledger. She gingerly pulls it out, careful not to disturb the contents of the safe too much.

She takes a step back and opens the ledger. She glances up one side, then down the other. Slowly, a smile uncurls across her face.

"What is it?" Ford presses, wondering what it could be that causes this reaction. It's hard for him not to notice how pretty her face looks in this low light.

"This is it. The motherload. The financials for the entire Raven Foundation—income, even from the variety show, expenses for recruits, their bar tabs, bank account numbers for all of it, and check stubs with amounts paid directly to Lucille Bontemps, housemom of the Thetas. That'll link us directly to the sex diary and then, once we crack its code, to individual Thetas. To all of the 'students' who testified against me at my hearing."

Margolis takes out her phone and starts taking photos of the pages.

"There's even a payout to Detective Pantucci—guess we can't trust her either," Margolis sighs. "And most of all—here it is—the way funds were flowing from Chet into the university. Even a slush fund for 'administrative entertainment.'"

"That's got to be for President Lane," Ford points out.

Margolis flips a page and takes more photos. After a few more, she slams the book shut and takes it back to the safe. She starts to wedge it again under the other stuff in the safe.

"What are you doing?"

"Putting it back."

"But we need that book. It ties everything together, just like you said."

"But it's inadmissible in court and would make for boring visuals in our film. Besides," Margolis grunts as she forces the ledger finally back into place. "We don't want to raise suspicions. We still have to finish this film and we need time. We won't have it if they know we're on to them, which they will if we take this book. Plus," she puts her hand on his shoulder, "I've got the pics. They'll be good enough to trace bank records and other paperwork, to corroborate the Slut Diary. Now we can connect the dots. With a little luck, it will even be enough to warrant a subpoena for this ledger and other files in Orchard's stash."

"Great, but," Ford glances at his watch, "now, it's time to go."

Margolis steps to the door and stops. "The camera cycle repeats every 80 seconds, right?"

"I don't know. You're the brains here!" Ford hisses.

Looking at her watch, she does the calculations in her head when the hall camera will rotate off the monitor. Ford impatiently waits for her to move. She puts her right hand on the doorknob, eyes still on the watch. When the second hand rolls around again, she pulls the door open.

"Go." Margolis steps into the hall and looks both ways. Ford follows her as she turns left, back the way they came. They practically tiptoe down the hall toward the stairwell exit. Out of nowhere, Margolis's pocket vibrates; she quickly pulls out the phone. A text from Sandy: "GUARD ON HIS WAY UP!"

They hear a *ding* and stop, frozen, right in front of the elevators. Margolis looks up. Ford can see the *O shit!* look on her face.

The doors open. Looking down at a clipboard, the security guard steps out, and when he lifts his head, surprise flashes over his face.

"Hey, who are you?" He stops dead staring them up and down with a glare.

A moment of hesitation, Margolis isn't sure what to do. Ford is freaking. Then she smiles. "My word!" A slight but definitely fake southern accent flips in her voice. "You scared me!" She giggles low and puts her hand to her chest. "I wasn't expecting anyone this late at night." The guard about to speak, Margolis jumps in, "I'm Cherry Valance. This is Johnny." She gestures to Ford without looking.

The guard looks at him, then back at Margolis, smile still lingering on her face.

"I don't remember you being on my list," he puzzles, pulling out his clipboard again.

Margolis takes a step forward. "Oh, that's because it was last minute, hon." She touches his hand holding the list. "We were just here to do a little research."

"Research?"

"You know, into the foundation. Johnny and I just inherited a large fortune and are looking for worthy causes—"

"That may be so, ma'am, but I can't let anyone up here after hours." He reaches for the radio on his shoulder and presses the com. "Um, central, I've got some unauthorized visitors..."

"Now there's no need for that, officer." Margolis removes her hand.

"...at the Orchard Building. Requesting back-up for assistance. Possible trespass—"

A deep voice comes from behind Margolis: "It's okay, P-Roe. They're with me."

P-Roe takes his hand off the radio. "Mr. Andouille! I didn't know you were—central, cancel that request, over."

Mickey walks up next to a stunned Margolis and smiles broadly at the guard. "I wanted to give them a tour of the foundation but knew I was going to be late. I appreciate your vigilance, but it's all cool." Mickey turns to Margolis. "Y'all were going to leave without me?"

Margolis shrugs.

P-Roe looks confused. "Why didn't I see them come in the lobby?"

"I don't know," Mickey grins as he escorts Margolis and Ford onto the elevator, "too much internet porn?"

P-Roe's face goes red.

"It's all good, I won't tell." Mickey's grin continues as the elevator doors close on P-Roe, left standing in the hall alone.

Down in the lobby, Mickey hurries Margolis through the lobby, his arm in hers.

Margolis: "Good thing you came when you did." She puts her hand on his arm. He notices.

"Thank Brie. She called the cavalry. But I had a feeling

something like this might happen. You know you're not a real sleuth, right?" He grins.

"Strictly amateur." She smiles back.

"Did you get what you need?"

"Yeah, I think so. There was so much—"

"Good. Then you better get outta here before P-Roe really does get suspicious and calls in reinforcements."

He takes a step back and points toward the door. Ford is already on his way out.

Margolis lingers for a moment, walking slowly backward facing Mickey. She mouths the words, "Thank you."

Mickey calls out as Margolis and Ford head for the door: "Hey, maybe we can get that date when all this is done!"

"Maybe," Margolis smiles over her shoulder.

Cut back to the women in the breakfast nook, later:

Eggy: "I gotta hand it to you, Santos. Brilliant plan."

Emma: "Except for the almost getting caught part."

Brie: "Yeah, *My Mom the Convict*. Our next movie."

Eggy: "Good thing Sandy was there for you."

Brie: "And Mickey. He really came through."

Emma: "As did Brie." They exchange a nice smile—they're both finally good.

They look over all the evidence spread out before them—invoices, receipts, memos, video footage on a tablet.

"Looks like we have everything we need to nail these guys," Eggy notes.

"Not everything—we need Theta confessions," Margolis sighs.

Emma: "And we have to put it together into a compelling film. If we don't, nobody will see it."

"Keep in mind," Sandy rains on the parade, "it's likely Orchard is going to find out you're on to him. No telling what he'll do."

They look at each other, a little worried.

Margolis: "Yeah. The clock is ticking."

Part 6: A Final

I.

A knock on the office door.

Ronnie, Chet's security chief, pops his head in. "Got a minute?"

Chet is busy at his desk, looking down at papers through reading glasses. "Better be important."

Ronnie steps in and strides over to Chet's desk. "I think you're gonna want to see this." He hands Chet a thumb drive.

Chet looks up at him blankly. "What is that?"

"A thumb drive," Ronnie says, matter-of-fact.

"Fool, I don't have a computer." Chet frowns.

Ronnie figuratively kicks himself and pulls his laptop out from his satchel and places it on the desk. He opens it and inserts the drive.

"It's the file marked 03/20. March 20th. Almost a month ago." Ronnie makes a few clicks. A video pops up on screen.

"What am I looking at?" Chet squints.

"Today in our security briefing, we were going over the unauthorized visitor policy for the building. One of the guards mentioned an incident on this date. This is the camera in the lobby—the relevant footage starts around the 8:42:00 pm timestamp."

"Who is this guard?"

"Paul Rover, the guys call him P-Roe for short."

"P-Roe?" Chet lifts his eyebrow. "My building is guarded by a dude named 'P-Roe'?"

Frowning, Ronnie points; Chet turns back to the screen.

Roll black-and-white security cam footage of Margolis, Ford, and Mickey entering the lobby with P-Roe. Chet's eyes dart between the three visitors, recognition rising in his face.

"They're coming from the elevator into the lobby before exiting the building, indicating they had been upstairs," Ronnie explains, "so I went to check the footage from the upper floors, and I couldn't see when they got in, which means they knew the security feed and were timing the cameras."

"Where did they go in the building?" Chet asks anxiously.

Ronnie reaches down and clicks on the keyboard. Insert more black-and-white footage of P-Roe with the visitors standing outside an elevator. "Your floor, the fourth."

Red starts rising from his collar, and Chet looks up at Ronnie. "Were they in my office?"

"I don't know for sure—there's no cameras in here, and this is the first time they show up on the security footage that day. I would assume the worst, sir."

Chet bangs a fist down on his desk—the laptop jumps with the blow. He sits back and puts his hand to his mouth, working frantically with thought. With a sudden realization, Chet looks at the portrait behind the desk and jumps out of his chair. He swings the picture back and wrenches open the safe.

"You should lock that, sir," Ronnie observes casually.

Chet ignores the remark and searches frenetically through the contents looking for anything missing. Gun, money, ledger, jewels—all there—*wait,* Chet always replaces the ledger spine out—he's a stickler for those rituals—lets him know if anyone has been fucking with his stuff. But he's taken it out so many times over the last month, he can't remember if it was ever different.

Chet turns around, leaving the safe open. On his face there's total calm but inside there's panic—he knows that he could be cooked.

"Ronnie, I want you to go through all my files—see if anything is missing. If Margolis Santos is able to do *anything* with these papers," Chet gestures back to the safe, "we'll all do a lot of prison time." He locks eyes with Ronnie. "Make sure that doesn't happen. You got me?"

"Understood." Ronnie heads for the door.

"Do I even need to utter the line about making it look like an accident?"

Over his shoulder, Ronnie gives an irritated glare. Then he

turns the knob and is gone.

*   *   *   *

"Okay, okay, listen up everybody. Today and for the rest of the month, we're talking about the western. It's our last unit before the final exam, and in some ways we've saved the most important for last. Who loves westerns?"

Margolis looks around the room to the tune of silence. Students look around dumbly at each other. No raised hands.

"See? The genre has fallen out of favor lately, so your generation has not been exposed to these films. Back in my day—way back in the stone ages of the late 20th Century (chuckles)—we had some of the greatest westerns, nay, greatest *films*, of all time: *Dead Man, Lonesome Dove, Silverado, Dances with Wolves, Legends of the Fall, Lone Star,* and of course, *Unforgiven.* Now you've got what? Bupkis.

"But make no mistake—the western is not only the most quintessentially American of movie genres, it's also the genre that defines cinematic form itself. The basic plot of all westerns—set-up, confrontation, and resolution through a 'showdown'—is the basic plot for almost every movie, particularly those made in Hollywood. Sure, the origins of this plot structure are ancient, but the western gave us the vocabulary that we best know it by. After all, what movie, no matter the genre, doesn't have a 'showdown'?"

Margolis shrugs emphatically, making a humorous face.

"We've talked about the American origins of many of the other genres, like film noir, but the western is the only genre that is almost exclusively set, and in fact, made possible by, America. There would be no such genre if it were not for the wide-open, vast scenery of the American West, stretching from the Plains through the Rocky Mountains to the Pacific Coast. And there would be no westerns without the particular history of America, including so-called 'manifest destiny,' the genocide of Native Americans, the Civil War over slavery, and the myth of the 'wild west.'

"Although they are uniquely American, westerns over their history became an international phenomenon. Almost always set in the American West, these films are made all over the world. The ones made in Italy after World War Two are lovingly referred to as 'spaghetti westerns.'

"Although I just said 'most,' westerns aren't always set in what we would think of as the 'Old West' either."

"Does *Serenity* count?" a student asks. "You know, based on Joss Whedon's awesome TV series, *Firefly*?"

"Absolutely! I mean, after all it is basically 'cowboys in space,' set in a dystopic future after a war that ended a libertarian rebellion against the federal government, where people have colonized other planets, and everybody cusses in Chinese. Hell, the characters even carry six-shooters in holsters—what's more western than that?!"

Margolis shrugs gleefully. The students are wondering, *why is she in such a good mood?*

"Finally, the western is the most basic film genre because it, more than any other genre, boils conflict down to its most essential form, that between good and evil. Hero versus bad guy. Law-and-order versus outlaw. Although some late westerns after the 1960s muddy these waters and show the grey shades between these two poles, especially with the advent of the 'anti-hero' (which we'll talk about next time)—"

As if "next time" were a cue, the students start packing up in a loud shuffle.

"I didn't say put away your things!" She looks at the clock. "It's not even time—I have one more point to make—most westerns center on the universal and timeless fight between what is right and what is wrong. Even a postmodern, revisionist western like *Unforgiven* has a moral center in which an aging gunfighter, who has done lots of bad things in his day, helps a group of abused prostitutes by taking out the corrupt sheriff and his henchmen in a blazing showdown that, for all intents and purposes, ended the western as we know it. It was that good.

"Okay, so that's all. Watch *Unforgiven* and we'll talk about the anti-hero next time."

II.

Although the campus of Athens U is green most of the year—what with the climate and all the evergreen live oaks and magnolias and such—it's particularly beautiful in the spring. That's when the flowers and all the literal birds and bees break out into a colorful frenzy. Now the walks and plazas are lined with pink azaleas, purple pansies, orange tiger lilies, and myriad other varieties that few know, except maybe Margolis. The lawn on the quad is the quality you'd find at Augusta National golf course, and sometimes you even see shirtless dudes out there putting and chipping away at their little white balls.

Granted, the admin spends a shitload on landscaping and water. There's always a mower, weed-eater, sprinkler, or blower going somewhere around the forty acres or so of greenery. Art Lane once announced smugly to the faculty senate that the U turned down an eco-friendly LEED rating because it would require them to turn off the sprinklers and replace grass with more local, drought-resistant species. Lane said no fucking way. But what he was really saying was that green is the color of the University, and without the green of the grass there will be less green in the coffers. In that sense, green is the color of every university.

Today, Margolis isn't noticing flowers or any of the beauty around her. She's not dressed in her usual, flamboyant flowing garb—she has on jeans, a t-shirt, leather jacket, and a baseball cap, which she pulls down as far as she can on her sunglasses. She doesn't want to be noticed—this place feels foreign now, oppressive, and it fills her with paranoia.

She passes by a "Lane for U.S. Senate" sign with a balloon tied to it, flapping in the breeze.

Although she feels better about being in her house, with the new security system and Mickey checking in often, it didn't seem right to keep all the footage there after the break-in.

Margolis herself in a fit of over-confidence told Emma and Brie, "We'll edit the film where they least expect it—right under their noses!" But now she's thinking it wasn't such a good idea to use the campus computer labs to finish the film. Too public, too exposed, maybe even vulnerable to hacking from administrators.

Margolis tugs at her cap again as she passes the frat boys and their golf clubs. Their eyes follow her as they ogle her over their cups of vodka and Red Bull.

What Margolis doesn't see is Ronnie walking 20 steps or so behind her. Frat boys pay him no mind neither, since he's dressed in a suit, could be any university pencil-neck. Unaware, Margolis keeps her head down and hurries on toward the lab. It's in her old building, Hartley Hall, which feels weird as she opens the door and steps into the cool air conditioning.

On the second floor, Margolis passes Sandy's office. *Shit.* Margolis doesn't want to see anybody because she's not supposed to be there. At first, Sandy doesn't wave or anything; she just watches Margolis knowingly; then, at the very end, just before she passes out of Margolis's sight, there's a nod. Of approval. Encouragement. It makes Margolis relax just a bit.

Ronnie makes his way up the stairs just in time to see Margolis slip into the computer lab. He avoids Sandy's office and takes a seat in the hall to wait.

In the lab, Emma and Brie huddle close to each other peering at a screen where we see Eggy's upper body and face but can't hear what she's saying—the girls have headphones on—and it just looks like they're watching a talking head. Margolis looks around at the other students in the lab and wonders what they'd think if they heard what Eggy was saying about their University. *Well, soon, they'll find out, I guess,* Margolis thinks.

"How's it going?" Margolis hushes, as she sits down next to Brie. They don't even look over.

"There," Emma blurts, pointing to the timeline of the

editing software.

Reaching for the keyboard, Brie hits a key, and the footage splits in two. "And another edit here?"

"Yeah."

Brie repeats the command and then deletes the clipped footage.

"Show her." Emma takes off the headphones.

"Hi, Mom." Brie looks over and gives a weak smile. "Tell me what you think?"

"You both look wrecked, working so hard," Margolis says. Then to Emma: "You should be studying for your own finals."

"It's gotta get done." Emma hands the headphones to Margolis who puts them over her baseball cap.

Brie clicks the space bar and the footage rolls in the upper right-hand window on the screen. Margolis watches, motionless, for the entire interview.

"It's good. Has the essence of the story." Margolis takes off the headphones and lowers her voice.

"You don't have to say it," Brie mimics her mother's voice. "'It's not going to mean anything without an eyewitness—'"

"Yes," Margolis agrees, smiling in spite of herself. "We need someone who will admit to participating in the ring and to say who paid them—we've gotta keep working on the Thetas."

Emma sighs again. "I'll take one more crack at it, but I'm telling ya, it's useless—they ain't gonna talk. I mean, would you? You won't let me film myself..."

"I didn't say you couldn't," Margolis corrects. "I just said I'd prefer if you didn't have to. But it may be our last resort."

*   *   *   *

Cut to Emma talking to Brooke in a sorority bedroom:

"Look, you two, the film is almost done. Would you please just let me interview you?" Emma begs. "All you have to do is tell the truth."

"You mean say we fucked guys for money? No way!" Brooke sneers.

Aria looks worriedly over at Emma. "I don't want to get in trouble."

"We're the victims here, Brooke! These boosters exploited us for the football team."

"It wasn't that bad," Brooke shrugs.

"Well, some of us didn't do it all that willingly," Emma insists. "Chet has dirt on my dad, and he held it over my head. What was I supposed to do?"

"Why haven't you interviewed yourself already?" Brooke asks knowingly.

Aria presses her, "Yeah, you're a witness or whatever. You banged that Ryan guy."

"But he was my boyfriend." Emma bends the truth. She wonders silently if she should tell them now. Confess that she too doesn't want to admit that she did such awful things. If she admits she's scared, then maybe it would motivate one of them to talk. But Emma hesitates and loses them.

"Whatever. I guess your shit don't stink..." Brooke raises her lip contemptuously.

"Look, if I testify on camera that I had sex with a recruit in order to get him to sign with Athens, will you do it too?"

Aria and Brooke look at each other, then turn back to Emma. Aria shakes her head sadly.

"No," Brooke bluntly states. "I've cut you slack since Stephanie died, but you need to decide where your loyalty lies, Barnes. If you're gonna be a traitor and tattle on all of us, you can just get your shit and move out. Otherwise, pull your weight."

Brooke gets up and walks past Emma into the hall. As she walks down the stairs of the Theta house, she takes out her phone. Once out the door and in the yard, she dials. As it rings, she turns back to look at the house to make sure no one has followed her.

There's an answer.

"It's me." Brook puts a hand on her hip. "I just found out that Professor Santos is almost done with her movie. And you won't believe who's helping her..."

*　　　*　　　*　　　*

Margolis looks nervously at her phone. She picks it up to dial and puts it down again. After a few repetitions of that, she finally lets it ring.

"Hello—can I talk with Detective Collins?"

She waits while the call is transferred.

"Detective Collins, this is Dr. Margolis Santos—I came to you with the information about sex-for-football at the Delta Delta Theta house?"

"Yeah, but that investigation was dropped."

"And you know why it was dropped, don't you, Detective Collins?"

Collins is silent on the other end. Cut to:

The police department loud with the sound of voices and ringing phones. Collins glances over at his partner, Pantucci, at the next desk typing away at a report.

"Yeah," he says finally.

Margolis's voice, tinny on his phone: "Well, I've got new evidence, and it's big. Meet with me, and I'll show you. And come alone."

"Alright, I gotta go." Collins hangs up the phone.

Pantucci looks over at him and then casually, "Who was that?"

Collins moves papers around his desk like he's distracted and then after a minute says, "Oh, just that crazy Athens professor." It's not really a lie. "She just won't let the football thing go."

"Crazy bitch," Pantucci remarks and then goes back to typing. "Did you tell her to fuck off?"

"Yeah, something like that." Collins surreptitiously checks his cell phone under his desk—he got a new text. It's from Margolis. It reads: "Meet me in the parking lot, Krune's Lake, 8pm."

Collins puts away his phone and watches his partner type for a while.

III.

"Can I have a minute, Coach?" Frank leans into Eggy's office.

"Sure." Eggy nervously slides the red Slut Diary into her desk.

"What was that?"

"Oh, nothing. An old journal," Eggy lies. "Been doing some reflecting on where I'm at."

She pushes her chair back. Frank settles in across from her.

"Ah, I see." He gives her a weak smile. "Hi."

"Hi," she says half expectantly, half braced for the conversation.

"I just wanted to see how you were doing." Frank hesitates, Eggy starts nodding her head, he continues, "I miss you."

"I miss you, too," she says between her teeth. "I don't think that this is the place to talk—"

"No, I know. But this is the only place I see you. You won't return my calls. You're never at home anymore."

"Frank, I—"

"I just want to know what happened to us. See if you might want to try again." He fumbles the words out quickly, afraid she might cut him off. She takes a breath in start of a reply, but he beats her to it: "Look, I know that the job changes things—we're in the same office now, you're a lead member on my staff, and it can't look like I'm playing favorites." He changes tack. "If we stay together, it looks like you got the job because of me and not because of you."

Eggy nods silently, lets him talk.

"And I understand that," Frank continues. "You're a phenomenal coach and you deserve everything you've achieved. That's why I hired you. But..." He looks pointedly at Eggy.

"But?"

"But I also have feelings for you, you know this. And I don't want to have to give us up just because of a public perception problem." He closes his lips tightly, giving her an almost pleading look. "Can't we just go back to the way things were?"

"On the sly?"

"Well, isn't that the only way to have our cake and eat it too?"

Eggy looks at him for a long time, considering her words carefully. She has all the fingertips of both her hands touching in the shape of a diamond. She's rocking slightly back and forth in her chair, quickly, like a fidget. "I know you think that it's just the favoritism that's the main reason why we're not together."

"Well what else is there?"

"My feelings have changed for you, Frank."

"How?"

"I've learned some things. Things that have made me question your character."

Frank is stunned.

"You've been so focused on football, do you even know that—" Eggy hesitates a second, not sure if she should say it.

"That what?" Frank begs.

"That your ex-wife is making a movie about the U?"

"What—so? I knew she was doing something about Stephanie Rogers, but now I guess that's moot."

"Because she's dead," Eggy mumbles.

Frank looks down at his hands. "That was an unfortunate situation. I just pray my players weren't involved like she said."

"Oh, but they were." Eggy's voice goes up. "They still are. I know for a fact because I saw them with Stephanie, Frank. I was there, and I told Margolis about it. For her film. I'm gonna be in it."

Frank is stunned into silence.

Eggy continues in hushed tones, "And that's not all. Margolis has found out somebody is paying Thetas to sleep with recruits when they visit campus so they'll sign with the team. I find it hard to believe that you wouldn't know anything about this."

"Eggy, I, I didn't—"

She doesn't wait for him to finish: "All this has happened on your watch. You say you don't know anything about it, and maybe you don't. I don't know what to believe about you anymore, Frank. All I know is that you hired me to join a sinking ship. And I can't be associated with it."

"What are you saying?"

"That I've already got my feelers out at other programs."

"But you haven't even coached in a single game yet—your historic position—you'd just give it up?" Frank pleads.

Eggy gets out of her chair. As she walks to the door, Frank talks faster, trying to keep her from leaving: "I mean, what if none of this stuff is true? Would you come back to me then?"

Eggy stops at the door and considers. "I don't know, Frank. I just don't know." With a quick turn on her heel, Eggy is out the door, leaving Frank crumpled in a pile on the chair, alone in her empty office.

*   *   *   *

Margolis sits at the breakfast table with her phone to her ear. She's talking to her agent, Jack Carnahan.

"Look, I thought of that already, Jack," Margolis speaks, animated. "I've cut together a few clips that we could use as a trailer or for a news story. We're ready to go." She listens for a long moment. "Well, no, we don't have any sorority girls pointing the finger at boosters who paid them to have sex, but—" Margolis cuts herself off, listening again. "I know that's what they want. I'm still working on it, but even without the eyewitness interviews, it's still a strong film. So much documentary evidence—tell 'em they don't want to pass up this chance, Jack, to have this kind of scoop." Another pause, pause. Pause, "Alright, just let me know. Please."

She hangs up the phone and flops back on her couch. She stares at the ceiling. Discouraged.

The front door swings open, and in steps Brie. "Hi, Mom." she walks over to the couch and plops next to Margolis. "How's it going?"

"Jack can't get any interest from distributors in the film, but other than that," Margolis says sardonically, "it's been a great day."

"Look what I got," she holds a white envelope out to her mother.

Margolis lifts her head. She's happy for the distraction. "What, is that your letter from Athens?"

"You bet!" Brie says excitedly.

"Well, come on, open it!" Margolis pats the space next to her on the sofa. Brie jogs over and sits down. She looks Margolis in the eye as she opens the letter.

Brie stops. "I'm afraid to read it."

"Oh, come on, Brie-Brie, let's see what it says!"

Brie finishes tearing open the flap, slides the letter out and unfolds it. As she reads, her face goes from intense eagerness to sagging sadness. She crumples it into Margolis's lap. Eyes on her daughter, Margolis raises the letter and smooths it out to read better. She now sees the reason for Brie's reaction.

"I'm so sorry, honey, I really thought that you'd get in."

Brie gets up slowly and turns toward her mom. A few months ago, she would have said something biting and blamed her mom for this disaster, but now she doesn't have to— Margolis already feels like shit, as she watches her daughter slouch upstairs and out of sight.

$$*\qquad*\qquad*\qquad*$$

A loud knock wakes Margolis up on the couch in the den. The light has moved across the room, but it's still day. A bit groggy, Margolis checks her phone. Another knock. She gets off her ass and goes to the door.

It's Frank.

"What's this I hear about a film on my football program?" He stomps past her into the den.

"Come on in," Margolis says with sleepy sarcasm.

"You told me you were doing it on the Rogers rape case, but this, these baseless allegations—what the hell?"

Margolis sighs. "It's not about your football program. It's about people who are doing illegal things to promote it."

Frank takes a breath, calms his tone. "Look, Glee. Please don't do this—don't release this film. I'm begging you. Let me handle it internally. I'll take your information to the president, start an investigation—"

"The president? Art Lane?" Margolis laughs. "You really don't know anything about this do you?"

"What do you mean?"

"Lane is part of the conspiracy, Frank. He's the one who gave the green light—how do you think a man like Chet Orchard has such open access to campus and places like the Theta house?"

Frank is dumbfounded. "Wait...no, it can't be true." But the facts are starting to dawn on him—his mind races back to the conversation with Lane back in August, about "doing more off the field to win." He remembers meeting Chet and Mickey for the first time on the practice field. The recruits and co-eds at the banquet, Colby Lennox, Stephanie—it all rushes upon him like a terrible montage. A sinking feeling falls over him, the emasculating sense that he isn't responsible for his own success, that maybe he didn't win his championship through hard work and smarts, that somebody else has been pulling all the strings. Fear of such failure has him paralyzed.

"Frank, I have to see this thing through to the end. It's going to come out one way or the other. At least this way, I can control the narrative." She smiles sadly at her ex-husband.

A sudden flash of anger in Frank's eyes: "Brie texted me

that she didn't get into the U—now we know why—putting your precious job before our family. Again."

"Frank, that's not fair, they are exploiting these girls—"

"And you're exploiting our family! Those girls choose to do illegal things—nobody forced them—they're adults! But Brie didn't choose this—she's collateral damage, Margolis, and you don't seem to care if she gets hurt just as long as you get to make your movie."

Instead of retorting that Brie is 18 and capable of her own decisions, Margolis musters as much empathy as she can—she knows this is hard for him—so she just watches him fume and fidget.

Frank takes his cap off, scratches his head. Resignation falls over him like a lull: "I guess you got what you wanted. I guess we're all ruined. Except you, of course. You'll be big shit after this."

Frank puts on his hat and leaves Margolis with a vicious stare.

*   *   *   *

Springtime is alive with sound. All through the surrounding woods, frogs, crickets, and cicadas fill the air with their evening lays, the harsh and heart-felt appeals for love resonating through their hollow bodies.

Detective Collins puts out a smoke on the gravel next to his car. He wonders if detectives are destined to smoke cigs just like Old West sheriffs are destined to smoke big, fat cigars. The movies didn't make that stuff up—they capture the occupational hazard that substances help one—cowboys, soldiers, cops—get through the stress of the job, and even worse, the boredom.

He's been waiting a quarter of an hour, when a pair of headlights cuts into the parking lot and pulls up next to him. It stops and out get two shadowy figures.

"Detective Collins?" It's Margolis, who closes the door to her Subaru. She and Mickey walk up to Collins: "This is my...associate, Mickey Andouille. He's been a source inside the foundation and the U."

Mickey reaches out to Collins; they shake hands. "It's a pleasure."

"So, you got the evidence?"

"Not exactly," Margolis cautions. "I needed to ask you a few questions first—make sure you're really on our side—you understand."

"Yeah, sure. Shoot."

"Does the name Chet Orchard ring a bell?" Mickey interrogates.

Collins shrugs, gives a price-of-tea-in-China look and ventures a guess. "You mean the oil tycoon. Runs Uncle Jim's Rice? Rich as fuck?"

"Yeah, that's the one."

"OK, so? Everyone in Athens knows who he is."

Margolis: "He's also a key founder of the Raven Foundation."

"The booster organization," Collins confirms.

"Yeah," Mickey answers. "But what most people don't know, but I do, is that he runs the foundation's," Mickey puts in scare-quotes, "'recruit assistance program,' a euphemistic way of saying that they do all they can to make sure the best players come to Athens to play."

"Like what?" Collins asks, dubious.

"Like pay off cops to hush investigations." Margolis hands Collins a tablet with a photo of Chet's ledger. "Do you see there?" She points. "That line indicates that Pantucci received $45,000 from this foundation subsidiary account last month on March 20. That was just one week before Stephanie Rogers's suicide. A day before Pantucci called off the investigation."

Collins looks at the image silently for a few minutes.

Mickey takes the tablet back from him, and Margolis cuts

to the chase: "I can tell you where you can get all these records, but I need something from you first—I need you to come with me to interview some of these sorority members, to assure them that they won't be prosecuted. And I need you to deliver that promise with the backing of someone in the DA's office that you trust."

Mickey: "Do you know someone?"

"Yeah."

"Can you deliver?"

"Maybe. But I gotta do some looking into these allegations about Pantucci—I can't just take on faith that my partner's dirty."

"I'd certainly want to know that myself," Margolis admits. "But, listen Detective Collins, if I'm wrong, you get to go on as you were, maybe have your partner sore at you for a little while when she senses your disloyalty. At worst, maybe she requests a new partner. But if I'm right? This is going to be the biggest case ever to hit Athens PD, and you'll be the one to break it. Imagine the press exposure for the cop who takes down a corrupt college football dynasty." Margolis pauses while Collins takes a long drag. "Anyway, it's gotta be soon—recruitment season is about to start again—and campus visits will mean—"

"More tricks are turned at the Theta house." Collins nods.

"Exactly, if you don't go now, you may miss your chance." Margolis takes back the tablet and looks sternly at Collins. "I'll text you the location of Orchard's records. You just go find out for yourself. Let me know in 48 hours, or I'll know that you're on their side."

With that, she and Mickey turn away. As soon as the engine turns over, they're gone.

* * * *

Inside the brightly-lit arena, the crowd is getting raucous. Chants of "Light-ning Lane, Light-ning Lane, Light-ning Lane!"

rise and fall through the cavernous space with increased frequency. The stage is festooned with balloons and bunting and flags, all in red, white, and blue, while throughout the crowd, there's more than just a splash of the grey, pink, and black.

Suddenly, the crowd goes berserk.

Up the stairs and onto the stage climbs none other than the man himself. The PA system booms, "NCAA national football champion and future Senator of the United States, Art 'Lightning' Lane!"

Lane waves to the ecstatic crowd, and we can hear the Athens's Raven cry of "caw-caw" from all over the building. He stands at the podium and waits minutes for the crowd to settle down.

"Ladies and Gentlemen, Raven fans everywhere..."

"Caw-caw!"

"I humbly accept your nomination to become the next Senator from this great state!"

The crowd roars. A Kid Rock tune blasts through the speakers, as Mrs. Lane joins her husband on stage. Arm-in-arm they smile and wave gratefully to the crowd.

*   *   *   *

With wipers flapping, Margolis and Mickey pull out of the parking lot and turn on to the road bordering the edge of Lake Kune and its surrounding woods. They pass a car parked on the shoulder but don't notice when it pulls out into the road behind them.

"Do you think he'll bite?" Mickey asks, referring to Collins.

"Do you mean do I think he'll help us? I don't see any reason not to if he finds out Pantucci is a bad seed."

"Yeah, but will he take that step?"

Margolis considers that question thoughtfully—it was a gambit to try to entice a cop into working against his partner, all for the sake of career glory—but Margolis knows that her investigation has gotten bigger than just something a filmmaker can handle. She needs the law on her side.

As she adjusts her rearview mirror, she can see two headlights speeding toward her. She watches in disbelief as the car doesn't slow down. It smashes into the back of her car, both her and Mickey lurching forward. The lights recede back in the mirror.

"What the fuck?!" Mickey yells, turning to look back over his shoulder.

Margolis can see the lights approaching again, faster this time. At the last second, the pursuer breaks around the outside of the Subaru, and the driver swerves the wheel so that the front of his car clips Margolis's back panel.

The Subaru begins to hydroplane on the wet road. Margolis steers frantically into the skid, but she loses control of the car, which starts to spin uncontrollably into the middle of the two-lane road. All goes black.

When she comes to, Margolis looks over and sees that Ronnie has the passenger door open and is beating Mickey senseless. With each punch, there's more and more blood coming out of his mouth and nose. Soon, Mickey is unconscious.

Undoing her seatbelt, Margolis pulls the latch and heaves against the door, but it won't open—the car is jammed against a thick hedgerow along the driver's side. With Mickey dispatched, the thug reaches across him and grabs at Margolis. Mickey groans.

Margolis uses Mickey's limp bulk as a kind of shield to climb toward the back seat. But the thug reaches around anyway and takes hold of her dress. She tries to tug free, but he's got her stuck between the seats. She bites down into his knuckles; still he won't let go. Margolis keeps pushing herself away from Ronnie and toward the back, Mickey's body acting like a fulcrum against the thug's arms.

After a few seconds, he can't hold any longer and must let go. As she scrambles into the back seat, she drags her book bag with her, and its contents spill all over the center console, some to the floorboards.

Ronnie pulls himself back and shuts the car door. Although she can't see where he is through the fogged windows, Margolis jumps forward, reaching through Mickey's seatbelt and locking the door. She lunges at the back door just in time to lock it before Ronnie pulls up on the handle. Locked out.

There's a brief moment of stillness before a loud crash shatters the back window. The elbow of a wool jacket flexes where the glass once was. Margolis jumps, tries not to scream.

Without bothering to open the door, he reaches into the back seat to drag her out. There's a kind of tug-of-war: he gets her neckline, but she falls back on the cushion, the gauzy fabric of her dress stretching to allow her to lay back, her feet braced against the door. She jams her head into the door on the other side, trying to get as far away from him as possible.

Bending at the hip, he leans further in, body more than halfway in the back seat, and grabs her with the other arm. She strains against the force of his grip, but he manages to pull her into a sitting position.

Their faces almost touch, eyes locked.

She recognizes him in an instant—he's the one who followed her, in the peacoat, who broke into her house when Brie was home, the one she pepper-sprayed in the face—Chet's thug.

Margolis suddenly thinks of Cicero and remembers the time after she got beat up again in elementary school. Flashback to the two of them standing in the back yard of their house. The lapels of her sweater all wrinkled, Margolis cowers in front of her dad who yells at her like she's a private: "Again. What if some punk grabs you here," Cicero takes her lapels in both hands, "and pulls you in close? You can't use your arms to strike back—does that mean you're finished? No! You got the

hardest part of your body available front-and-center!"
Margolis's face frozen in a helpless stare, Cicero head-butts
her. Not that hard, but hard enough to knock her head back.
Margolis sees stars.

As Margolis rears her head back, her black hair whips
forward as her forehead crashes into Ronnie's. He staggers
back from the blow, his crown hitting the top of the car window
as he pulls himself out into the street. He tries to shake it off.
With a snarl, he reaches into his peacoat and pulls out a large
handgun.

Margolis desperately looks around the back seat for a way
out and there, on the armrest between the front seats, she spies
a pen-like object.

Her laser pointer.

Ronnie steps forward, extends the gun, and takes aim.

Exactly then, Margolis shines the pointer into Ronnie's
face. The red dot wiggles around his brow and forehead, but in
a second, the beam finds his pupil. He puts his hand up to the
blindness.

In his hesitation, Margolis lurches for the latch. She thrusts
her legs forward and her feet propel the door open with
explosive force. It hits Ronnie square in the abdomen, and as
he flies back his frightened eyes linger momentarily on
Margolis.

Then, WHAM! A speeding truck pancakes him straight out
of view.

Margolis gawks through the back window, trying to see
where he went, but she can't—too shaky. She falls back on the
seat. For what seems like the longest moment, she hears the
squeal of the tires against blacktop as the truck grinds to a halt.

When it does, all Margolis can hear is the dull idle of the
truck's engine. Everything else is still.

Suddenly, Mickey comes to, coughing blood onto the
windshield. He looks around, dazed, then frantic. He finds
Margolis lying in the back seat.

"Margolis." He panics when she doesn't respond. "Margolis!"

Margolis slowly opens her eyes, arms up across her forehead, and looks at him.

"You okay?"

She nods.

He sighs in relief, then with a quizzical look: "How'd you get back there?"

Margolis's mouth crinkles into a deep laugh that shakes her entire upper body. Once she starts, she can't stop. Mickey struggles with his seatbelt but gets it undone. He belaboredly exits the car and surveys the carnage in disbelief. He sees two long black and one red skid-mark that lead up to the truck, an Uncle Jim's Rice truck, Mickey ironically notes. His eyes follow the trail to the mangled figure in the middle of the road; the peacoat now torn and bloody.

Mickey looks back at the still-laughing Margolis as he touches the contusions on his face gingerly. Sirens begin to wail in the distance. The rain has stopped, but droplets continue to fall from the leaves above them.

Margolis's laugh gradually shifts into profound sobs.

*   *   *   *

"The one necessary condition—the one ingredient that all westerns share—is the gun.

"Now, I'm not saying that any movie with a gun is a western. No. Gangster films almost always have guns, as do action films. What I'm saying is that every western has a gun in it. It cannot be a western without a gun."

"And perhaps that's one of the reasons for the decline of the genre. Sure, most American movies have guns in them, but we just don't expect everyone to wear a gun walking around in real life. For the majority of the 20th century, guns were a non-issue in politics. In fact, society's advancement was once measured by how little one needed guns. Now? They are a huge controversy. And in that climate, maybe the idea of the shootout or the gunslinger just isn't that entertaining anymore..."

*   *   *   *

Sitting at his desk, Collins strains to look out of the corner of his eye at Pantucci without being detected. She pours over case files in a large stack in front of her. Her jacket is off. The back of her grey blouse hangs untucked through the seat of her office chair. She looks haggard with wisps of long hair straying from the tight bun on the back of her head. Since she's so absorbed, he hopes that he can just stand up and walk out with her saying a word. He's got another meeting with the professor in ten minutes, and he should have left five minutes ago. He watches the clock nervously. *Now. Wait, no. Three, two, one. Okay, now.*

Collins pushes back his chair, grabs his coat off the rack, and heads out of the cubicle.

"Where you going?" Pantucci asks, as she casually leans back in her chair. "It's a little early to cut out." She looks at her watch.

Collins stops, rolls his eyes in mock indignation. "Dentist appointment," he says. "Fucking root canal."

"No shit. Really? That sucks ass. I didn't know you had a bum tooth. Hid it well."

"Pain killers." He points to his jaw.

Pantucci jerks her head up once slightly in understanding. "Be sure to save a couple for me," she smirks and turns back to her stack.

Collins relaxes in relief and takes a step toward the door.

"Oh, wait!" Pantucci calls. Collins turns back and peeks over the divider wall. "Did you hear that Athens film professor was involved in a big smash-up?" she inquires. "Guys in Traffic say there were reports of a struggle, some kind of attack. Perp got hit by a truck. Weird, huh?"

"No, I hadn't heard," Collins replies as evenly as he can. He looks plainly at Pantucci who looks back searchingly, as if plumbing him for unseen depths. *Don't react,* he reassures himself, *it's just a detective habit—she has no reason to suspect you.*

She holds his eyes for what seems like another 30 seconds.

"Okay," she relents. "Maybe we should look into it. You know, just to make sure. Probably isn't a connection."

"You got it."

"Get the hell outta here, would ya? Just the sight of your mouth is making *my* teeth ache."

Without a word, Collins turns on a heel, and we see him walk out, tension draining from his face.

*   *   *   *

Margolis sips coffee and wonders why Detective Collins wanted to meet in public, particularly if he's afraid of his partner finding out. Then the thought occurs to her, maybe he isn't. Maybe he wants Pantucci to know. The thought of all the subtle politics of law enforcement excites her, but she tries to tamp it down. *Stay cool.* But for once it seems like everything is going her way. Collins's voice brings her out of her thoughts.

"Are you sure it was Chet's guy—how do you know?"

"Of course I know it was Chet's guy—I saw his face, didn't I? Though from what I hear it's hardly recognizable now..."

"The coroner is working to identify him through dental records. Fingerprints aren't in the database."

"Fine. Whoever it was tried to kill me, a nobody college professor. Why? Because I've uncovered their shithole secret. Are you convinced now?"

"Well, it certainly seems that you've stirred a hornet's nest."

"And are you gonna help me get rid of it?" Margolis raises her eyebrows.

"I did some looking into Pantucci's relationship with Orchard, and there definitely is one—call logs and duty sheets at the department—she's called and visited him multiple times. But it could be for anything."

"Without you there? Doesn't that seem very suspicious to you?"

Collins pauses, blows on his coffee, and sips. "Yeah. Yeah, it does."

"So, you're on board."

"I'm on board. But you understand I can't work as a detective, right? My involvement would simply be on the side, as a consultant on your film until it comes out."

"I understand. Will you do it?"

Collins grins. "Alright. What's first, Detective Santos?"

A new sense of purpose swells up in Margolis. "Let's start with the Thetas. We need them to talk."

*   *   *   *

Margolis returns home after her midnight meeting with Collins to find all the girls still up—Eggy, Brie, Emma, and Sandy. They've basically moved in and taken a bunker mentality since the attempt on Margolis's life, but she's hoping that the news about Collins will lift their morale.

When Margolis walks in the door, the girls look up at her, silent, like they've just been talking about her.

"What?" Margolis asks. "What is it?"

They all look at each other, wondering who'll go first. They all are sitting up straight on sleeping bags and comforters strewn across the sectional in the den. Junk food and soda cans litter every surface in the room. Glued to the TV, they haven't left since the accident.

"We've been talking," Brie starts. After all, Margolis is her mom, they figure.

"Obviously."

"And we're scared, Margolis," Sandy confesses.

"Breaking into buildings was one thing," Emma points out. "That risk was kinda fun even."

"Yeah," Brie agrees, smiling at Emma, who turns her face away.

"But people trying to kill you? And Mickey?" Eggy adds. "That's fucked up."

"They've broken into your house, Margolis. Your house, with Brie in it!" Sandy implores Margolis but points at Brie.

Eggy adds, "When will they stop?"

"Like Sandy said," Emma mumbles hesitantly, "we're scared. We don't think we should work on the film anymore." She looks guiltily at Margolis; Emma knows she's let her down.

"Yeah, let's stop it now before anyone else gets hurt," Sandy rejoins.

Egg adds pointedly, "It could be one of us next."

Nods and noises of agreement around the room. Except Brie. She's hoping her mom can talk them all out of this funk.

"But," Margolis objects energetically, "I was just coming home to tell you that Detective Collins has agreed to help us. He thinks he will be able to offer any Theta who talks a deal to avoid prosecution."

"He thinks? You mean it's not a done deal."

"Well, he's got to work on the DL unofficially with us for now to avoid raising suspicion, but when the story breaks, he'll be able to negotiate with the DA officially."

"You mean *if* the story breaks."

"We may not survive to make it."

Sad and uncertain looks cloud all around the room.

"Come on, guys!" Brie interjects. "You're letting your fear talk for you. Don't you understand how huge Collins's involvement is? We can finally get our interviews!"

"It's not about interviews anymore, Brie." Emma says

sadly. Brie feels cut.

"And it's not about us or us getting stuff on film." Eggy puts her hands in her lap.

"Or the glory of bringing down bad guys."

"This is no longer about you, Margolis."

Margolis stops, deflated. It's not that she feels betrayed exactly, but guilty. She's been blind to the risk she's been putting these people in, these women she loves and respects. They've become sisters-in-arms through this ordeal, she knows it in her bones, but perhaps they are right. Perhaps she's let that feeling of camaraderie blind her to the danger. She can't risk anything happening to any of them. It would be on her conscience forever.

"OK, you're right. It's too risky. I'll pull the plug. Hand it off to Collins."

The room releases tension with a collective sigh of relief.

*   *   *   *

Margolis lies awake in her bed—she can't sleep—so she swings her legs out and gets up to leave. At the bottom of the stairs, she stands, looking at the four women sleeping peacefully in her living room. The glow from streetlamps against the blinds floods the room with a faint light. She can see the relief on their faces, the innocence that comes from certainty, from not having a terrible decision to make.

Cicero stands next to her, but she doesn't look at him. He doesn't look at her.

He speaks: "You may be able to head-butt some two-bit thug, Glee, but these bigshots—Orchard and them? You'll never touch them with all their money and influence. They've got your balls in a sling."

"I don't have any balls, Dad. I'm a girl," Margolis responds dispassionately.

"Face it, babe." He says, with a strange soothing voice,

"You're finished."

Margolis draws her shoulders back, turns around, and marches decidedly up the stairs.

Margolis goes to Brie's room, tentatively pushes open the door. "Bee?"

A moment of silence, then, "Yeah."

Margolis shuffles to the bed and sits down next to her daughter. She strokes Brie's hair in the faint light. "They are right you know."

Brie bristles under the covers and turns her back to Margolis.

"You are my fighter," Margolis says soothingly. "You always have been. You have such strong convictions, passions, and I admire you for it."

"I sense the world's biggest 'but' coming..."

"You have the world's biggest butt, ha ha," Margolis jokes.

Brie can't help but smile.

"I want you to leave town, go to Grandma's—"

"But I could help you! We could finish this thing together, remember? Mother and daughter!"

Margolis feels the strong pull of that, yet: "No, it's too dangerous, and you are already too wrapped up in all of this...Theta business."

"But Mom!"

"Don't argue with me. I want you to promise me that you'll leave first thing in the morning."

Brie is silent.

"Brie!" Margolis insists.

"Okay, okay. You win. I'll go." Brie sighs.

"Thank you," Margolis leans down and kisses her only child on the forehead. "There will be other battles. I'll let you know when it's safe to come back. Alright?"

"Alright."

Margolis stands and opens the door. She looks back longingly at Brie. Such a big girl now. A woman, it seems. She slips out of the room and shuts the door.

Behind Brie's back, we see both of her hands, double fingers crossed.

IV.

From inside the grey metal safe, we peer out at Chet's face. He's looking over the things stacked in there and frowns. He reaches his arm inside, and it hovers there, casting a shadow over the leather-bound ledger. Suddenly, he grabs it, along with the gun, and shuts the safe.

Chet strides through his office and a door to his reception area. Chet's secretary, Birdie Johnson, sits at her desk, focused on the screen two feet from her eyes. Even with glasses, she's squinting.

She hears the door open and doesn't even turn. "The funeral parlor called, Mr. Orchard. Ronnie's body has been prepared."

"Yeah, such a terrible thing," Chet mumbles. He stands there looking at Birdie, gauging how much he can trust her. "How long you been workin for me, Birdie, twenty years?"

It takes Birdie a second to pull away from what she's doing, but hearing his tone, she looks up at Chet. "Twenty-two, sir."

"And I'm so glad you're here to help me get through these hard times."

"I was so sorry to hear about Ronnie. What an awful accident."

Chet bows his head slightly at the sympathy. "Thanks."

He's looking down at the ground, doesn't move. From behind Chet, we can see that he has the gun tucked in his belt at the small of his back.

"Oh, would you take care of this?" Chet insists, holding the ledger out to her at arm's length.

She looks at it but doesn't take it just yet.

"What would you like me to do with it?" Birdie asks dutifully, as she puts her hand on the book.

Feeling she has it in her grip, Chet shifts the bulk of the weight of the ledger to Birdie's hands.

"Burn it," he quips and leaves her there, still holding the

ledger high in the air.

*   *   *   *

Margolis sits at her computer in the dining room. Headphones over her black, trestled mane, she's leaning forward intently, watching footage of Stephanie. She's editing film.

Emma walks in the front door carrying books and a laden backpack. She sees Margolis and plunks her stuff on the couch. She speaks, but Margolis can't hear.

Outside, Chet Orchard sits in his sedan and watches the lights coming from inside the house. They've been on the whole time he's been sitting there, so he's sure someone is home. Without shifting his gaze, he reaches down on the seat next to him and picks up the gun. He holds it for a second, then looks down on it. He opens the revolver and checks the ammo. Full. He punches the cylinder back into the pistol and puts it in his suit-jacket pocket. Heaving against the door, he's out of the car and moving across the street toward the house.

At Margolis's shoulder, Emma reaches out—the older woman jumps at Emma's touch and yanks the headphones off her head.

"Oh my god, you scared me!" Margolis pants.

"What are you doing?" Emma asks, incredulously.

"Look," Margolis raises her hand in a conciliatory gesture. "I know I said we'd give up the film."

"Yeah, we did."

"That's fine for you all. But I can't, Emma. I just can't."

Just outside the house, Chet walks normally up the walk, like he's going to ring the bell for tea, but he slips into a shadow by the garage, out of the glare of the streetlight.

He sidles up to the porch and is quickly next to the darkened door. He raises the gun and listens.

He can hear voices coming from inside.

333

Cut to:

Margolis, who stands and faces Emma. "Look, I know you're scared, Emma, but we can't quit now. We're so close to putting the pieces all together."

"But you agreed!"

"I know I did. But I went to the cemetery today." Margolis stops, looking intensely at Emma, who slumps her shoulders when she realizes what Margolis is saying. Emma is suddenly overcome with guilt; her eyes well with tears.

"I know remembering Stephanie and what happened is hard," Margolis says softly as she moves to Emma's side. "We'd all like to forget and move on with our lives, but I have a chance to do something about this. Right now." Margolis puts her hand on Emma's arm. "Despite the risks, it just feels like my whole life has been coming to this—everything I've ever done preparing me to make this movie." Margolis smiles faintly. "That's why I have to finish it." Cut to:

Exterior.

Chet gently tries the knob on the front door, and it gives slightly. It's unlocked. His face shows an ashen grin from the shadows at his good fortune. With a tightening of the knuckles, he renews his grip on the gun and puts his weight against the door. He counts inside his head, ready to go on three. Cut to:

Interior.

With Margolis's hand on her shoulder, Emma looks around. "Where is everyone?"

"I sent them off," Margolis replies. "Brie to her grandmother's upstate, Eggy to her folks on the coast. At least for a few days."

Emma turns back. There's fear in her eyes.

Margolis tries to reassure her. "That's why I need you. You're the strong one. You can do this. You want to finally end the threat to your father? This is how you do it—punch the bully in the nose." She lifts Emma's face up to hers. "Will you help me?"

With a saddened look, Emma relents. She nods. Then an idea occurs to her; her face lightens. "Actually," Emma admits, "there's someone I think we can see who will talk to us. About the whole thing."

Chet bursts through the front door into Margolis's living room. He swings the gun around toward the sound of voices.

The television is on—some late-night talk show with the actress Kerry Washington being interviewed, something about "It's on Us"—the volume is loud.

Chet swings the gun around to the other side of the room. Then from one corner to the next.

Scratching his head, Chet curses. Then he notices the computer in the dining room. He goes over to it and recognizes Eggy on screen. He picks up the headphones, presses play, and listens to the footage as it rolls by.

In a sudden rage, Chet tears off the headphones and grabs the monitor. In one swift motion, he lifts it and brings it down on the table with a massive WHACK. He throws the keyboard over his shoulder and starts ripping cords out of the back of the machine like a madman.

With the hard drive under his arm, Chet moves quickly toward the front door. He hears something. Stops.

Brie stands at the foot of the stairs. "Mom?" She's groggy, rubbing her eyes.

Chet cocks his head and smiles. "Why hello there!"

He raises the gun.

*   *   *   *

Emma's Car—night. Emma drives, while Margolis talks into the phone: "Can you meet us there? My office. We'll probably arrive right around sunrise." Margolis listens then ends, "Great. See you then." She hangs up and puts her phone in her lap.

The two sit silently for a while, staring out the front

windshield. After a moment, they look at each other. Lady Gaga wails on the stereo. They smile at each other. Margolis reaches over and turns it up.

They speed down the highway and out of sight into the darkness.

*　　　*　　　*　　　*

Margolis sits in a plush chair in the living room of an upper middle class home. A camera hums on a tripod over her shoulder. Emma stands next to the camera, headphones over her ears.

"Just for the record, are you still a recruit for the Athens University football team?" Margolis asks.

"No, I decommitted last month."

"Decommitted?"

"I changed my mind. I'm going to Alabama to play instead."

"So, what were you told when you arrived on Athens's campus and by whom?" Margolis leans forward.

Ryan Cavanaugh looks back at her uneasily and shifts in his seat. For a moment, he glances up at his parents who huddle nervously in the back corner of the room, then at Emma who gives him an encouraging look.

He turns back to Margolis: "The older guys, the captains of the team, kinda gathered us up and said that someone had arranged 'dates' for us to go out with on our visit. At night."

"Was there any discussion that sexual favors would be involved in these dates?"

"No, but it was implied—you know, lots of laughing at joking about getting laid—er, sorry."

"No, no. It's okay to speak freely," Margolis assures him. "Did you avail yourself of such favors during your date?"

"Me? Um, no." Ryan swallows. "But I did start seeing my date later—she was a nice girl."

Emma flinches at a little pang inside. She had feelings for

him and wished it had worked out better.

Margolis continues, "Did other recruits take advantage of the sexual opportunities presented to them, as far as you know?"

"Well, I didn't see anything, you know, myself, but let's just say there was a lot of bragging the next day. On the team busses and stuff."

"Then how do you know such transactions were happening, sex for recruits?"

"Because someone came to me..." Ryan fades out.

"You'll have to speak louder," Margolis says calmly.

Ryan clears his throat, "Because a booster from the Raven Foundation came to me later and asked me why I didn't—um—have sex with her."

"And what did you say?"

"I, uh—this is kind of embarrassing..."

Margolis gestures subtly for him to continue.

"I, uh, wanted to wait for my wedding." Ryan shifts again. "And she was really pretty." Ryan glances up at Emma, who smiles back at him.

"Fair enough." Margolis points out, "But you did eventually have sex with her."

Ryan nods sheepishly. Emma blushes.

The confession made, Margolis moves on: "Who approached you and encouraged you to have sex, do you remember?"

"Yeah," Ryan replies. "It was a man named Chet Orchard."

Cut to:

Inside the car, later that day, Emma hangs up her phone. "It was Aria. She got my message about Ryan's confession. She says she'll talk too if Detective Collins is there."

"We'll film her as soon as we get back." Margolis nods and presses down on the accelerator.

*　　*　　*　　*

Margolis's classroom, ACC. This time, Emma sits in the chair across from the interviewee, Aria, who looks nervously around the room.

Mickey stands at the door, leaning back against the jamb—he still has bandages from the accident over parts of his face—Collins stands behind him. Margolis introduced him to Aria as "security" to make her feel safer. So, she tells the story of Chet Orchard paying her $5000 to have sex with one of the Raven Foundation's boosters after the variety show.

When they're done, silence settles on the room.

Margolis's phone rings, and she answers it, thinking it might be Brie. She hasn't heard from her since she left yesterday morning.

"Yeah." A beat. Margolis's face is disappointed; it's not Brie. "This is she." Margolis listens for a moment, then she looks directly at Emma. "Okay, that's great. Thanks, Jack." Margolis hangs up. She takes a breath, then addresses the room: "Well, that was my agent." She pauses. "*60 Minutes* called—they want to feature us on the show!" Margolis smiles and raises her hands in victory.

Everyone claps except Aria. "Oh my god," she groans.

Emma takes Aria's arm, "No, that's good—it means people are going to find out about what's going on at Athens—you're helping to get the word out."

Aria nods reluctantly.

"Holy crap!" Mickey exclaims. "What did they say?"

"Lesley Stahl will be here Wednesday next week—they want to feature us the following Sunday!"

"Hold on just a minute," Collins warns. "Are you sure about this? It could blow our cover, and the DA will flip—there goes Aria's immunity down the drain." Aria looks up at him, alarmed. "Not to mention, Pantucci won't be happy." Collins frowns.

"Then we'll just have to make sure we do the interview right, won't we?" Margolis says unperturbed. "I'll get Jack back on the phone—then we'll have to see if we can finish this film over the weekend!"

"OK, then," Collins concedes, "if we're gonna go all out, then here's the plan..."

V.

TV anchor: "In light of the rumors of a sex for hire scheme at their daughter's sorority, Delta Delta Theta, the parents of deceased Athens's student, Stephanie Rogers, have filed a civil wrongful death suit against both the Thetas and the University. In response, Art Lane, the current president of Athens and candidate for U.S. Senate, issued a statement denying any culpability for either scandal, stating, quote, 'the University is not responsible for the insane actions of a few bad apples,' end quote..."

*　　*　　*　　*

Art and Chet stand next to each other at the window of the president's office overlooking the campus from the top floor of the administration tower. Lane is holding the football in his hands.

"Yeah," Lane says, almost matter-of-fact, "I saw on the news your response to this Sunday's story—disgruntled professor breaks into the office of a highly respected local businessman, makes outrageous claims against Athens U—it's a clever way to get in front of the story, to discredit Santos before she goes public. Well done."

"Thank you kindly," Chet retorts in faux formality. Then his tone gets darker: "I've seen the footage they got for this so-called 'film'—mostly interviews with sluttish young Thetas and hearsay. That turncoat Eggy Compson."

"Oh, she's done at Athens for sure. Frank Sinoro and his experiment with female coaches. What a joke."

"It'll be easy to cast reasonable doubt on all that horseshit. I've agreed to go on *60 Minutes* myself, since they got nothing on me."

Chet regales Lane with his plan. He says that he'll tell Santos that he'll tie it up in court, snow her in with legal fees and endless motions to dismiss. He'll deny it until she and the DA and God himself runs out of money. "Cause the Lord knows I won't!" Chet cackles.

"That's great, Chet. I'm happy for you. Well played." Lane pauses, spinning the football in his hands. "But I'm afraid that my office will have to deny any ties to you and the Raven Foundation. With the campaign under way, we can't have this kind of bad press." Lane walks back to his desk, sits down. "I'll have to launch an official investigation into your dealings with the football program." Elbows on desk, Lane folds his hands with satisfaction.

Chet turns, slightly surprised: "I don't think you understand, Lightning, my fine-feathered friend." He walks over to Lane's desk and points. "Santos broke into my office. Rifled through my files. That means she probably has evidence linking you to me. You can't wash your hands of this one."

Chet walks toward the door.

Lane calls after him: "We agreed when we started this thing that there'd be no paper trail, Chet!"

"What can I say, Artie. I always like to carry insurance. You know how it is..."

"Oh, so you're saying you fucked me on purpose?"

Chet stops at the door. "No, just a little mutual assured destruction, to keep everyone honest." Chet pauses for emphasis, then adds: "Don't worry, old pal, I'm taking care of this."

"You had better fucking take care of this!" Lane thunders, "Or you can kiss access to my senatorial office goodbye—I don't care how much money you've given to the campaign!"

"Let's just hope there is a campaign." Chet pauses. He holds up his hand and looks at it. "You give me some cover by denying all allegations, and I'll make sure that movie never gets made."

*　　*　　*　　*

Margolis sits at her classroom desk going over some notes in preparation for the interview. "How many is that now?" she asks Emma, who is seated at a computer.

Mickey looks up from filing his nails; he's at his usual perch leaning next to the door. Clips from Aria's interview play on Emma's screen. She answers, "That's six now."

"Six?" Margolis is incredulous.

"Yeah, since Aria came clean, five more Thetas have come to Jesus."

"Keep 'em coming out of the woodwork, Emma. Good job." Margolis then asks, "This room still sufficing for an interview space?"

"Yes, with the books, desks," she looks around, "they feel comfortable here."

"Okay, I can take over editing as soon as I finish—"

There's a sudden loud knock on the door.

Everyone freezes.

Mickey stands to attention and lifts a hand for everyone to be quiet. He looks out the window.

"It's some old lady." Mickey looks over at Margolis.

She scrunches her nose and nods once—it's okay. "Come in!" she yells.

The door opens and in walks a woman dressed in proper old-lady, southern fashion.

It's Birdie.

She hesitates just inside the door and clutches a purse under one arm and something in a bag under the other.

"Can I help you?" Margolis calls mildly across the room.

Birdie looks up at Mickey and his imposing biceps, then over at Margolis. "Are you Professor Santos?"

Margolis smiles. "Yes."

"I'm Birdie Johnson, secretary to Chet Orchard."

Margolis suddenly stiffens, and Emma looks at her worriedly.

Birdie notices everyone's apprehension. "I have something

to give you, something you may find very useful." She holds it up to Margolis.

"Chet's ledger." Margolis gasps, then asks in true shock, "What have you gone and done, Mrs. Johnson?"

Birdie hands it over to Margolis who sits dumbfounded, turning the leather volume in her hand.

"Consider it amends—for working in that office too long—he told me to burn it. I figured you might have some better use for it."

"I do," Margolis admits.

*   *   *   *

"Since your final is the day after tomorrow," Margolis announces from the front of the classroom, "I only have one last thing to say about the western, but you can bet this is going to be covered on the exam."

She pauses for emphasis and looks around the room. The students all wait, breathless, pens poised above paper.

"The western—in fact, every film and all stories, really—is defined by its ending. The showdown."

Cut to:

An Athens auditorium full of students hunched over blue exam books with pencils scribbling madly. It's dead silent with the exception of a shuffle of paper here or a cough there.

Emma takes a final exam.

She looks across the rows and sees Brooke staring at her. The sorority president draws her thumb across her throat and then flips Emma the bird. Brooke's face is deadly serious.

Emma swallows hard and goes back to her exam. Cut back to:

Margolis's ACC classroom.

"In every narrative, just as in every western, the conflict must be resolved. The good guy must face the bad guy. It's essential. In fact, the good guy has no choice but to face up to his foe because the foe is so good that he's left our hero no choice. It's fight or die."

*   *   *   *

On the Athens U campus, it's Wednesday morning.

Margolis walks quickly, again incognito, down the quad toward the administration building. With hat down over her sunglasses, she stops at the door to the tower and looks around to check if she was followed. She looks both ways, then pulls the door and enters.

President's office. In the reception area, Margolis marches past the secretary before she can even protest. Margolis opens the door and strides, fully confident, up to Lane's desk.

Lane notices the unannounced visitor and says into the phone, "I'm gonna have to call you back," as he hangs up.

Before he can speak, Margolis smacks something down on his desk. Lane looks down and sees a DVD case.

"Your boy tried to kill me before I had a chance to finish this, my movie. Because he knows you're finished. You and your kind."

Lane nonchalantly reaches for his phone and dials, "Yes, I need campus security to my office immediately, thank you." As he hangs up, he looks coolly at Margolis: "You haven't even done your interview with Stahl yet—I know the president of CBS and can just get him to delay it until you get arrested for breaking and entering, shut your film down. I know you broke into athletics and Orchard Industries. And you're trespassing now."

She retorts, "You try to do anything to me—send Pantucci or any of your other lapdogs, and this movie goes out, even without *60 Minutes*. It'll go out to all local and national news outlets, theaters, community playhouses, if necessary—I'm sure at least one of them will find it interesting that the national champs had to pay girls to seduce good players. Plus,

I have distributors lined up all over the country, and copies are all ready to go. Now, I'm leaving. Watch it now. Or you can just tune in on Sunday. Your call."

* * * *

Later that day, the sun is down, and Margolis's interview with *60 Minutes* is over. Mickey walks up to Margolis at her desk.

"Since Ms. Stahl has left, I'm going to go ahead and take off." Mickey points over his shoulder toward the door. "You good?"

"Yeah, I'm almost ready." Margolis looks up from her computer. "Just waiting for the final cut of the film to render before I pop it over to the show's producers. I think it looks pretty good."

"Alright," Mickey notices how tight her face is but heads for the door. With a change of heart, he stops and walks back toward Margolis. He takes her and pulls her up into his arms. He looks sincerely into her eyes.

"Hey, Glee?"

"Yeah?" She looks back at him.

He kisses her lightly on the lips.

He smiles, then says, "You done good. Real good."

Margolis can't help but smile at the compliment. "Thanks, Mickey. For everything."

He lets her go and strides toward the door. "Don't thank me yet." He cocks his head. "It ain't over!"

He winks and leaves Margolis alone. She watches the space he just vacated for a long moment. The cool thrill of attraction mingles with the savory pleasure of being appreciated by a solid man. The feeling washes through her body, a feeling she hasn't felt in such a long time.

She looks around her room at Athens Community College— this hasn't been a half-bad place to work, she thinks. Although she misses the pomp of the Athens U campus, this place has been intimate, inviting. Like with Mickey, she's felt safe here.

When the computer dings that the film is finished, a sudden pang twists in the pit of her stomach. She knows what's coming—knows it's the right thing—but somehow, she's still scared. *What will happen?* She pushes the question out of her mind as she gathers the rest of her things.

Margolis exits the front of the building as usual, her keys brandished, and heads down the lidded block. It's late, so the street is deserted and made lonelier by the lights that keep changing even though there are no cars stopping at them.

At the end of her building, she takes a right, like she always does, down the alley that leads to the parking lot. She's not worried about Chet's thug anymore. With him out of the way, she has bigger fish to fry.

At the instant she thinks it, Chet Orchard steps out of the shadows. *And there it is*, Margolis tells herself, unsurprised. Even though he has a gun, hip high, leveled at her, Margolis reminds herself to stay cool.

"Good evening, Professor Santos," Chet says in a cheerily normal voice. "I'll just be relieving you of that bag of yours and your purse." He points with his gun.

"Ah," Margolis retorts as she lifts the straps over her head and hands them over. Chet lays them on the ground. "The old 'make it look like a robbery-gone-wrong,' huh?"

"You know it. Best trick in the book."

"I'm just impressed you'd have the guts to do it yourself."

"Well, I'm fresh out of henchmen at the moment. Plus, you know what they say: If you want something done—"

"I do, but I thought it might be Lane, though."

"Naw, he's too big a softy. Wants to be Senator. Doesn't have the stomach for breaking-and-entering. Or murder."

"You know I already gave my interview with CBS this morning, right? Like I told Lane, it's going forward, whether I'm dead or not."

"I know. That's why I gave Ms. Stahl my interview today, too. Couldn't have you hoggin the spotlight. Gotta plant those seeds of reasonable doubt, you know."

Margolis looks at Chet's hands, the fingers gripping and releasing nervously on the gun handle. He can feel everything closing in on him. He shakes it off.

"Oh, you didn't think I'd face this bullshit in public, huh? Why not? It may all be true, what your movie says, but all I have to do is taint it with the stink of half-truth, exaggeration, and make-believe, and the average person won't believe it."

Margolis can hear a muffled sound from the shadows but can't tell what it is. Chet's voice distracts her.

"People won't believe it," Chet gloats, a little too loudly, "because they don't want to. They'd rather not know that public figures they admire do bad things—that upstanding pillars of the community would pay young girls to have sex. It clashes with their worldview. That's why we can get away with it. The Big Bad Rich Guy story doesn't float anymore. People love a success. The richer we are, the more people think we've earned whatever we do. Essentially, no one will ever suspect the man who built this town and its university."

"If everyone will believe you and not me, then why be so cliché and pull a gun?"

Margolis's eyes dart from doorway to trashcan—looking at hiding places, looking for weapons or ways out.

"I don't like letting my enemies go scot free. Not when they've fucked with my business."

"So that's why you want to kill me—because you can?" Margolis says calmly.

"Oh, I'm not just going to kill *you*, my dear." Chet reaches into the shadows where the sound was and pulls out Brie, mouth taped, hands tied.

She stumbles, imploring Margolis with widened eyes and muffled screams.

"No, no, no, no. You leave her alone. Please!" Margolis begs, hand raised. She feels the electric pulse of panic.

"Oh, now you're asking me nicely," Chet screams, sweat on his brow. "I guess you realize you've lost your leverage, you cunt piece of shit!"

"Please don't hurt her. I'll do anything."

"That's more like it. Now," Chet forces Brie down on her knees. "You're going to call off the *60 Minutes* thing and give me everything that you have on the Raven Foundation." Margolis is frozen. Chet yells, "Now!"

"Yes, done." Margolis is rocking frenetically on the balls of her toes.

Chet puts the gun to Brie's head and cocks it, his hand shaking.

"And you're going to burn that fucking film. Every last megabyte." He raises his head to Margolis, his eyes aflame. "And I'm gonna keep her until you do."

Suddenly, there's a snap to Chet's right. His head swings around toward the noise.

There, in the streetlight, stands Eggy, arms raised. "Who's the sissy-boy now, perv?"

Out of reflex and surprise, Chet swings the gun toward her, taking aim off Brie.

Margolis dives for her daughter and covers her with her body.

From out of the shadows, an arm comes instantly down on Chet's hand and in one smooth motion twists it behind his back.

Detective Collins. He has the old man in a pincher hold that makes Chet wince loudly and release the gun. It falls harmlessly into Collins' other hand, which slides the piece into his coat pocket and deftly produces his cuffs. He pushes Orchard to the ground and clips them on the twisted arm, then the other.

"That should be enough to convict," Collins smiles.

"You better have recorded all that," Margolis snarls

urgently. "My fucking daughter's life was on the line."

Collins nods and pats his chest pocket. Microphone.

"Sorry about Brie. We didn't know he had her. Unavoidable complication."

"Unavoidable complication?" Margolis laughs as she rips the tape of Brie's face and hands. "You okay?" They embrace, sobbing.

"You'll need to get a warrant to make any of that admissible, shit-for-brains," Chet yells hoarsely from the pavement.

"I did. Just got back from the capital. Federal judge. Not one of your state cronies. Racketeering, conspiracy. Should be enough to make the DA want a piece of the action on your pandering charges. The FBI even deputized me to serve it! Plus, you know, assault with a deadly weapon, kidnapping. Shall I go on?"

"I'll have your job for this, spook-ass motherfucker!" Chet yells over his shoulder as Collins carts him away. "Pantucci will have your head—"

"Pantucci has her own problems," Collins mumbles. Cut to:

Pantucci sitting at her desk. She's on the phone looking over a file on Collins. There's a map with his address, other known hangouts—she's obviously looking for him. In the foreground, several men in black suits stand behind her, surrounding her desk. She looks up at them. Badges say FBI. One reaches down and takes her sidearm before she can react; two others take her by the shoulders and pull her out of her chair. They slap cuffs on her—we hear them reading her Miranda rights.

Back to the alley.

Slowly, other figures emerge from the shadows—Mickey, Emma, Sandy, even Mark and Farrah—they circle around Margolis.

Brie hugs her and asks if she's alright. Margolis nods and laughs at the irony, the stress releasing into smiles.

"Thanks for being my back-up, all of you." Margolis sniffles and looks around gratefully at her people. "You risked your lives for me."

"We weren't going to let you face this punk alone, Glee!" Sandy states. The others agree.

Mickey adds: "Anyway, Collins took the real risk, tackling Orchard and advising us to leak the story to the press—he coulda got himself killed."

"I thought he was just making himself scarce to avoid his partner and leaving you two alone. But the whole time he was working the federal angle. Smart guy."

"I'm not sure we could have gotten this thing done without him," Margolis marvels, watching him escort Orchard out of the alley. "Especially since Orchard had Brie." She strokes her daughter's hair lovingly.

"Now all we have to do is wait," Eggy adds.

"And finish final exams," Emma blurts. "Well, some of us."

"I think you just passed," Margolis rumbles wryly.

*   *   *   *

Sunday night. The moment of truth is here. We can hear the ticking stopwatch from the opening title of *60 Minutes* coming from the TV around which everyone is gathered: Brie, Emma, Eggy, and Sandy snuggle on the couch in Margolis's den. Mark and Farrah in chairs, and of course Margolis, who sits by herself farthest away, back toward the kitchen. They've all got drinks and are tossing popcorn in their mouths out of big bowls. Nervous smiles are exchanged. All except Margolis, who bites her nails, eyes riveted to the television.

Leslie Stahl's gumshoe voice: "Tonight, sex, lies, and corruption at the highest levels of one of America's premier universities. And it all starts with football..." There are highlights from the national championship game with shots of screaming, cheering Athens fans in the stands. A cut to the now famous picture of Eggy jumping into Frank's arms.

Everyone laughs and razzes Eggy a bit before quieting down again as Stahl continues, "A new documentary by filmmaker and former Athens University professor, Margolis Santos, has uncovered a vast conspiracy of alleged crimes ranging from bribery to sexual assault and prostitution..."

Well, this is it, Margolis thinks to herself. She looks over at the girls who are so excited to see their handiwork broadcast to millions of viewers around the world, and she wishes she could share in their joy. But Margolis can't be sure if this is the end or the beginning. Will this story finally end rape, assault, and trafficking on her campus, or will it just kick the ant hill, bringing to life an entire network of evasion, stonewalling, and denial from men in organizations even more powerful than Orchard's? She doesn't know.

Mickey comes in from the kitchen with drinks and stands behind Margolis. He reaches over her and hands her a glass of wine. She barely raises the corners of her mouth at him before turning back to the TV. He puts a hand on her shoulder for a brief moment.

A seated Margolis appears on screen and a shout goes up in the room. Margolis hushes them.

Stahl starts off by hitting Margolis hard: "You were fired from your position at Athens..."

Margolis: "Yes."

"...for an inappropriate relationship with a student."

"Yes. A student from another school."

"But he was young. Nineteen."

"The mistake made me realize that I needed to focus on what was important in my life, my family and my art."

Stahl changes the subject. "Let's talk about your art. Isn't this a documentary in which you allege," Stahl looks down at her notes, "that the Raven Foundation paid girls from the Delta Delta Theta sorority to have sex with football recruits, that current and future players raped Stephanie Rogers, and that the university knew about it and did nothing, creating, in your words, an unsafe environment for women and promoting the culture of rape on campus?"

"Yes," Margolis replies. "That's correct."

"Some might ask, isn't this all just sour grapes for being fired, a disgruntled employee seeking revenge? Why should anyone believe a professor who sleeps with young students?"

"Well, I didn't make anyone at Athens do these things. I just uncovered them and my film documents them. I didn't make any of this stuff up."

"Good answer," Sandy looks over at Margolis.

The next thing Stahl asks her about is her marriage.

"You husband is the football coach at Athens—"

"My ex-husband," a contrite Margolis says solemnly. "We're divorced.

"All of these allegations occurred under his watch—he had to have known about them—otherwise it just seems like he was willfully ignorant of what was going on in his own program. Why did he never speak up and stop them—were you protecting him?" Cut to:

Frank sitting on the edge of his couch watching TV and nervously rocking back and forth. He has a pillow pinched in the vice grip of his knees. He's alone. He waits for his ex-wife to answer.

The TV cuts to a close-up of Margolis's face.

"He did know," Margolis says evenly.

Brie looks over at her mother in shock. Margolis does not return the glance and says nothing. Brie watches the screen.

"He did know," Stahl repeats, eyebrows raised in surprise.

"After the Rogers case, Frank came to me with more information of what was going on inside the locker room. We knew that we needed more evidence in order to fully understand the scope of the cover-up, so we agreed that he'd stay silent. Otherwise, the real culprits would have just run to ground. That's when he gave me insider access to invaluable resources inside his office—coaches, staff, and documents related to recruiting. Frank not only fully cooperated with my investigation, he participated in it whole-heartedly. Without Frank, there would be no documentary." Cut to:

Frank lays back against his couch and lets out a huge sigh of relief.

Flashback a few days ago to:

Interior. Parking Garage—night

Margolis and Frank standing facing each other. The place is empty and the fluorescent light makes it seem eerie and clandestine. If you didn't know better, you'd think they were lovers, from the posture of their body language.

"This may not work, you know," Margolis points out. "They might still think you lied to cover your ass or, worse yet, that you and I were somehow involved together in covering things up. Therefore, responsible for Stephanie, the variety show—the whole thing."

"I know. But at this point, it's the only play I got," Frank bows his head. "I just wanted to win football games. Do something that Brie...and you...could be proud of." He looks Margolis square in the eye.

She sees the sincerity there—she can't stop thinking how he just didn't know what he was getting into—pity wells up in her, and she just reaches out for him instinctively.

They hold their embrace for a long moment, then part.

She turns and starts walking away.

After a few seconds: "Hey, Glee!" Frank calls. She turns. "Thanks," he smiles at her. She nods and continues walking and disappears down a stairwell. Back to:

Margolis sitting in her den—she's leaning forward and listening intently.

Stahl's narration over a montage of images from Athens: "The coach's cooperation opened Santos to the secret world of athletics boosters, where wealthy patrons, mostly of the football program, work outside the jurisdiction of the university to support, and in some cases stack the deck for, their team's efforts to get the nation's best high school players. At the center of this booster universe for Athens is one Chet Orchard, energy magnet and rice baron from the gulf coast, who once played for the Raven himself..." The bio of Chet goes on for a little while.

Cut to a shot of the room, where Farrah looks knowingly across at her friend. She knows this was the part Margolis was dreading—the last words of Chet before Collins took him away hanging in her mind like an omen—*This won't stick, all I had to do was stir up a shadow of doubt in your crazy story, you can't stop all of us.*

"Mr. Orchard, were you involved in or have any knowledge of a sex-for-recruits operation going on at the Delta Delta Theta sorority?"

"No, ma'am," Chet nods, comfortably and calmly, as if he'd been grilled by investigative journalists on TV all his life.

"But you do have connections to the Theta house, do you not—you donated hundreds of thousands of dollars for a remodel of the house." Stahl holds up a sheaf of papers that look like invoices.

"Well, I support hundreds of charitable organizations all over campus and give millions to worthy causes." Chet smiles. "I didn't know generosity was a conspiracy." He laughs.

"Of course it's not," Stahl presses. "But you also had personal connections to some of the girls in the sorority."

"I'm not sure to what you're referring." Chet cocks his head.

"Emma Barnes, you were in business with her father."

"Well, I can't rightly recall..."

"In the film, Ms. Barnes claims that you threatened her father in order to blackmail her into prostitution. She agreed to let us play this for you." Stahl points to a monitor off screen. Chet looks over at it, smile on his face nowhere to be seen. Cut to:

A close-up of Emma's face. Her eyes are red, she's been crying. "I couldn't pay my tuition or my dues to Theta. That's when they approached me with the proposition to escort recruits on dates."

"And there was the expectation of quid pro quo sex from you?"

"Um, yeah. Other girls were already doing it. The housemom would keep record—we called it the 'slut diary,'" Emma chuckles through a stuffy nose, "of all the girls, who they went out with, and how much they earned." Cut to:

A shot of Stahl leafing through the diary. Her voice-over goes: "Professor Santos agreed to let me look through the diary, which was encrypted, a code she says it took a month to crack. Of the thirty names listed, seven of the girls are interviewed in Santos' film, a shockingly high number, considering how underreported sexual crimes are..."

A graphic shows photos of Aria, Emma, and five other Thetas. Clips from several of them play, each admitting to selling sexual favors for money.

Cut back to interview with Emma:

"And when you refused to have sex?"

"That's when Mr. Orchard threatened to frame my dad."

Cut to shot of Chet:

"Look, I'm in business with thousands of people at hundreds of firms all across the globe. Most are upstanding, but I'm sure not all are. With the amount of business that I do with Mr. Barnes's firm, it must just be coincidence that my company was involved when he committed his malfeasance..."

Stahl: "But Orchard Industries documents, obtained by *60 Minutes*, indicate that you were pleased with Mr. Barnes's services right up until his daughter, Ms. Barnes, alleges you contacted her."

"Well, that's a simple matter of—"

"In fact, after that, your involvement in his corruption case only increased and his attorney claims it was testimony from

Orchard operatives that provided the bulk of evidence against his client that threatened him with jail time. Until they were withdrawn. Why were these documents withdrawn, Mr. Orchard? They certainly seem to suggest blackmail."

"Ms. Stahl, these are complex business matters completely unrelated to my volunteer work with Athens." Cut to:

An animation on screen in which several pages of documents stack over each other, piling up. Stahl's voice narrates over them: "The heart of Professor Santos's film links Orchard's Raven Foundation directly with the university, particularly university president, Art Lane. We confronted President Lane with some of the evidence." Cut to:

A full-body shot of Lane sitting across from Stahl in his ornate office. You can see some of the lighting equipment to each side of the shot.

"Have you ever seen this binder before, Mr. Lane?" Stahl reaches across and hands Lane the leather-bound ledger.

The look of shock in his eyes is palpable. He leafs through it slowly.

"Do you recognize that hand writing?"

Lane is silent.

"This ledger records hundreds of payments the Raven Foundation made to university students, employees, and administrators, including to you university president, Art Lane."

"This could be a fake, a forgery. I've never seen this before."

Over a montage of images from campus—the Theta house, the Tower, Boom Fisher, etc.—Stahl's voice continues: "Mr. Lane vehemently denied any payments, as did Mr. Orchard, but *60 Minutes* was able to verify many of the transactions detailed in the book: construction invoices obtained by Professor Santos and confirmed by contractors; several of the Thetas provided bank statements verifying cash deposits of the same amounts shown in the ledger, and cancelled checks to two key athletics department employees all lead back to Mr. Orchard.

"What's most troubling about the records contained in the ledger is an apparent quid pro quo between Orchard and Lane: university resources flowed into the Raven Foundation, donations to President Lane's Senate campaign flowed out."

Chet Orchard: "No such transactions ever occurred. This is a liberal media witch hunt against hardworking Americans who pay their taxes, create jobs, and generously share their wealth with outstanding institutions like Athens U..."

Stahl: "A warrant for a search of university financial documents as well as Mr. Orchard's own bank records is currently pending in the Athens County District Court...President Lane abruptly ended his interview with CBS."

Insert footage of Lane standing up, taking off his mic, moving around the lighting equipment, and walking out of his office.

Cut to:

A shot of Margolis across from Stahl who asks, "Is the university culpable for what happened to these girls at Athens?"

Margolis answers unerringly, "Yes."

"Even Stephanie Rogers, her suicide?"

"When a university puts image and income above the health and safety of its female students—all in the name of preserving their 'brand'—then they, especially university presidents, are responsible for the human cost. Stephanie was the cost of doing the business of recruiting football players illegally. Did these girls in the Theta house make bad choices? Yes—anyone would admit that—but they were placed in a rigged system that makes sex a glamorous tool with the promise of riches and celebrity at the end of it. Very few of us could resist such temptation. The university gave them little choice: on the one hand, play the game or be left out in the cold with the wolves; on the other hand, win fortune and attention or suffer the shame of being a victim. It's as simple as that."

Stahl sits on a dark sound stage in front of the iconic 60

Minutes logo to deliver her epilogue: "What Professor Santos's documentary highlights for us is that college football is no longer an innocent affair. It's a high-stakes lure for billions of dollars in TV contracts, product endorsements, ad revenue, and big donations for universities and their athletics programs. The temptation of fortune and fame drives people—educated and otherwise normal people—to do things they might not otherwise do. Professor Santos's film shows us the secret ecosystem that sustains that nefarious game in which there are winners and losers, predators and victims.

"After we recorded our story, Chet Orchard was arrested on attempted assault charges when he allegedly drew a gun on Professor Santos outside of her workplace. Along with these charges, Mr. Orchard faces dozens of counts of state and federal crimes, including racketeering, pandering, solicitation, and conspiracy to commit a felony.

"Margolis Santos's documentary, *Ivory Tower*, opens nationwide in theaters next month."

Fade to black.

*   *   *   *

Local TV news announcer: "In shocking events over the weekend, the University of Athens finds itself the subject of an investigation. After the airing last night of an episode of *60 Minutes* detailing an elaborate sex-for-play scheme inside the U's football program, the Athens County prosecutor has decided to file charges against those implicated in the documentary made by former Athens professor, Margolis Santos...Warrants were issued and investigators walked out of Chet Orchard's office with a large cache of documents..."

President's office, reception. Lane's secretary, Susie, sits at her desk like normal among the display cases of football trophies, the new national championship trophy displayed prominently in the middle of the room in its own glass case.

The white noise of sports announcers hums from the mounted TVs around the room.

From the hallway, a large band of men in FBI jackets and local police uniforms rounds the corner and marches purposefully toward the president's door. Collins is among them.

Susie picks up the phone, "Sir, there are—"

She is interrupted by Collins who unrolls a search warrant in front of her face.

The men barge through the door and swarm into Lane's office.

He stands, startled, and looks around the group. "What is the meaning of this, I—"

Two uniformed officers cuff his hands behind his back. Collins steps up to Lane's desk. "You have the right to remain silent. Anything you say can and will be used against you in a court of law."

"I was just going to announce my investigation into athletics today," Lane protests to deaf ears.

"If you cannot provide your own attorney, one will be provided for you..."

"Susie, get my lawyer on the phone."

Collins marches around to the other side of the desk and takes Lane by the arm.

Cut to:

A cuffed Lane emerges from the tower escorted by Collins. A crowd of reporters and TV cameras surges in around them as they start down the walk toward the quad. Photos flash and questions fly in a roar of inquiry and confusion.

"What was your relationship with Chet Orchard?"

"Did you pay co-eds to sleep with football players?"

"What's the university's role in Ms. Rogers's death?"

"Will you continue your Senate campaign?"

Lane lowers his head and just lets the volley of questions bounce off of him. Collins calls for everyone to make room for them as they make their way slowly down the lawn.

Off to the side of the crowd stands Margolis who watches the crowd flow away through the campus. Somehow this isn't enough. She can't help but feel—with Stephanie gone, dozens of women used, lives ruined—that this is a hollow victory, come much too late.

She looks across the plaza and sees Mickey and Eggy waving. Next to them stands Frank. He smiles and nods once in acknowledgement.

A single reporter steps in the way and blocks her view.

"Professor Santos," he interrupts. "I'm Derek Beagle from the *Athens Observer*. I'd like to ask you a few words about your film."

"OK," Margolis replies as she heads the other way, away from the crowd. The reporter follows her and struggles to keep up with her stride.

"Some are calling you 'the woman who brought down a dynasty.' How do you respond to such praise?" Cut to:

Mickey, Eggy, and Frank—from their perspective, we watch Margolis and the reporter walk off into the setting sun.

Epilogue: A Graduation

I.

Outside a classic, ornate theater where the marquis reads *Ivory Tower Premiere*, hundreds of people line velvet ropes along the sidewalk leading to the street. Lines of limos pull up, disgorge their glittery cargo, and depart.

Margolis, Brie, Emma, and Eggy walk slowly down the red carpet to the dizzying flashes of paparazzi camera bulbs. All listed as producers on the film, they are dressed in sparkly evening gowns of gold, red, and silver. Margolis smiles and waves to an adoring crowd.

An *E! Entertainment* announcer describes the event: "*Ivory Tower*, the documentary by Margolis Santos that uncovers corruption and sexual abuse in the storied Athens University football program, opened last weekend to rave reviews. Apparently, filmgoers approve too. In just three days, it has already grossed $20 million dollars, making it the most successful documentary at the box office since Michael Moore's *Fahrenheit 9/11*, but Santos's controversial film was not without its detractors."

Nearby, a small but vocal group of protestors hold signs that say "Athens Football Forever" and "We Love Lightning" and "You Can't Just Fire Champions." Somewhere in the middle is one that reads, in small handwriting: "Go Home Wetback!"

They chant slogans like, "We Are. Ra-ven," and "So-ur Gra-aapes. So-ur Gra-aapes."

As Margolis approaches the entrance to the movie house, a protestor rushes up and slings something brown and sticky at Margolis. It drips down her silver dress.

Margolis stops, looks down—it's ruined.

She raises her head at the protestor and freezes for a moment. The protestor sneers. But Margolis keeps her face calm and serenely strides past her into the theater without a word. Security guards tackle the protestor and drag her off.

With serious faces, Brie, Eggy, and Emma follow Margolis inside.

Cut to:

An ESPN sportscaster speaks to the camera from an elaborate set: "Today, the NCAA, the national governing body that oversees all college sports, handed down the dreaded 'Death Penalty' to the Athens University Raven football program. The team will not be allowed to play games for three seasons and after that will be restricted to half of their allotted scholarships and barred from postseason play and television contracts for five years...

"Also, at Athens today, Frank Sinoro resigned as head coach of the football team, even though he was cleared of any involvement in the illegal activities that brought down the program and its booster organization, the Raven Foundation."

Frank sits at a table with microphones in front of his face: "I want to give Athens a fresh start. My players and the fans deserve that. After all that they've been through, it's the least I can do. I'm grateful to the NCAA and to Athens Community College for allowing me to start over again too. As of today, I will be taking over as the coach of Athens Community College's junior division football program, which will allow me to not only build on relationships I've made with people in the community but to also stay near my family..."

Cut to:

David Muir sits as the ABC news desk with his perfect hair and addresses the camera: "The Board of Trustees at Athens University announced today that they have fired President Art Lane for his involvement in and knowledge of the alleged sex-for-play scandal involving sorority members and football recruits. In a statement, they acknowledged that 'Lane has severely besmirched the reputation of the University' and that they 'hope to move forward and do everything possible to restore confidence in Athens as an academic institution that values the lives of young women.' Lane will also be investigated, according to state prosecutors, for his relationship to booster billionaire, Chet Orchard, who was arraigned last week on charges of pandering, racketeering, and reckless endangerment..."

Footage shows Chet in grey wool business suit being led by two beefy bailiffs to the defense table in a bright, modern courtroom. His face is cleanly shaven, looking haggard but defiant.

Judge: "How do you plead to these charges?"

A lawyer goes to answer, but Chet interrupts him: "Not guilty, your honor. Completely not guilty."

Off Chet with an easy grin opening to his crooked bottom teeth.

Cut to:

A local news announcer stands in front of the Athens administration tower holding a microphone:

"It seems that jurors in the wrongful death suit filed against Athens University by the parents of Stephanie Rogers have already reach a verdict. After only two hours of deliberations, the foreman told the judge they had reached a decision of 'guilty' in the case. This means that Athens could be forced to pay millions in damages to the Rogers family and could be open to a federal Title IX investigation..."

*   *   *   *

Emma sits at the computer in Margolis's house scrolling down what looks like a website for the Delta Delta Theta. She reads intently for a moment, then turns eagerly over her shoulder.

"Hey, Brie, come here. You gotta see this."

Brie gets off the couch and bends over Emma's shoulder, "What is it?"

"Here, look," Emma points. "The national chapter has stripped Brooke of her office."

"Really?" Brie reads, her face brightening. "That's awesome. I thought for a second that she'd have enough support from alums to hang on."

"Are you kidding? The parents wanted her ass out."

"I know I did," Margolis pipes up from the other side of the room. "If my daughter is going to be a Theta, that troubled girl had to go. And the housemom, whatever her name was, Ms. Slut Diary."

"Lucille," Emma offers.

"Yeah, her too."

"I'm just glad," Brie adds, "that national didn't shut us down. At least I get to be a Theta when I start at Athens next year. It would have sucked without it."

"And I'm sure the house will take a whole new direction with you as president."

"Whatever, I have no idea what you're talking about."

"I'm serious," Emma says. "I got together with the juniors, the other girls, they all want you to be president next year. For saving their asses from jail and stuff." Emma laughs.

"My daughter, the sorority president."

"First freshman Theta president ever," Emma crows.

Margolis shakes her head. "Who woulda thunk?"

Off Brie, glowing a smile.

*   *   *   *

Eggy and Frank stand outside his apartment next to a moving van.

"Are you sure that I can't talk you into joining my staff at ACC?" Frank asks, trying to hide his longing.

Eggy looks at him sadly. "I told you. I've already accepted a position at Georgia State."

"Not as good as Athens, but okay," Frank jokes. "And ACC will have better athletes..." He fades away and just stands there, looking into Eggy's eyes.

She reaches up and touches his face.

"No, baby." She smiles. "But I am grateful for the opportunity you gave me. The trust. I don't think I would have gotten this job if you hadn't taken a chance on me in the first place."

"It wasn't chance, Egglebert Compson." Frank smiles back sadly. "You earned it."

Eggy holds Frank's face for a moment.

"I gotta go."

Frank moves to take her hand, but she's withdrawn it.

"Hey, Eggy!" a voice comes from behind where the two are standing.

It's Margolis with Brie in tow.

"What are you still doing here," Margolis ribs her, "aren't you supposed to be in Georgia by now?"

"Margolis!" Eggy laughs. "Brie."

Margolis walks up and takes Eggy into her arms. "I'm gonna miss you." Margolis pulls back and looks Eggy sincerely in the eye. "Thank you for all you did. You're one brave woman."

Eggy turns to Brie, "Hail, president of Theta!"

She high-fives Brie. They hug. "I know you're gonna take care of my Theta girls."

"You know it," Brie smiles as she releases Eggy.

Eggy looks around and then slaps her hips. "Well, I guess it's time for me to mosey."

She opens the truck door and climbs up inside. In a moment, she's revving the engine and pulling out of the parking lot.

Frank, Brie, and Margolis wave after her. Eggy honks twice in goodbye.

Under her breath to Frank, Margolis whispers: "I'm sorry things didn't work out."

Frank: "With Egg?"

Margolis: "Or anything else in Athens."

"It's how things come and go, Glee." He girds himself, then turns to Brie and says in a louder voice, "Hey Brie-Brie, how about a hug for the road."

"You're leaving too?" Brie asks as she readily jumps into her father's arms.

"No rest for the weary." Frank hugs her. "Gotta hit the recruiting trail again.

"Even for community colleges?" Margolis asks. "I thought it was more laid back in that league."

"Oh, no," Frank whistles. "It's just as bad. Maybe worse. There's more dumb jocks at that level." He laughs—he's just kidding. Sorta. "They can't get into places like Athens. Gotta start 'em somewhere."

Margolis nods as if she just learned something new.

"Nice southern accent, Dad," Brie teases.

Frank tickles her as she walks toward his door. "You'll house-sit while I'm gone?"

"Only if I can have a wild party," she muses sarcastically, raising her hand without turning around.

Frank chuckles and throws a pebble after her.

Margolis watches, happy to see Brie and her father so engaged.

"Our daughter's grown up," Margolis observes. "I know this year has not been easy on her."

"No, but she got through it somehow, in spite of her parents," Frank smiles wryly.

"Listen, I'm sorry you lost your job, I—"

"I know you never meant me to." Franks takes off his hat. His tone is philosophical: "So, I lost a job? Not the first, probably won't be the last. But thanks to you, I didn't lose my career. I can still coach at least."

Margolis reddens and toes a stone at her feet. "Well, I love my family. And you're still part of it." She looks up at him in all seriousness.

"That's one of the reasons why I got you this little thank

you gift." He points across the parking lot.

Margolis's eyes follow his fingers at the end of which dangle a set of keys. She looks out toward the parking lot.

There sits a brand-new Mercedes, shinier and better than the old one she sold to finance the film.

Margolis's mouth drops just a little bit open.

"I may have resigned from Athens," Frank says, "but only after they guaranteed me my salary through the end of my five-year contract extension. With all the yet-unseen dirt I have access to, they weren't in any position to say 'no.'"

"But, Frank I—"

"Go ahead, take it." He shakes the keys at her.

Margolis takes them and walks trance-like toward the car. She looks back, still in shock, at Frank. He waves her on, smiling.

When she gets to the car, she starts laughing, walking all around it, kicking the tires. Then she gives a little hop and claps her hands.

"You did not have to do this."

"It's one of the best uses I could think of for Chet Orchard's money, don't you agree?"

Frank walks up to the car, pleased at how tickled Margolis is. She jumps on him and gives him a big hug of thanks.

"Maybe you can take Mickey out on a date in this thing. He'll be impressed."

Margolis looks over at him, seriously for just a moment, and then punches him lightly on the shoulder. "Thanks, Frank."

*   *   *   *

"Hey, stranger," Margolis greets Mickey outside the doors to the Athens U administration tower. "Fancy meeting you here."

"Yeah," Mickey sighs. "I just came from Concord's office."

"That's just where I was headed. How did it go?"

"Pretty good," he exhales. "She just made me the new athletics director."

"Mickey! That's great!" She reaches out for him with both hands. He steps into her embrace. They hold it for a little bit longer than necessary. "I think we'll have to celebrate the occasion."

He looks at her face—it's clear that she's happy for him.

"You're on," Mickey grins. "Later tonight?"

"You bet. Now, I don't want to be late to my meeting!" She gives his hand a squeeze. He smiles watching her go in.

Margolis enters the heavy doors and ascends the old, art deco elevator. Only a few people could fit in there with her, it's so small. Her curly hair brushes the top of the car.

It dings, she steps out. Lane's old floor.

Walking into reception, Margolis notices a huge change— the televisions, the trophies and sports paraphernalia—all gone. Most of the shelves sit empty, only dusty rings marking the spots where the spoils of championships used to sit.

In one glass case, Margolis sees something that wasn't there before—books. She steps over to it. The books are all written by Athens faculty, and in the stack is the one by Margolis, *Femmes Natales*.

"The president will see you now."

Margolis steps through the door and sees Gloria Concord rise from her seat behind the desk.

"Margolis!" Concord smiles. "Welcome. Have a seat."

Margolis takes her hand before sitting down.

"My, you certainly have made some changes around here," Margolis wonders looking around at the new décor—art, statues, and artifacts in deep earth tones from all around the world—no footballs or cowboy statues in faux-bright southwest colors. Concord was originally a professor of anthropology, and it's certainly clear now in her new office.

"Do you have any inkling why I asked you here, Margolis?"

"No," Margolis answers warily. "The last time I was in your office, I was being grilled about my personal life."

"Yes, I know. And please let me apologize for that now. I admit that I was quite misguided in your case—I had no idea what was really going on in the previous administration."

"I'm sure you didn't, Gloria. That's why they made you president." Margolis hoped that didn't come across as defensive.

"I understand your caution. But I want you to know that my goal as dean was always to keep standards high at Athens, and I plan to continue that as president."

"Of course."

"That's why I want you to rejoin our faculty."

"What?" Margolis almost chokes.

"Yes, I want to restore you to your full position—tenure, research account, everything." Concord folds her hands decidedly. "After observing your class last fall—which was not my choice, just for the record—I realized how excellent you are as a teacher. And everyone knows now, after *Ivory Tower*, how good a filmmaker you are."

Margolis lowers her head humbly and plays with her purse strap.

"What do you say, will you come back," Concord reaches a hand out to her, "Professor Santos?"

Margolis stands and grips Concord's hand. They both smile heartily, simultaneously a tacit exchange of regret and promise of future cooperation.

*   *   *   *

Pomp and Circumstance plays soberly as scads of grey-robe clad students file onto the field of a sunny Athens Stadium. We see Emma with Aria and some of her other Theta sisters in line—all of them have some sort of sorority message on their caps—"Thetas Rule!" or "The Class of Kicking Ass" or just

"ΔΔΘ," the Greek symbols for Delta Delta Theta.

Next, the faculty, including Goldberg and Margolis, process down the center aisle all dressed in their formal academic regalia. When the line bottlenecks, Margolis turns her head to search the student sections.

After a moment, her eye catches Emma's, those golden irises as hungry and clear as ever. Dressed in cap and gown, Emma leaves her seat and hurries over to the professors.

"Professor Santos! Professor Goldberg!"

Emma takes Goldberg's hand and shakes it heartily.

"Well, done, Ms. Barnes," Goldberg congratulates her. "They're gonna love you at USC—you're just gonna kill it in grad school."

"I hope so, sir." Emma turns toward Margolis. "I've had the best faculty to prepare me."

Emma sets her jaw and nods slightly, as if to tell her, *I owe this to you.* Margolis nods silently in reply.

The line starts moving again, and Margolis lets go of Emma's hand with a smile. She follows Goldberg up the steps. They take their seats on stage.

As Emma returns to her chair, she passes in front of Brooke Golindy.

"Emma, congratulations," Brooke reaches up to her.

"Thanks, Brooke, you too."

"Listen, I—"

"No, it's cool," Emma waves her off. "We're good." Emma looks firmly at Brooke, then smiles. "Gotta live for the now, right?"

Brooke smiles wistfully, "Right."

From the stands, Emma hears her name yelled loudly. She looks up at the stands and sees Farrah, Sandy, and Brie waving ecstatically at her. She smiles, waves, and puts her hand to her heart.

*　　*　　*　　*

Three months later.

Inside the Great Hall of Theta house, Brie stands on stage surrounded by a semi-circle of seniors. One of them, Aria, reaches up and pins a badge on Brie's lapel. Another places a sash over Brie's head and straightens it over her navy blazer.

Aria now turns to the crowd of girls.

"Although it feels like she's been a sister long before she pledged, I now present to you, new Theta and unprecedented freshman president, Brie Sinoro-Santos!"

The crowd, including Margolis and Mickey dressed in finery at the back of the room, cheer as Brie smiles and steps to the podium. The girls stomp and whistle, yelling 'speech,' insisting that Brie say a few words. She looks out at her mom, who nods in encouragement, and so Brie speaks. And after a few stumbling words of thanks, Brie comes to this:

"After all this chapter has been through, I take this office very seriously. In the name of those Thetas who have left us," there's a shuffling in the crowd as the other Thetas look sadly at each other or bow their heads in memory of Stephanie Rogers, "I vow to renew our purpose as a sorority. For service and excellence in everything we do, standing strong as women!"

The Thetas, heartened by Brie's words, cheer and call out her name, hopeful for a new beginning. Mickey glances over at Margolis who surreptitiously wipes an eye and smiles full of pride.

$$* \quad * \quad * \quad *$$

Margolis plops down on her couch and cuddles close to Mickey who puts his arm around her.

"What a night, huh?" Mickey says. "The future looks bright for the Thetas, and I didn't think I would ever be saying that."

Margolis turns to face Mickey and says seriously, "Well, I

never thought I'd be saying the future looks bright for Athens athletics either, but here you are."

"Here *we* are," Mickey points out. "Gonna make this place right together."

"Yeah." Margolis puts her hand on Mickey's chest.

As always, he's taken by her modesty. "You know," he changes tack a bit, "it's been more than seven months since our first date—"

"You mean, when you forgot and awkwardly asked me out for a first date on Valentine's Day?"

"Yeah, you know me," Mickey laughs good-naturedly. Then after a pause, "Maybe it's time for the next step." He looks, now seriously, into her eyes.

"What's the next step?"

"I don't know. You tell me. What is the next step for Margolis Santos?"

Margolis is stumped a bit by the question. She looks off, contemplating for a moment.

Cut to:

Margolis stands in front of a large hearing room, the same room where her appeal was held almost one year ago. But the deep shame and desperation she felt then is all gone.

The chamber is filled mostly with women, who chatter loudly and don't notice Margolis yet. To her left, Brie watches her mother rise and quiets herself in anticipation. To Margolis's right, sits Sandy, the president's new Title IX coordinator.

No one in the crowd sees Margolis—they continue to talk. There's a gavel next to Margolis's hand, but she doesn't use it. Instead, she just lets the chatting go on, as if she doesn't exist. While it does, something in the back of the room catches her eye. She looks up.

It's Cicero.

He's wearing a golf shirt and goofy, plaid pants again. But he's smiling right at Margolis, and she stares right back, braced for a sardonic quip or gesture. But he just raises his hand. In salute or goodbye, Margolis can't tell. But in an instant, he's gone, and Margolis turns to the microphone and just starts talking over the static.

"Welcome, everybody," she says, clear and loudly. The room immediately beings to hush. "Welcome to the first meeting of NACSA, the National Network Against Campus Sexual Assault."

Margolis gestures beside her to Brie and Sandy. "In addition to our Athens representatives," she then gestures behind her at two screens, "we are joined this morning by reps from our sister campuses."

Margolis points to one screen. "Former alum, Emma Barnes at the University of Southern California."

"Hi, Athens!" Emma waves to the camera, her head ten feet tall on the back wall.

"And over here," Margolis turns, "Eggy Compson from Georgia State."

Eggy waves, "Hello!"

Margolis, to the room: "Please welcome our guests." Her applause is joined by the dozens of Athens students and faculty in the room.

"Now," Margolis continues, literally rolling up her sleeves, "let's begin. We have a lot of work to do..."

Acknowledgements

I would like to thank the many readers who gave invaluable feedback during the writing of this book. To my writing group—Sloan Davis, Jeff Van Hanken, Josh Parish, and Keija Parssinen—their insight, close reading, and comradery made me believe that this was a story worth telling. Other very important readers include Joanne Davis, Brian Riley, Gary Sutkin, Timothy Bradford, and Jennifer Wills. This book was made possible in part by The University of Tulsa's Office of Research and Sponsored Programs, Dean of the College of Arts & Sciences, and Faculty of English Language & Literature. Thanks to my family who suffered through the arduous process of my writing this novel, along with viewing lots of sports events and journalism on television. Special thanks to my editor, Kyle McCord, whose input made this a better book. And, finally, I also sincerely appreciate the support and belief that Nick Courtright and Atmosphere Press have invested in this book.

About Atmosphere Press

Atmosphere Press is an independent, full-service publisher for excellent books in all genres and for all audiences. Learn more about what we do at atmospherepress.com.

We encourage you to check out some of Atmosphere's latest releases, which are available at Amazon.com and via order from your local bookstore:

To the Next Step: Your Guide from High School and College to The Real World, nonfiction by Kyle Grappone

The George Stories, a novel by Christopher Gould

No Home Like a Raft, poetry by Martin Jon Porter

Mere Being, poetry by Barry D. Amis

The Traveler, a young adult novel by Jennifer Deaver

Breathing New Life: Finding Happiness after Tragedy, nonfiction by Bunny Leach

Mandated Happiness, a novel by Clayton Tucker

The Third Door, a novel by Jim Williams

The Yoga of Strength, a novel by Andrew Marc Rowe

They are Almost Invisible, poetry by Elizabeth Carmer

Let the Little Birds Sing, a novel by Sandra Fox Murphy

Spots Before Stripes, a novel by Jonathan Kumar

Auroras over Acadia, poetry by Paul Liebow

Channel: How to be a Clear Channel for Inspiration by Listening, Enjoying, and Trusting Your Intuition, nonfiction by Jessica Ang

Love Your Vibe: Using the Power of Sound to Take Command of Your Life, nonfiction by Matt Omo

Transcendence, poetry and images by Vincent Bahar Towliat

Leaving the Ladder: An Ex-Corporate Girl's Guide from the Rat Race to Fulfilment, nonfiction by Lynda Bayada

Adrift, poems by Kristy Peloquin

Letting Nicki Go: A Mother's Journey through Her Daughter's Cancer, nonfiction by Bunny Leach

Time Do Not Stop, poems by William Guest

Dear Old Dogs, a novella by Gwen Head

How Not to Sell: A Sales Survival Guide, nonfiction by Rashad Daoudi

Ghost Sentence, poems by Mary Flanagan

Such a Nice Girl, a novel by Carol St. John

What Outlives Us, poems by Larry Levy

Winter Park, a novel by Graham Guest

That Beautiful Season, a novel by Sandra Fox Murphy

About the Author

Grant Matthew Jenkins teaches literature, television, and creative writing. He lives in Tulsa with his four kids and two cats. A life-long college football fan, he attended the University of Texas and Notre Dame. Although he is a published poet and scholar, *Ivory Tower* is his first novel.

CPSIA information can be obtained
at www.ICGtesting.com
Printed in the USA
LVHW021303220221
679634LV00001B/76